REVIEWS

from bestselling authors

"*The Savannah Project* signals the arrival of a new member to the thriller genre. Chuck Barrett. The tale contains all of the danger, treachery, and action a reader could wish for. The intrigue comes from all directions, slicing and stitching with precision. A worthy debut from an exciting talent."

— Steve Berry, *New York Times* bestselling author

"From the tree-lined streets of Savannah to the mossy stones of an ancient Irish castle, *The Savannah Project* weaves a fast moving tale of murder, mystery and suspense. Chuck Barrett has written a winner here. A must-read novel for thriller lovers."

— William Rawlings, bestselling author of *The Mile High Club*

from book reviewers

APEX REVIEWS

"*The Savannah Project* is a bona fide suspense thriller. Rife with abundant mystery and intrigue, author Chuck Barrett's standout tale takes the reader on a tortuous path of all-engrossing action and adventure. A highly recommended instant classic."

THE MIDWEST BOOK REVIEW

"*The Savannah Project* is an exciting thriller that will prove hard to put down."

FOREWORD CLARION REVIEWS

"*The Savannah Project* represents a superior effort for this newly-minted novelist."

THE SAVANNAH
PROJECT

THE SAVANNAH PROJECT

A Thriller

Chuck Barrett

Switchback
PUBLISHING
An Imprint of Wyatt-MacKenzie

THE SAVANNAH PROJECT
by Chuck Barrett

SECOND EDITION

ISBN: 978-1-936214-07-5
Library of Congress Control Number: 2009943341

The Savannah Project is a work of fiction. Names, characters, places and incidents are products of the author's imagination or are used fictitiously. Any resemblance to actual events, locales, or persons, living or dead, is coincidental.

Cover design by Mary Fisher Design, LLC, www.maryfisherdesign.com
Interior Illustrations by Johnny McNabb

Published by Switchback Publishing
An Imprint of Wyatt-MacKenzie

www.switchbackpublishing.com

For Debi, Brittany, Chase, Christa, and Kates

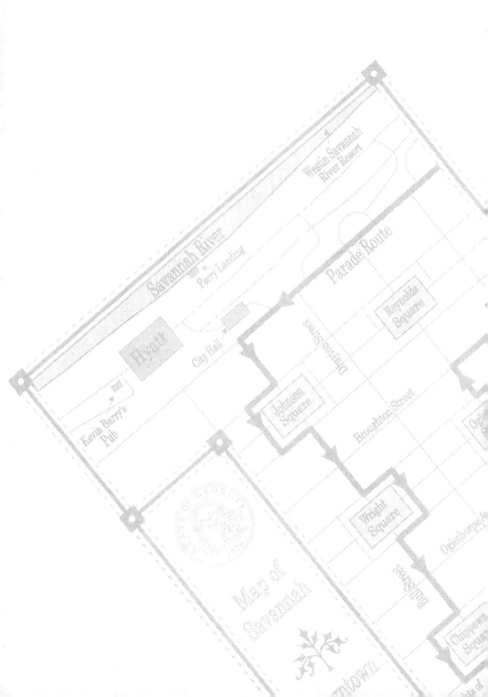

*In memory of George Fontaine—whose untimely departure from this
world has left a void in the lives of many, certainly mine.
You are sorely missed
—CYP*

ACKNOWLEDGEMENTS

First and foremost, I want to thank my beautiful wife, Debi, for all her support and assistance. She is my best friend, biggest fan, and toughest critic. Without you, this would never have been possible.

I want to recognize Nancy Cleary and Wyatt-MacKenzie Publishing for making this possible and for her guidance and patience as I stumble through this process for the first time.

A special thanks to Jennifer Munro for talking me into starting a lifelong ambition. Without her positive thinking and encouragement, I never would have picked up a pen.

For their editorial skills, guidance, and advice to a neophyte, my sincere gratitude is extended to Emily Carmain and Arlene W. Robinson. You too, Terry.

To my good friend Mary Fisher—Wow, what an amazing book cover! You're the greatest. Thank you.

Thanks to my friend and co-worker Johnny McNabb for his graphic illustrations of Savannah and Dromahair.

Another special thanks to my group of readers—Bob DeBrule, Chris Klein, Jim Dwyer, Marlena Collins, George and Karen Mills, Jennifer Montgomery and Charles and Doris Barrett. Thank you for taking time from your busy lives to read this book and provide me with your valuable input and advice.

I would also like to thank Jim Wilson and my critique group at the 2009 UNF Writer's Conference for helping me shape and reshape the beginning of this book.

My good friend David Cook (the real life Cookie) allowed me to steal his identity for this book. I hope you're not disappointed. Thanks.

I want to recognize a few others whose input helped with the creation of this book. David Rigney, Aimee from Barry's Pub for the use of her personality and appearance, the management of the Savannah Westin for their hospitality, Dr. Jonathan Kantor for his evaluation and diagnosis of Ian Collins' medical condition, and my co-workers at Jacksonville ARTCC for providing me with an unlimited pool of personality traits from which to choose.

For the Second Edition, I want to extend a special gratitude to Rebecca Mills for her assistance in making *The Savannah Project* an even better book.

The world breaks everyone and afterward many are strong in the broken places.

But those that will not break it kills.

It kills the very good and the very gentle and the very brave impartially.

If you are none of these you can be sure it will kill you too but there will be no special hurry.

Ernest Hemingway,
A Farewell to Arms, 1929

PROLOGUE

St. Patrick's Day
Savannah, Georgia

Jake cradled her head in his lap, hand cramped from applying pressure to stem the fountain gushing from her neck. Warm, sticky blood oozed through his fingers, pooling on the floor beneath his legs.

He brushed his thumb across her cheek wiping away a tear. "Hang on. Help is on the way, just hang on."

The historic old house reeked of burnt gunpowder. Its acrid tang stung his nose, his eyes filled with water. Water that threatened to turn to tears. He couldn't let that happen. He wouldn't let that happen. He had to be strong. For her, maybe for himself.

It had happened so fast, the massacre that left death all around him. A bloodbath—the result of an aircraft accident investigation gone horribly wrong.

"Jake? Jake, where are you? I can't see anything, Jake. I'm scared."

"I'm right here." He stroked her hair. "I'm right here with you."

His pulse quickened when he saw the man propped against the closed front door—lifeless eyes open, two gunshot wounds to the chest. A trail of blood smeared down the inside of the front door where he'd succumbed to death.

Across the living room lay two bloody figures. One dead, draped over a coffee table, the other curled on the floor in the fetal position. A bullet in the gut.

Another body lay behind a black leather recliner. The impact of the bullet at close range had blown part of the man's head off. Blood, bone, and brain matter stained the wall and floor a sickening pink.

He retched.

Movement caught his eye. He turned to see the assassin staggering down the hall toward the back door. The man moved in slow motion, clutching his left shoulder as he bumped against the wall.

In a weak voice, she said, "Jake, I don't want to die."

"You're not going to die. I won't let that happen."

He brushed away another tear.

After the last barrage of gunfire, the house had become eerily quiet—the silence was deafening.

Sunlight beamed through the slit in the curtains. Like a still photograph, dust particles hung motionless in midair.

The calm *after* the storm, only devastation remained.

The past few minutes were a blur. It made no sense. How did a simple investigation end like this? A nightmarish scene of blood and gore, spies and assassins, betrayal and deceit.

His usual foresight had failed him this time. It had never been a problem before. Dammit, why hadn't he seen this ending? Clueless. Until it was too late.

Rocking back and forth, stanching the flow of blood, he prayed. Prayed she would survive. Prayed his efforts would prove worthy, all the while reassuring her that she would be okay. Reassuring himself that she would be okay.

Banging on the front door broke the silence like thunder clapping—drawing him back into reality.

Voices on the street below screamed and yelled. Sirens wailed. Police whistles blew. A groaning mutter from the air traffic controller on the floor was laced with profanity. Sounds filled the room, growing louder and louder with each passing second, rising into a chaotic roar.

Jake looked into her terrified eyes, and he knew what he had to do. Anger cleared his mind.

He caressed her cheek. "You'll be alright. I'll make everything right. But you have to fight. Don't give up."

"Please...don't let me die." Her words were barely audible.

"I won't let that happen." *I'll kill that bastard or I'll die trying.*

She didn't hear him. Her body went limp as she drifted into unconsciousness.

A plan had formulated in his mind and his resolve became clear. He knew what he had to do.

He knew who he had to call.

CHAPTER 1

Three days earlier, the assassin had arrived at Sanders' Dallas apartment, quietly knocking on the front door while calling him with his cell phone.

"Hello?" Sanders answered.

"Duane. It's Ian. Open the door, it's urgent."

"Ian?"

Ian hung up but kept knocking on the door.

Seconds later the door opened. Sanders was barefoot, wearing blue jeans and a crumpled white t-shirt. He rubbed his eyes. "Ian? What the hell are you doing here?"

Ian looked at the five-foot-five mechanic. "We have work to do on Challenger Three Charlie Bravo."

"Three Charlie Bravo? She doesn't leave for Savannah for over twenty-four hours. We have all day tomorrow to work on her—whatever it is can wait until a decent hour."

"We have something to install now. It won't take long, now come on." Ian grabbed Sanders' arm.

Sanders jerked his arm away. "Hell no. I'm not installing *anything* on an airplane at two o'clock in the morning."

Ian pointed the weapon at Sanders' forehead. "Oh, but you are," he said. "I anticipated that you might need a little incentive so I went to see your girlfriend a few hours ago. I think you'll agree to come with me now." Ian pushed his way into Sanders' apartment and closed the front door.

He reached into his pocket and pulled out a photograph. "Just so you won't try anything stupid." He handed the photo to Sanders.

The mechanic fell to his knees. "My God. What have you done?"

Ian snatched Sanders from his knees and shoved him into a chair. "Come on, Duane. What does it look like I've done? I drugged your girlfriend, tied her up, and strapped an explosive device to her chest." He held up his cell phone. "And all I have to do is press this button and boom."

"Who the hell are you? What do you want?"

"Who I am is none of your concern but it should be obvious about now. What do I want? What I want… is your full cooperation without any more stupid questions. Is that clear, Duane?"

Sanders nodded. "Okay, I'll do whatever you want. Just don't hurt Heather."

Ian smiled. "Good choice, Duane. I thought you'd see it my way."

When they arrived at the hangar, Ian gave Sanders the schematics and the parts. He watched carefully as Sanders installed the device into the Challenger 604 Business Jet. When Sanders finished, Ian activated a switch. A series of lights blinked as it performed a diagnostic check. A steady green light came on, indicating a proper installation.

Ian waved the weapon motioning Sanders out of the aircraft. "Let's go."

He closed the aircraft cabin door and together they walked to Sanders' pickup truck.

Sanders started shaking. "I…I did what you wanted. I don't care what any of this is about. We won't talk. I promise. Just let Heather go."

Ian backhanded Sanders across the face. "Shut up or I'll kill both of you. If you do as I say, I'll let you both go *after* Three Charlie Bravo leaves for Savannah. But, Duane, know this, if I find out you talked, I'll track you down and kill you. Are we clear on that?"

"I understand, I understand. I'll do anything you say, just let Heather go."

Ten minutes later they arrived at Heather's house. Ian opened the front door with Sanders' key and shoved Sanders inside. When Sanders turned around, Ian fired the weapon.

The assassin smiled as the mechanic collapsed to the floor.

His eyes traced the copper coils of the Taser M26 down to the man lying on the floor. The needle-tipped darts stuck in Sanders' chest delivered fifty thousand volts when the assassin squeezed the trigger.

How easy it had been. His master plan had worked flawlessly, and Duane Sanders would be the first fatality of the Savannah Project.

He squeezed the trigger again and watched Sanders lose consciousness.

* * *

Sanders awoke to water splashing over him. His blood-stained shirt clung to his chest. His head pounded. He couldn't move his arms and legs, they were duct-taped to a chair.

Music played from the stereo.

The lights were off.

The afternoon sun beat against the closed blinds.

Heather was moaning.

Ian was sitting on the edge of Heather's bed. The Taser was gone. In his hand he held a pistol.

"Welcome back, Duane. You've been out quite a while." Ian stood and walked toward Sanders.

"I thought you were going to let us go. I did what you wanted."

Ian smiled. "I lied."

The color drained from Sanders' face. "What are you going to do with us?"

"What do you think, Duane? I would just leave and let you two walk away? You're a liability." Ian leaned close and whispered, "But first, I'm going to enjoy Heather. And you're going to watch."

The thought of Ian touching her made him want to vomit. He wanted to save her, but how? Ian was a huge man with a body builder physique. He was a small man bound to a chair. What chance did he have against a man like that, a killer like Ian?

"Ian, please don't hurt her. Do what you want to me, but let her go. I beg you, please."

"No begging, Duane. It's very unbecoming." Ian smashed the butt of his pistol into the side of Sanders' head.

When Sanders regained consciousness, Ian was wearing only a towel wrapped around his waist. The humid smell of soap and shampoo filled the room. Heather was naked on the bed, bound to the corner bedposts.

Ian sat on the bed next to her. He ran his large hand along Heather's tanned body, caressing her breasts. He skimmed his hand along her curvy anatomy.

Sanders tried to scream, but was gagged with one of Heather's socks.

Ian stood up. "Duane, I've decided to honor your request. I'm not going to kill Heather—only you."

Sanders struggled against the bonds holding him to the chair—but to no avail.

A shadow loomed over him. He looked up and saw Ian pointing a pistol at him.

"Goodbye, Duane."

CHAPTER 2

Ian Collins folded his newspaper, tucked it between the cushion and the armrest, and studied the eighteen-foot sculpture that dominated the lobby of the Dallas Adams Mark. It was a Remington-style metal sculpture—a cowboy falling off the back of a rearing horse. The high ceilings gave the foyer an open feel. Outside the large plate glass windows overlooking the valet station was a line of taxis, each driver waiting for his next fare.

He glanced at his reflection in the window and noticed his white hair visible beneath his cap. He readjusted it on his head.

His most notable and quite prominent features were his white forelock and mismatched eyes—one eye had a light brown iris, the other a vivid sapphire blue. His appearance always commanded second and third glances from passersby.

His profession as a hired assassin mandated that he maintain a low profile, which was difficult due to his size and unusual physical features. He had tried several disguise techniques—hair dye, head shaving, and hairpieces. None suited his taste, so he opted for the sole use of hats to conceal his hair.

His eyes were much easier. Brown-colored contact lenses were easily obtained, drew no suspicion, and masked his mismatched eye color.

He had been in Dallas for only three weeks, but it seemed like three months. A dirty city, he thought. Then again, Belfast was far worse. Even so, he couldn't wait to get home to Ireland. He despised the United States.

Collins had already killed one person and critically injured another—both aircraft mechanics. He'd raped the girlfriend. Of course, that part was enjoyable. Icing on the cake. The women usually were. No doubt when she came out of her drug-induced stupor, her life would never be the same.

He'd submitted a résumé to the manager of Longhorn Aviation, a fixed based operator at the Dallas Love Airport under the assumed name of Ian McDonald. The manager seemed impressed by the credentials and references he provided for the same type jet aircraft that Longhorn Aviation operated. The assassin knew there wasn't an opening. Not yet. Just laying the foundation for his plan.

Two weeks prior, he began following the two mechanics at Longhorn Aviation and studying them closely—watching both men at work and play. Lurking in the shadows, he'd learned their individual traits, habits, mannerisms and, more importantly, their weaknesses. Sanders' weakness was his trophy girlfriend, a former NFL cheerleader. Duane Sanders had been a likable little man, amicable and gullible.

This worked to Collins' advantage. He chose Sanders as his mark.

Sanders was one of the two jet mechanics at Longhorn Aviation Services.

Collins' knowledge of automobiles made it a simple task to engineer the accident that incapacitated Sanders' coworker, leaving him comatose and creating a job opening.

Collins had used coercion to get Sanders to install the bomb.

Sanders installed it correctly.

The plans and materials for the device came from a contact he made while working a job in Libya. His contact had sent the device in three shipments from three different countries. Each shipment in and of itself benign. But when assembled—deadly. A fourth was shipped directly to Savannah, a harmless radio remote control. The radio remote matched the discrete frequency of the device Sanders had installed in the aircraft.

The assassin kept his true identity and personal details a closely guarded secret. His clients accessed him only by email. An anonymous email account on an anonymous server.

THE SAVANNAH PROJECT 11

Only two of his closest friends knew his real name, Ian Collins, and how to reach him other than by email. He went by the online username "Shamrock," a name also given to him by Interpol because of his trademark left on the victim after each hit—a shamrock.

The Savannah Project was a unique assignment in two ways. One, it was the first time he actually *knew* one of his targets. And this job had several targets, each a necessity to reach his ultimate mark, a man he'd met as a teenager and despised ever since.

Second, it was the only time he'd ever used anyone else on a job. He had known them since childhood, one was his former best friend. Both of them knew everything about him.

For his friends, though, he knew this wasn't just an assassination—it was far more than that. It was a cause. A cause for their homeland, a cause for their people, a cause for all those, like themselves, who had watched as their loved ones died at the hands of a traitor.

This job would take the lives of innocent people. An acceptable consequence. Their cause was more important. The end justified the means. He knew for last pastners, this was all about revenge.

An eye for an eye.

A blood vengeance.

For Collins, it was also about revenge. And money, a lot of money. Unbeknown to his friends, though, he had planned a fitting payback for his mark. Payback for all the pain and anguish and humiliation he had suffered because of his final target. A game of sport. A well-conceived plan in which Collins planned to lure his target into a deadly trap.

He'd never had any remorse for the lives he had taken. He did his job well, separating his emotions from his work.

Collins was still staring at the sculpture when his BlackBerry vibrated. He glanced down to see the Caller ID of the incoming text message, 555-545-5426, a number he knew too well. The number belonged to one of his friends and co-conspirator. The number was not just a random phone number generated by the phone company, but a vanity number—numbers chosen to correspond to the letters in the person's first name.

545-5426.

Jillian.

The text message was short: **CALL ME.**

He glanced at his watch, calculating how long it would be before the target and his entourage came through the lobby. Plenty of time, he thought, so he pushed the call button and dialed the number.

"Jillian," answered a woman with a commanding raspy voice.

"It's Ian," he said into his Bluetooth headset.

"Ian, good. Is everything all set?"

"Yes, just waiting in the lobby for O'Rourke and his escorts to come downstairs."

"What are you doing there? You could be recognized. Ian. We worked too hard and too long to make any mistakes now. We *have* to succeed. Then O'Rourke will have paid for what he did—what he did to our family. What he did to you."

"Relax, Jillian. It's been too many years for O'Rourke to recognize me. Besides, I have to see him. I might not get the chance tomorrow. I have to see him one more time, up close. I want to remember his face."

"Perhaps you're right. Have all the loose ends been tied up? No way to trace anything back to us?"

"Yes, all taken care of. The device is in place and ready to go. The mechanic has been silenced."

"What about the girlfriend? How did you handle her?"

"The same way I handle most women. Besides, she knows nothing. The cops will just think some pervert stalked and raped a Cowboys cheerleader, killing her boyfriend in the process."

"Can she identify you? Aren't you worried about DNA samples?"

"Don't worry, Jillian. She was blindfolded the whole time and never saw my face. I've left DNA samples all over the world. What's one more with a washed-up bimbo? Remember…I don't exist. They'll be chasing a ghost."

"Ian, I hope you know what you're doing." Jillian paused. "I'll need to know the specifics about the flight as soon as possible. Text me when you know something. I have everything worked out on my end. I'll be ready."

"As soon as O'Rourke gives his speech tonight," Collins said, "Sullivan will brief him about his schedule for tomorrow. I'll intercept it then. The bug I planted hasn't failed yet, no reason to think it will now.

"Listen, Jillian, we've been over and over this plan—nothing will go wrong. I do this for a living, remember? You don't need to worry. The plan is foolproof. O'Rourke will die. Your parents will be avenged. And we'll have the satisfaction of knowing we got to him first. I know for a fact there are several contracts out on him. There are quite a few parties interested in ensuring that he never gets to deliver his 'revelation' speech in Savannah."

He hung up and for the first time in his life felt an emotion he'd never dealt with before—remorse. Remorse for his friends. Although out of touch for nearly a decade, these friends had been more like family, the only family he had left.

The Savannah Project might cost them their lives. They would never see it coming.

He'd thought it through many times—every scenario, every possible angle—and came to the same inevitable conclusion each time.

His friends were a liability.

CHAPTER 3

A Lincoln Town Car stretch limousine drove toward the Dallas-Fort Worth Airport on the John W. Carpenter Freeway taking Michael Sullivan to catch a flight to Savannah. He was going in advance of Laurence O'Rourke to identify and neutralize the threat of a planned assassination attempt on O'Rourke.

"Are you sure your source is reliable?" O'Rourke asked.

"Totally reliable. Matter of fact, he's never been wrong," Sullivan said.

"Yet. He's never been wrong, yet. Always a first time, you know."

"He's not a problem, Laurence."

"I don't guess you'll tell me who *he* is, will you?"

"Laurence, we've been together a long time. Have I ever told you who any of my sources are? No, and for good reason—plausible deniability. You're a public figure, I am not. It would not be good for you to know all the details. That's why our relationship has worked all these years. You trust me and I trust you. I cover your ass and you cover mine."

"You're right, of course, Michael. I guess I'm just curious as to where you always get your information. Are you sure it's safe for me here without you? What if this is a plot or a decoy to lure you out of Dallas so they can make their move here, whoever *they* are?"

"Don't worry about safety. These two," Sullivan motioned at the bodyguards flanking O'Rourke, "will keep you safe. They have their orders, you're in good hands. However, what you need to ask yourself is why the Irish Republican Army would put a contract out on you now, of all times. Why hadn't they done it long ago? It doesn't make sense."

"I've already asked myself that question, Michael. I'm not so sure it is them. I can think of some others who might want me dead more than the IRA."

The limousine pulled up to the curb. Sullivan opened the door and got out. He looked back at O'Rourke and said, "Just stay out of sight and strictly follow the plan. All the arrangements have been made. Nothing will go wrong if you stick to the plan. I'll see you in Savannah tomorrow night."

"I hope you're right, Michael."

"I am. You're not to worry."

The limousine pulled away from the curb and retraced the same route back toward the hotel. O'Rourke thought about what Sullivan had said and about who else might want him dead. Want him dead enough to put a contract on his life. The list was long, he was sure of that. And one man kept coming up at the top of the list. A man he hadn't thought about for a long time—the Commander.

It had been more than twenty-five years since he'd last encountered the Commander. He could remember the exact date, September 23, 1983. It was just two days before he escaped from the H.M.P. Maze prison in Northern Ireland. That night's events were etched into his consciousness, a time he could never forget. A time that still haunted him.

He lay dreaming on his prison cot. Hazy light beamed through the bars casting an eerie shadow across his blanket. A noise startled him, awakening him from his dream. He was drenched in sweat. Panic swept over him.

He'd opened his eyes only to see two silhouettes rapidly approaching from the cell door. The larger shadow held him down against the cot while the second shadow stuffed a rag over his nose and mouth. O'Rourke fought back. A fist slammed into his stomach. Gasping for air, he felt the burn of ether. Another slam to the stomach caused him to inhale even deeper, the ether filling his lungs. The figures grew darker in the pale moonlight. Desperately trying to hold on to consciousness, he held his breath.

One more blow to the stomach.

He now inhaled involuntarily, his lungs full of the tainted air.

His throat burned. His lungs burned. His head felt light.

His arms and legs became too heavy to lift. Needles prickled his entire body.

The room faded to darkness.

He tried to resist but his body went limp.

The Maze had been a horrendous prison with a dreadful reputation. Black mold grew on the walls and ceilings of the H-Blocks at the Maze, located in Lisburn, Ireland, just over fourteen kilometers outside of Belfast. The dismal corridors between the rows of cells were lit only with low-wattage bulbs wrapped in wire cages.

"O'Rourke, O'Rourke, wake up."

A single light shone down on the chair in the middle of the cold, dark interrogation room. A black chair made of solid wood with wide armrests, stout legs, and a tall headrest sat anchored to the concrete floor. Leather straps with buckles fettered his arms and legs. His head was immobilized by another leather strap, wrapped around his forehead and secured tightly against the headrest.

As he surfaced from his drug-induced stupor, he tried to move, but couldn't. His bare feet tingled against the cold floor. Wearing only boxers and a tattered t-shirt, he shivered.

"Mr. O'Rourke, are you awake?"

Footsteps in the darkness, two sets. The voice calling his name—British. That voice. Then he remembered.

His SIS handler. The man who recruited him as a spy for Her Majesty's Secret Service. The man who trained him. The man who arranged his initiation into the Irish Republican Army. The man who was responsible for him being imprisoned here.

"Commander?"

"I see you haven't forgotten. Good. Your time at the Maze is almost at an end. It is now time for the next phase of your mission," the Brit said. "You have been a liability for me lately. Now you have a chance to redeem yourself. Do you understand?"

"I understand."

O'Rourke's eyes followed the voice as it moved around the dark room. At times he heard another set of footsteps shuffling in the darkness, but only the Commander spoke. The footsteps stopped in front of him. His handler's voice remained behind him. Struggling to focus through the darkness, he could only make out shoes—high-quality dress shoes.

Who is this man?

The Commander droned on for over an hour. A drill he'd been through before, but not this way. Never beaten up and drugged.

The first time was different. A clandestine meeting. A meeting he thought would shape his future. Indeed it did shape his future, just not in a way he would have ever imagined. On his last attempt to gain admittance and acceptance into the IRA, he was sold out and ended up here, in the Maze.

The Commander unveiled his elaborate plan, then went silent.

O'Rourke heard a third set of footsteps approaching. Boots stomping across the concrete floor. He immediately recognized the boots when the large man stopped in front of him.

The prison guard.

O'Rourke noticed a shadow move above him just as the guard's fist smashed into the left side of his face. Blood spurted onto his bare leg when his eyebrow split open. Swelling closed his eye. Blood oozed down the side of his face. The guard's other fist struck his right jaw, busting his lip open against his teeth.

He remembered the Commander's final words: "It was necessary to drag you in here this way to avoid suspicion. There are eyes watching. We cannot jeopardize this mission. Be careful, Laurence. Trust no one."

The ether soaked rag reappeared. He didn't have the strength to resist.

Two days later O'Rourke left his cell in H-Block 4 for the final time. He hid the handguns under his coat—handguns left in his cell by the Brit—and took his place in the meal line. If he was to see freedom, then the actions of the next few hours must be executed with extreme precision and flawless timing.

Thirty-eight men, O'Rourke included, overpowered prison guards, then hijacked a meals lorry and smashed their way through the gates and to freedom. He followed the Maze's Provisional IRA leader out of the prison walls, just as the Commander ordered, until they were clear of the Maze.

He broke away from the others and started his long journey toward the town of Londonderry. Several other escapees hid in ditches and bogs. Nineteen were later recaptured. Republic-friendly families throughout Northern Ireland harbored several of the escaped prisoners.

O'Rourke had a long way to travel and found transportation waiting exactly as the Commander had assured him. He took a circuitous route, changing vehicles in Antrim, Galgorn, Dunloy, and Coleraine. He arrived in Londonderry at three a.m.

When he reached his destination, he hid underneath a porch across the street from his new refuge and waited for the all-clear sign. His orders were to wait until the fourth occupant left the house in the morning, then the house would be empty. He was to let himself in the back door and find his way to the cellar, where he was to stay until the man of the house returned. He sat and watched the house. Minutes seemed like hours and fatigue set in, he drifted off to sleep.

Cold and wet, he awoke to the sound of a starting truck engine. Overcast skies spat small raindrops down on him. He gazed through the bushes as a man drove away from the house. Thirty minutes later three teenagers, two boys and a girl left the house with school books in hand. One of the boys was tall. Very tall and muscular with a prominent white streak down the middle of his hair. The other boy was rather stocky with reddish brown hair and a ruddy complexion. The girl, thin with red hair and freckles, walked close behind them.

He waited another fifteen minutes to make sure the coast was clear, and then made his way to the back door. As he started up the steps to the small back porch, he caught a glimpse of a woman in the kitchen.

Damn—the house should have been empty. The Commander was wrong.

He ducked underneath the back porch, out of sight.

The woman was slim with long, thick auburn hair, and sparkling green eyes. The kind of eyes that captivate you. Stop you dead in your tracks. Her skin was smooth and porcelain white against her red dress. She stepped out from the kitchen, pulled a scarf around her neck and draped her coat over her left forearm as she closed the door behind her.

Spellbound, he watched her walk down the steps to the street. She stopped and glanced back toward the house. He noticed her shapely figure. He had been in the Maze for nearly a year and longed for the touch of a woman.

Her perfume lingered on the porch. He imagined her soft skin against his, the touch of her hair, the smell of her clean body. She was small, maybe five-foot-two, he figured. Probably topped the scales at a hundred and five, maybe a hundred and ten pounds—easy enough to overpower.

She stared at the house for several seconds.

He froze with fear, sure she had seen him.

She put her coat on and cinched the belt snug around her trim waistline, then turned and walked down the street.

When she was out of sight, he raced up the steps to the back door. It was unlocked as the Commander had promised. He made his way down to the cellar, where he found a change of clothes, provisions and a pallet with blankets. The next three days would be spent there, until his next transport would take him out of the country.

Fatigue from the last twenty-four hours took its toll. He lay on the pallet but was unable to sleep—his mind consumed with the woman. The loveliest woman he had ever seen. His desire grew with each passing thought until he made himself a final vow. He would not leave Londonderry until he had her.

O'Rourke stared trancelike out the window of the limo, a smile crept across his face as he remembered the woman. His thoughts returned to the Commander—the smile vanished. Unresolved issues remained between them. Issues that must be settled.

He had abandoned his handler before completing the assignment. He had expected some sort of fall-out—but none ever came. That's what worried him.

An inevitable confrontation loomed on the horizon. Only one way to handle it, he thought. He had to make the first move. The Commander would never expect it—O'Rourke confronting him. Especially *after* O'Rourke delivered his speech in Savannah.

A St. Patrick's Day for all to remember.

*   *   *

At the Dallas airport, Collins watched the American Eagle regional jet push back from the gate and taxi for departure. Michael Sullivan occupied seat 7A.

He'd listened to O'Rourke's exchange with Sullivan in the limo. Now he knew O'Rourke's plan. The bug worked perfectly. All the pieces were falling into place.

The assassin had carefully devised the ruse of the IRA hit man and used his contacts to get that information relayed back to Sullivan—and through him, to O'Rourke. His plan to separate Sullivan and O'Rourke had worked flawlessly.

He typed quickly on his Blackberry, addressed the message and pressed send:

O'Rourke and Sullivan separated
Sullivan enroute to Savannah - arrives tonight.

CHAPTER 4

The morning sun peeked over the eastern horizon and glistened across the Dallas skyline, announcing the arrival of a new day. A cold front had passed through the Dallas area the night before and left it unseasonably cold. The forecast high less than forty degrees. The low-pressure system that passed through Dallas two days ago had now become a severe winter storm along the Eastern seaboard, wreaking havoc with airline schedules. A northwest wind blew across the airport, carrying with it a chill that cut through the assassin's layers of clothes.

Ground crews scurried on the tarmac of the Dallas Love Airport readying several business class jets for whatever journeys awaited them. Parked on the ramp in front of Longhorn Aviation was a chartered business jet.

The Bombardier Challenger 604, a long-range wide-body corporate jet, could fly at speeds of four hundred sixty knots for a distance of nearly thirty-eight hundred miles. Equipped with state-of-the-art instrumentation, the jet sported what was known as a full "glass cockpit," rapidly becoming the norm among general aviation aircraft. Sixty-eight feet long and nearly twenty-one feet tall, the jet had a wingspan of just over sixty-four feet. Although not nearly as corpulent as airline aircraft, the Challenger dwarfed the ground crew.

The jet's paint scheme was unusual, with both wings and the underside of the aircraft burgundy, and the top two-thirds painted white. The required registration number was painted across each of the two General Electric CF-34-3B turbofan engines in burgundy twelve-inch-high numbers—N319CB.

While the Challenger was being fueled, the lineman buried his hands under his armpits in a vain attempt to keep them warm, all the while bouncing on his toes.

Two men in pilots' uniforms, with classic leather bomber jackets, gloves and aviator-style Ray-Ban sunglasses, walked around the aircraft conducting a preflight inspection. One of the pilots pointed to the landing gear door at the nose of the Challenger.

Another man, in a considerably different uniform, loaded food and beverages from the catering service van onto the aircraft.

Out of the cabin doorway stepped a large man wearing a jump-suit with the Longhorn Aviation logo on the left breast pocket and carrying a toolbox and a clipboard. He adjusted his cap against the gusting wind, then descended the stairway and walked over to the pilots. He set his toolbox down on the tarmac and handed one of the pilots the clipboard. The man cupped his hands in front of his mouth and blew his breath into them. A puff of steam slipped through his fingers. He spoke to the pilot, who signed the clipboard and handed it back to him. Tucking the clipboard under his arm, the man picked up his toolbox and disappeared into the hangar.

The lineman secured the fuel pump, logged the number of gallons pumped on his clipboard, tore off the top copy and handed it to the copilot. With the sheet in hand, the copilot climbed the stairs into the aircraft to make required weight and balance computations.

The black limousine pulled onto the tarmac and drove toward the Challenger, stopping within thirty feet of the cabin door. Two men in navy blue trench coats scurried from the limo, taking their places next to the rear passenger door. The men could have passed for brothers except for their age—maybe father and son. Both were large, six-four, maybe six-five. Both had broad shoulders, red hair and freckles—the elder's hair a shade darker than the younger man's.

Their trench coats draped over them, concealing their weapons. The bodyguards scanned the area, moving in synchrony, each keeping one hand in his coat pocket and using the other to open doors and move luggage. The elder of the two men opened the limousine door and a tall man dressed in a dark brown three-piece suit stepped out.

Laurence O'Rourke had gained more than twenty pounds since his days in the Maze prison. Weighing in now at one hundred ninety pounds, his six-foot-three frame made him look tall and lanky. He stepped from the limousine, a gust of wind rocked him backwards and tousled his gray hair. He placed his hand against the limo to catch himself. He took off his silver metal-framed glasses and tucked them into his vest pocket, retrieved his briefcase from the seat, and walked toward the jet, flanked by his two bodyguards.

The pilot greeted O'Rourke with a handshake. The lineman took the baggage and secured it in the aircraft while the pilot escorted O'Rourke onto the aircraft.

The lineman spoke into a handheld radio and one of the pilots closed the cabin door. Within two minutes the left engine started the familiar whirling sound of the turbines spooling up, followed by the thundering sound of ignition. The smell of burning jet fuel flooded the tarmac.

The Challenger remained motionless for several minutes. Then, with a short burst of power, it started to move. As the jet taxied away from the hangar, the right engine ignited with another roar. The aircraft disappeared from sight as it taxied to the departure end of the runway.

Standing by the edge of the hangar, the assassin watched the Challenger thunder down the runway, past the hangar, becoming airborne and then banking into a climbing left turn. He unzipped his coveralls and stepped out of them, revealing his new appearance—khakis and a button-down blue oxford shirt. He wadded up the coveralls and tossed them into the corner of the hangar. He slipped on a brown corduroy sport coat with brown leather elbow patches, threw his mechanic's cap onto the crumpled coveralls, put on his Donegal tweed cap, and grabbed his travel bag.

Casually walking into the parking lot, he pulled out his Blackberry and sent a message:

O'Rourke enroute to Savannah, departed 7:40 lcl, expect arrival approx

10:40 Eastern Time

As before, he sent the message to more than one recipient.

Finally, he could get the hell out of Dallas. The first stage of the project was complete. What a God-forsaken piece of land Texas turned out to be. And these people, their obsession with the Old West, couldn't they just move on?

O'Rourke was finally on his way to Savannah where the assassin's trap awaited him.

Collins parked Sanders' old pickup in long-term parking and discarded the keys in a trash bin along the walkway to the terminal building. Arriving at the ticket counter, he reached into his coat pocket and pulled out his Southwest Airlines ticket, a ticket for a nonstop flight from the Dallas Love Airport to Jacksonville International Airport. There, his leased black Cadillac Escalade was waiting for him in another long-term parking lot. Within a few hours he would be in the Escalade driving to Savannah for the final stage of the Savannah Project.

CHAPTER 5

Gregg Kaplan stood inside the doorway of the radar room at the Savannah Air Traffic Control TRACON, as the Terminal Radar Approach Control was known.

The TRACON was the portion of the air traffic control facility that handled arrivals, departures and over flights by providing radar separation between aircraft. The control tower cab, recognized by its stereotypical glass enclosure at the top of the tower, handled clearances, ground movement of aircraft and other vehicles, and cleared aircraft to taxi, take off and land. The control tower and the TRACON worked in concert to sequence and choreograph arrivals and departures from the Savannah International Airport. The timing had to be precise. The air traffic controller could never make a mistake. Mistakes could cost lives.

Kaplan stepped forward, headset in his hand, and waited at the front line manager's desk while his eyes adjusted to the darkness of the radar room. "Front line manager" was the coined title the Federal Aviation Administration decided to call supervisors after the agency imposed work rules on the air traffic controller workforce in 2006. An imposition that lasted three years.

In the center of the radar room the manager sat at a gaudy rectangular behemoth the FAA called a desk. It was made up of two three-section consoles, each wrapping around a hundred eighty degrees. A space between the sections allowed the managers to walk through and sit in the seats in the middle. From the center of the radar room, the desk overlooked the four radar scopes.

Four radarscopes and the flight data position, lined up next to each other, occupied the fourth wall. Three walls in the nearly square room were devoid of any air traffic control equipment. No pictures. No tables. No chairs. Nothing—just empty, black walls.

Kaplan's eyes adjusted to the darkness within a couple of minutes and he saw only two radar positions open. The other two radar scopes were unmanned and their traffic combined on the open scopes, standard procedure when traffic volume decreases or staffing is inadequate.

The West and North Radar sectors were combined on the North Radar scope. The South Radar position provided final approach service to inbound aircraft by providing vectors for the approach, prior to transferring control of the aircraft over to the control tower when the planes got within a few miles of the airport. The air traffic controller up in the control tower cab then cleared the aircraft to land.

The South Radar position appeared very busy, with two controllers and a front line manager plugged into the same position. The flight data controller turned around, and seeing him, raised his hand in acknowledgement. Gregg Kaplan motioned him over.

The controller rolled his chair back without getting up, and Kaplan whispered, "What's going on over there? Looks like Annie's down the crapper."

The controller replied, "It's been like this all morning, a steady stream of inbounds. I hate St. Patrick's Day. It's getting worse than Thanksgiving. Everybody's comin' to the party."

Kaplan walked up to the South Radar position, plugged his headset into the slot next to Annie's and said, "Tuber!" She grinned at the word, a dig made among controllers when they got extremely busy.

The term supposedly originated from the dropping of flight plan information printed on strips, usually several in rapid succession, down a tube from the control tower cab to the radar room signifying that there would soon be a departure push and the controller would get very busy—otherwise known as "going down the tubes."

Annie Bulloch, Kaplan's girlfriend for more than ten years, had tucked her long auburn mane in a bun. She wore khaki capri pants, his favorite, and, as was her style, a blouse that accentuated her shapely five-foot-three figure. A splash of freckles showed across her upper back just above the low neckline of her shirt.

"I can't do a repeat of last night if I have to open the next morning," she whispered. "I'm just getting too damn old to make that kind of turn-around on that little sleep."

"You didn't seem too old last night. If I recall correctly, you had enough energy for three rounds."

She shot him a dirty look. "Have I told you lately that I hate you?"

"No, you don't, you love me."

"Dream on, lover boy. You know the attraction's purely sexual."

"Whatever. I'll come by after work and maybe we can head down to River Street. I hear there's a pretty good Celtic band at Barry's."

"Okay, it's a date."

Their romance started fast, with fire and passion. At first he likened it to something along the lines of what is now called *'friends with benefits.'* And the benefits were awesome. Later he realized their commitment to each other was at a deeper level. She had mentioned marriage to him more than once. He wasn't thrilled with the idea, and deep down he didn't think she was either. His mindset was that their current arrangement had suited them well, so why change it?

He leaned over and looked at the radar scope. "Mac said you are going home early, give me a briefing."

Annie pulled up the automated position relief-briefing checklist. "You are working South Radar and Arrival, the weather at the field is marginal VFR with strong winds from the west. The ceiling is low enough to require instrument approaches so we're using the GPS Runway 27 almost exclusively.

"Some aircraft have used other approaches but all have to circle to land on runway two-seven. Equipment is up and operational except for the primary radar. There is no back-up but it hasn't caused a problem this morning."

She continued, "Traffic has been steady but seems to have

tapered off for now. Flow control, to Atlanta as usual. They just canceled the ground delay program for Atlanta, but there are ground stops for several airports in the New England states due to the winter storm. You're working these four here," she pointed to the data block tags for the aircraft. "This is new business, and it looks like you have another inbound. Any questions?"

"No questions, I got it."

She unplugged from the position, got out of her chair, kissed him on the cheek and left.

Kaplan, in his usual unflappable fashion, worked his sector load…

"Savannah, Challenger three one niner Charlie Bravo descending to one one thousand with Foxtrot."

"Challenger three one niner Charlie Bravo, Savannah Approach, roger, turn right heading one one zero, descend and maintain five thousand, Savannah altimeter two niner niner eight."

"Challenger three one niner Charlie Bravo roger."

"Departure, Cheyenne three one four six two off two-seven out one thousand for three thousand."

"Cheyenne three one four six two, Savannah, radar contact, fly heading two niner zero, climb and maintain one zero thousand."

"Heading two niner zero and up to ten, Cheyenne four six two."

Static…unintelligible.

"Aircraft calling Savannah, transmitting carrier only, unreadable."

"Attention all aircraft, Savannah ATIS information Golf now in use."

"Challenger three-one-niner Charlie Bravo, the one-five-five-

> one METAR wind two eight zero at one-zero, gust to one-five, visibility seven, one thousand six hundred overcast temperature one-one, dew point zero-eight, altimeter two-niner-niner-eight, cleared direct WORIB, expect GPS runway two seven approach."

He was somewhat relieved that this was his last inbound of the rush to Savannah. He had issued the same weather sequence to every aircraft. The same clearance to the same approach with the same instructions. Boredom took over quickly.

> *"Challenger three-one-niner Charlie Bravo copy the weather direct WORIB at this time."*

> "Cheyenne three-one-four-six-two proceed direct Dublin, contact JAX Center one three two point five."

> *"Direct Dublin thirty-two-five, Cheyenne four-six-two. Tell the tower thanks for the graveyard tour."*

> "Will do."

> *Static...unintelligible.*

> "Aircraft calling Savannah unreadable."

> "Challenger three-one-niner Charlie Bravo maintain two thousand five hundred until initial approach fix WORIB cleared GPS runway two-seven approach at Savannah, report over final approach fix SINBY."

> *"Two thousand five hundred until WORIB, cleared for approach, call SINBY, Challenger three-one-niner Charlie Bravo."*

Kaplan leaned back in his chair and readjusted his headset. Air traffic volume at Savannah had calmed down after the arrival rush from earlier in the morning. With St. Patrick's Day just two days away, many revelers were already flying in for the Irish festival, among the largest in the nation. March 17th was a day when the entire city turned green in celebration. Children and adults looked forward to the excitement as the whole community, regardless of ethnic background, went into a celebratory mode. For Savannah, this time of year turned into a prodigious festival. Vendors would line the streets peddling trinkets and beads, hats and horns, and t-shirts galore, all of them shamrock green or trimmed in neon emerald

The river turned green, the fountains turned green, even the beer turned green. All of this in anticipation of the hordes of people who migrated to Savannah once a year to lavish in the traditional revelry.

What earlier seemed like an endless stream of inbounds had dwindled down to one business jet, two turboprops, and a single-engine Cessna.

A cold front had passed through Savannah overnight. The low pressure center stalled over New Jersey and shut down airports in the New England states with record snowfall and ice from Virginia all the way to Maine. Even the best-equipped airports couldn't de-ice aircraft fast enough to allow for takeoffs, and with visibilities approaching zero, no landings were being accomplished or attempted for that matter. Hundreds of flights in and out of the Northeast had been canceled and it would be days before the airlines could resume normal operations.

Meteorologists were forecasting this freakish winter storm to stall for the next three days and anticipated snowfall in the Northeast to be measured in feet rather than inches. In its wake it left Savannah with overcast skies and exceptionally strong winds from the west. With winds calming by evening, the temperature was expected to drop, bringing thick fog to Savannah by morning.

"Savannah, Challenger three-one-niner Charlie Bravo, roger, coming up on SINBY leaving one thousand eight hundred"

"Challenger three-one-niner Charlie Bravo, roger, radar service terminated, contact Savannah tower now, one one niner point one."

"Nineteen one, nine Charlie Bravo."

"Mayday, Mayday, we just had an—"

"Challenger three-one-niner Charlie Bravo, Savannah."

"Challenger three-one-niner Charlie Bravo, Savannah."

He pressed the tower cab button and called the controller in the tower cab.

"Local," the tower responded.

"Jerry, did nine Charlie Bravo come over?"

"Not yet."

"Well, try him and see if he's sitting there, will ya?"

"Okay, stand by ..."

"Gregg, he's not here."

"Well, shit, that's what I was afraid of."

He turned around and stolidly called to the front line manager, "Hey Mac, I might have just lost one."

CHAPTER 6

Jake Pendleton stood in the cold rushing water of Mountain-
town Creek in Ellijay, Georgia. The pressure built against his waders,
but he wouldn't yield. He'd been stalking a rainbow trout that had
taunted him for two days—he wasn't about to quit now. Overcast
skies kept the temperature pleasantly cool. A passing cold front left
it breezy down in the valley by the creek where it was generally shel-
tered from the wind. The breeze ruffled his dirty blond hair as he
watched the rapids. With each gust of wind, a weeping willow
reached down to take a sip from the creek.

Twenty feet from the willow was a fire pit. Oak logs still smol-
dered from the fire he'd started earlier that morning. His gear bag sat
atop a pine picnic table next to the pit.

A red-tailed hawk flew down from his nest across the creek,
swooping toward the water in search of food. The hawk screeched,
protesting the man's presence, and then soared upward on a wind
current and back into the trees.

He couldn't see her, but he knew Beth was swinging in the rope
hammock on the porch of the log cabin he'd built high above the
creek. That's where he'd left her when he started down the serpen-
tine walkway from the cabin to the creek.

Thirty-three years old and a former Naval Intelligence Officer,
Jake worked as an accident investigator at the Atlanta Field Office of
the National Transportation Safety Board. Raised in the small Georgia
town of Newnan, Jake had lived his life, and certainly his career, over-
shadowed by his father's legacy.

Jake knew his coworkers at the Atlanta NTSB respected his intelligence. After all, he did graduate number one in his class at the

United States Naval Academy with a bachelor of science in aerospace engineering and a minor in political science. But he also carried the stigma that his father, a former NTSB chairman, not only had secured him the job with the NTSB but also was instrumental in his placement at the Atlanta Field Office. It was a stigma Jake desperately wanted to destroy. No matter how good he was at his job, he wondered if he would ever be seen as anything besides "JP's boy."

He waded fifteen feet from the creek bank and cast a gold bead head pheasant tail fly toward some rocks to entice the elusive rainbow trout. His Sage fly rod and Tibor reel gleamed as he cast upstream past some rocks along the far shoreline. As the fly floated past him, he mended his line to ensure a clean presentation. Then, with repeated strips—slow ten-inch pulls of the line—he began retrieving the fly.

On the fourth strip, the water roiled when the trout swallowed the fly. He raised the rod tip to set the hook and the trout broke the surface of the water, trying to free itself from the hook. It was the big one, the one he'd been chasing for days.

His pager vibrated. He ignored it as he kept working the fish. The trout was only ten feet from him when it made another run for the rocks, but not before Jake caught a glimpse of the size of this fish, an easy four pounder.

The pager vibrated again. He glanced down and saw the number. It was Patrick McGill, his boss, manager of the Atlanta Field Office and a good friend. The pager was only used for official NTSB business. Any personal contact was always done via cell phone.

"I'm on vacation," Jake grumbled. "What the hell does he want?"

He ignored the pager.

He worked the trout closer to him—almost within netting distance. He patted his chest pocket, an unconscious reflex, ensuring his camera was in his pocket. This was a picture he *had* to have. Proof of his conquest. Lifting the rod high with his right hand, he reached behind his back for his net. As he brought the net around, the trout made a leap into the air, thrashed in the water, spitting the fly free from its mouth.

As if taunting him, the fish rolled away and slapped the surface of the water with its tail before disappearing out of sight beneath a rock. Jake stood still, staring at the water in disbelief. Robbed of his trophy trout. "Son of a bitch."

He waded backwards toward shore, searching for any sign the trout had returned. After putting down his rod, he fumbled in his bag for his cell phone, never taking his eyes off the creek.

He pressed #3, speed dial for McGill, then pressed dial. The phone rang only once.

"Pat, it's Jake."

"Jake, hey buddy. I really hate to bother you while you're on vacation, but there's been an accident in Savannah and I really need you on this one"

"Savannah? What kind of accident?"

"A Challenger 604," McGill said. "Carrying an Irish high-profile who was supposed to speak and marshal the parade. It crashed while shooting an approach. The weather on the Eastern seaboard has closed most of the airports so the Go Team in DC can't get out for a few days, if at all. Our office is the Go Team, and the Director named me as IIC."

"Well, Mr. Investigator in Charge, what's the plan?"

"The plan is," McGill said, "for you to get your butt down here as fast as you can so we can get mobile."

"Pat, it'll take me a good two hours to get there," Jake said. "I've got to secure the cabin, pack a bag, and drop Beth off at her apartment. You should get on the road. I'll be a good hour behind you to Savannah. There's no way in hell you can wait on me and meet your two hour response time."

"No, I need you with us on the ride down, so we'll just wait for you." McGill said.

"Okay, but I can't make any promises on the time."

"Don't worry about the time, we're only going to get in an initial walk-through today because of weather and tides, then kick it off full bore tomorrow morning."

"Weather and tides? What do you mean, tides?" Jake asked. "Where did it crash?"

"In a tidal marsh," Pat said. "But I'm told it's easily accessible. You might want to bring those fishing waders you're no doubt wearing right now. You know, just in case."

"Pat, I still think you should just go on to Savannah without me. You can just brief me when I get there."

"Jake, you're not listening. The time doesn't matter, just get here ASAP."

"Fine, I'm on my way."

CHAPTER 7

Jake stored his fishing equipment in his bag and started up the incline to his cabin.

He wondered about the crash. A Challenger 604. He'd never worked an accident involving a Challenger. He'd investigated several business jet accidents, a couple of Learjets and Falcons, a Westwind, and a lot of business class turboprop accidents, but no Challengers yet. And this Challenger crashed in the marsh—a tidal marsh. *That should be interesting.*

He recalled some accident sites in the woods, along river banks, one actually in a river. Two small single engine piston powered aircraft, a Cessna and an experimental in the Okefenokee Swamp and countless numbers in open fields and hillsides.

As he approached his cabin, he thought about how disappointed Beth would be about canceling their plans. Hiking Amicalola Falls, walking around Dahlonega's town square, and her shopping trip to the outlet stores in Dawsonville would all have to wait again. How would he explain that his job had cancelled another one of their trips?

Jake walked to the side entrance of the cabin and onto the screened porch. He removed his boots and waders, then hung the waders on a rack to dry.

Beth was not where he'd left her, reading in the hammock. She'd been barefoot, wearing blue denim jeans, rolled up to mid-calf. She was wearing his long-sleeved cotton flannel shirt, the red and black plaid one, unbuttoned with the sleeves rolled up, and the shirt tail pulled up and tied into a knot at her navel. He smiled when he remembered her parting shot as he left with his fishing gear.

As he was walking away she had said, "You know I'm not wearing any underwear."

He turned to see her with shirt pulled open and her breasts exposed. "Tease."

He hurried upstairs to the master bedroom looking for her. No Beth. He grabbed his traveling toiletries and shoved them into his suitcase. He packed several changes of clothes, then hauled his suitcase downstairs and placed it by the door. He checked the guest room. No Beth.

Damn, where is she. I got to move it.

Jake hauled his bags outside to the driveway and placed his suitcase in the trunk. "Beth? Beth, are you out here?"

Where the hell is she?

He reset the thermostats and made sure the windows were latched.

"Dammit Beth, where the hell are you? I've been called in."

Then he knew. A smile crept across his face as he headed for the back porch.

She was naked in the hot tub on the back porch with the jets whirling the steamy water around her body. Her clothes piled in a chair next to the tub. She was stretched in the corner of the tub, her tanned arms resting on the edge. Her shoulder-length chestnut hair was pinned up. Her brown eyes turned a sparkling hazel in the sunlight. He looked at her scarlet nail polish and knew her sexy toes were painted to match.

Catherine Elizabeth McAllister didn't fit the traditional mold of a Southern belle, despite coming from a family with extremely conservative values. She worked at her father's bank in Newnan, a mundane nine-to-five job, but it paid the bills and offered her plenty of time off, an extra benefit of being the owner's daughter. Jake knew Beth's father still thought of her as Daddy's little girl, something he saw her exploit every chance she got.

"Babe, I've got some bad news," he said. He squatted down next to her and ran his fingers along her wet shoulder. "I've been called back to work and have to go to Savannah to investigate an accident."

"Old news, Jake. Pat called me when you didn't answer the page. He apologized for ruining our vacation, again. This is becoming a pattern, Jake. We hardly get away and you get called back to work."

"I know you're upset, but I promise to make it up to you."

"Upset? You have no freaking idea how upset I am. Do you realize the wedding is in less than three months and I still don't have a dress? I've got so much to do to get ready."

He smiled. "I know. I'm sorry, but right now you need to get packed, so we can get on the road."

A teasing glint in her eyes caught his attention. She raised her toes out of the water, tempting his foot fetish.

Beth had the advantage and he knew she was about to exploit it.

"I'm already packed, bag's in the car and ready to go, but first we have to have one last dip in the hot tub, so you better move it and get your ass in here!" She raised her body just enough to let her breasts break the surface of the water.

He tried to stay focused. "Hey, that's not fair. I need to get on the road. Quit fooling around. This is important. I don't have time."

"Jake, you owe me this one. I'm not going anywhere until you join me."

"Dammit, Beth. It'll have to wait, I have go. We have to go, now get dressed"

She slowly stood up. Steaming water droplets raced down her smooth skin. She turned her backside to him, teasingly bent over and shook her tight round ass at him. "You see something you like, big boy?"

He grabbed his shirt and ripped it off. As he tossed his clothes on the deck, he said, "Alright, you win. I lost my fish this morning and it waved its tail at me in mockery, but I'll be damned if I'm going to let this tail get away."

Laughing, she turned around just in time to see him jump into the tub with his socks still on.

He pulled her naked body against his. "Pat is going to be pissed."

CHAPTER 8

Four men sat in the conference room at the Savannah air traffic control facility, listening to a tape recording. It was the recording of the actual transmissions during the time frame when the aircraft accident occurred. Kaplan was saddened by the accident. He figured whatever happened to cause the accident probably happened inside the aircraft.

He'd been involved in two other accidents in his career as an air traffic controller, but this was his first involving a fatality. Kaplan felt sure he did everything by the book and would not be held liable in the accident. But the NTSB has been known to make issues out of procedures and working habits that controllers take for granted as safe operating practices.

The first accident for Kaplan occurred when a Piper Cherokee he was working ran out of gas. The pilot landed in a nearby field and tore up his airplane, but he walked away with only minor injuries. His second involvement was as a tower cab controller—local controller—when a pilot of a light twin-engine aircraft landed gear up. The only injury in that accident had been the pilot's pride.

The other men at the table were the Air Traffic Manager of the Savannah facility and the front line manager on duty at the time of the accident, and Kaplan's good friend, David Cook, the facility representative for the National Air Traffic Controllers Association (NATCA), the air traffic controllers union at the Savannah facility.

Kaplan trained Cook when he was hired fifteen years earlier, the best trainee Kaplan had ever had. They were both ex-military with similar exercise regimens and Kaplan quickly formed a lasting friendship with the forty-five year old Cook.

They sat on one side of the table while the air traffic manager and supervisor sat across from them in classic labor-versus-management style.

Cook and the supervisor took notes as the recording blared through the speaker.

Cook glanced at Kaplan, "You've been through this before, it's all standard protocol for accident investigations. Besides we want to listen to the recording before you write your official statement. Sometimes you hear things that you may not have remembered without listening."

"Thanks Cookie," a nickname affectionately given to Cook by his fellow controller. "I thought I did everything by the book—so far it sounds good."

Cook twirled his pen. "Gregg, everything I've heard so far is by the book. I don't think you have anything to worry about."

At the end of the tape, the air traffic manager said to Kaplan, "I didn't hear you read any of the weather strips. You know, the NTSB is going to bust our asses on that one."

"None were given to me so I never saw any," replied Kaplan. "I did read the local weather shortly after he checked on."

The manager rapped his fingers on the table, turned to Cook and said, "Cookie, the Region informed me this is a covered event for drug and alcohol testing, so Gregg will be required to remain here until they show up and administer the tests. They should be here in an hour or so."

Cook gave the manager an irritated look. "Gregg was clearly by the book. There's no reason for testing of any kind."

"The Region made the call. I have no choice in the matter," he replied and then paused. "You'll just have to deal with it. And by the way, Gregg, the NTSB will be in here tomorrow and you will be interviewed. Whether or not Cookie is invited is entirely up to the NTSB investigator."

Cook pushed his chair back abruptly and stood. "Might I remind you that Article 6 Section 1 entitles the union to be present at meetings with the NTSB?"

The manager said nothing.

Kaplan looked over to see a slight smirk on the supervisor's face. "I'm on annual leave tomorrow. I won't be back until next week."

"I'm canceling it. Part of it anyway. Be here no later than nine o'clock in the morning. You'll meet with an FAA attorney at nine, then with the NTSB at ten."

Cook shook his finger at the manager. "You can't cancel annual leave that's already been approved. Gregg may very well have made plans by now."

"Well, I am—file a grievance if you want to." The manager turned to Kaplan. "Be here tomorrow morning at nine o'clock and that's an order. And Gregg, one more thing, you're relieved of air traffic control duties until the NTSB gives you the green light."

"You can't do that, you have no cause," Cook said. "You heard the tapes, Gregg was by the book."

"I just did. The phone hasn't stopped ringing, the newspapers, TV stations. I'm not taking any chances. That's the way it's going to be."

The manager turned and left the room.

"I'll talk to him, maybe I can change his mind." The supervisor handed Kaplan an accident statement form. "I'll need this before you go home, okay, Gregg?"

Kaplan nodded. "Yeah, no problem."

He started writing his statement for the accident, recalling the events of the morning. His mind replayed the scene.

He'd plugged his headset into the slot next to Annie's and joked with her a few minutes before she briefed him. He'd sat down and taken over as she left. It had seemed like a busy morning with the heavy inbound push but quickly turned into a routine day. Nothing had occurred to raise unusual tension in the room, until he heard that "Mayday" from the corporate jet making its approach to the airport.

Kaplan finished writing his statement, omitting only the personal byplay between him and Annie, and then handed it to Cook to proofread.

"Thanks, Gregg. I trust you, just give it to Mac. I'm going to talk to that asshole in the front office and see about getting you back to work."

"Good luck with that, Cookie. I wouldn't worry with it too much. I'm on leave for the next few days anyway."

"I know, Gregg. It's just the principle of the matter. The prick stepped over the line, and in my eyes, that's tantamount to starting a fight. I don't like it when he picks on one of my troops."

Cook left the union office.

Kaplan found the supervisor in the hall and handed him the statement. "Here you go, Mac, all done."

"I talked to the son of a bitch but he won't budge. I left when Cookie showed up. He's in there yelling at him now. The drug and alcohol testers are already here," the supervisor told him. "Check in with them and when you're done you're excused for the rest of the day. I'll take care of the CRU-ART," making reference to the automated sign-on/sign-off program used by the FAA, similar to punching a time clock.

Kaplan raised his arm to acknowledge and headed for the designated drug testing room.

After the tests were administered, he walked to the parking lot and climbed onto his black Harley Davidson Fat Boy. Kaplan slipped on his sunglasses, fired up the 1584 cc Twin Cam 96B balanced engine and pulled out of the airport parking lot. He waited impatiently as the security gate slowly opened, twisting the throttle rapidly, revving the engine. Before the gate had fully opened, he sped out.

Kaplan had lived in Savannah for nearly twenty years, getting hired after the hiring spree that followed the 1981 Professional Air Traffic Controllers Organization strike.

He had grown up near an airport in Fayetteville, North Carolina. As a young boy he would ride his bicycle to the airport and sit for hours watching the airplanes take off and land. One of the Fayetteville air traffic controllers noticed Kaplan out there nearly every day. On one occasion, he invited young Kaplan up into the tower.

He was an instant favorite in the tower. He still remembered the amazement on the controllers' faces when they saw how well he knew and recognized the different aircraft, in some instances better than some of the controllers. When asked where he learned so much, he told them he spent a lot of time at the library reading about airplanes from the library's copy of Jane's *All the World's Aircraft*.

After high school, he attended North Carolina State University for two years. When his parents were killed in an automobile accident, the financial burden forced him to drop out of college and work full time at a hardware store in his hometown. Eventually Kaplan got bored and joined the Army. Upon enlistment, he requested flight training to be a pilot, either fixed wing or helicopters. He didn't care as long as he was flying. He was informed that there were no slots available, nor would there be for a couple of years. After some soul-searching, he enlisted as a private in an infantry division.

At a solid, muscular two hundred twenty pounds, his strength was impressive. His personal regimen was strict.

He received accolades in marksmanship, self-defense, and field navigation, and after two years, became part of the Special Forces Airborne Division in Fort Bragg, North Carolina. At the end of his four-year enlistment, the Army offered him a lucrative reenlistment incentive and, seeing nothing in civilian life very promising, he stayed in four more years.

He'd earned respect from his fellow soldiers and his superiors alike for his calm demeanor in the face of adversity, his intuitive instinct, and his survival skills—skills he shelved in civilian life, not knowing that one day they might save his life.

CHAPTER 9

The black 1967 Pontiac GTO screeched to a stop in the NTSB designated parking area at the Atlanta Federal Building. Four men stood next to the two Suburbans belonging to the NTSB Atlanta Field Office—some with their hands in their pockets, some with arms folded, all with an agitated look as they stared at Jake with Beth McAllister riding shotgun.

Beth raised her eyebrows. "It looks like the natives are growing restless."

"You think? Should I tell them the real reason I'm late?"

She smiled.

He parked next to the white Suburbans brandishing the black block letters NTSB on the sides and rear, retrieved his bag from the trunk and handed her the keys. "Take care of her."

"Don't worry, Jake. I promise I'll keep it under a hundred."

Jake had always been a fan of the classic muscle cars—the GTO was his favorite. He bought the GTO from a man who was desperate to sell after going through a divorce. The man had started the restoration process when he had to sell—part of the marriage dissolution decree. Jake had spent the last ten months and over ten thousand dollars bringing the GTO to mint condition.

As she stepped out of the car, Pat McGill greeted her with a hug. "As always, it's nice to see you again, Beth. Sorry again about ruining your vacation."

"It's nice to see you too, Pat. Don't worry about it. Jake was getting to be a real pain in the ass," she laughed. "God, all he wanted to do was eat, fish, and have sex and not necessarily in that order. I needed a break anyway."

"Hey, I resent that remark," Jake said. He held up his hands. "Which vehicle am I in, Pat?"

McGill pointed to the Suburban next to the GTO. "You and I are in that one and actually, you're driving." McGill tossed him the keys.

McGill looked over at Beth and winked. "What are you going to do without him?"

"Get a little peace and quiet." She grinned. "Or maybe just one good night's sleep."

"Funny girl," Jake said. "I'll call you when I know something."

She slipped into the driver's seat of the GTO, put it in gear and drove off. Jake put his bag in the back of the Suburban and closed the back door.

"I thought you were taking her to Peachtree City first?" McGill said.

"Well ... it took us a little longer than I planned to get away from the cabin."

McGill laughed, motioned all the investigators into a small circle and said, "I've done as much of the pre-launch checklist as I can, which I mentioned on the phone. The command center will call while we're en route with more details. Let's move out. We're already well over our two hours."

Within minutes of leaving the Federal Building, the two Suburbans were cruising down Interstate 75 southbound toward Macon. McGill leaned over and picked up one of the two-way radios. "Unit one to unit two, how do you read?"

"Pat, we got you five by five." It was a reference to the old military scale of one to five, or loud and clear.

McGill keyed the microphone. "When we get south of Macon on I-16, I'll give the briefing to everyone at once, so keep the radio on."

He put the radio down and turned to Jake. "It's been a long time since I've been back to Savannah, much less for St. Patrick's Day. It's a shame we won't get to enjoy the big party."

"Can you believe it? I've lived in Georgia off and on my whole life and I've never been to Savannah. I've heard it has great food and plenty of beer."

"It's a historical town," said McGill. "I lived there for several years after we moved from Ireland."

"Okay. I know you've been in the states a long time but just how long did you live in Savannah? And what do you mean, *we*?"

"I moved to Savannah twenty-five years ago, with my aunt and my cousin."

"With your aunt and cousin?" Jake asked. He slowed the Suburban for a construction zone on the interstate.

"My parents died when I was five," McGill said. "My aunt and uncle took me in and raised me."

"You've been here twenty-five years and in all that time you've never lost that Irish accent?" Jake laughed.

"No, I guess I haven't."

"What part of Ireland are you from?"

"Northern Ireland, actually. A little town in the northwestern corner called Londonderry. We left because of the Troubles in Northern Ireland. It got to be too much for my aunt to deal with."

"What were the Troubles?"

"I thought you minored in political science? Don't they teach you prep boys anything?"

"I thought that was just some religious tension stuff."

"It's more than that. It's political, religious, ethnic. But mostly just a dark time in Ireland's history. And, although it has gotten a lot better in recent years—mostly due to the 1998 Good Friday Peace Agreement and the formation of the New Northern Ireland Assembly—Northern Ireland still has a long way yet to go before we have true peace."

Jake noticed a change in McGill's expression, an introspective stillness. McGill was never one to talk about his past. It quickly became apparent he wasn't going to talk about it now either. Something was bothering McGill, Jake knew that for sure.

CHAPTER 10

She stood in front of the mirror while waiting for the hot water to work its way through the pipes from her basement to her third-floor master bathroom. The volume on the TV was barely loud enough for her to notice the broadcast interruption from the news station. The news flash was reporting an aircraft accident that just occurred near the Savannah River. She ran into the bedroom, grabbed the TV remote from her nightstand and turned the volume up.

> *"A corporate jet has crashed while on approach to the Savannah International airport. According to sources, the crash site is on or near Hutchinson Island. Rescue, fire and police units are responding. Traffic has the Talmadge Bridge gridlocked and authorities have temporarily closed the bridge so rescue and emergency vehicles can access the scene. We will bring you more as developments occur."*

Annie looked at the clock next to her bed and knew that Gregg Kaplan must have been working the aircraft that crashed. She had been a controller for over fifteen years but had never worked an aircraft accident. She had heard the stories of stress and trauma from the air traffic controllers involved with accidents and could only imagine the emotions they felt.

She reached for the phone and started to dial Gregg's cell phone, but then hung up. She didn't know what to say to him. Tears rolled down her cheeks as she replayed the morning's events.

Immediately after Kaplan had relieved her from the controller position, she had signed out for the day, headed to her locker, put up her headset and grabbed her purse. Kaplan's suggestive remarks had distracted her with the thought of last night's garden tub adventure. The events rolled through her mind as she exited the front door of the facility and headed across the parking lot to her car.

She slipped into the front seat and checked herself in the mirror, put on dark red lipstick, her sunglasses, put the key in the ignition.

The red Mazda Miata MX-5 came to life. The engine quietly hummed as she lowered the convertible top and secured it. She unclipped her hair and shook her head, then pulled her hair back into a ponytail and slipped on her baseball cap. After a few more seconds, she gave herself one final primp check in the rearview mirror, pursing her lips.

She pulled away from the tower, out the gate and onto Gulfstream Road. She accelerated the car, her auburn ponytail whipping in the air. A hundred thoughts invaded her mind, from Kaplan's disheveled appearance this morning to the items on her day's "to do" list.

Distracted, she suddenly realized she was about to miss her exit, she swerved across two lanes of traffic amid the blaring horns of angry motorists and down the off ramp. Her house was only five more minutes away.

She pulled into the alley behind her home on Oglethorpe Street, across from Colonial Park Cemetery in the historic district. She opened the rear gate and drove into the garage, leaving the garage door open for Kaplan. She climbed the stairs to the door that let her directly into the kitchen.

Scout, her overweight tortoiseshell cat greeted her, rubbing against Annie's legs before walking over to her food dish. "Okay, I know, it's time to eat," Annie said as she reached down to pet her.

She tossed her car keys on the counter next to her mail basket. Her day had started without her normal regimen of fifty sit-ups followed by forty-five minutes on her StairMaster. She grabbed a bottle of water out of the refrigerator and headed upstairs. Annie took off her work clothes, slipped into her workout clothes, and walked into her exercise room on the third floor.

Twenty minutes later she abandoned her workout. Something wasn't right. She just couldn't get into it. She stripped off her workout clothes, tossed them into the hamper and turned on the hot water in the shower.

After showering, she wrapped a towel around her wet hair like a turban. She dried off with another towel and then draped it over the glass shower enclosure hanging it equal lengths from the top on both sides. She needed to hurry—Kaplan was probably already on his way to her house.

CHAPTER 11

Tehran, Iran

"Son of a bitch!" The Persian grabbed the metal statue from the table and hurled it at the television. The statue smashed through the screen, sending glass shards onto the floor. Smoke billowed toward the ceiling, sparks flew.

His two children, a girl and a boy, ran into the room. "Father!"

His wife followed them and saw the television. "Farid Nasiri—the children. What have you done?"

The Persian, born in Tehran, Iran, in 1975, was the son of a wealthy businessman. He inherited the business when his father was killed in a tunnel bombing in Afghanistan after the United States retaliated from the Al Qaeda attacks of September 11, 2001. He had a ruthless business style and was known for his foul temper and unscrupulous dealings. On more than one occasion he had double-crossed his contacts, keeping both the money and the merchandise. His contacts were reluctant to do business with him, mostly out of fear. And he'd just learned that Laurence O'Rourke's chartered jet had crashed in Savannah, Georgia.

He turned to his wife and glared. His hard black eyes cut at her from underneath his traditional headwear.

She lowered her eyes, looking at the floor. "I beg your forgiveness."

He motioned with his hand, muttering, "Leave me." She ran to the kitchen, hurrying the children to their bedrooms.

How could this have happened? Who would want O'Rourke dead? A question he knew didn't need answering.

While in Dallas, O'Rourke first made contact with the Persian through an Iranian singles web site, the Persian's usual method of conducting business.

He had contacted O'Rourke yesterday to confirm the offshore account number. The money had been raised and a substantial deposit made in O'Rourke's Cayman bank account.

The disappointing news of Laurence O'Rourke's death could have a devastating impact on the plans of the terrorist cells.

How would the news be taken by the leader?

Even more troubling, how would the Pakistani take the news? Salim Malik, Bin Laden's number-two man, was known for his barbaric methods of punishment.

No sooner had the disturbing thought passed through the Persian's mind when his cell phone rang. Malik.

"Hello?"

"Your failure is not looked upon favorably by our leader, Farid."

"How could this be my failure? These are not circumstances I have control over."

"You should have planned better. You should have realized the dynamics surrounding this man O'Rourke and planned accordingly. These things should have been taken into consideration before you disclosed your intentions to our leader."

"But the situation—"

"Enough," Malik said. "He will give you one more chance. Another failure on your part and you will never see paradise. Is that clear, Farid?"

Before the Persian could answer, Salim Malik hung up.

CHAPTER 12

Ian Collins yawned as he rode down the escalator at the Jacksonville International Airport, his overnight bag slung over his left shoulder.

He had tried to sleep on the airplane but the woman in the seat next to him was a talker. A baby two rows back cried half way to Jacksonville. And there was the nine-year-old kid in the seat behind him who got bored and started kicking the back of his seat. Collins had stopped that quickly. He removed a contact, leaned around the seat and gave the kid an evil look. "Don't do it again."

The petrified boy didn't move the remainder of the flight to Jacksonville.

He held his Blackberry in his right hand, reading his new messages. The first of the four messages was from Savannah:

Call me when you arrive JAX—Jillian

He remembered how anxious she sounded on the phone the night before about her part of the operation—he shook his head. He advanced his Blackberry to the second message. Message number two was from Belfast:

Request immediate update on O'Rourke.

The third message was also from Belfast, although from a different sender. This sender had an opposite agenda from the others.

Word is phase one of Savannah Project complete. Please confirm.

The fourth message was a follow-up message from Jillian.

LO crashed the party about twenty minutes late. Surprise party was a success.

He walked across several lanes of traffic in front of the baggage claim area to the area designated for courtesy vans. Several passengers were taking advantage of this first opportunity to smoke a cigarette since leaving their departure points. Annoyed by the smoke, Collins moved to an isolated section of the waiting area. He placed his bag on the concrete and leaned back against the metal rail separating the waiting areas from the lanes of traffic.

While waiting for the courtesy van to pick him up, he typed out replies to some of his messages. First, he responded to Jillian's:

Happy to hear party went as planned. We must still monitor the situation closely and keep away uninvited guests. Find Sullivan location. Will call when arrive SAV.

The next message was sent to Belfast. The message was short and to the point:

LO sanctioned.

The interest in Laurence O'Rourke from so many different parties in Belfast had aroused his interest from the onset. It was a risky game he was playing—pitting several dangerous parties' interests against each other, all for the sake of the money—a lot of money. If he was successful in executing his plan, he would collect from all three parties and they would each get what they paid for. If he failed, he was virtually out of business and would have a contract placed on his head.

The final message also went out to Belfast:

Phase one complete. Savannah Project progressing as planned.

Sullivan in Savannah, location unknown.

He hit the send button as the courtesy van pulled up to the curb. The driver tried to take his bag to place it in the baggage area but he refused. Finding a seat in the front row, he placed his bag in his lap. As the van pulled into the parking garage, he received a reply from his last message.

Sullivan deemed a liability to Savannah Project. Additional sanction. Commensurate supplement as previously agreed.

The elimination of Michael Sullivan didn't really come as a surprise to the assassin. It was something he was prepared to do but wanted to avoid. The Savannah Project was going to cost him enough personally as it was. The betrayal of his childhood friends was already a struggle. He didn't need the additional burden of eliminating another, even closer relationship.

CHAPTER 13

McGill's cell phone rang. Jake could see the caller ID. It read "Headquarters." McGill answered, "Pat McGill."

He could only hear McGill's side of the conversation but it was enough for him to know that more details about the accident were available.

He saw a sheepish grin come across his friend's face. McGill spoke into the phone, "Really? The Westin, huh? Wow. Okay, we're just south of Macon now so we should be there in a couple of hours. I'll have Carol call you with our arrival time."

McGill hung up the phone and glanced at Jake. "Well, Junior, it looks like Daddy came to the rescue again. He called the mayor of Savannah and found out they always book extra rooms downtown for dignitaries and VIPs.

"JP snagged us six rooms at the Westin Savannah Harbor Resort located on none other than Hutchinson Island. He also arranged for two conference rooms and the Westin is furnishing dedicated phone lines, a fax machine and a copier."

McGill added, "The Westin is right across the Savannah River from the historic district with water taxis running back and forth all day and most of the night. It's even better for us because we can stay out of the historic district mob."

Jake clenched his jaw and muttered under his breath, "That meddling son of a—"

McGill interrupted. "Come on, Jake, give the old man a break. It's in his blood. You, of all people should know that by now. He's just trying to be helpful. It's hard for your father to let go. It's killing him that his health took him out of the game."

"I know, I know. He just won't leave my life well enough alone. It's a hard shadow to get out from under and just when I think I'm almost there, he does something like this."

"Why don't you call Beth and have her come down," McGill said. "She'll have a good time. Just tell her she will only get to see you at night."

"Good idea, I think I will." Jake smiled as he picked up his cell phone.

While he was talking to Beth, McGill's phone rang again. Jake didn't notice the caller ID this time but from the snippets of conversation that he overheard, he could tell McGill was meeting someone in Savannah.

He and McGill ended their conversations simultaneously. Jake said, "That girl was already packed. I guess she must have known. Did headquarters call you again?"

McGill held up his cell phone. "My cousin in Savannah returning my call."

He picked up the radio and asked, "Are you guys ready for the briefing?"

"Whenever you are, Pat," was the reply through the speaker.

"This morning at approximately 1510 Zulu or 1110 Eastern daylight time, a Challenger 604 en route from Dallas Love to Savannah crashed while shooting a GPS approach to runway 27," McGill said, flipping through the initial accident report.

"The controller had switched the aircraft over to the tower frequency and subsequently heard a 'Mayday.' He noticed the Challenger fly about a mile off the final approach course when the radar target disappeared. The flight plan indicated six souls on board. The fixed base operator stated that there were two male pilots, a female flight attendant, and three male passengers.

"The aircraft was equipped with all the latest and greatest avionics, a full glass cockpit, the Collins ProLine 4 EFIS system, I believe, including a flight data recorder and a cockpit voice recorder, which we'll concentrate on locating first. The aircraft's equipment list showed dual ELTs, a 406 MHz, GPS enabled and a TSO-91A transmitting on 121.5 MHz."

Jake listened intently. So far, it was all basic facts.

"The crash site is solely contained in a brackish water marsh. I want everyone in coveralls, boots, rubber gloves under leather gloves, facemask and goggles. The DC Go Team can't make this one until later in the week, if at all, due to the snowstorm in the mid-Atlantic and New England states. They have their hands full with a regional jet that crashed departing Reagan National and the two airliners that slid off runways this morning in Dulles and Boston.

"Gulfstream Aerospace Corporation in Savannah will be in on this one as an industry volunteer and they have made an old empty hangar available for us. Gulfstream indicated they won't need the hangar for at least a couple of months. They have been granted Party status. Others granted status as parties to the investigation are Bombardier, General Electric, Collins, Honeywell, and NATCA for ATC. There are others but those are just a few."

McGill folded the report and placed it in his lap.

"The FAA will no doubt have someone there waiting for us on site, thinking he's in charge. I'm sure there will be other parties showing up tomorrow. I think that about wraps it up except for one more thing."

He looked over at Jake and grinned. "It looks like Junior's dad got us all rooms at the Westin by pulling a few strings with the mayor."

Before Jake could even say a word, the jokes started flying from the radio. He just shook his head and shot McGill a dirty look. "Thanks a lot, asshole."

McGill laughed, then continued talking to the group over the radio, "We'll head straight to the crash site and start stakedown procedures. Carol went ahead this morning in a company car and will set up the conference room and pressroom at the Westin. Since there were no survivors—this is recovery only, so we'll be working daylight hours only. There will be an organizational meeting this evening in the hotel at 1830 and a short press conference at 1900."

Traveling to Savannah about thirty minutes ahead of the team was Carol Martin, McGill's administrative assistant. Her superior organizational skills kept the office running smooth regardless of the chaos at hand.

McGill had told Jake that he first met Carol when he worked in the D.C. office as part of the D.C. Go Team. As he was promoted through the ranks, he came to rely on Carol's ability to handle all the small details. When McGill became manager of the Atlanta office, he offered her a job as his assistant. At first reluctant to leave the D.C. area, she refused until her husband died of a heart attack a month later. When McGill called with his condolences, Carol asked if the job offer was still available. Even though he had already hired someone, he gladly told Carol the job was hers for the asking.

McGill continued, "We'll meet back in the morning at 0700, just the Board members. At 0730 I will call all the groups together and we'll officially kick this thing off at that point. I'll inform you as to who is the leader of which group at the organizational meeting tonight. Some of you will no doubt be leading more than one group. We'll talk again as we get closer to Savannah."

As McGill spoke to the team, Jake sensed edginess in his voice. Edginess that he'd never heard before.

This investigation would be different from all the other investigations.

CHAPTER 14

Kaplan pulled into the alley behind an old three-story duplex on the edge of Savannah's historic district. He unlocked the gate with his keys and drove his Fat Boy into the back yard, parking it underneath the second floor balcony.

As soon as he turned off his motorcycle Kaplan heard a familiar female voice call out, "I called the facility. Mac said you already left. Come on up and tell me all about it."

He hung his black half-shell Harley helmet on one of the motorcycle's mirrors and walked through the garage next to her Miata, climbed the stairs to the second floor and entered into the kitchen. Annie kept her house spotless, and the modern kitchen lined with white cabinets was where she spent most of her time. The bright sunny room always energized her, and that's where he found her, sitting on the bench in the oversized bay window next to the kitchen, a book in her hands, Scout in her lap. The cat jumped down from Annie's lap, landed on the floor with a thud, then walked over to Kaplan and purred as she rubbed against his pant leg.

Annie's face had a youthful glow—younger than her thirty-nine years. She looked up at Kaplan. "Rough day at the office, I hear."

"I've had better."

He took in her sweat pants, form-fitting short-sleeved crop t-shirt and white socks, her hair pulled into a ponytail. She smiled at him, her green eyes sparkled in the light from the bay window. A splash of faded freckles ran across the bridge of her nose.

"And to top it off, I have to go in tomorrow for interviews with an FAA lawyer and the NTSB," Kaplan said. "It shouldn't take long. Then it's just you and me and thousands of visitors." The crowds attracted by St. Patrick's Day wouldn't be clearing out for a few days.

"That sucks. Why do you have to go in when you're on leave?"

"The manager ordered me in to meet with the NTSB and relieved me from ATC duties until the investigator clears me back to work. I didn't even know they did that kind of thing. I think he's just flexing his muscles to piss off Cookie."

"Did it work?"

"Oh yeah. When I left, Cookie was in his office giving him an earful."

"I would love to have been a fly on the wall for that conversation." She stood, and threw her arms around his neck. "How about a beer?"

"Two. Get me two beers, please. I think I'll skip Barry's tonight—I'm not really in the mood. I hope you don't mind."

"No, I don't mind. I kinda figured we'd stay in tonight anyway."

"Great. So what'd you do all day?" he asked.

"The usual, pined for you all day, wondering when you would get here to tell me about your day."

Kaplan walked into the living room and fired back, "Liar."

Scout followed him into the living room. Kaplan found a seat on the long leather sofa. Scout jumped into his lap, padded her paws on Kaplan's leg, then settled in for a comfortable nap.

Kaplan first met Annie when she transferred to the Savannah facility from Augusta, Georgia. On her first day at the Savannah facility, she went into the radar room to observe and ran right into him as he was walking out. They stood an inch apart, staring at each other in the doorway to the dark radar room.

Kaplan looked down at her and said, "Are you coming or going?"

Flustered, she said, "Depends." It was the only response Annie could think of.

"Depends on what?"

"On you." She smiled.

"Well, I'm going to the break room—care to join me?"

"Sure, I'd like that."

Annie's confident, brash manner intimidated a lot of men, but not Kaplan. He was the only man who ever made her feel "weak in the knees," she had told her best friend soon after the relationship with Kaplan began. Her demeanor was different around him. Subdued. Submissive. Even their coworkers remarked about the different tone in her voice when he was around.

The day they met, the two of them talked for thirty minutes until Kaplan's break was over. Annie asked him if she could sit and observe him in the radar room while he was plugged into position—an opportunity neither of them let pass by.

After work, they went out for dinner, and later sat on a bench on River Street for hours talking. That was more than fourteen years ago.

Annie walked into the living room with the beer bottles and placed them on the coffee table. "Here you go—for my two-fisted drinker."

Waving her arm down toward Kaplan's lap, she said, "Okay, Scout, scram. Shoo. This is my time with Gregg."

Scout ignored her and didn't move, so she picked her up and moved her to the opposite end of the sofa where the cat curled up in a ball. Positioned just right so she could see Kaplan and Annie.

Annie unbuttoned Kaplan's shirt down to his navel, started rubbing his chest and said, "Now, tell me about the accident. And don't leave out any details."

Kaplan removed her pony tail holder, letting her hair fall to her shoulders. Placing his hand on the back of her neck, he ran his fingers through her thick red hair.

"Well, it all started when I let a good-looking redhead off position so she could go home and goof off."

"Goof off!" She punched him in the stomach lightly with her fist. "I'll have you know I came home and did my workout, cleaned up around this house, and … well, I did take a little nap right after lunch," she said, shrugging her shoulders. Then her smile faded and she grew serious. "Just tell me what happened."

"I had a Challenger coming from the west. I set him up for the approach to runway 27. Everything seemed fine until I tried to switch him to the tower. Then I heard a couple of maydays. He just disappeared from radar."

"No other signs of trouble?"

"No, actually, he had been the least of my worries."

"What do you think happened?"

"I don't really have a clue, but I can only guess that since he was slowing and lowering his gear and flaps for final approach, he had some sort of mechanical issue that caused him to lose control of the aircraft."

Annie nodded and reached for her beer bottle. "The news said there was an Irish bigwig on board. He seemed sort of controversial, the way they described him."

"That's what they said at work. They came out and made me pee in a cup and blow in the tube," Kaplan said.

Annie chuckled.

Stretching out on the couch, she accidentally kicked Scout, who jumped off the couch, letting out a squawk in protest.

Looking up into Kaplan's eyes, Annie finished unbuttoning his shirt and said, "You look tense ... why don't you let me help you relax a little?"

She slid her fingers down his chest, stopping at his belly button. "We could play good cop, bad cop," she murmured.

"Not tonight. I'm a little stressed, you know how we hate to lose one. Maybe I'm just tired and need some time to think. No games tonight."

Grinning, she jumped up amid his protests and said, "What you need is a distraction."

"Annie, not now."

"I'll be right back." She jumped off the sofa and removed her t-shirt, revealing her firm, round breasts. "I won't need this." She tossed the shirt onto his lap.

He watched her strut topless toward the stairwell and up the steps. She stopped midway, removed her sweatpants and tossed them over the balustrade. They landed on the sofa next to Kaplan. She turned and disappeared into the bedroom wearing only her white socks.

Kaplan flipped through the channels on the TV and found another news broadcast on CNN Headline News about the accident. He fell deep into thought about the next day's interview with NTSB and how that would pan out.

Focused on the information the newscasters were reporting about Laurence O'Rourke and the accident, Kaplan didn't notice Annie come down the stairs.

"Ahem," she called from the stairway.

She stood there in a black thong, thigh-high black fishnet nylons and black stiletto heels. On her head perched a dark blue police hat. Smiling, she turned her back to him and slowly held up a pair of shiny silver handcuffs and dangled them.

In a sultry voice she taunted, "I've been bad—very, very bad."

He laughed. "Annie, you sure know how to take a man's mind off of his troubles."

He got up and walked over to her.

She pushed out her derriere.

The sound of the handcuffs clamping around Annie's wrists sent Scout darting down the hall and out of sight.

CHAPTER 15

Jake spotted the accident scene as the Suburban crested the top span of the Talmadge Memorial Bridge toward Hutchinson Island. As they crept across the bridge, McGill pointed to the smoke rising from the still smoldering crash site. "There it is."

"I see it." Jake said. "But at this rate it'll take us an hour just to get to it. Damned at the cars."

McGill looked at Jake, "Since we seem to have time, you ready for a history lesson on Hutchinson Island?"

"Do I have a choice?"

"The first settlers of Savannah used this island as a place for duels before it was turned into a communal farm. Slaves planted hay and rice as well as built the Savannah waterfront and warehouses. As the population started getting sick from fever, the mosquitoes from the rice fields were linked to the illnesses, so the rice fields were destroyed.

After that, the island was turned into an industrial center with the arrival of the Seaboard Railroad in 1896. Then in 1919, a fire destroyed most of the cotton and turpentine warehouses."

Jake interrupted, "Good, we're moving again. Thanks for the history lesson. Am I going to be tested on it later?"

"Maybe." McGill laughed at Jake's sarcasm. "Learn from history, Jake. That way you don't make the same mistakes."

At the bottom of the north end of the bridge, law enforcement officers directed traffic. A Georgia state trooper feverishly waved his arm demanding travelers to South Carolina keep moving. Another trooper directed all cars exiting onto Hutchinson Island toward the resort end of the island or toward the scene of the accident. A staging area near the exit ramp had been designated for the press. No press was allowed closer than the bridge to view and report on the accident.

The highways in the Savannah area were already jammed with travelers making their way into town for St. Patrick's Day. Savannah, rich in its Southern heritage and claiming a larger than average population of Irish and Catholic descent, boasted the second largest St. Patrick's Day parade in the United States.

Jake looked at the sky, noticed how the overcast had reduced their available light, then glanced at his watch and calculated the Go Team had only about two and a half hours of daylight left at best. The long line of rescue vehicles looked like an arrow pointing the way to the accident with their flashing lights. The visibility had fallen to less than five miles and dropping, and the cloud ceiling had lowered below one thousand feet. Low, transparent white wisps of clouds scudded quickly across a darkened overcast sky.

The Suburbans exited the bridge and followed the police blockades to an unpaved access road, then followed the road until they reached a large sweeping left turn, where a Georgia State Patrol officer stopped them.

After showing their credentials, the Go Team was directed off the access road onto a two-rut road. Within fifty feet they reached an impasse of vehicles of every type, rescue, fire and police, and were directed to park in an area just cleared by a bulldozer. A Georgia trooper was arguing with a reporter and his cameraman, apparently disgruntled about being told to move the TV station's van back to the media staging area. A truck was hauling a small trailer into the clearing to serve as the NTSB's temporary on-site command center.

Team members put on their standard issue NTSB coveralls and caps, donned their gloves, face masks and goggles, then sealed their gloves and boots to their coveralls with duct tape. Grabbing their cameras, markers, tape, and an assortment of other necessities, they strapped on their accident packs and made their way down a muddy path.

The first person to meet them was FAA Accident Investigator Aaron Kowalski, who oversaw the initial site security. After introductions, Kowalski explained his earlier actions at the site and issues involving the tides and the marsh. "We cordoned off the area as instructed. The fire burned pretty hot and several hotspots reignited and had to be extinguished again. All those on board perished so the bodies or what's left of them were left the way we found them. We're hauling in sand bags to place around a wide perimeter to help with the water intrusion. The first truckload should arrive any minute now." He pointed and led them toward the still smoldering wreckage. "If you're ready."

As they reached the clearing, they could see the twisted airframe and other debris resting in a salt flat about the size of a football field, a small area for an aircraft accident Jake noted as he stepped over the yellow police tape marking the perimeter of the crash site.

It was low tide so the site was relatively easy to navigate, but Jake knew at high tide it would be much more difficult.

*   *   *

The smell of burnt metal, fabric, wiring, and jet fuel filled his nostrils. A smell all too familiar to McGill. The tang brought a flood of memories back of the first time he inhaled it. When he found his calling.

In 1988, while studying at Georgia Tech for a degree in Aerospace Engineering, McGill learned his aunt in Savannah had died of a stroke. He and his cousin took her remains to Scotland, her birthplace, to be buried. The cemetery was at a church on the outskirts of the small village of Tundergarth. Almost on cue with the closing "amen" of the ceremony, flaming debris rained down from the sky littering across the open expanse next to the church. Suitcases, clothes, twisted metal of all shapes and sizes, showered across the rolling fields. Mourners scattered about, running for cover, but McGill stood there staring into the debris field.

As if in a trance, he slowly started walking into the field until a thunderous crash stopped him dead in his tracks. The ground shook. He turned to see the right half of a Boeing 747's cockpit lying on the ground only thirty feet from where he stood.

He walked toward the wreckage. It groaned as it settled onto the ground. He stood back from the cockpit and noticed the words "Maid of the Seas" painted on the side of the aircraft shell. Looking around the area, he noticed no other large debris. He felt a sense of urgency to know where the remainder of the airliner went and what caused such a large, sturdy aircraft to destruct in mid air.

McGill and his cousin left Tundergarth and headed back toward Lockerbie. They saw more debris in fields and on the roads. Civilians and authorities pitched in to move debris out of the roads to make them passable. In Lockerbie, they saw the largest devastation. The bulk of the Pan Am Boeing 747 had plowed through the town, destroying more than twenty homes and forming a linear crater. Lockerbie lay in shambles.

Looking at the huge hulks of twisted metal that were once a fuselage, he had an epiphany, his destiny called him. Most people would have nightmares at seeing such horror and destruction, McGill was excited and charged with passion.

Immediately upon arriving back in the States, he started taking the first steps toward a career as an aircraft accident investigator.

*   *   *

McGill cleared the stakedown area of all personnel except for his team. The Go Team would walk the perimeter of the main wreckage taking notes and discussing anything peculiar that might be observed.

After the perimeter walk, McGill would assign duties and responsibilities to each member, and the site would be secured, this time for the evening. The team would leave the site en route to the organizational meeting, and if necessary, McGill would conduct a press briefing.

It had been several hours since the accident occurred. Rescue personnel had been advised to remove only those who might still be alive. The remains of the dead were to be left undisturbed, orders of the NTSB Command Center and the FAA. The site was treated by the police as a crime scene—necessary to avoid compromising an investigation by inadvertently tainting evidence. The fire department was allowed to put out and contain any fires. Six red body bags lay empty on the marsh, one for each reported person on board.

The team made their way across the tidal marsh. Low tide had been more than thirty minutes prior and the smell of exposed mud and sea life still hung in the air. The tide had turned and the waters rose. Tiny crabs and spiders worked their way to the tops of the saw grass blades and jumped on the pants legs of the team members in hopes of hitch-hiking a ride to dry ground.

Across the marsh beyond the wreckage McGill saw Back River, the river that constituted the state line between Georgia and South Carolina.

Most of the wreckage was situated on the hard-packed sandy portion of the salt flat, although some debris lay in the softer muck. The muck made walking difficult, and McGill told them it would be increasingly harder to work as the tide came in.

The sawgrass, brown as winter approached its end, stood tall, sometimes as high as four feet. With each gust of wind the dense grass did "the wave" around the accident—bowing down and rising again. Thousands of tiny holes dotted the harder packed marsh flats, little mounds of dirt piled next to each hole. Fiddler crabs scurried in and out hauling food to and from their homes.

A great blue heron swooped in low across the wreckage and landed near Back River. Several white ibis worked their way through the marsh in search of food. A diesel bulldozer revved its engine and moved across the marshlands, startling the birds. They flew off, only to circle and land in a different section of the same flat.

McGill pulled out his compass and turned until it aligned with the aircraft's direction of impact. "The aircraft was headed almost due south. That's almost ninety degrees off from the final approach course."

The nose of the Challenger faced directly toward them as they squished through the marsh.

Dave Morris pointed at the aircraft's nose cone. "Look at that lateral tear across the nose cone. The damn thing's grinning at us."

Dave was a short, rotund man, only five-foot-six and carrying two hundred ten pounds, best known for his uncanny resemblance to the comedian Danny DeVito, especially when he walked. The forty-four year old was the prankster of the Atlanta office. He and Jake had teamed up several times on aircraft accidents.

"I'm really surprised the debris field isn't more expansive. It's really just confined to this small area." McGill motioned circles with his hand.

"Well, you gotta figure the aircraft had slowed down to approach speed and then hit here at high tide which abated the impact substantially. I mean, look at the impact crater." Ben Lewis pointed at the crater. "It's relatively shallow—all things considered. That also explains why the wreckage is still basically intact."

The only black team member at the Atlanta Field Office, Ben stood six-foot-four, just over two hundred sixty pounds. Ben had played nose tackle in college at the University of Michigan. For the last ten years, he'd kept his head shaved and sported a graying goatee. Jake nicknamed him "Mr. Clean." Friendly, docile and jovial, Ben was known for his smile, showing a mouthful of large white teeth.

The salt marsh was unfamiliar territory for McGill as well as the rest of the team. He was intrigued by the fiddler crabs skittering away from his feet.

The Go Team surveyed what remained of the aircraft. Larry Kirkland, clipboard in hand, sketched out a rough diagram of the crash site with the approximate location of the larger sections of wreckage. Later, measurements would be taken and all the data entered in a computer program.

Kirkland was the oldest of the Go Team members at fifty-nine. A slide rule geek, he wore black plastic rimmed glasses and a pocket protector with his usual three pens and one mechanical pencil. All business—no play—he had difficulty with the constant bantering between the other members of the team. Kirkland was best known amongst the team members for his hair. As it thinned on the top of his head, he let it grow long on one side and then combed it over with the help of a little styling gel. When in the field, the wind would lift his comb-over, causing it to flap on his head. The other members, not allowing the moment to pass, teased him by mimicking his comb-over with their hands on their heads.

McGill looked at Jake. "Okay, hotshot, what do you see?"

"Okay. Three main sections to deal with here. Starting from the rear, a shear across the fuselage separating the tail section from the main cabin area. It tore immediately behind the wings, obviously after the wings were sheared off. Then a second tear between the cockpit and the main cabin, immediately behind the cabin door and bulkhead."

Jake pointed to the two wings in the marsh. "Both wings were ripped off, rupturing the fuel tanks and causing an inferno that engulfed the cabin section. Destruction of the aircraft occurred so quickly that the occupants were probably killed on impact. In all likelihood, everyone on board realized their impending fate as the aircraft plummeted from the sky"

McGill looked at the other team members. "Does everybody concur with that?" The others nodded. "Okay, let's move on."

Dave Morris pointed at the nose of the aircraft. "It looks like when the floor of the cockpit fell free, the forward momentum jammed the pilots, seats and all, underneath the nose section. That probably lifted the shell of the nose section upward from the rear and buried the pilots under the rubble. They'll be a mess to remove."

McGill said, "Since the tides are rising and fog is rolling in, we'll recover the pilots' remains first thing in the morning. Besides, we'll need the crane and it can't get here until morning anyway."

They moved toward the second section of debris, the main cabin compartment. Jake whistled and pointed to something in the tall marsh grass.

"Whoa, what have we here?"

The team moved forward to see. An Uzi machine gun lying next to a white IPod and a gray laptop computer.

"Bodyguards." McGill placed a yellow flag next the gun. "He had his bodyguards with him all the time."

Jake marked the other items with yellow flags.

Dave stuck his head inside the main cabin, then leaned back out. "From the outside, the main cabin section appears by and large intact, although somewhat charred, but the inside—holy crap, it's a scene from hell. The fire burned hottest here."

The cabin configuration had two sets of facing leather seats on the left side of the aircraft and two individual seats plus a couch on the right side. A wood partition in the front of the cabin that separated the galley from the seating area had been ripped free and hurled toward the rear of the aircraft with enough force to sever two seats just above the armrests. On impact, the floor buckled and collapsed, breaking free the couch, which smashed into the seated flight attendant, crushing her. Her body was still strapped to her seat, charred stumps sticking out where her knees should have been.

The breeze shifted slightly, blowing ash and smoke from the smoldering cabin toward the team. The smell of the muck and the marsh mixed with the odors of jet fuel, burnt plastic and leather was tolerable. But the pungent stench of charred flesh was too much for Larry Kirkland—he doubled over and vomited in the marsh.

Ben reached in his pocket and pulled out a ten dollar bill. "Here, Dave. You win again."

Dave grabbed the bill. "Like taking candy from a baby."

In the split second before the fireball consumed the cabin, the passengers had suffered blunt traumas as projectiles flew through the cabin at speeds faster than any human can react.

Ben pointed to a body with no head. "Another decap." He moved closer and saw the head dangling from the back of the seat by the burnt sinews in the man's neck. It would later be determined that the older red-haired bodyguard died when the seat in front of him broke free and hit him in the face, knocking his head over the back of his headrest and snapping his neck on impact.

Pat McGill pointed to the lower half of a body still strapped in a seat. The second of the two O'Rourke bodyguards had died when, with the twisting of the metal fuselage, cabin spars tore into the cabin and impaled him, then with a secondary impact ripped free, leaving him disemboweled and dismembered—scattering pieces of his upper body out onto the debris field.

The remains of the passenger identified as Laurence O'Rourke had no discernable blunt trauma. His charred blackened body sat upright in his seat, his scorched briefcase still on his lap.

The rear section of the Challenger lay in the muck turned slightly upward. The engines were still attached but mangled, several turbine blades in each engine were missing. The rear bulkhead had burned through, exposing several metal strips that were ripped and twisted upward.

The team located the left wing alongside and slightly behind the main wreckage by nearly fifty feet. It had been sheared off and lay flat on the marsh with the left main gear protruding, tires upward, through the wing.

The right wing was about one hundred feet north of the main wreckage, indicating the aircraft first struck the ground in a slight right-wing low configuration, ripping it free on impact. McGill noted this would have pulled the aircraft slightly toward the right, and when the aircraft hit the ground, the left wing had sheared off as the Challenger plowed into the marsh.

The marsh, normally filled with a variety of aquatic and insect species, was now littered with mechanized death. Aircraft debris and body parts were strewn in every direction from the impact.

Ben Lewis tripped on something and fell face-down onto the marsh flat. "Shit." He rolled over—coveralls coated in muck.

He had tripped on a mud-covered shoulder and a right arm.

He stuck a red flag in the ground. "God, sometimes I really hate this job."

CHAPTER 16

He stood on the balcony of his sixteenth floor room looking into the foggy evening. The lights below him accented the Savannah Westin's pool—barely visible. A hint of the Savannah River glinted below as the fog rolled across the water.

Jake wondered if the water taxis would operate in these conditions, but that question was answered as a ferry eased into the dock, blasting its horn to announce its arrival.

"How much longer?" He called into the room.

"Don't rush me," Beth said from the bathroom. "I'll be ready in a few minutes. My hair doesn't like this humid Savannah air. I'm going to have to pin it up. Tell me about the walk-through and your meeting."

"Oh, nothing out of the ordinary, just Uzis scattered at the crash site?

"Uzis? You mean, like *the gun*?"

"Yes, precisely like the gun. This guy O'Rourke had two body-guards and they were packing some serious firepower. Uzis. Beretta pistols, with silencers no less."

Jake walked into the room and closed the door to the balcony. "There were a few other things worth noting, too."

"Yeah, like what, babe?" She asked, while she struggled to fix her hair.

"Are you asking just to placate me or are you really interested in what went on today?"

She stuck her head out of the bathroom. "Maybe a little of both."

"That's what I thought."

"Come on, Jake, what other things?" She moved back into the bathroom.

"Little things, really. After the aircraft took off from Dallas, the crew got a cabin door warning light and instead of turning around they just leveled off and made a quick stop at Longview, Texas."

"Is that unusual?"

"It's certainly out of the ordinary, but it does happen from time to time. Then controller gave him a through clearance in and out of Longview."

Beth stuck her head out of the bathroom door. "Come on, Jake. You know I don't know what that means."

"A through clearance is basically a clearance to make an approach at the airport, stop for a short time interval and a clearance to depart by a certain time. It's what it sounds like, a clearance through an airport. But I haven't seen a controller use a through clearance in years. It completely blocks an airport, nobody in or out until the through clearance aircraft has departed, which is something controllers usually don't want to do."

Jake stepped into the doorway to the bathroom. Beth leaned forward to the mirror putting on mascara. She wore a white terry cloth robe.

"Five minutes, Jake. That's all I need."

"I'm just looking."

"How about the meeting? How'd it go? Was Pat boring again?"

"The *meetings* are boring—not Pat. He's just reads the same damn script with adjustments for each individual accident. It's boring and dry. Puts everyone to sleep."

"Did Pat give you anything new this time?"

"Nope. I'm working with Dave on the Structures group and heading the Air Traffic Control and Operations groups. I'll be working with some woman named Donna Greene from the Arlington, Texas, Field Office." Jake spun her eye liner pencil on the counter.

"I need that Jake. Now don't mess me up or it'll just take longer. So, why is someone from the Arlington office on an accident in Savannah?"

"Ms. Greene will get the information about the aircraft and crew and the owner from Dallas. Then she'll get the ATC data from the facilities involved and send it to me here. She'll get maintenance logs and training records and anything else we may need."

She turned to Jake. "What time do you start in the morning?"

"Seven."

"That's not too early."

She removed her robe and hung it up in the closet. "How do I look?"

"You look wonderful as always. Better take a coat though, it'll get chilly tonight."

"How long do you think this investigation is going to take?"

"I imagine we'll be here at least a week, maybe more. Maybe less."

"Well, then I'm not waiting around. I have too much to do. I'll stay until the day after St. Pattys then I'm going home. You'll just have to wing it without me."

"Why can't you stay? It'll only be another couple of days after that, I'm sure."

"Because I'm sick and tired of your job always cancelling *our* plans. I'm making plans of my own."

She walked out of the room.

CHAPTER 17

The elevator door opened. Jake and Beth walked out into the lobby. McGill was waiting in the foyer with Ben, Dave and Carol.

Dave shouted, "Hey, pretty boy, you noticing a common thread here? We're always waiting around for you to show up."

"Whatever." Jake rolled his eyes at the group. "Kirkland bail on us again?"

"I made the cursory offer, but you know how he is," McGill said. "C'mon, let's go. The ferry's this way."

The receptionist informed them that the water taxis would run until two a.m. The hours had been extended past the usual last run at midnight due to the extra crowds for the holiday.

The group walked out the side door from the Westin. The fog had thickened to the point River Street was no longer visible, not even the glow from the lights.

The landing was situated at the end of a U-shaped drive located between the Westin and the Savannah International Trade and Convention Center. They walked down to the ramp at the landing, as the Savannah Belles Ferry vessel *Juliette Gordon Low* pulled into the dock. The ferry, formerly a tug, was about forty feet long with a large black smokestack protruding upward immediately behind the pilothouse. The cabin had been converted into a seating area with painted bench seats.

Crossing the river in the fog gave Jake an eerie feeling as the lights from the hotel dock disappeared. Although there was plenty of room inside the ferry for passengers to sit, most wanted to stand on the deck as the ferry made the crossing. Dave and Ben stood on the bow. Jake, Beth and Carol stayed inside. Carol recapped her day with the media to Beth. Jake stared out the window looking at McGill, who stood just outside the port-side door, talking on his cell phone.

The single beam of the tug's spotlight shone into the darkness ahead revealing nothing. After two minutes of what seemed like an eternity in the black void, the sky brightened. The lights from River Street came into view. The captain pulled the ferry up to the City Hall landing and docked next to the Hyatt.

Jake grabbed Beth's hand and they followed McGill and the others on the short walk up River Street to the pub. River Street, he found, was not paved but rather constructed entirely of cobblestones, historic but rough on pedestrians and vehicles. The stones were laid by slaves nearly two centuries ago and were actually ballast stones taken from the bowels of the ships as they docked on the riverfront to load cotton from the warehouses.

Cotton warehouses sprang up along the Savannah River in the early 1800s. Carts were used to carry cotton down to the ships but kept getting stuck in the soft sand. So, Savannahians unloaded the ballast from ships returning from England and used the rocks to line the waterfront and create ramps down the bluff from Bay Street. Masonry walls were constructed along the sandy bluff lining the ramps creating a barrier to prevent erosion.

Walkways built over the ramps were used by merchants and buyers to observe and inspect the cotton as it was carted down below. These walkways make up Factor's Walk. Cotton merchants, or factors, built a row of warehouses along River Street between East Broad Street and Bull Street. Known as Factor's Row, these warehouses were later converted to offices, shops, hotels, restaurants and pubs.

River Street was bustling with tourists. Peddlers confronted pedestrians and pushed their goods.

Still two days away, vendors were already gearing up for the big St. Patrick's Day celebration.

Beth smiled at Jake. "Isn't this exciting? Look at all the stuff."

She pointed at an older man. "Look. He's making flowers out of palmetto fronds."

Street performers lined the street playing guitars, some singing, in hopes that passersby would throw spare change into the open guitar cases. Three young black men sang "Amazing Grace." A cappella.

Jake elbowed Beth. "Get a load of this guy." He pointed to a religious fanatic carrying his Bible in one hand and his doomsday sign in the other while shouting words from "Revelations" at the top of his lungs.

McGill led the group up the walkway between the river and the Hyatt, avoiding the crowded tunnel for easier walking. As they came around the end of the hotel, he gestured to the first building across River Street, Kevin Barry's Pub.

The pub occupied the bottom two stories of a five-story building. The other stories were accessible only from the Bay Street side at the top of the bluff. The pub had two entrances on the front facing River Street with two windows between the doors. American flags, Irish flags, and POW/MIA flags hung from the roof of the second floor balcony bar. Below the windows was a row of shamrocks and musical notes, all in vivid green.

Irish music spilled out onto the streets from the live entertainers who lent Kevin Barry's its authenticity and Irish flavor. The group entered the main bar and a waitress cheerfully told them to find any open tables downstairs or upstairs. A U-shaped bar extended from the rear of the room toward the front with bar stools lined along the outside, fast-moving bartenders served patrons from a walkway extending down the middle.

Beth stumbled slightly on the uneven rough-cut timber floor. Jake caught her by the arm. "Careful there, Grace."

"I don't get out very often. Can you tell?" She said.

They laughed.

The dark stone and brick walls, low rough-cut lumber ceilings and low lighting added to the dimness of the room. A haze of cigarette smoke cast a halo around the lights. The group wandered around downstairs looking at pictures on the walls. The crowd was loud as they tried to talk over the Irish band playing on a small stage in another room.

McGill located a place for them then Dave and Ben helped him push three of the round tables together to make one table large enough for everyone to sit together. They all pulled up chairs and sat down.

The barmaid approached and pulled out her pad. "Will this be on separate tabs?"

McGill spoke first, "Black and Tans for everybody. First round's on me."

She smiled and put away her pad. "Okay, six Black and Tans it is."

Jake grabbed her by the sleeve. "What's a Black and Tan?"

She grinned. "You'll like it. The bartender makes it with half a mug of Harp's pale lager, and half with Guinness Draught, a dark stout beer. It's a great combination."

"Sounds good—bring 'em on."

The waitress walked toward the bar. Jake turned to thank McGill when he noticed McGill staring at a man at the bar. The man was tall, exceptionally tall, with mile-wide shoulders and a white triangular-shaped forelock in his hair. Even in the dim lighting he noticed something strange about the man's eyes. The irises were different colors—a brilliant sapphire blue iris in the right eye and brown in the left.

McGill was still looking at the big man. Jake leaned in toward him and asked, "Do you know that guy?"

The waitress returned with their first round, placing the mugs in front of McGill and Jake first before serving the rest of the group.

McGill broke eye contact with the stranger, looked at Jake and shook his head. "No, he just looks freaky. I knew a family like that in Ireland, but I haven't seen anyone like that since my aunt's funeral."

Jake grinned and raised his mug. "Well, if you don't quit staring at him, you're gonna piss him off. He might come over here and kick your ass."

"Yeah, I guess you're right. And he looks big enough to kick it all the way back to Atlanta."

They laughed.

Beth was eavesdropping. "It's called Waardenburg's Syndrome. It's quite common on my father's side of the family. I'm sure he's probably self-conscious about it."

Jake looked over at the stranger again and then turned to Beth. "Maybe he's one of your relatives."

He laughed and winked at McGill, then turned back toward the bar. The man was gone. He looked around the room. The stranger was nowhere to be seen.

"Hey, Beth, does that Whataburger syndrome also let you vanish into thin air?"

"Waardenburg—smart ass."

McGill laughed at Jake. "Yeah, smart ass. He's gone now anyway."

The conversation at the table turned to the crash scene and some of the details that were observed during the initial stakedown. Beth and Carol objected a couple of times at the more graphic details. The conversation was interrupted periodically by the waitress as she delivered more rounds of Black and Tans. Carol raised her hand in protest and stopped drinking after the second round.

The group got louder with each drink. Ben asked, "Who was this guy O'Rourke anyway?"

McGill quickly spoke up. "Laurence O'Rourke is a bastard, I tell ya. When I was but a wee tyke, he started his killing for the IRA. The Irish Republican Army, for those of you who don't know."

His Irish brogue now thickened by the alcohol, he said, "Mr. O'Rourke worked his way up the ranks in the IRA very fast. Innocent people died because of him. His plans backfired about as often as they succeeded. IRA men died. The Constabulary men died. He was promoted to the IRA's internal security unit called the Nutting Squad."

"What's a Nutting Squad?" Dave asked.

"It's like … maybe like internal affairs with the police but with much graver consequences. They police their own. Anyway, as a member of the Nutting Squad, O'Rourke killed many IRA members for squealing when the Constabulary arrested them."

Jake interrupted, "Sounds like you knew him personally, Pat?"

McGill picked up his glass and looked around the table, his eyes hard. "The bastard was a ruthless murderer. He was arrested in 1978, and thrown in prison where he participated in the 'Dirty Protest' at the H-Block. He was released, then arrested again in 1982. And once again he was thrown in the Maze. Then in September of 1983, I did meet Mr. Laurence O'Rourke. "

There was a long silence as he stopped talking. McGill took several hard swallows from his fifth Black and Tan of the night. Still gazing at the ceiling, his eyes glassed over, McGill finished his story.

"My family, my cousins' family—we were always IRA sympathetic. Even though my uncle never participated, we supported the IRA's efforts in many ways. In 1983, there was a prison break from the Maze and Laurence O'Rourke hid in our basement for three days while authorities combed the countryside. I was sixteen at the time. Three months later, my aunt, my cousin and I moved to the States to get away from the Troubles. We moved here, to Savannah."

Jake studied McGill's face, now as grim as it had been jovial earlier in the evening, deep furrows in his brow and hatred in his eyes. "I don't get it, what makes him so special?"

"That's what I'm getting to. Mind your horses…Jake."

Jake threw up his hands. "Sorry."

"O'Rourke left the internal security unit when he was appointed IRA Quartermaster General," McGill said. "His job was to obtain, conceal and maintain the stores of weapons and arms of the IRA. Then, around 1995, he left the IRA and joined Sinn Fein where he spent several years working toward unifying Ireland. The 1998 Good Friday Peace Accord was the first real step toward peace. But even it had problems.

"Now the IRA has disarmed. The only way there will ever be peace is through mutual giving. The unilateral disarming of the IRA ..."

McGill dropped his head and stared into his beer mug.

Beth elbowed Jake in the ribs and taking the hint, Jake said, "Come on, folks, it's getting late, we have a busy day tomorrow, and we should head back to the ho—"

McGill interrupted, "A spy! Now he's a spy. You see, it all makes sense now. All those loyal IRA men he killed or that were killed when one of his plans backfired. He was a British spy."

"That was *this* guy, the guy on our plane? I remember reading about him in the paper a few weeks ago but I couldn't remember his name. I didn't realize that was *this* guy," Dave said.

McGill mumbled, "The bastard, the bastard."

The ferry ride back to the Westin was relatively quiet. McGill muttered about Laurence O'Rourke while Carol urged him to drink the coffee she had talked the bartender out of prior to their departure from Barry's.

Ben and Dave were talking about the accident, both making "educated guesses" about the angle of impact and speed at impact—using their hands to simulate airplanes angling downward. They discussed what time the flatbeds should show up to start removing the wreckage and relocating it to the Gulfstream hangar.

Beth snuggled close to Jake in the chill of the damp night air.

He put his arm around her. "I've never seen Pat like this before. He's mentioned a couple of things about his past before, but usually he's very private."

"He's just had too much to drink," she said. "He'll feel it tomorrow."

The ferry pulled into the dock next to the Westin.

"I'll make sure he gets to his room okay."

The elevator took them to the sixteenth floor, the top floor of the hotel. Dropping Beth off at their room, he walked McGill down the hall to his room. McGill fumbled with his keycard, finally making a clean swipe and unlocking the door. Jake stayed long enough to make sure McGill was coherent enough to get ready for the day tomorrow.

"Pat, are you going to be alright? Can I get anything for you before I go?"

Jake had known his boss had a past he didn't like to talk about. Now he was starting to understand that part of McGill, although he really wasn't sure what to say to him.

McGill looked at him. "Thanks for being a good friend. I'm fine—just too much to drink is all."

"Pat, since you knew O'Rourke and all, do you think you should recuse yourself as investigator-in-charge?"

"Nonsense, Jake. How was I to know that someone I met nearly thirty years ago would be on that airplane? Besides the investigative procedure is the same regardless of who's on board."

"Yeah, I guess you're right. It really shouldn't matter one way or the other."

McGill smiled. "You better get back to Beth before she gets jealous. I think she's on to us."

They laughed and Jake walked out.

He stood outside the door until he heard McGill lock the dead-bolt. As he walked down the hallway toward his room his mind had questions. Why was McGill so upset about someone he knew such a long time ago? This O'Rourke sounded like a pretty bad guy, but why did McGill hate him so much?

At his door, he slid his keycard into the lock, saw the expected green light and heard the click of the release of the door lock. He opened the door—the room was dark except for the light coming in through the sliding glass door. In the darkness he could see the shadowy silhouette of Beth sitting on the bed.

He closed the door behind him—locking the deadbolt.

"Alright, are you naked?"

A man swiftly moved from the bathroom and placed the barrel of a silenced pistol next to Jake's right temple.

With a heavy Irish accent he said, "Not a sound. I want you to know something about a man named Laurence O'Rourke."

CHAPTER 18

The next morning, the Go Team assembled in the conference room shortly before seven a.m. Carol had prearranged breakfast for them. Six silver platters were brought in by the hotel servers.

McGill pushed his meal away and drank only coffee. Jake grinned, an expected repercussion from McGill's excess the night before.

McGill stood. "I want to start this by apologizing for my lack of tactful behavior last night. The fact is we're working a crash where someone I once knew was onboard. My past relationship has no bearing on how we do business or conduct this investigation. We have procedures and we'll follow them. I'll follow them. Any questions or comments before we move on?"

Jake wasn't listening. He was troubled about the stranger in his room last night—the first time he'd ever had a gun pointed at him. The man put the gun away after Jake and Beth agreed to listen quietly.

Beth was angry at him for not calling security after the man left. But, if what the man said was true, Jake would need time to investigate the man's allegations covertly.

Covertly and carefully.

Breakfast was cleared away. McGill unlocked and opened the conference room doors for the group members awaiting the seven-thirty briefing.

During the briefing Jake relayed to the assembly that he had scheduled a call with Donna Greene, the NTSB investigator in Texas. She was to make an early morning visit to the FBO but because of the time zone difference, her briefing to Jake would be around or slightly before noon.

"I will be meeting today with a representative at the Gulfstream plant to check out the facility they've donated for the wreckage," Jake said.

"The Air Traffic Control group should meet at the Savannah Air Traffic Control Tower (ATCT) by ten a.m. for data collection," he added. "This group will review data logs and radio transcripts of the accident, then the hearing with the air traffic controller will follow around ten forty-five."

Dave Morris gave a quick briefing and his group left for the accident scene.

Ben Lewis' group sat at a table with a stack of manuals and specifications on the Challenger 604. After a quick overview of the material, Ben took his group to the accident scene.

Larry Kirkland made arrangements for delivery of information on the pilots' logbooks, duty logs, and pilot certificates and ratings. The National Weather Service information was already on site and ready for review.

McGill excused himself to make a quick statement in the press briefing room as the investigation of the crash of N319CB got started.

Jake scanned the room, nearly empty. Kirkland was on the phone and Carol Martin was loading paper into a copy machine. He glanced at his watch, it was already after eight o'clock—he had to hurry. He was due at the Savannah air traffic control facility by nine o'clock but had business at the Gulfstream aircraft facility first.

As he walked to his car, he couldn't shake the image of the silencer next to his head or the words that the strange man said.

CHAPTER 19

Early morning fog clung to the ground. Thicker near the river and marsh than inland. The forecast called for clearing skies by noon and then clear skies for the remainder of the week with high temperatures around seventy. Jake turned the black Mustang rental car into the main entrance at the Gulfstream Aircraft Corporation. He mused that Carol Martin had arranged for the Mustang knowing his affinity for sports cars, but knowing Carol, she paid the same rate as a standard vehicle. He was still distracted by the late night visitor but knew he must concentrate to push it out of his mind. At least for the next few hours.

The guard at the gate checked his credentials and issued him a pass, which he placed above the dashboard in the corner of the windshield. He gave Jake a small map of the Gulfstream complex, then showed him how to get to the empty hangar.

A Gulfstream representative met him at the hangar. "We haven't used this hangar for quite a while and won't need it for a few months, but the boss man wants me to find out how long the NTSB anticipates needing it."

Jake replied, "I'm sure the IIC will release the wreckage back to the operator within a few weeks at the most."

He and the representative discussed the security requirements and check-in procedures for NTSB personnel and vehicles.

Twenty minutes later he made the two-minute drive from Gulfstream to the Savannah air traffic control facility. He announced his arrival into the speaker at the gate.

The red brick building served as the administrative area and housed the TRACON and the air traffic control tower. The building was of newer construction and well maintained, unlike most of the other FAA Air Traffic Control facilities he had visited. He was accustomed to visiting FAA facilities in worn and dilapidated condition due to lack of proper maintenance and upkeep.

He walked toward the building and noticed a black Harley Davidson Fat Boy motorcycle parked in the lot with a fly rod case attached to a pack on the sissy bar. On the front of the motorcycle was a small tag with a fly fishing graphic in the center and the words "Bite Me" written beneath it. He wondered what type of fly-fishing there was in Savannah.

The Quality Assurance and Training Specialist, or QATS as the FAA calls it, greeted him at the front door and escorted him down the hallway to the conference room.

The ATC group was already seated at the conference table awaiting his arrival. Seated around the table were the National Air Traffic Controller's Association's Aviation Safety Inspector, a representative from the FAA Air Traffic Safety Oversight Service, the Savannah facility's air traffic manager, and an FAA Airways Facility representative.

The air traffic manager informed Jake that the FAA attorney was interviewing the air traffic controller involved in another office prior to the hearing.

"I called yesterday and made a request for data extractions, statements, certified ATC recordings, certified transcripts, notes, outages, and the like—how are we doing on all that?" Jake asked.

The manager replied, "We have everything you asked for except the information from Jacksonville Center." He was referring to the Jacksonville Air Route Traffic Control Center that overlies Savannah ATCT and TRACON airspace. "It will be this afternoon before that data is available. I had one of my staff specialists drive to Hilliard to pick it up."

"How long will that take?" Jake asked.

"It's a good two-and-a-half-hour drive each way so we better allow for approximately six hours."

"That's considerably longer than I wanted to wait for the data. Any way we can just get a courier to deliver it?"

"It's too late for that now, he's probably half way there."

"I guess the Jacksonville Center data will have to wait until tomorrow, then."

The QATS brought over a stack of data and explained to Jake and his group the details. The group read over the statements and the outage log, noting only one pertinent outage, the primary radar site. He gave a brief introduction to the group about Savannah TRACON and ATCT. "Savannah has an automated radar tracking system, the ARTS IIE, with both primary and secondary radar displayed on the air traffic controllers' scopes. However, yesterday morning, the Savannah primary radar was taken down for four hours."

Jake interrupted, directing his question to the Airways Facility technician. "Explain to me why the primary radar was taken out of service."

"The primary radar was due for its PM's, preventive maintenance, and a couple of days ago we got an alarm," the technician replied. "We've had to do a couple of resets in the last few days, so we figured it was better to take it down yesterday for three or four hours than risk it failing today."

"Why is that?" Jake asked.

The manager replied for the technician, "St. Patrick's Day is a high traffic volume period for Savannah. It's busier than most holidays. The aircraft start trickling in a couple of days before the holiday and then there's a huge rush in the day before and out the day after St Patrick's Day. As a matter of fact, with the low visibilities this morning, they're up to their assholes in alligators right now—very busy. I don't like to have any equipment outages during St. Patrick's Day week."

The QATS continued, "The ATCT is equipped with digital bright radar indicator terminal equipment, D-BRITE, which provides radar information from the approach control to the tower for purposes of aiding in identifying and sequencing of aircraft. The weather at the airport was marginal visual flight conditions, but due to the low ceilings, instrument approaches were required. The winds were quite strong from the west and runway two-seven was the only runway being used for both takeoffs and landings—"

"Okay, let's listen to the tapes," Jake said.

The QATS turned on the tape player, noting that the actual recording started two minutes prior to when N319CB checked in on frequency. As the group listened to the recording, Jake jotted down a couple of notes, as did the rest of the group. The tape ended two minutes after the last transmission.

When the QATS switched off the tape player, Jake asked, "There were a couple of moments of static, what was that?"

"It could have been some interference from another site or, more likely, an aircraft transmitting on the same frequency, just too weak to understand," the Airways Facility technician said.

"Why wouldn't we be able to understand it if it was another aircraft?"

"Well, roughly speaking," the technician continued, "the frequency is 125.3 MHz and we have a twenty-watt transmitter/receiver located here at Savannah. It's twenty watts because we are a terminal and we don't want our transmissions to interfere with any other facility also using 125.3. But it is possible for an aircraft to have line of sight with Savannah and be talking to another facility using the same frequency. The aircraft's radio though, doesn't have enough power to transmit clearly over that same distance so all we hear is static."

"Is that the only time you get the static?" Jake asked.

The technician shook his head. "No, there are a multitude of instances that can give us the same result. Sometimes bad weather, like thunderstorms in the area, can cause static. Some aircraft have lousy radios and are extremely difficult to understand. Some handheld radios don't have enough power to modulate until they are much closer to our site, the same with some older radios. Sometimes even the aircraft's angle to the site with direction of flight will influence signal. And, just like with our radar, we have blind spots or weak spots that are the results of geographic phenomena that we just can't explain. There really is no way to determine the source of those carrier signals unless we can actually hear the voice modulation."

Jake nodded. "Well, that's all I have for now. Does anyone else have any questions?" No one raised an issue so Jake looked at the manager. "I guess we're through with this group for now. Is the controller ready?"

"I'll check and the rest of us will get out of your hair," the manager said. "I'll send him right in."

"Good, I'm quite interested in his perspective of the accident."

CHAPTER 20

Gregg Kaplan walked out of the briefing room with Cook and the lawyer sent down from the FAA Regional Office. He'd interviewed with the NTSB once before but never with an FAA attorney and it wasn't something he wanted to do ever again. The lawyer had briefed him on what to expect at the NTSB hearing and interview. The lawyer had been rude and disrespectful, especially when, against the attorney's advice, Kaplan chose his NATCA Facility Representative to be his representative during the interview with the NTSB. Some investigators had been known to rake the controllers over the coals. His previous encounter with an NTSB investigator had not been a good one and he hoped this one would be better.

Kaplan and Cook walked into the conference room and sat down.

Jake introduced the individuals in the room and then said, "My name is Jake Pendleton. I work for the NTSB, Atlanta Field Office, and I'm the lead for the air traffic control portion of the investigation into the crash of N319CB. I want to put your mind at ease, this should be short and relatively painless. This is not going to be an inquisition as you may have been led to believe. That's not my style.

"I'll start with some basic background stuff then move into questions that are related to the accident. If any of us ask anything you don't understand, please don't hesitate to ask for clarification, we want you to be as comfortable as the situation will allow. Do you have any questions before we get started?"

Kaplan shook his head. "None that I can think of."

"Let's get started," Jake said. "When were you hired by the FAA?"

"March 5, 1990."

"Did you have any prior air traffic control experience?"

"None."

"Did you attend the FAA Academy?"

"No, I was a direct hire to Savannah under the Veteran's Rehabilitation Act."

"How long were you in the military?"

"Eight years, from 1982 until 1990."

"What branch?"

"Army."

"What did you do in the Army?"

"Special Forces Airborne Division."

"I'm impressed. You had to stay in good shape for Special Forces, I bet."

"Oh, yeah. It was a very strict routine, and very difficult."

"What about now? Do you do the same kind of routine?"

"I have a very strenuous exercise regimen of running and weight lifting. Nothing like the Army, though. I have no health issues at all other than just getting older."

Jake smiled. "Don't we all. What about sleep? Do you have trouble sleeping?"

"Not really. I usually get a good six to seven hours every night."

"What about last night? Did you have trouble last night?"

Kaplan smiled. He couldn't tell the investigator about his "good cop, bad cop" adventure with Annie. "Actually, I slept like a baby."

"I saw your work schedule, you work shift work," Jake said. "Do you get fatigued from shift work?"

"No. We don't work mid-watches at Savannah so fatigue isn't an issue—not for me anyway." Kaplan said. "With all due respect, Mr. Pendleton, what does any of this have to do with the accident?"

"Yeah, I know. I'm sorry." Jake said. "I was just trying to ease any apprehension you might have before we get into the specifics of the accident."

"The only thing bothering me is that I was supposed to be on leave today but got ordered in here to talk to you."

"I wasn't aware of that." Jake said. "Then let's get down to business so I can get you out of here."

"I appreciate that." Kaplan smiled.

"When you were working N319CB, did you read him the weather?"

"Yes, I did. I make it a habit to read them the weather on initial call or very soon thereafter."

"Why is that?"

"So the pilot has plenty of time to get set up for the approach and isn't rushed at the last minute finding charts and setting up his equipment."

"Did you issue SIGMETs or AIRMETs?"

"No, none were given to me."

"Were there any active for this area?"

"None that I was aware of."

"When you plugged in to relieve the controller before you, did you use the checklist?"

Kaplan nodded. "Yes."

"Was the position relief briefing complete?"

"Yes."

"Did you record the briefing?"

"Yes."

"Did the previous controller tell you about any equipment outages?"

"Yes, she did. The primary radar was out."

Jake flipped to the next page of his notepad, then leaned back in his chair. "Take your time and give us a brief rundown of what you remember. A sequence of events, if you will."

"When the aircraft checked on frequency, I issued a turn and descent clearance to get him away from my departures. Do you want to know what I did with the other aircraft on frequency also?"

"No, just the aircraft in question will be fine," Jake said.

"I read him the weather sequence and told him which approach to expect, and cleared him direct SINBY, the initial approach fix. I later gave him an altitude to maintain until the initial approach fix and cleared him for the approach. I also asked him to report over SINBY—"

Jake said, "Why did you need to do that?"

The question puzzled Kaplan. *Surely he's seen this done dozens of times.* He gave Jake an almost unnoticeable shrug. "Don't guess I needed to. But that's a good time to switch him over to the tower frequency. And the pilots are generally used to it. It's just a good reminder. In case I get busy or get sidetracked with something else. A good work habit."

Jake nodded.

Kaplan fidgeted in his chair. "When he reported over SINBY, I switched him to the tower frequency. He acknowledged and read back the frequency. Then within a few seconds I heard a mayday on my frequency that sounded like him. I called for him a couple of times with no response. I noticed the aircraft veered slightly off course, then his transponder disappeared, so I called local to see if he was talking to him. He wasn't, so I reported it to my supervisor."

"How busy do you think you were at the time of the accident?"

"Not busy at all. I had just finished a little push, but I never really got very busy."

"Over the years, different controllers have told me that they can usually sense things about certain pilots—you know, good vibes, bad vibes. Did you sense anything about this aircraft and its crew?"

"No, actually he was quite professional from beginning to end … I really had no concerns with him at all."

"How do you feel about losing an aircraft?"

Kaplan stood and leaned over the table. "How the hell do you think I feel? It sucks. No one likes losing an aircraft. But I know I didn't do anything wrong or contribute to it. The whole thing, you know, whatever happened to the aircraft was out of my control."

"You're that confident about your performance?"

"Absolutely."

Cook pulled Kaplan back into his chair.

"I do have a question that may not be related. I noticed on the tape a pilot said something about a 'graveyard tour.' What's that?" Jake asked.

Kaplan explained, "When the east/west runway was built, there was a cemetery in the way. All the families chose to have their family members' graves relocated to another cemetery at the airport's expense, except for one family. They refused to allow their family members to be moved. So, near the middle of the runway about fifty feet north of centerline are two headstones inlaid in the asphalt. Actually, they're really plaques, not true headstones, but they're on top of the gravesites.

"When traffic at the airport permits, we allow the aircraft to taxi down the runway past the graves so the captain can give the passengers a unique glimpse, gravestones in a runway." Kaplan grinned. "Thus the name, 'Graveyard Tour.' I'll bet you've never heard of that before. Where else but Savannah, huh?"

"You're right, I haven't heard of anything like that before."

Jake asked questions for another ten minutes, then looked around the room. "That's all I have for now. Do any of you have questions for Mr. Kaplan?"

Some of the other air traffic control group members had a few questions, which Kaplan answered in the same commanding self-assured manner he answered Jake's questions.

*   *   *

Jake dismissed the group members and all the participants with the disclaimer that they might have to return for a follow-up as the investigation continued.

The room emptied and as Kaplan was getting out of his chair, Jake stood and shook his hand. He glanced down and noticed Kaplan's riding boots. "That your Harley outside?"

Kaplan smiled. "Yeah. You ride?"

"Never have. But I saw the fly rod on the pack. Do you fly-fish?"

"Oh yeah. My favorite pastime. Been fly-fishing ever since I moved here."

"What do you fish for?"

"This time of year, usually trout."

"There are trout streams around here?" Jake asked with a puzzled look.

"No, all my fishing here is salt water fly fishing. I fish for speckled trout and redfish mostly."

"I've never fly fished in salt water ... How is it?"

"When you get a redfish to swallow a fly, there's no experience like it. The first thing he'll do is run you into your backing. He'll make three or four runs before he tires, then just reel him into the leader."

"That sounds like fun."

"What about you? What kind of fly fishing do you do?"

"I usually go up to north Georgia. I have a cabin on a creek and fish for brookies or rainbows. Sometimes I'll drive on up into Tennessee or North Carolina. I have a few favorite spots on some smaller rivers and creeks. My father owns a place outside of Atlanta that has a lake stocked with bass and bream. I fish there too. My father taught me to fly fish when I was a kid. He said it was the only 'real fishing.' He got me hooked, so to speak. It's relaxing. I could do it all the time."

"I know what you mean. I feel the same way," Kaplan said.

"Someday I'll have to give salt water a try."

"I'm telling you it's a blast, Mr. Pendleton."

"Please, call me Jake."

"Okay, Jake. What are the chances you'd let me come out to the crash site? You know, just to check it out. I've never seen one up close."

"It's really not procedural since you're somewhat involved, but I might be able to arrange an observer's pass. You'll have to keep a good distance though."

"My girlfriend might like to come along, if that's okay. She's a controller here too."

Jake pulled out his cell phone and dialed Carol. He talked to Carol for a couple of minutes, then snapped his phone closed and looked over at Kaplan.

"Gregg, you and your friend go to the Westin and ask for Carol Martin. She'll give you two observer passes. Those will get you onto the site. You'll have to show Carol your FAA badges to get your pass. You'll have to stay outside the perimeter tape, okay?"

"No problem. Thanks, Jake, I really appreciate it. Hey, maybe sometime after this investigation is over, you can come back down and I'll take you on a redfish adventure and show you what real fly fishing is all about."

"It's a deal." Jake's cell phone rang. It was his employer, but a number he didn't recognize. He held up a finger to Kaplan, flipped open the phone. "Jake Pendleton."

"Jake, this is Donna Greene from the Arlington NTSB office."

"Yes, Ms. Greene, I was told you would call—"

"This is a very strange case you have here, Mr. Pendleton."

Jake felt his jaw tighten. "How so?"

"You have something to write on?"

He slid his binder closer and reached for his pen, then said, "Yes, go ahead." He motioned to Kaplan that he must excuse himself to take this call.

"About three weeks ago, on a Monday, a man named Ian McDonald came in, looking for a mechanic's job at the FBO that operates the aircraft that crashed. The FBO manager said it was an impressive resume, quite a list of references, but the manager didn't need any more mechanics just then. Just stuck the resume in the file cabinet and forgot about it."

Jake listened, clicking his pen. "With all due respect, that doesn't sound too strange—"

"It's about to. A few days later, one of the mechanics is in a car wreck. Ends up in a coma. The manager called some of Ian McDonald's references. Glowing praises all around, so he hires him.

The guy works hard and does a great job all week. Before the aircraft departed yesterday, McDonald worked on a couple of squawk sheet items, then left, saying he was headed home."

"What kind of squawk sheet items?"

"Just minor things, a couple of panel light bulbs, a rattle or two. Nothing to ground an aircraft over."

"We need to talk to him."

"Sure, but here's where it gets weird. He didn't show up for work today. When the manager tried to call, the phone number had been disconnected. The address he gave doesn't exist either. When he called the reference numbers back, they were disconnected too."

"Yep, definitely weird. What about the other mechanic?"

"It's his day off. The manager's tried to get him all day. So far, no answer. Figures he's off with his girlfriend somewhere."

"Do we have a physical description of the new guy he hired? What's his name, Ian McDonald?"

"Yes, that's his name. The manager says he was a big guy. Real tall, he guessed six-five or six-six, maybe two-fifty, muscular, brown eyes and reddish-brown hair with a white streak running down the middle of his head and a heavy accent—"

"What?"

"He had a white streak running through his hair and a heavy accent. Thinks maybe Irish or something like that—"

"No, no, I heard you fine. I saw a guy that fits that description. Here, last night. He didn't have brown eyes. He had one brown and one blue, but everything else fits him to a tee."

"That's a strange coincidence."

"Alright, Donna, fax all that stuff over here, you have the number, right?"

"Yes, I have it."

"Fax all maintenance records and personnel data including that man's resume."

Jake hung up his cell phone and tried desperately to absorb the information Donna Greene had just given him. For the first time feeling the sweat that had formed on the back of his neck. It all led him back to the man who was in his room the night before. The man was right. Maybe this "crash" wasn't an accident at all. Could it be that sabotage was what caused the crash?

The man in the pub, is that the same man from Dallas? What was the involvement of the man who came to the room? Could he be trusted? Who could be trusted? The man said to trust no one. What was it he said? "The enemy is closer than you think." What the hell did that mean?

As the questions chased each other through his mind, he wondered if his chance to finally make a name for himself might have arrived. No more living in the shadow of his father.

Not an accident, in spite of the evidence so far. Sabotage. His mind told him this could be the case.

His gut feeling told him this *was* the case.

But how could he prove it?

CHAPTER 21

J ake arrived at the crash scene at the same time the cockpit voice recorder and the flight data recorder were being pulled from the debris. He noticed Dave Morris carrying the flight data recorder toward one of two ice chests located by the perimeter tape.

Dave had already located the "black boxes" submerged in salt water and muck. The boxes weren't located the night before due to rising tides, darkness and the amount of mud covering the units. The impact of the crash had forced the "black boxes" several feet into the muck. The rising tide hampered recovery efforts until the marsh drained itself during low tide.

The name "black boxes" was something of a misnomer since both boxes were actually painted Day-Glo orange. The boxes contained the cockpit voice recorder and the flight data recorder. Each unit recorded different data and comprised completely different and independent systems. The recorders primarily used solid-state technology, much more reliable than the older magnetic tape models and were able to store more data in less space.

The recorders used stacked arrays of memory chips with no moving parts. No moving parts meant fewer maintenance problems and less chance for breakage during a crash. These stacked memory chips were housed in a "crash-survivable memory unit."

The cockpit voice recorder was located in the rear of the aircraft. Several microphones were built into the cockpit to track and record all conversations of the flight crew. All microphones in the cockpit were connected to the recorder. These microphones recorded all ambient noise in the cockpit as well as the pilot's headset, the co-pilot's headset and the headsets of any other crew members for a duration of two hours.

Both boxes had sustained heavy damages during the crash and would be packed and sent to Washington, D.C., for examination and data extraction. Dave brought along two large special purpose chests for storing the recorders once they were located. Because the recorders were submerged in salt water, they would be rinsed off, stored and shipped in fresh water.

While Dave and Ben were busy preparing the recorders for shipping, Jake started telling McGill about the briefing he had received from Donna Greene. When Jake reached the part of the briefing about the missing mechanic, a furrow in McGill's brow deepened.

McGill said, "Call Donna back and tell her to get local authorities involved in locating the whereabouts of both mechanics."

Jake nodded. He then revealed his theory to McGill.

Dave and Ben stopped working on securing the recorders at the sound of McGill yelling obscenities while waving his hands in the air.

CHAPTER 22

Due to heavy gray rain clouds, darkness settled early upon Northern Ireland. In the Stormont Parliament Building in Belfast, the Commander stared out the window at the rows of street lights reflecting off the wet pavement that lined Prince of Wales Avenue. The bronze statue of Sir Edward Carson, the man touted as the "uncrowned King of Ulster" for his successful resistance against the British Government's attempts to introduce Home Rule for all of Ireland, was barely visible through the mist gently falling across the Stormont grounds.

A voice called out from behind him, "Is O'Rourke dead, do we know for sure?

With as much confidence as he could muster, he replied, "It would appear that is the case. There were no survivors. All the dead have been identified ... including Laurence O'Rourke."

"Do the authorities think this was an accident or sabotage?"

"The Americans are investigating it as an accident. There has been no mention of sabotage from my source. The Washington investigators are not available to conduct the investigations because of the weather in the D.C. area, so the Atlanta office is in charge. Oddly enough, the lead investigator is an Irishman from Londonderry."

"Is he your source?"

"No, sir, I don't know anything about the man."

The room went silent while he peered out across the lawn in front of the Stormont Parliament building. The death of O'Rourke was unexpected but could prove beneficial. The Commander had worked arduously to train O'Rourke with tremendous successes and very few failures. O'Rourke's ultimate betrayal had left him in a compromising position.

"Send someone to Savannah to positively identify O'Rourke," the man said.

"I have already dispatched a man. Dental records for all the occupants have been sent so the Americans can make positive matches."

The man turned to the Commander, his aging eyes glaring. "I presume we never acquired the location from O'Rourke?"

"No, sir, but we still have another chance—if we can find Michael Sullivan."

"I wasn't aware that Mr. Sullivan wasn't on board the aircraft when it crashed."

"We believe Sullivan went to Savannah a day early," the Commander explained. "But as of now, his whereabouts remain unknown. All those on board have been tentatively identified and Sullivan was not among them."

"He could be a problem. You need to find him, extract the information we need from him and then have him eliminated. Those documents O'Rourke possesses could ruin everything we've worked on the last several years. Might I remind you that those documents could also land us both behind bars—or worse?"

"I have already made arrangements for someone to handle Sullivan."

CHAPTER 23

The woman listened to the man on the phone. "I'm telling you for the last time, we had nothing to do with the plane crash. It was either an accident or someone else sabotaged that airplane. What would I have to gain? If anything, I would rather have O'Rourke alive. We had nothing to do with this."

The man was the "unofficial" chief of staff of the Provisional IRA.

Mairéad Brady, newly elected president of Sinn Fein, the first woman ever elected, was sure of one thing, the man did have information about the crash of Laurence O'Rourke's airplane. She also knew the band of members known as the Provos had a lot to lose with the death of O'Rourke.

Sinn Fein, founded in 1905, is the oldest political movement in Ireland. Representing Irish Republicans, Sinn Fein works for Irish people as a whole to attain national self-determination.

Brady, a tenacious woman, worked her way to the top of the Irish Republican food chain by her aggressive nature and the backing of her political ally at the time, Laurence O'Rourke.

When the news had leaked that O'Rourke was a British spy—a sleeper who had infiltrated the IRA—the Provos initially wanted to have O'Rourke killed. Not a pretty, clean death but a long, slow, agonizing, and above all public death. A message sent to the world of his betrayal. Several unsuccessful attempts had already been made on his life. But the existence of a secret location containing mysterious evidence against Sinn Fein had surfaced. Evidence of extreme significance to all of Northern Ireland. The site and its contents were sought after, but known only to O'Rourke.

Mairéad Brady also wanted to know the location. She needed the contents destroyed. The hidden information, if revealed, threatened all the work and progress Sinn Fein had accomplished over the last several years. It threatened the sanctity of the New Northern Ireland Assembly.

O'Rourke's demise was good news for her.

Good news for Sinn Fein.

Good news for the future of Northern Ireland.

She hung up the phone and punched the speed dial button and hoped for an answer on the other end. After the third ring a familiar voice answered. It wasn't the voice of the man she was calling, though, but that of a man she despised.

"Commander, is the Secretary in?" she asked.

"Hold the line." She heard a click, followed by recorded music. She counted to three before the music ended.

"Mairéad Brady, how may I be of assistance to you on such a dreary evening?" the Secretary asked.

"I called to express my condolences about O'Rourke and to inform you that certain parties to whom I have spoken have disavowed any involvement in his death."

"I'm certain they have," he said. "They would no doubt prefer Mr. O'Rourke alive. It is you, madam, I am concerned with. You have everything to lose and nothing to gain with O'Rourke alive. What is *your* involvement with O'Rourke's death?"

"Mr. Secretary, I assure you we had nothing to do with this incident and I resent your implications to that effect."

"Be that as it may, it does lead one to wonder, with his death arising at such an opportune moment for Sinn Fein. Maybe, though, it was just a stroke of good fortune on your behalf."

She bit down on her lip hard enough to taste blood. Her face flushed with rising emotion. "I don't consider anyone's death to be fortunate. I called as a matter of respect and decorum. Good night, Mr. Secretary." She hung up without affording the man a reply.

He was right, though, and she knew it. That's why she was so upset. She regretted making the call. She *had* wanted O'Rourke dead.

Sinn Fein, unofficially, wanted O'Rourke dead. He was a threat. A threat that could only be dealt with in one way. That's why she had commissioned the assassination of Laurence O'Rourke.

CHAPTER 24

Farid Nasiri reached up and removed his headdress, and heard the familiar buzzing of his Blackberry announcing the arrival of another message. He read his messages. The one that caught his attention was the email from the Iranian singles web site announcing a personal message awaiting him on the web site.

He put down his Blackberry and turned on his laptop computer. After it booted, he opened the web browser and logged onto the singles site.

> Circumstances not as grave as they seem—rendezvous still on. Will contact with place and time. Michael Sullivan, Personal Assistant to Laurence O'Rourke

The Persian felt a burden lift from his shoulders and he rejoiced in the good news. His euphoria was short lived as he wondered who Michael Sullivan was and, more importantly, how he knew about the deal and the method of contact. Could this be a trap? The CIA had been after him for years, but he'd managed to avoid their trickery. He decided he would proceed with caution and expect the unexpected.

He picked up his cell phone and called Salim Malik.

The Persian explained the fortunate turn of events and the anticipation of successful completion of his assignment.

Malik's only response was, "For your sake, I hope you don't fail us again."

The phone line went dead.

CHAPTER 25

Kaplan and Annie rode down Broughton Street on their way to the crash site. Motorcycle riding became a passion for Kaplan after he bought his first motorcycle in college—a Honda 250 street bike. Since then he had owned several motorcycles.

He bought his first Harley Davidson when he was in the Army, a Sportster 1200. His previous bike was a Dyna Wide Glide—very sporty but lacking the comfort he wanted for longer road trips. Then two years ago, he'd bought a Fat Boy.

Annie had pulled her auburn hair into a ponytail before sliding on her half-shell motorcycle helmet. She wore blue jeans, a black fitted Hard Rock Café t-shirt and a black leather Harley jacket.

As they reached the apex of the Talmadge Bridge, he held out his left hand, pointing in the distance to the commotion associated with the crash site.

"I see it." She said. "Now, both hands on the handlebars, please."

After they picked up the NTSB observer passes from Carol Martin at the Westin, they drove toward the accident site.

A Georgia state trooper waved them through the first checkpoint when they produced their FAA identification badges and NTSB observer's passes. The second check point was closer to the crash site. The trooper stopped them and would not let them proceed on the motorcycle, demanding they park and walk the remaining distance to the crash site.

He and Annie walked down the dusty gravel road a hundred yards until they reached the access point to the wreckage. They carefully stepped on and over the broken limbs and branches the bulldozers had knocked down while clearing a path for the cranes.

When they reached the marsh clearing, they saw several people scurrying around performing their duties. Two men were strapping silver duct tape on two strange looking chests. One man, with comb-over hair flying wildly in the wind and a pocket protector full of mechanical pencils, was measuring debris from the wreckage, and then logging it on a sketch pad.

Several men were helping move huge planks. The creosote planks were being laid side by side in a long row, creating a mat for the heavy equipment to traverse the marsh without bogging down in the soft muck.

Kaplan pointed to two men arguing and said, "That's the guy that interviewed me, the younger one. His name is Jake Pendleton."

With a sly grin Annie said, "He's cute."

"He's not your type." He pointed at the marsh. "Watch your step, it gets kind of mucky in the marsh."

*   *   *

Jake and McGill noticed them at the same time. Kaplan was pointing at the ring of sandbags and probably explaining their purpose to the woman standing next to him.

Kaplan lifted his hand in a waving gesture at Jake.

McGill shook his head and frowned. "Who are they and what the hell are they doing here?"

"He's the controller who was working this aircraft when it crashed. I didn't see any harm in letting him and his girlfriend see the site from a safe distance. She is also a controller," Jake explained, while giving Kaplan and the girl a "stay there, I'll be right over" return wave.

"I'm up to my ass in shit and you invite two observers out here without my approval. I don't need any more problems."

"I didn't think it would be a problem. I couldn't get hold of you and besides, he's been very cooperative."

McGill's face turned beet red, veins bulging on his face. He raised his index finger and shook it in Jake's face, "That's the problem, Jake, you're not thinking. You know you must run this by me first. I make the call—not you. Get them out of here."

"Okay, okay. I'll give them a quick overview and then send them on their way."

McGill didn't say a word, just turned and motioned for the crane operator to start lifting the main fuselage slowly out of the clinging muck.

He walked over to Kaplan. "Hey, Gregg—not a pretty sight, is it?"

Before Kaplan could answer, Annie held out her right hand and said, "Annie Bulloch."

"Jake Pendleton, nice to meet you."

"Likewise."

"We didn't cause you any problem, did we?" Kaplan asked.

"No. Don't worry about it. My boss is under a lot of stress and has been on edge ever since this investigation started."

Jake explained what they were doing. "As you can see, we're trying to ease the fuselage out without compromising any evidence that may lead to a probable cause indication. Plus, we still have two bodies that haven't been recovered yet—the two pilots. If we rush the debris removal, we could compromise the remains. Under these conditions, the extraction is slow and laborious.

"The sandbags help a little but the tide is coming through anyway and the marsh is getting softer by the minute. We already located and removed the black boxes, both the cockpit voice recorder and the flight data recorder. They're in those chests over there, ready to ship to D.C."

The wind shifted and smoke from the smoldering wreckage drifted over them.

Jake stopped when he noticed the grimace come across Annie's face. Looking into her big green eyes, he said, "The smell?"

"Eww." She nodded. "What is it?"

"A combination—burnt electrical wiring, jet fuel, fabric from the seats and insulation in the cabin. And then, of course, the burnt flesh … that's the worst."

Kaplan noticed some commotion and a gathering of NTSB investigators at a certain spot under the fuselage. He pointed. "It looks like they found something important."

Jake turned around and saw the gaping hole in the bottom of the fuselage's forward portion, directly behind and below where the cockpit door would have been.

*　　*　　*

Jake told Kaplan and Annie to stay outside the stakedown tape. They could stay for a few more minutes and observe, but he had to get back to work.

He walked over to the fuselage, leaned in and pointed toward the hole. "Looks like some sort of explosion did that."

McGill jerked around and glared at him. "Just how did you make that determination, Einstein?"

Jake said nothing.

"You see these blue streaks. Look. Blue paint inside this dented area here, and here." McGill patted another dent. "And here. I've seen this before. This is paint transfer, not an explosion. Someone bring me my handheld radio. Dave, can you get to the 91A?"

"Yeah, give me a couple of minutes," Dave said. "I gotta crawl back to it."

McGill ordered, "Someone get Kowalski over here."

Dave squeezed into the aircraft's tail section and searched for the emergency locator transmitter.

Ben Lewis walked up at the same time as the FAA accident investigator, Aaron Kowalski. Ben handed McGill the handheld VHF radio.

McGill asked Kowalski, "Has an aircraft been reported missing?"

"Yes, as a matter of fact, an ALNOT was issued yesterday for a vintage Cessna Skyhawk overdue in Augusta from Hilton Head. The Civil Air Patrol was dispatched this morning. They have two aircraft in the air right now, one in Augusta working south and the other in Hilton Head working north. The aircraft got a late start this morning due to the fog. They're running search grids along the river."

An ALNOT was an FAA search and rescue Alert Notice, issued when an aircraft was overdue at its destination by thirty minutes or more.

Looking at Jake, McGill said to Kowalski, "Is the aircraft blue?"

"Actually royal blue with white trim, no electrical system to speak of, no transponder and only a handheld VHF radio, VFR daylight only restricted," Kowalski said. "The seventy-year-old owner uses it to travel back and forth to his beach house in Hilton Head. According to his wife, he is intimidated by Air Traffic Control and follows the Savannah River from Augusta to the coast, then the coastline over to Hilton Head and back, giving Savannah a little wider berth and staying below thirteen hundred feet in order to avoid the Savannah Class C airspace.

"The wife said when the weather is bad he will scud run down the river, duck under the first shelf of the Augusta Terminal Radar Service Area and get a Special VFR clearance into Augusta Bush Field," Kowalski said. "He called her before he left yesterday but never showed up in Augusta and never called back."

Dave stuck his head out of a gash near the tail of the aircraft and yelled, "Ready when you are, Pat."

McGill looked down at his handheld and dialed in 121.5 MHz, the emergency frequency used in aviation, and the same frequency the emergency locator transmitter, or ELT, sends out after a predetermined impact triggers the device to operate. McGill turned up the volume and they heard the familiar *whooup, whooup, whooup* sound that the ELT transmits.

McGill called Jake over. "According to the equipment list for N319CB, the Challenger was equipped with a TSO C126 ELT transmitting digitally information on 406 MHz and the older TSO 91A ELT transmitting on 121.5 MHz."

"That's right, so?" Jake asked.

"Well, Jake, the satellite already identified the Challenger's C126, so the ELT was ignored ... an assumption was made that it was this crash. If I'm right, when Dave turns off the Challenger's 91A, we'll still hear another ELT transmitting in the area."

"*If* there was a midair," Jake said.

"That's right."

McGill looked at Dave. "Alright, turn off the 91A."

When Dave disengaged the ELT, the volume level dropped on the handheld but another ELT transmission was still heard, although not as clear and distinct.

McGill turned to Kowalski. "Have CAP come up here ASAP. I think we found your missing aircraft and may have just stumbled on probable cause."

Jake shook his head, he was dumbfounded.

Then he noticed McGill marching toward Kaplan, yelling something to him at the same time.

McGill put his face inches from Kaplan's face and barked, "You have quite a lot of explaining to do now. It looks like you ran two airplanes together. You need to go back over to the tower and we'll be there in a couple of hours. This 'accident' is now a midair."

Before Kaplan could respond, Annie pointed toward the FAA investigator and said, "Hey, wait a minute. Didn't that man just say the Skyhawk didn't have a transponder?"

"Yeah, so what?" McGill said.

"Well, our primary radar was down yesterday morning, so there is no way Gregg would have seen a non-transponder-equipped aircraft flying along the river."

McGill looked at Kaplan and then over to Jake. "Is that accurate?"

"Yes, it is. I haven't been able to brief you on equipment outages," Jake said.

McGill shook his head and turned hard brown eyes back to Kaplan. "Well. I guess that lowers your culpability. For now."

McGill turned his glare to Annie, but his order was for Jake: "Get them out of here."

McGill walked away.

Jake was about to speak to Kaplan when he heard Ben Lewis yell, "Remains."

Without thinking, Jake, Annie, and Kaplan turned to see Ben hold up a portion of an arm with a hand attached.

Annie's face turned white. She hunched over and vomited.

Jake felt his stomach tighten. *This is getting out of control fast.*

CHAPTER 26

The two tractor/trailer flatbeds that delivered the lattice-boom crawler crane, loaned by the Savannah Port Authority, were moved as close to the Challenger's crash site as possible so the wreckage could be loaded for transport to the Gulfstream hangar. The crane, with its two-hundred-thirty-foot boom length and one-hundred-ton lifting capacity, slowly lowered the Challenger's main fuselage on the first flatbed. The cockpit and tail section pieces, along with some of the scattered debris were loaded on the second flatbed.

The site would be scoured over the next hours and days to collect any remaining debris, using metal detectors and other equipment deemed necessary to locate anything still buried in the marsh.

Dave Morris pulled away from the site following the two flatbed rigs heading for the hangar. Kowalski walked over to McGill and Jake with a Cheshire cat grin. "The Civil Air Patrol found the wreckage of the Skyhawk."

McGill asked, "Well, don't keep me in suspense—how far away is it?"

"As the crow flies, maybe a mile or two, but by road several miles. The Jasper County deputies are en route as we speak. Here are the coordinates the CAP radioed in."

McGill whistled for Jake and Ben to follow. The four men walked over to the Suburban where McGill pulled out an area map and laid it across the hood. "Alright, here we are." He pointed to the spot on Hutchinson Island. "If we follow these coordinates ... that puts the Skyhawk right around here." He tapped his finger on a spot on the map, then circled it with his pen.

Jake watched as McGill ran his finger from the coordinates fix of the Skyhawk location toward the Savannah International Airport.

Looking up at Jake, McGill said, "Almost in a direct line from the end of Runway 27."

McGill's argument of a midair had just gained credence. The gaping hole underneath the cockpit could easily be explained away by other causes, even though the outward ripping and rearward curled strips of the metal hull were usually indicative of an outward blast. Even the royal blue paint transfer might have been explained away by a careless aircraft tug operator, but Jake knew there were now too many coincidences.

His earlier assertions of an explosion had damaged his credibility with McGill and shaken his own confidence in his ability to maintain an objective assessment of all the evidence. The evidence was telling him one thing but his instincts were telling him something entirely the opposite. Too many things were happening too fast and they seemed connected somehow. The man in the pub and the man in Dallas.

His thoughts drifted back to the man's words from the night before in his room. *Things aren't as they seem. The enemy is closer than you think.*

He jolted back to the present. He was about to tell McGill about the man in his room, but then had second thoughts. He knew McGill would be furious he hadn't reported the incident to hotel security, the police and to him. McGill would see it as a potential compromise to the investigation and would likely have Jake dismissed.

McGill said, "Take the cockpit voice recorder and the flight data recorder to Carol. Have her ship them out ASAP to D.C. Then go back out to the TRACON and pull all the maintenance logs for the last three months. I want to know everything about that radar."

He turned and looked at Ben, "Ben, you and Kowalski are going with me to check out the Skyhawk."

*   *   *

Jake loaded the two chests in the back of the black Mustang. He was driving toward the Westin when his cell phone rang.

"Jake, it's Dave."

"Yeah, Dave, what's up?"

"Can you get over here right away? I'm at the Gulfstream hangar. I was unloading the fuselage and … well, there's something here you really need to see."

"Come on Dave, don't keep me in suspense. What is it?"

"I think you might have been onto something but I'm not sure. You'll have to look at it yourself."

"Okay, Let me drop off the recorders for Carol to ship out and I'm on my way—"

Dave's line went dead.

He had barely hung up his phone when it rang again. He recognized the number of Donna Greene in Dallas and answered.

"Ms. Greene, what'd you find out?"

"Jake, things have turned into a mess here. The police originally couldn't find either of the mechanics. Their names were Duane Sanders, he'd been at Longhorn for a couple of years, and of course, Ian McDonald."

"Were?" Jake asked. "What do you mean *were*?"

"As I was about to say," Greene said, "the police entered Sanders' home and no one was home. It looked like he hadn't been there in a few days. Eventually they tracked down where his girlfriend lived, but no one answered the door.

"They heard some groaning and knocked down the door only to find an extremely gruesome scene. The girlfriend was tied to the bedposts of the bed, blindfolded, gagged, and naked. Sanders was duct-taped to a chair with a bullet through his left temple. They'd both been hit with Taser darts. When the girl settled down, she told the police that she couldn't remember much about the last couple of days."

"The last couple of days? How long had he held them?"

"We don't know for sure. Never will, probably. Anyway, Sanders had told her about the new mechanic. He came over to her apartment under the guise that he was meeting Sanders there. As soon as she opened the door he met her with the Taser in the chest, then it was lights out. She remembered hearing him talking on the phone and moving around the apartment. She can't remember anything he said, though. She's suffering from post-traumatic shock."

"Did he drug her or something?"

"Apparently so. The medical center is pulling a tox screen to see what he gave her, but the doctor said she was unconscious for most of it. She remembers being raped, though. She said she knew she was being raped but her body wouldn't move. And he did it more than once, she remembered that much. Not much else. They took semen samples and hope to find a match from the DNA database."

"He sounds like a monster."

"He is. He drugged her and raped her while she was incoherent. The cops think it was some sort of an Ecstasy and sedative cocktail."

"What about the FBO manager? What did he say?"

"He said the guy he hired had brown eyes, quite certain of that, was quiet, kind of an introvert but did excellent work … in the short time he was there. He said McDonald and Sanders became friends right off the bat. They would go out after work for drinks. Nothing really out of the ordinary."

She went on, "There's something else too. I ran a check on his Social Security number and it checked out with an Ian McDonald living in Tacoma, Washington. The locals there are going to check him out."

"Donna, fax everything you can over to Carol, police reports, descriptions, everything. Do it right after you get off the phone. I've got someplace to go first, and then I've got to find Pat."

CHAPTER 27

Jake pulled into the Westin's front entrance, identified himself, and gave his keys to one of the attendants with instructions to put the two chests in the hotel manager's office under lock and key. He then headed to the Riverscape meeting room, where the NTSB had set up its command center. The room cluttered with telephones, fax machines, copy machines, files, and file cabinets with Carol sitting in the middle of the mess.

Phone lines ringing, copy machine printing, and a fax machine negotiating an incoming fax call. Carol was punching the buttons on the phone, stating, "NTSB, hold please."

She shot Jake an exasperated look. "Jake, what's going on out there? It's been like this all morning."

He looked down at her, the most efficient administrative assistant he'd ever seen, and said, "I'm here to save you, come with me. Just let the phones ring. Better bring your cell though."

"What about all this?" she waved her arms over the room of actively buzzing business machines.

"Leave it. They'll call back if it's important. I need you now."

He walked Carol downstairs, showed her the chests and gave her McGill's instructions. He grinned. "Pat said make this your number one priority, so I guess the madhouse will just have to wait."

"Yes! Thank the Lord," she replied, giving him a big hug. "I could use a break."

Jake hugged her back. "Also, Donna Greene from Dallas will be faxing some information here soon. It is very important. Can you let me know as soon as it gets here?"

"Sure, Jake, I'll call you the moment I get it."

"And Carol," Jake said, "for the time being, this is strictly between you and me, okay?"

"Why, Jake? We don't keep secrets."

He smiled. "I'm not keeping secrets but I need to check out a few details first to make sure the information is...credible."

"Are you sure?"

"Please Carol. As a favor to me. You know I wouldn't ask if it weren't important."

"Okay, Jake. I'll do it for you."

As he left the manager's office, Beth was walking back in from the front of the hotel. She came straight to him, smiling.

"I thought that might be your Mustang outside," she said.

"Yeah, I just stopped by to drop off the recorders so Carol can ship them to DC. I'm on my way back out to the airport now, to Gulfstream, then over to the TRACON. What are you going to do today?"

"I was about to go get lunch—can you go with me?"

"No, I don't have time. I'll just grab a burger on the way and eat it in the car. Where are you going?"

With a disappointed look, she said, "I'm going over to River Street. I want to check out the shops and eat lunch at Tubby's Tankhouse. The valet said they have a good shrimp basket."

"How about I walk you to the ferry and catch you up on everything that's happened so far?"

They walked slowly toward the ferry landing while he explained all the gory details of Donna Greene's call, his strange phone call from Dave, and the overwhelming evidence that McGill had about the midair collision.

Beth slugged Jake as hard as she could on his arm. "Dammit, Jake, I told you to call security last night. We could have been killed."

He looked down at her while rubbing his arm. Her face was pale. "Wha— I thought you trusted me!"

"This isn't about trust. That guy last night was a nutcase, babbling on about some dead man you don't even know. And he spoke in riddles, too. Who talks like that anyway? He was crazy."

Jake grabbed her trembling shoulders and turned her toward him. "Baby, this isn't something you need to worry about. You go shop and try to take your mind off last night. Okay?"

"You should tell Pat."

Jake looked up as the ferry announced its arrival at the dock. "I'll think about it, okay?"

"Jake," Beth called out over the ferry's engine, "please be careful."

He grinned. "Me? I'm always careful."

* * *

Jake grabbed a burger, fries and a soft drink at a drive-through on the way to Gulfstream. As he turned on Gulfstream Boulevard, several police cars and an ambulance passed him, going the same direction. Lights flashing, sirens wailing. The emergency vehicles pulled into the Gulfstream entrance. He got an uneasy feeling in his stomach, so he sped up to the guard shack and flashed his credentials at the guard.

"Terrible thing about that accident," the guard said. He motioned Jake through the gate.

When he saw which hangar the vehicles went to, the sudden implication of the police cars and ambulance hit him. A wave of nausea swept over him as he saw the paramedics running over to the crumpled fuselage lying on the hangar floor. Jake skidded to a stop outside the entrance of the hangar, jumped out of his Mustang and ran toward the hangar.

A policeman moved toward him with his hands up, motioning for him to stop. Jake flashed his credentials and pushed his way past the police. He fought his way through the people huddled around one side of the wreckage.

Then he saw the body. Only Dave's head and left shoulder were visible from underneath the wreckage. A paramedic nearby was shaking his head, giving a "no" signal to the police officer, indicating Dave was already dead.

Jake stepped closer to one of the policemen. "What happened? How did this happen?"

"One of the Gulfstream workers, that guy over there," the policeman pointed toward a small Hispanic man. "His name's Hector Rodriguez. He saw this man standing underneath the wreckage while it was suspended in the air. He said he didn't think anything of it until he heard a crashing sound. He came over here to see if he could help and that's what he saw."

The officer went on, "The wreckage had been unloaded off the flatbed over there by this crane, an all-terrain lift and carry crane that moved it into the hangar."

"How did it fall?" Jake stared up at the crane, his eyes hard.

"We don't really know yet. Maybe it lost hydraulic pressure or something."

Jake looked at the officer. "Is this everybody that was working here?"

"As far as I know. Mr. Rodriguez said there was no one else around at the time he heard the crash."

"One question, where's the lift operator?"

CHAPTER 28

The NTSB Suburban whisked past an old farmhouse on the South Carolina gravel road, leaving a quarter-mile trail of dust behind it. Following the directions of the CAP aerial crew, the Suburban pulled up to the crowd of vehicles parked near a tidal creek. Three Jasper County deputies, an ambulance with two EMTs, and the farmer were awaiting the arrival of the Go Team.

McGill approached a deputy, "What have you got?"

The deputy pointed to the creek. "The Cessna Skyhawk is located about thirty feet from the creek bank. It's low tide right now so it's exposed. It's also inverted and its tail is missing."

The elder EMT spoke up. "The body's still intact with massive head trauma. Probably what killed him. I'm sure there's internal damage too. We didn't remove the body just like you ordered."

"Fine. I guess we'll wade out there and take a look." McGill pointed Ben to the Suburban.

McGill and Ben sat with Kowalski on the tailgate of the Suburban donning their boots over their coveralls, then pulling the Velcro straps snug so the boots wouldn't slip off in the mud. They put on their gloves and grabbed walking sticks, then made their way down the embankment and into the marsh.

The men made slow progress toward the aircraft and keeping their balance in the mire proved a challenge. Ben fell into the thick mud twice before reaching the Skyhawk, Kowalski three times. McGill was the only one who didn't fall.

Arriving first at the aircraft, McGill noticed the propeller and half of the engine nacelle buried in the muck. The Skyhawk struck at a vertical angle, nose down. The wings bent forward from the impact.

The pilot and passenger doors ripped off and lay beside the aircraft. The accident occurred just after high tide.

The tidal slough, full of brackish water, dampened the impact. Some debris could be seen farther down the slough as the falling tide washed some of the lighter debris toward the main river channel until it also became lodged in the mud.

The inside of the Skyhawk was full of fiddler crabs that went skittering as McGill approached the cabin. The body of the old man hung upside down, suspended by his seatbelt. The shattered windshield and smashed dashboard covered in blood. His face covered with the marsh creatures that will feed on anything dead. The man's arm looked strange, somehow shredded, but not from the impact.

McGill reached in the cabin in an attempt to unbuckle the seat belt. He noticed something large moving toward him from the rear of the cabin.

"Shit!" he yelled as he jumped back out of the cabin, falling against Ben, who was leaning in to get a look. They both fell backwards, landing in the soft mud.

All three men made it back to the bank in less than half the time it took them to traverse the same distance to the aircraft. As they arrived on shore, one of the deputies asked if they had seen the alligator.

"You knew about the gator?" McGill screamed. "Why the hell didn't you share that with us before we walked all the way out there?"

The deputy took off his hat and scratched his balding head. "Well, you were in such an all fire hurry, I didn't want to slow you down."

"You idiot. That's how people get hurt. And I don't appreciate it one damn bit."

"Well it is kinda funny."

"How's this for funny?" McGill stepped close to the deputy. "You and your men go out there and retrieve the body while my men and I comb these fields for debris. Oh yeah, and be careful, there's an alligator out there."

"Why us? It's not our investigation."

"Mostly because I said so. And I'm federal and you're county. That means you serve at my leisure."

A crane arrived on a flatbed as McGill reached the Suburban.

The three men removed their rubber boots and mud-coated coveralls, replacing them with spare coveralls from the Suburban. They put on clean boots and gathered around the tailgate waiting for McGill to assign duties.

McGill pulled out his map and his compass. "Here we are." He pointed to the map. "This way is opposite direction of flight so we'll spread out."

In the distance, McGill noticed an old man on a tractor. "And walk through this guy's field looking for debris."

The diesel engine on the crane roared to life just as McGill's cell phone rang. Glancing at the crane with an annoyed expression, he answered the phone, "Pat McGill."

"Pat, it's Jake."

Covering one ear to drown out the noise of the crane and turning his phone ear away from the crane, McGill yelled into the phone, "Jake, I can barely hear you. You'll have to speak up."

Jake, shouted, "There's been an accident."

"An accident—what kind of accident?"

"At the Gulfstream hangar, it's Dave."

"Dave—what about him?"

"Pat, Dave's dead. He's dead. Did you hear me, Pat? Dave's dead."

CHAPTER 29

She opened her green eyes and Kaplan looked down into them. "Starting to feel better?"

"A lot better. I'll get out in a minute."

Kaplan sat on the edge of the tub while Annie finished soaking in the bathtub. He had noticed that whenever she felt bad, a hot bath always made her feel better. Her fair skin had turned rosy red from the steaming water. Her eyes were closed, as though she still felt the shock of the experience at the accident scene.

On the way back to Annie's house, Kaplan had had to stop his motorcycle twice so she could vomit. Before he could get his Harley to a full stop behind her house, she had jumped off and run inside.

"Would you like some wine to help you relax?" Kaplan asked.

"Not right now," she said. "Maybe later."

"Whatever you say."

"How can people do that for a living?" Annie asked. "You know, going to all those accidents. Seeing all that carnage. The smell, the gore. Do you think they ever get used to it?"

"I imagine it's like anything else, over time you get desensitized to it."

"Do you think the investigators ever puke at accident scenes?"

"I'm sure there are those who do and those who don't. But I'll bet the ones who do outnumber the ones who don't."

He stood up and grabbed a towel as she pulled the plug on the tub. Handing her the towel, he said, "I think I'll head to work and revise my statement on the accident. I didn't make reference to the static noises I heard, so I think I'm going to correct that."

"That guy Pat, he was a real jerk, wasn't he?"

"I don't think I'll put him on my Christmas card list," he laughed.

* * *

Kaplan turned on Gulfstream Road heading back to the TRACON. As he approached the gate at Gulfstream Aircraft, he noticed an ambulance and a rescue unit at the guard shack and saw Jake standing next to the ambulance, talking to the driver and the guard.

The black Harley coasted up to the guard shack just as the emergency vehicles pulled away from the Gulfstream facility. Jake raised a hand to acknowledge him.

Kaplan pulled off his helmet and said, "What's going on?"

"There was an accident at the recovery hangar. One of our investigators was killed."

"My God, how did it happen?"

"A crane somehow lost hydraulic pressure and dropped the fuselage while he was underneath examining the damage, and it crushed him."

Jake motioned for Kaplan to follow him as he walked away from the guard shack. Kaplan pushed down the kickstand with his foot, dismounted his motorcycle, hung his helmet on the left mirror and walked over to Jake.

* * *

Jake stared out at the woods across from Gulfstream without really focusing on anything. The investigation seemed to be getting out of control, but only from his perspective. He had talked to Beth. She's always asking questions about his work but she really didn't understand the aviation industry and the lingo. She also couldn't identify with his situation.

He needed an insider, one who dealt with the same stuff every day. Someone he didn't have to explain everything to in such painful detail. He usually had McGill to bounce things off of—but not now. He and McGill certainly weren't seeing eye to eye right now. And worse still, he'd been withholding information from McGill about the investigation. He knew McGill would have no choice but to toss him from the investigation. That would damage his career, maybe irreparably. He needed a confidante. Someone he could trust. He didn't know who, though.

"I take it that investigators don't usually die on the job?" Kaplan said quietly.

Jake looked at him for a moment without speaking, and then replied, "You think?"

Kaplan's face was intent but calm. "Jake, this is high profile accident investigation. Now one of your investigators is dead. Sometimes accidents aren't what they seem."

Jake studied Kaplan. He recalled Kaplan's Special Forces background and his candor and professionalism during the investigation team's interview. Somehow he sensed that Kaplan had the kind of honesty and integrity that he could trust and the intelligence that might be a help to him. He was the second person to tell him things aren't what they seem.

Jake figured he'd already put his career at risk so what would it matter now.

"I'd like to run something by you, get your opinion. But disclosing information about an ongoing investigation could get me fired, or at the very least, removed from the investigation," Jake said. "I shouldn't talk about this, I know, but now I don't know who else on the Go Team is safe to talk to—or whether I'd be putting them in danger if I do tell them. Hell, I may be putting you in danger if I tell you."

"Sounds like you're between a rock and a hard place," Kaplan said. He leaned against the front fender of the Mustang. "I'm a good listener and I can take care of myself."

Jake made a quick decision. He lowered his voice. "I'm about to make a huge breach of protocol on my investigation. Hear me out and maybe you'll understand."

Jake began recounting to Kaplan all the things that had transpired so far in the investigation. He told him about the two mechanics in Dallas, the visit from the stranger in his hotel room, the man with the streaked hair and strange eyes, and the phone call from Dave right before the accident.

Kaplan threw his head back, furrowed his eyebrows and said, "That's a hell of a lot of coincidences, don't you think?"

"Yes, it is. But my gut instinct tells me I'm right. I just haven't figured it all out yet and I don't believe in coincidences."

Jake noticed the NTSB Suburban coming down Gulfstream Road. "Here comes Pat. He's been pissed at me ever since I told him my theory the first time. He won't like seeing you here either. Please don't mention any of this to anyone. I want to stay on this investigation until it's resolved."

Kaplan nodded. He looked at McGill then Jake. "My lips are sealed. Your boss, Pat. He has an Irish accent, doesn't he? Where is he from?"

"He grew up in Northern Ireland, Londonderry, he said. Then he and his cousin and aunt moved here to Savannah."

"Londonderry?"

"You better go now," Jake said as he walked over to the Suburban.

McGill stared as Kaplan mounted his Harley and rode off. He glanced up at Jake and said, "What the hell did he want?"

"Nothing. He was on his way back to the TRACON, like you told him to do, and saw the emergency vehicles and me, so he just stopped to ask."

"What'd you tell him?"

"I just said there was an accident at Gulfstream."

"Okay, so tell me what the hell happened to Dave?"

CHAPTER 30

She sat in her dark house peering through the gap in the drapes, listening to the man on the other end of the phone. The afternoon sun beamed through the window and washed over the side of her face. Her hair was pulled tight into a bun on the top of her head.

She hung up the phone and let it fall to the table. She stared out the window.

After two minutes, she stood, turned around, and talked toward the darkness, "Mr. Jake Pendleton is going to cause us problems. We need to ensure he stays out of our business."

A large figure rose up from a chair and moved through the dark room toward the woman. He stepped into the light. A streak of white hair down the middle of his head. His irises—one blue, one brown.

"I'll take care of Mr. Pendleton and anyone else who gets in our way, Jillian."

"Have you located Sullivan yet?"

"No, but I know he's here, and I believe he's talked to Pendleton too."

She raised her voice. "What would make you think that?"

The assassin moved to the window, stuck out his hand and parted the drapes. The sunlight brightened the room. "How else could Mr. Pendleton have become suspicious so quickly?"

"He's supposed to be quite an adept investigator," she replied.

"No, he's not that smart. He was tipped off about the bomb. This is one case he won't get a chance to solve."

She grinned. "Well, this time knowledge comes with a price."

CHAPTER 31

Jake and Beth listened to the music playing in the restaurant on River Street. Island reggae sounds of Bob Marley's *Get Up, Stand Up* filled the air, adding to the calypso flavor of the room. Bamboo-bladed ceiling fans turned slowly, enhancing the festive atmosphere inside the restaurant. Their waitress delivered a plate full of cracked conch fritters to the table, and poured them each a glass of red zinfandel, their favorite.

Taking a bite of fritter, he looked at Beth, picked up his glass and took a sip. This might not be the ideal time and place, but he knew she wanted to hear about what he was doing.

"I know it sounds coincidental but I have a gut feeling about this one," he said. "There are too many suspicious circumstances to just dismiss the possibility of sabotage. The whole mechanic scene in Dallas, the man shot in the head. The missing mechanic who just happens to look like the guy we saw here, the one with Whataburger syndrome. The girlfriend drugged and unable to recall anything that happened for a two-day period. Dave being killed in some freak accident. And don't forget the section of the Challenger missing from beneath the cockpit—"

"Here's what I think," Beth said. "First of all, it's Waardenburg's Syndrome. Second, I think that the crazy man who broke into our room is the reason you're so suspicious. He planted this whole sabotage thing in your head—for what reason? I don't know. He wouldn't give his name, he held a gun on us, and then he gave us some cryptic conspiracy theory with no proof. I think he was just some Irish crackpot—*and* I still think we should have called hotel security or the police. Let's just say, for a minute, that all that stuff is true, how do you explain the midair?"

"I can't. That's the one thing that keeps baffling me about this investigation. Without the midair, there are too many indicators to not to seriously consider sabotage. Without all the other factors, the Irish man, the two mechanics, Dave's phone call and death, it would scream midair only," Jake argued. "But for a sabotaged aircraft to have a midair while it's falling out of the sky—well, the odds must be staggering."

The waitress returned with their order, cutting their conversation short. "Blackened grouper for the gentleman and fried shrimp for the lady."

She refilled their wine glasses and asked if she could get them anything else. When they said no, she smiled and returned to the kitchen.

"Exactly. The odds are staggering. Too staggering. Somebody's playing games with you, Jake. Can't you see that?"

"Yeah, maybe you're right."

"It's horrible about Dave," she said. "He was such a funny little man. The way he walked and talked reminded me of Danny DeVito. He even had that little yarmulke-looking bald spot on the back of his head. I'm going to miss him. What did Pat have to say about the accident at the hangar?"

"Just that, it was an accident. The authorities said the crane either lost hydraulic pressure while Dave was under the fuselage, or the lever worked its way loose and Dave didn't notice until it was too late. He apparently was alone." Jake raised his finger. "That's another thing that bothers me. Dave never worked without a crane operator before—so why start now?"

"Maybe due to the urgency of the investigation, he was unable to."

"Perhaps."

"What happens next, Jake?"

"Pat suspended the investigation for the rest of today, discussed it at an early organizational meeting and later announced it at the press conference. He's giving everyone on the investigation the day off tomorrow for two reasons. One, because of Dave's death. And two, because of the St Patrick's Day crowd. But mostly, because of Dave. Pat said Carol took it hard."

Beth fell silent for a moment.

Jake gazed over her shoulder out the window overlooking River Street and noticed a man staring at him through the window.

The man they had seen in Barry's Pub.

The man who met the description of Ian McDonald, the mechanic in Dallas.

The man with the white streak in his hair and the mismatched eyes.

Jake stood and ran outside eager to put an end to the mystery surrounding this man. The man was gone.

CHAPTER 32

At that same moment, Pat McGill pulled the NTSB Suburban to the curb as his cell phone rang. The caller ID stated only Chatham County. He flipped open his phone. "Pat McGill."

"Mr. McGill, this is Jim Anderson, Chatham County Medical Examiner."

"Yes, Mr. Anderson, what can I do for you?"

"It's about Dave Morris. I found something you should know about."

"What was that?"

"When I started cleaning Mr. Morris' chest and removed his clothing, I noticed a lot of cuts and gashes and puncture wounds. Nothing I wouldn't have expected to find, until I cleaned him thoroughly. Then I saw a puncture wound that looked a little different so I opened him up. That's when I found it."

"Found what?"

"Gunshot wound through the heart. Mr. Morris was dead before that airplane fell on him."

"A gunshot wound? Are you sure?"

"Oh, yeah, I have the bullet right here to prove it. I bagged it and have it ready to send to ballistics. By law, I had to notify the local authorities so an investigation can be initiated."

"Very good, Mr. Anderson, I appreciate everything you've done. This is a federal investigation and as such, additional notification must be made to the FBI, actually they will have jurisdiction. Also, due to the sensitive nature of this investigation, I must ask you not to discuss this with anyone other than the local police investigator or me until the FBI arrives and views Mr. Morris' body. This aircraft accident involved a very influential and controversial political figure and must be handled with considerable delicacy."

"Okay, Mr. McGill, I understand. What about next of kin?"

"Mr. Morris was married but had no children. I called his wife and broke the news to her. She took it pretty hard. I won't tell her he was shot until the FBI gives me the green light."

"Alright, I appreciate that. Are you going to call the FBI?" Anderson asked.

"No. I'll let the local police make that notification. I'll give them a calright now."

He ended the call with Anderson, got out of his car and walked up to the front door of a home in the historic district.

The door opened after one ring of the doorbell.

"Pat, what are you doing here?"

"Cousin, we've got one hell of a big problem."

CHAPTER 33

Thirty minutes later Kaplan let himself into Annie's house through the garage entrance. As he opened the door from the stairwell into the kitchen, he found Annie sitting in the bay window reading a book, Scout curled up in her lap. Seeing him, Scout jumped down and scampered over to rub lovingly against his legs.

Annie marked her page with a bookmark, placed the book next to the window and walked over to him, placing her head against his chest and giving him a hug. Barefooted, her head didn't reach his chin.

She unbuttoned his shirt halfway down and kissed his chest, then said, "How'd it go at work?"

"I never actually made it to the tower."

"Where the hell have you been then?"

"I saw a lot of commotion at the Gulfstream plant. You know, ambulances, police, a rescue unit—"

She interrupted. "Yeah, I saw something on the news about an accident, but I didn't catch any details."

"Anyway, as it turns out, one of the NTSB guys had a huge piece of the wreckage fall on top of him and it killed him. Then I talked to Jake Pendleton and he told me a few things that are bothering him about the investigation."

"Like what?"

He spent a few minutes talking about Jake's theories about the crash, with a brief interruption for a beer and snacks.

As he finished, Annie looked at him curiously. "So he believes that something strange went wrong with the airplane causing it to fall out of the sky?"

"Yeah, basically, either a mechanical failure or some sort of explosion."

"So how does the midair factor into all this?"

"Jake said that was the one piece that doesn't fit the puzzle."

"I'd say that's one pretty damn big piece, wouldn't you?"

Just as he was about to respond, her cell phone rang. She picked up the phone, flipped it open, and placing it next to her cheek, said, "Annie Bulloch."

"Who? … No, I'm afraid you have the wrong number." She hung up.

He walked into the den and sat in the big leather loveseat and placed his beer on the coaster on the wrought iron end table. Turning around and looking over his shoulder toward the kitchen, he called out, "You're originally from Ireland—have you ever heard of this O'Rourke guy?"

She came in, put her beer glass on the opposite end table, and sat down next to Kaplan. She spun sideways in her seat, placing her feet in his lap. "Of course, I've heard of him—he's been in the news for months."

"You never talk much about your past," he said. "How come you moved away from Ireland?"

"Where I grew up was a dangerous place at a dangerous time … during the 'Troubles.' My mother was raped and my dad couldn't deal with it so he left her. We moved here. Then my dad was killed." She lowered her chin.

"I don't talk about it because it's painful. I just try to forget about my past before I moved here."

"Where in Ireland did you grow up?"

"Northern Ireland, a town called Londonderry."

*   *   *

Later that night, Collins lay in his hotel room, curtains drawn, room dark. The buzz of his Blackberry vibrating on the nightstand stirred him from a restless sleep. He reached over and picked it up to read the message that displayed in all caps.

BIG PROBLEM. MUST MOVE QUICKLY. JILLIAN.

He sighed.

What is the problem?

A minute later, the Blackberry vibrated again. The reply simply stated:

Jake Pendleton is getting too close. Stop him ASAP. And his girlfriend. Bring them both to me.
J.

He deleted his messages, rolled over and went back to sleep.

CHAPTER 34

Holding his binoculars to his eyes, Jake stood on the balcony of his sixteenth-floor room overlooking downtown Savannah and the Savannah River. Wisps of steam rose from the warmer river waters. The waters were calm except for the wake from one of the ferries that had already started making its way from the City Hall Landing to the Trade Center Landing.

The morning sky was clear and the rising sun lit up the gold dome on the top of the Savannah City Hall, reflecting it directly at the Westin. Jake squinted as he looked out over the city. The spires of the Cathedral of St. John the Baptist towered above the trees and stood prominently in the Savannah skyline. The early morning temperature was a cool forty-two degrees with an expected high of seventy-four, perfect for a St. Patrick's Day celebration in Savannah.

Across the river along River Street, vendors had started setting up for the day's festivities. Exhaust from the few vehicles allowed on River Street billowed from their tail pipes. Pedestrians' breath was clearly visible as they spoke to one another on the street. A young boy swept the sidewalk under the yellow and white striped awning of Spanky's Restaurant, a cloud of dust rising up with every stroke of his push broom. Next to the sweeper Jake saw a young girl in shorts and a jacket under a red and white striped awning, wiping off the benches in front of the Shrimp Factory. Two men were opening the windows at the twin buildings that made up the River Street Marketplace.

He knew there was something else, something he was missing. His gut told him that the unknown man was right, the crash *was* a result of sabotage. But how could he prove it without riling McGill and getting tossed from the investigation? And how could he explain the other aircraft and the midair?

The odds were staggering that it was just a coincidence. Yet he knew it couldn't be *just a midair*.

There was more.

He was determined to find out what it was.

He heard Beth protesting behind him.

"Jake Pendleton, it's cold. Close the door." She rolled over on her stomach and pulled the covers over her head.

He turned and went inside, closing the sliding glass door behind him. He sat on the edge of the bed and said, "Babe, I'm going to run out to the airport. I'll be back in a couple of hours, probably less, and then we'll go have breakfast."

"You're not leaving me here alone. That, that weirdo might come back. Besides, I thought Pat gave everybody the day off."

"He did, but there are a couple of things I want to look into, then I'll come right back. Look, you'll be just fine here. Deadbolt the door when I leave and no one can get in, not even me and I have a key."

"You promise you'll only be gone a couple of hours?"

"Of course."

She grumbled from under the covers. "Say it, Jake."

"I promise," he replied.

"Jacob Pendleton."

"Alright, alright. I promise I'll be back in two hours—or my ass is yours and you can have your way with me." He grinned.

CHAPTER 35

The guard at Gulfstream stepped out of his guard shack, held up his hand and stopped the black Mustang. He pointed to an old white Ford F150 long-bed pickup truck with homemade wooden bed walls parked in a visitor's parking spot.

The guard said, "He's been waiting here since sunrise. He said he will only talk to an NTSB agent."

"Agent?" Jake smiled. "Did he say what he wanted?"

"No. He's got a lot of junk piled in the back of his truck and threatened to dump it in the parking lot if someone didn't show up soon."

He walked over to the pickup. An elderly man sat behind the wheel, his head leaned back on the headrest, and his hat pulled down over his eyes. Jake tapped on the window and the old man jumped. He held his NTSB identification badge up to the window. The old man rolled down the window.

He stepped back and said, "I'm Jake Pendleton with the NTSB. The guard there said you've been here a while. Is there something I can do for you?"

"It's about time one of you boys showed up. You boys must work banker's hours."

"I beg your pardon?"

"Never mind. I think I found something you might need," the old man said. "It's in the back." He pointed with his thumb.

Jake and the old man walked around to the back of the truck. The bed was filled with debris. A lot of debris. Many shapes and sizes—all of it twisted and torn. One piece in particular caught Jake's eyes. It was a large burgundy piece that almost filled the bed of the truck. One end was curled back and shredded into smaller strips of the metal, each about eight inches wide, twisted backward nearly a hundred and eighty degrees.

He looked at the old man's tired face, his bushy gray eyebrows, over a decade in need of a trim, reminded him of Andy Rooney. "Where did you find this?"

"On my property, over in South Carolina just across the river. It looked like something off of an airplane and I heard about a crash over here so I figured I'd bring it on over. I busted a shear pin on my bush hog when I hit some of it," the man said, pointing to a blue piece of the tail section of the Skyhawk. "It stopped my mower blade just like that." He snapped his fingers for emphasis.

"You ran over it? You hit it with the mower?"

"Not the big piece—I ain't blind, sonny. Some of the smaller chunks were hidden in the taller grass. I bumped over something with the tractor, then I heard the mower blade whack something hard. That's when the pin sheared. It took me nearly a half hour with a crowbar to get that piece off my blade."

"You found it this morning?"

"Naw. I did this yesterday right after dinner."

Jake leaned over to look closer at the big chunk of wreckage. "Why didn't you bring it yesterday or call or something?"

"Well, young feller, I ain't no government worker like you. I had a lot of work to do. I picked up as much as I could find and then finished my mowing. I hit a few other smaller pieces but I could never find 'em after I hit 'em."

"Can you show me where you found this?"

The old man looked up at him and shook his head. "Can't right now, but I figured you boys would want to go look see for yourself so I drew you a map to my place. Yer welcome to go look around all you want, take whatever ya need." He pointed at the bed full of debris and asked, "Where do I dump all this trash?"

He rode with the old man back to the recovery hangar where they unloaded all the debris. He escorted the man back to the gate, took his name and phone number. The old man pulled out of the parking lot, blue smoke billowing from the back of his pickup as he accelerated down Gulfstream Road.

Jake returned to the hangar and laid the debris on the floor, separating the pieces as best he could. Then he studied the largest piece. It was the missing section from the underside of the Challenger. The section below and just behind the cockpit. The strips of metal on one end were curled backward and outward. The green side of the metal was the inside and the burgundy side was the painted side of the metal, the exterior.

He studied the green side and noticed something peculiar. What he saw made his heart jump in his chest.

Residue.

Residue from a fire—or an explosion. He preferred explosion. But he had to be sure.

He grabbed his field kit and started the preliminary tests. An excitement took over when he saw the results, explosive residue.

He was right all along. Sabotage. A stretch maybe to call it sabotage at this point, but his instincts told him otherwise. And better yet, it confirmed what the strange man had said. He needed to call McGill. They needed to call the FBI.

*   *   *

On the fourth ring, McGill answered his cell phone. "Hello, Jake, what do you want?"

"Pat, I'm at the Gulfstream hangar—"

"Jake, I said take the day off. I meant it."

Jake heard the ire in his voice.

"I know, I know. I couldn't sleep, so I got up and figured I'd look things over out here. Anyway, when I got here there was this old farmer from South Carolina waiting with a pickup full of debris he found on his property. Some of it was compromised by his mower but most of it is okay.

"Pat, there's something here you need to see. The missing section from the Challenger is here, and it has explosive residue on it. You need to get over here right away."

"Okay, I've heard enough about explosions. Are you sure? Did you check it?"

"Yes, Pat, it checked out positive. Come see for yourself."

"Alright. I'll leave right now. I'll be there in twenty or thirty minutes. Secure the hangar. Let no one, I repeat *no one* in until I arrive. I'm bringing my kit and for your sake, Jake, you better be right. After I look at the debris, if I'm not convinced, then you're on your way back to Atlanta. Do I make myself clear?"

"Crystal."

Exactly twenty minutes later, McGill's NTSB Suburban pulled into the hangar. McGill and Jake spent the next hour studying and discussing all the ramifications and details of what the old man had brought in his pickup.

McGill conceded, "Jake, this changes things. Although certainly not conclusive, it's enough to warrant suspicion and notify the FBI. For the record though, I'm still more than a little upset that you've gone behind my back, not followed orders and withheld information."

The last comment startled Jake. Did McGill know about the man in his room? "What did I withhold?"

"That piece about the primary radar being out?"

"I didn't withhold it Pat. I just hadn't had an opportunity to share it with you yet."

Jake knew he needed to tell McGill about the man but now he realized that if McGill knew, he would certainly relieve Jake of duties. He couldn't allow that. He had to work this investigation to its conclusion.

Just then Jake's cell phone rang.

"Uh-oh, It's Beth. She's probably pissed."

"Why is that?"

"I told her I'd be back in less than two hours … and it's been much longer than that."

"You better answer it then."

Jake flipped open his phone. "Beth, I'm sorry. I know it's been longer than two hours, but something very urgent came up at the hangar."

"Jake, that's not it. Are you alone?" Beth said.

"Nope, I'm standing here with Pat. We were just going over a few details on the crash."

"Listen carefully, just listen. I just got a phone call from Gregg Kaplan, that air traffic controller."

"Uh huh, I remember," he said, smiling at the phone. He noticed McGill making the call to the FBI.

"You need to get away from there right now. This Kaplan guy told me some things. I believe him. It all makes sense now. Jake, you were right. Remember what that guy said in the room, 'Trust no one.' Well, he meant it. Don't trust anybody. Kaplan wants to meet you right away. He said to meet him at Barry's Pub on River Street in one hour, that's eleven o'clock. I'll be there too. Hurry."

She hung up.

A quiver of panic ran down his spine.

He glanced at Pat. "Alright, babe. An early lunch would be great, we'll beat the crowds ... yeah, I love you too. Bye, now."

He hung up his phone. McGill did the same.

McGill walked over to Jake. "The feds will be here in a couple of hours. I called the Atlanta office. They have to call it in to D.C., and then they will dispatch a Special Agent from Savannah. The efficiency of the federal government. You'd think I could just call the Savannah office myself and save everyone a lot of time."

"Good. That was Beth. She wants me to come have an early lunch with her like I promised. I hope you don't mind. I should be back by the time the feds get here."

"Yeah, that's fine. No problem."

As he walked toward the Mustang, McGill shouted out, "Jake. That was good work."

"Thanks, Pat."

He drove the black Mustang out of the hangar.

In his rear view mirror, he noticed McGill on the phone again. But his mind was on the phone call from Beth. Is she alright? Did he make a mistake in telling Kaplan his suspicions? Could he be trusted?

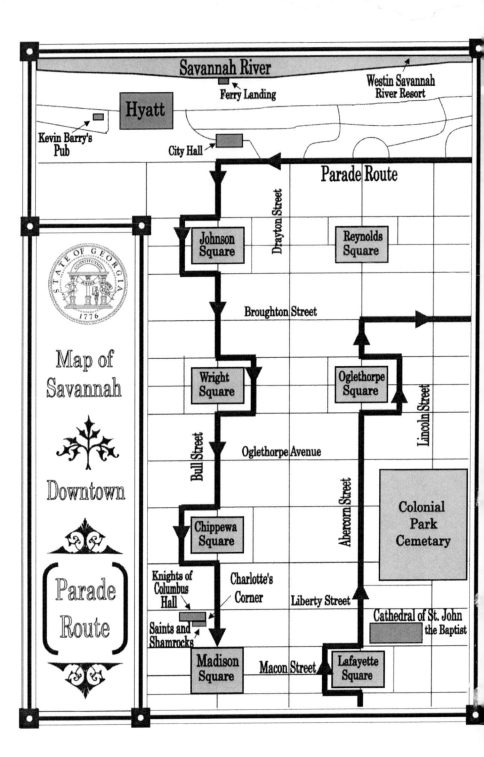

CHAPTER 36

The drive back to the Westin took him longer than anticipated. In the Westin parking lot, he called Beth's cell number to see if she was still at the hotel, but there was no answer. He assumed she was on River Street and, with the already crowded festival, might not have heard her phone ring.

After waiting in the long line at the landing, he boarded the second ferry that arrived. The ferry was at capacity. He stood on the bow for the three-minute trip to the City Hall landing, wondering what Kaplan so urgently wanted and why Beth had a tone of panic in her voice. He disembarked and walked along the river, as the group had the first night, thus avoiding the always overcrowded tunnel where River Street went under the Hyatt.

The breeze tousled his hair. When he left for the airport earlier in the morning, he had dressed for the cool morning—blue jeans, a long-sleeved yellow button-down, brown leather jacket and Timberland hiking boots. He was comfortable now but realized soon he wouldn't be and wished he had changed his shirt and dropped off his jacket while he was at the Westin. It was too late now.

He rounded the corner of the Hyatt and right in front of him was Kevin Barry's Pub, looking much different in the daylight than at night. The sunlight revealed its age. Faded wood panels had long since weathered and were in desperate need of paint. Sun bleached letters had lost their Irish green luster.

To his right a crowd had gathered around a young man break-dancing to funky Irish music playing from a boom box. He was dressed in traditional St. Patrick's Day style—green. The music was loud.

He made his way toward the pub, craning his neck to see through the crowd watching the dancer and looking for any sign of Beth or Kaplan.

He turned around toward the pub and ran into four young men, college age, with painted faces. Painted green. Two of them wore tall fuzzy hats. Green and white. *Cat-in-the-Hat* style hats. The other two wore wigs—one, a green Afro-style wig, and the other, green dread-locks. All of the young men held mugs of green beer, not their first mug of the day.

Jake worked his way through the crowded entrance of Barry's and looked in. The pub was busy yet there seemed to be seats available at the bar. He noticed the sign over the bar he'd seen on his first visit. It read "CE'AL MI'LE FA'ILTE" across the top and, in an arch in the middle, "Kevin Barry's." He had no idea what the words meant.

A few patrons had come in for an early lunch. He looked around for Beth and Kaplan. He moved through to the main restaurant and scanned the dining area. A band was setting up equipment. He went upstairs and checked the Balcony Bar and Liberty Hall dining room. No Beth. No Kaplan.

He took a seat in the Balcony Bar. He figured it an ideal spot as it offered a clear view out over River Street. He should be able to spot Beth and Kaplan without much difficulty.

A female bartender walked up behind him and said, "Hello, welcome to Barry's—may I get you something?"

He looked at her big brown eyes, warm and inviting. She was attractive, mid twenties, with thick brown hair pulled back in a pony tail. She wore a clingy white knit skirt that stopped just below the knees, along with a t-shirt bearing the Barry's Pub name and logo. "Not right now," he replied. "I'm waiting on a couple of friends."

He noticed her right forearm and wrist were wrapped in a black Velcro arm splint. "What did you do to your arm?"

"I broke it last week snowboarding," she replied.

He detected her Northern accent and smiled. "Your accent, I can't quite place it. Somewhere up north, certainly not Savannah," he said.

"Nope. I'm from Michigan. A little town just north of Detroit."

"So, are you a Yankee, or a damn Yankee?" Jake quipped.

"What's the difference?"

"A Yankee comes down South, then goes home. A damn Yankee comes down here and never leaves." He gave her an impish grin.

She waited a second or two, then smiled back. "I'm just a Yankee. I'm going back home when I finish school in Savannah."

"What school is that?"

"SCAD."

He looked puzzled.

"Savannah College of Art and Design," she said.

"Oh yeah, I've heard of that. I've seen the signs around town."

"Just give me a shout when you're ready to order."

She moved to another table.

He took out his cell phone and placed a call to Beth. After the sixth ring, it went to her voice mail. After waiting for ten minutes, he decided to go ahead and order something to eat. He hadn't eaten breakfast and the hunger pangs got stronger with each whiff from the kitchen.

He leaned back and waved at the waitress to get her attention. She nodded and gave him the "be right there" wave. He turned around and faced the window again, scanning the crowd for any sign of Beth or Kaplan.

A man stared up at him from the street.

Jake instantly recognized him.

CHAPTER 37

Jake stood abruptly and took two steps back away from the glass, bumping into the waitress. He turned to her, opened his mouth, but said nothing.

"What's wrong? You look like you've seen a ghost," she said.

He struggled to think of an explanation and finally said, "Do you see that big man with the streak in his hair?"

"Yeah, I've seen him in here before. He's creepy looking, his eyes and all. He's rude and a bad tipper."

"What's he doing now?" he asked.

"He's trying to get across River Street. Looks like he's coming in here."

He needed to find Beth. He was worried about her safety and with the current path the investigation was taking, this man now could be a threat. He needed a cover story. He couldn't just tell the waitress his suspicions.

"That's my ex's new boyfriend. He's real jealous and he's real mean."

"And real ugly." She said, "There's something's wrong with your ex if she traded you in for him."

"Is there another way out of here?"

"Yes. There are two doors on this floor that exit onto the alley in the back. One is just under that exit sign and the other is through that door." She pointed to a small door bearing the sign, "Office."

"But you have to zigzag through the kitchen to get out that way," she said.

"Which one is quickest?"

"Just go through that door at the exit sign and you're in the alley."

"Thanks. I owe you one," Jake ran for the door.

*　　*　　*

Kaplan stood outside the doorway of the Riverhouse Bakery, two doors down from the entrance to Kevin Barry's Pub. Bubbles rained down on him from the Loafer's Loft gift shop directly above him.

He watched the man in the doorway to the pub, looking around, blocking the entrance. Two college-aged girls tried to squeeze around him. One said, "Do you mind?" The other, "Puleeze, how rude." The man didn't move.

He had noticed the man following Jake as soon as Jake got off the ferry. He recognized him from the description Jake had given him the day before in front of the Gulfstream plant. He had been on his own way to catch up to Jake when he picked up on Jake's tail by chance.

When Jake stopped, the man stopped. When Jake turned around, the big man ducked to conceal his presence.

When Jake had stopped at the green-faced boys, Kaplan stepped to the other side of the break-dancer in order to observe both Jake and the big man. No doubt about it, the man was following Jake.

He looked at the two doorways, the only ways in or out of Barry's Pub from the River Street level. He repositioned himself next to the Hyatt tunnel for a better vantage point. The big man disappeared inside. Jake was still inside. At least, Kaplan thought Jake was still in there, until he saw someone moving out from behind Barry's on the second-floor level. He saw Jake run across the ramp and over to the stone steps that led up the bluff to the front of the Hyatt at the Bay Street level.

He glanced up at the balcony bar window and saw the big man grab the waitress. He shook her and she pointed toward the rear of the bar.

He moved to warn Jake when he spotted the man again, coming out from behind Barry's Pub at the same place Jake had come from.

The man moved quickly to the stone steps, shoving people out of his way. He could see Jake was nearly at the top of the steps when the man reached the bottom of the stone steps.

Stalking the big man reminded him of a time long ago when he first encountered covert urban operations.

In December 1987, he had been dropped into a remote portion of the Panama jungle on a covert mission with three other soldiers. Their mission was to scout, locate, and map the position of target officials and facilities of Panama as intel for what became Operation Bushmaster. Operation Bushmaster was an operation that used infantry units to supplement military police patrols in Panama, specifically the areas immediately surrounding the Panama Canal and American installations. Their mission was primarily executed under the cover of darkness and they were told that, in the event of capture by General Noriega's forces, the U.S. government would disavow their operation and claim they were merely mercenaries.

When Operation Bushmaster became official, he and his team were extracted and returned to the United States.

In early December 1989, he received an acceptance letter from the FAA, his start date would be in March. However, on Christmas Eve 1989, Kaplan found himself on another C-130 Hercules transport plane leaving Hurlburt Air Field in the Florida Panhandle in the dead of night, headed for Panama again.

This time his main target was General Noriega's second-in-command, Raul Diego. He'd acquired his target and followed him through the streets of Panama City. Diego drove from bar to bar ending up at the doorstep of an ill-reputed whorehouse with his favorite prostitute, Angelina Vasquez. He stayed close but out of sight and when Diego arrived, he radioed his squad, "Blue jay is in his nest." The squad moved in through the rear entrance, as prearranged with Vasquez, and captured Diego, literally with his pants around his knees.

The extraction went as planned and when placed in confinement, Diego divulged enough information to make the operation a success.

He'd all but forgotten Panama and what it had taken to survive there, sure that he would never need those skills again—that is, until now.

He knew Jake was in big trouble.

He also knew he had to help.

CHAPTER 38

Jake heard the noise of the parade, already in progress along Bay Street. He moved fast to the stone steps leading to Bay Street and into the mob of revelers watching the parade. He hoped to blend in with the crowd. When he reached the top of the steps, he turned east toward the Hyatt entrance.

He paused at the corner of the hotel, pulled out his cell phone and hit redial. Still no answer. Where was Beth?

Jake looked over his left shoulder, one last look down at River Street.

He saw the big man.

And the man saw Jake.

He jammed his phone back in his jacket pocket, turned back toward the east, and walked as briskly as the crowded sidewalk would allow. He turned around again to look for the big man. The one advantage Jake had was his size, not too tall to stand out. The big man's height was a disadvantage and Jake spotted him right away, now walking across the Hyatt driveway looking straight at him.

He tried to think rationally. What could this man want with him? He could just be doing what the other thousands of people here were doing, enjoying the St. Patrick's Day festivities.

He looked back at the man again and his instincts told him—*run. This man is trouble.*

He ran across the brick driveway toward City Hall. A drunken college student wearing a huge green foam cowboy hat was taunting a pretty girl with his beads. His buddies were chanting words of encouragement egging her on. Looking up, Jake could see the clock just below the gold dome of City Hall.

The clock showed 11:55.

The music was louder as the bands in the parade marched down Bay Street. Another roar from the college boys behind him. He turned around to see the young woman pull the front of her shirt up to her neck and shake her breasts. Her nipples were covered with green shamrock pasties.

The throngs of revelers packed the park in front of the Hyatt entrance, obscuring most of the parade from view. Only the floats were visible above the crowd.

He stopped at the corner of City Hall and looked back across the front of the Hyatt. He had a relatively clear view of everyone coming across the entrance as the swelling crowds jammed up next to Bay Street to watch the parade.

Then he spotted the man with the blaze in his hair. The man stopped and looked around. Jake tried to round the corner of the building but wasn't fast enough. He peered back around the corner and saw the man coming toward him fast.

He pushed his way through the massive crowd packed in front of City Hall, where the distance from the building to the street was much smaller. He bumped into a man wearing a camouflage baseball cap and a green wife-beater shirt.

"Hey! What's your problem, man?"

"Sorry, man," Jake said, and moved as quickly as he could past City Hall.

He walked east in front of the old Savannah Cotton Exchange, now Solomon's Lodge Freemason Hall. A red-winged lion guarded the front of the old Exchange.

He stopped for the parade at the corner of Bay and Abercorn streets. Looking up at the old majestic live oaks, still bearing their leaves, he saw Spanish moss hanging from the limbs and gently swaying back and forth in the breeze.

He looked around at faces, searching for his pursuer. A vendor selling beads, hats and trinkets stood next to the light pole on the corner. Three teenage girls walked by giggling, each with a headband supporting two shamrock antennae.

He heard one of the girls say, "Did you see his hair? And his eyes ... they were creepy looking."

A flood of panic swept over him.

He scanned the area.

He saw nothing.

He feverishly looked around, jumping up to see over the sea of green headwear.

Then he saw the man.

Twenty feet away, coming right at him.

*   *   *

Without hesitation, Jake ran into Bay Street, cutting through the middle of a high school marching band. He almost made it across the street without running into anyone, until a band member raised his trombone to play. He collided with the shining brass horn, knocking it free from the musician's hands. The horn bounced twice on the red brick crosswalk.

Jake jumped over the horn and kept running. The band member shouted at him in anger.

He turned south down Abercorn. Looking back over his shoulder as he ran. He made it forty feet before he lost his footing when the sidewalk suddenly dipped at an entrance to a parking garage. He tumbled onto the concrete entrance landing hard on his left shoulder. A sharp pain shot through his shoulder and into his neck. He rolled over and looked at his shoulder, his leather jacket was scuffed and stitching had pulled loose. He was glad he was wearing the jacket now.

He jumped to his feet. His left shoulder throbbed from the impact on the pavement. Farther down the sidewalk, a vendor selling green beer in two-foot-tall plastic glasses looked at him, then shook his head in disgust at what appeared to be just another drunk.

Glancing back the other way, he saw the huge man crossing Bay

Street. Jake had increased his lead to a hundred feet.

Almost all of the streets in the Historic District were closed to vehicular traffic during the parade. Jake stepped into Abercorn and ran down the middle of the street until he reached Reynolds Square.

The square was full of revelers. A vendor selling strands of green beads to two teenage boys had set up his station next to a park bench, not far from the statue of John Wesley that stood in the center of the square.

Panting, he slowed to a brisk walk, weaved through the mass of people, looked around and saw the man gaining on him again.

He broke into a full sprint out of Reynolds Square, south on Abercorn past the Lucas Theatre. As he approached Broughton Street, he saw the parade coming north on Abercorn. The parade turned east at Broughton, so he turned west.

The corner and surrounding streets were lined with people, some having camped out for hours ahead of time in order to get a good view of the parade. Many had set up chairs with their coolers close by. A few even set up umbrellas for shade, but Savannah's Finest made them take the umbrellas down for safety reasons as the crowds grew.

He ran diagonally across Broughton Street at the Broughton Municipal Building toward the Marshall House. Two blocks farther, he reached Bull Street, where the sidewalks were again jammed with parade-watchers.

The parade was moving south on Bull toward the end of its route. The route had started on the southern end of the historic district, looped through downtown, then ended back just a few blocks from where it began.

Jake weaved through the crowd, stopping underneath the awning at Starbucks. He looked back and hoped he had lost his follower. The aroma of the coffee shop made him realize he hadn't eaten all day. His stomach growled at him in protest. He paused, looking around for a few moments to get his bearings, until his angst pushed him onward. He followed alongside the parade down Bull Street.

He crossed through a break in the parade and into Wright Square. In the southeast corner of the square, Jake stopped by a granite boulder big enough to hide him from view. He drew several deep breaths and rested a moment. A plaque indicated the boulder was from Stone Mountain and commemorated the burial in 1739 of Tomo-Chi-Chi, Chief of the Yamacraw tribe. He didn't read it—he was looking for the man.

On the other side of the square, he merged back into the parade and celebrators, trying to get lost in the multitude of green. The thought struck Jake, if the man was a threat to him, he was certainly a threat to Beth. He pulled out his phone and redialed her number. Still no answer.

At Oglethorpe and Bull he saw a big green landmark sign marking the birthplace of Juliette Gordon Low, Girl Scouts founder. He moved much faster than the parade itself, traversing the two blocks to Chippewa Square in surprisingly good time given the holiday crowds.

He stopped at the corner of Hull Street and Bull Street beside the square. Surely he had lost the man by now. Tired and out of breath, he rested his hands on his knees while he gulped in air and stared back at the crowd. He thought he saw a fleeting glimpse of the white-blazed hair but couldn't be sure. Then it was gone.

After he caught his breath, he started running again. Heading diagonally across Chippewa Square, he crashed into a young couple getting up from a park bench. The man yelled, "Hey, asshole. Watch where you're going."

Jake looked back into the square and saw the big man moving toward him again.

Jake hurdled some bushes, crossed through the parade again, then darted through an open wrought iron gate into the backyard of a home on the corner of Perry and Bull.

A fountain in the garden spewed water up to a bowl held up by three cherubs. He didn't really have time to study it. The water cascaded down into a basin filled with lily pads and goldfish.

A twin wrought iron gate was directly across the yard from the one he entered. It opened into an alley. A table with plates of appetizers was set up near the second gate. Three couples sat on a brick patio near the back of the yard in the shade, drinking their cocktails and enjoying the sunshine and the sounds of the parade.

As he crossed the yard toward the far gate, a dignified Southern voice said, "May I help you?"

He turned and smiled at the man. "No, thanks, just passing through."

As he passed the table he grabbed a handful of what looked like stuffed pretzels, then darted into the alleyway. He heard a female voice protest, "Of all the nerve ... how rude."

A small parking lot filled with cars was straight ahead. A muted yellow building on the left cast a shadow onto the lot, keeping the cars in the shade. A red brick building on the right had nearly disappeared as ivy covered its walls.

Jake walked through the parking lot toward Liberty Street, eating the pretzels. They were good, but they weren't pretzels. They were mini-rolls, stuffed with what tasted like crab meat. The food felt good on his empty stomach.

Liberty Street was one of the few Savannah historic district streets with a grassy median dividing the traffic. Directly across from him, he saw a Mellow Mushroom restaurant. To the left of it, the Savannah Council Knights of Columbus Hall. Beside the hall was Charlotte's Corner and a mob of party-goers, drinking and talking loud. Above the corner store, the Knights of Columbus had a patio deck filled with people, most of them also drinking enthusiastically.

An exhausted and breathless Jake approached. He noticed a difference in the crowd compared to the partiers downtown. This crowd was much better dressed, preppie looking. They were older too, in general, and appeared more affluent.

On the Knights of Columbus patio stood men in coats and ties, and women in long dresses, some formal. Wine glasses instead of beer bottles prevailed. The crowd appeared to be locals who came to socialize and watch the parade in a somewhat tamer environment. The music playing on the patio was drowned out by the bands in the parade.

He stood at the edge of the gathering of Savannah socialites, scanning for the man. He thought of Beth and how they'd attended those debutante balls in Newnan. Then a wave of fear hit him like a blow. Where was she?

After a minute of looking around, he convinced himself that he had shaken off his pursuer. He merged into the crowd and took a well deserved breather.

He looked to the south, the parade was disbanding one block away. He decided to walk to the end of the parade route, then work his way back to the Westin.

The sidewalk in front of Charlotte's Corner and the Saints and Shamrocks next door was packed. He had to walk sideways next to the buildings. Sidestepping to the right with his back to the glass store windows, he inched his way south. Twenty feet away was an alleyway and the crowd thinned.

He pushed his way toward the alley, his back to the wall. He looked ahead and saw he would have to get past the last glass window, across an open stairwell leading to the Knights of Columbus patio, and then edge along the remaining wall to the alley. Keeping his back to the window, he moved into the stairwell. He stood facing the street while he surveyed the mass of people he would have to squeeze through before reaching the alley.

Suddenly his heels came off the sidewalk as he was lifted by a mighty force into the stairwell landing. Something sharp and painful jabbed into his right side. A gloved hand covered his mouth while the sharp object dug deeper into his side. He felt the leather on his coat give way to the knife blade.

The point of the blade broke his skin. He felt a trickle of blood run down his side. The man slammed him hard against the wall. Pain screamed through his already injured left shoulder. The hand on his neck was strong, stronger than anyone he had ever felt. His left side was held firmly against the stone wall. He was no physical match for the man who held him.

The man spoke.

A deep low voice with a strong Irish accent.

"No tricks, no yelling. If you ever want to see your pretty little girlfriend again, then you'll do exactly as you are told. You're coming with me now. Someone wants to talk to you."

CHAPTER 39

The man pushed the button on the doorbell again and again. Four times in less than fifteen seconds.

The door was jerked open by a woman who stared at the impatient visitor.

"What's so damn urgent?"

"Jillian, we have a big problem now. We need to go into the damage control mode right now. Jake Pendleton figured it out. Somehow he figured it out to the last detail. He's found enough evidence to get the feds involved. What are we going to do?" The man stepped inside.

"Relax, the feds won't get involved. Jake Pendleton won't say a word. Ian has been tailing Mr. Pendleton for a while and will bring him here shortly." Jillian pointed to a chair. "Have a seat."

The man hesitantly sat and said, "The feds will get involved. Ian shot one of my men and the medical examiner already called it in."

"That is a problem, but one I'm sure Ian can fix."

"Why is Ian running around town? Is that wise? He's too obvious, too easily recognized. He shouldn't be out in public."

"He's not going anywhere until we wrap this thing up. We need him. He's experienced in these types of things. You know that better than me. He was your best friend. Haven't you even seen him since he got here?"

"I caught a glimpse of him the other night in the bar, but I wasn't able to talk to him. I've talked with him on the phone, same as you, swapped emails with him a couple of times. He's not the same person we grew up with. The years have changed him. He's colder. Meaner. He scares me."

"He's changed, but so have we. We're not innocent either. When Ian brings him in, I think we will be able to persuade Mr. Pendleton into staying quiet for a while," said Jillian.

"Yeah, how are you going to do that?"

"I have something he wants, something he desperately wants."

"What is that?"

Jillian smiled. "His fiancée."

The man stood up, his hands balled into fists. "I thought we agreed not to involve anyone else. No one else was to be harmed."

"Circumstances changed."

"I'll have no part of this."

"You're in this just as deep as anyone else, maybe even more so. You will go along with this. And if Mr. Pendleton and his fiancée have to die, it'll be for our cause. It's too late for you to back out now."

"I don't like it. I don't like it one damn bit."

Jillian raised her hand. "That's enough. What's done is done."

"Where is she? Is she hurt?"

"No, she's unharmed. She's upstairs, tied up in the closet." Jillian pointed up the stairwell.

* * *

The closet was dark, even darker with the sleeping mask over her eyes. Her arms and shoulders ached. Her leg muscles were cramped. Her feet were tied together. Her hands bound behind her back. Straps binding her elbows behind her made her shoulders throb. Duct tape over her mouth. She had been lying there for several hours, long enough for her to lose track of time. Her head pounded, radiating from the bump on the back of her head where she was struck.

She heard sounds in the house, voices, too hushed to understand. The man Jake warned her about, the man with the strange eyes and streaked hair had grabbed her at the Westin as she walking to the ferry.

He'd grabbed her arm and quickly forced her at gunpoint into the underground garage where his Cadillac was waiting. That was the last thing she remembered until she woke up in the dark.

She hadn't listened to Jake. His hunch was right. The man who came to their room that night really wasn't a crackpot. But it was too late to warn Jake now—Kaplan would have to handle it alone.

She had no idea where she was, she just knew she was in a house. She could tell by listening to the sounds a house makes. Toilets flushing, water running through the pipes, a refrigerator cycling on and off, the distant sounds of cars and trucks on the street outside. Musty. That musty, older house smell.

Occasionally she heard footsteps on stairs. She detected a slight echo with each step. Two of the steps creaked when stepped on. A door would open. She would sense a change in the darkness, and then the door would close. For hours the footsteps seemed soft. Over time her sense of hearing became more acute.

She heard different footsteps on the stairs. Heavier than before. The first person checking on her must have been a woman, she thought. These footsteps belonged to a man. Maybe the big man was coming back for her. Beth felt a surge of panic.

The door opened. She squirmed to the back wall, heart-pounding. She heard a voice mutter, "Hold still, it's okay." She started crying out of fear.

The sleeping mask was quickly removed. The sudden light blinded her. She kept her eyes closed to a tiny squint, allowing her eyes to adjust to the brightness of the room. The man reached down and jerked the duct tape from her mouth.

She looked up as the shadow leaned in, pulling her to a sitting position. Her eyes were still unable to see anything more than a shadow. He cut her feet and hands and arms free from their bindings. The man had a gentle demeanor, it wasn't the one who had brought her here.

She sat still, and her eyes slowly adapted to the light. The man knelt down in front of her and in a flash she recognized him. Her eyes lit up and a smile broke through her crying.

"Oh, Pat, thank God it's you."

Then she remembered what Kaplan had told her.

CHAPTER 40

Jake was held firmly against the wall. Every time he moved, the man pushed the knife blade a little deeper into his side. The pain grew so intense that Jake stood on his toes, arching his side away from the blade.

The man leaned in close to his right ear. "Don't try anything stupid, Mr. Pendleton. If I had my way you'd already be dead, but someone wants you alive … for now, and that's how I'm going to deliver you. Unless, of course, you try something stupid. Then you'll die on the sidewalk. By the time anyone can get to you, it will be too late. Do you understand what I'm saying to you, Mr. Pendleton?"

He nodded.

"Good. Now we're going to take a little walk. Nice and slow. Calm and relaxed. Okay?"

"Okay."

Jake heard the click from the hammer of a gun. The big man froze. A voice spoke. A voice Jake had heard once before. The man from the hotel room.

"Let him go, Ian," the newcomer said.

Jake recalled the name Ian from Donna Greene's briefing. *This has to be the same man—the assassin.*

"Sullivan! You son of a bitch. How did you—"

"Let him go, I said."

"What if I kill him? Right here, right now," the big man growled.

"Then I'll kill you. Right here, right now," the other voice said.

"Can you do that, Michael? Can you kill one of your own?"

"One of my own? You stopped being one of 'my own' years ago, Ian. You have betrayed us. You have betrayed everyone. Your pig-headed attitude will be your undoing. I owe you one, though. You warned me and saved my life. Now, I'll do the same for you. But make no mistake, if you kill him, I *will* kill you. Now let him go."

The assassin slowly pulled the knife blade away. Jake felt the blade pressure stop, but the pain was still there. He was bleeding. Bleeding a lot, he thought. Jake pressed his hand against the cut. The blade had cut deeper and wider than he thought. He felt his blood-soaked shirt sticking to his skin.

He heard a thud and felt the assassin's body go limp behind him.

Sullivan said, "Get out of here. Go back to the Westin. Wait for me. Don't call the police yet, I need to find Ian's partners and neutralize them. When I do, I'll come get you and we'll go to the authorities together."

Sullivan pushed him hard out onto the sidewalk, not giving Jake a chance to respond.

He took two steps. He looked into the street and saw the multitude of people.

He stood still, almost dazed, as the last few seconds replayed in his mind. It had seemed so quiet, as if they were totally alone.

He turned to speak, "Where—"

Sullivan and the assassin were gone.

He walked slowly south down Bull Street, holding pressure on his wound. He stayed on the sidewalk, paralleling the parade. The marchers disbanded at Madison Square, a square named for President James Madison. He walked into the square, still in a daze, replaying the past few moments over in his head.

He stopped in front of a monument of Sgt. William Jasper, Hero of the Siege of Savannah in 1779. Jake was in a daze. He looked around, wondering which road to take. Trying to get his bearings.

He wandered east on Macon Street, his right hand still holding his side. The knife wound throbbed. He released some pressure. The bleeding felt like it had stopped or at least slowed to a trickle.

He stumbled on a sidewalk stone that a tree root had pushed up out of place. He grabbed a pole to catch his fall. Honeysuckle draped across the coral colored wall, its blooms full of nectar ... and bees. Its sweet smell filled his nostrils.

He reached another square, stopped and looked at the tall spires of a church across the square. People moved in and out of the tall cathedral doors. The steps were lined with parade viewers, starting to break up as the tail end of the parade finally moved past.

Jake could think of only one thing to do.

Police.

Find a police station.

They've got Beth.

Find a police station and find it fast.

Even though Sullivan had told him otherwise, Jake made that his resolve.

As he moved through Lafayette Square, he asked passers-by if they knew where a police station was. No luck. He saw an old homeless man sitting on the steps in front of the cathedral panhandling for money.

Jake walked over to him then stepped back. The man's ragged clothes reeked. "Police station. Do you know where there is a police station?"

The old man looked up at him, squinting at the sun. "Yeah, sure. Two or three blocks that way." He pointed north up Abercorn Street. "Right next to the cemetery."

"Thanks," Jake said.

The old man stuck out his hand and said, "Hey, buddy, can you spare a dollar?"

He reached into his front pocket, pulled out his money clip and, with his bloody hand, tossed the man a crisp new twenty-dollar bill.

He walked to the corner of Abercorn and Liberty. He looked west, toward Charlotte's Corner, as he crossed Liberty Street.

That's when he saw the man Sullivan had called Ian, the assassin from Dallas.

CHAPTER 41

The assassin wasn't looking in his direction, he was looking down at the sidewalk while he rubbed the back of his head with his right hand. Jake saw him look at his hand as if checking for blood.

He briskly walked halfway across Liberty Street to the median and glanced back. The assassin was looking up, looking in his direction. Jake could tell that the man hadn't recognized him yet. He was still half a block away from the intersection.

Jake crouched low and darted the remaining way across Liberty, using other pedestrians to screen him from the assassin's view. He stayed crouched while he moved swiftly down the brick sidewalk allowing the azalea bushes to provide cover. He looked up Abercorn. He saw the end of the parade less than a hundred feet from him. The fire trucks blared their horns and sounded their sirens signifying the end. He took off running in a full sprint.

As he approached the southwestern corner of Colonial Park Cemetery, his cell phone rang. He looked at the number ... Beth.

He stopped at the corner and quickly flipped open his phone. *It's about time.*

"Beth, are you alright? Where are you? Did they hurt you?"

He strained his head around in search of the man called Ian.

A woman's voice answered. A voice with a slight Irish lilt. "This isn't Beth and if you ever want to see her again you'll do exactly as I say."

"Who is this? Where is Beth? What have you done to her?"

"She's safe for now and unharmed. If you want her to remain that way, listen carefully and do as I say."

His pulse raced. "Not until I know she's alive. Let me talk to her."

"No! We're not negotiating here. You're in no position to negotiate. You'll just have to believe me," the woman said.

He stood still, staring at the cemetery. Seeing nothing. He needed proof that Beth was still alive. The woman wasn't cooperating, she wouldn't let him talk to Beth. Why?

He had an idea, not a good one, but maybe one that would work.

"Who is this? What's your name?" he asked.

The woman replied, "You can call me Jillian. Now are you going to do as I say or not?"

"Okay, Jillian. Use Beth's phone. Take a picture of her, then send it to me. I'll know she is still alive when I receive the picture. Then call me back and I'll do what you ask."

The phone was silent. After ten seconds of silence the woman said, "I don't see that a picture would hurt. I'll do it. This is all you get, though. After this, if you don't do exactly what I tell you, she will die. Do you understand?"

"I understand."

"I'll call back in a few minutes."

His phone went dead.

He closed it and put it back in his pocket. Then a hand grabbed his sore left shoulder. The hand pulled him backwards, spinning him to the left. One brown and one blue eye stared back at him.

The assassin.

Ian.

CHAPTER 42

At that moment Kaplan was on the other side of Abercorn Street watching. He saw the man reach out for Jake. He called out but the blasts of noise from the fire trucks drowned out his yells. Then it was too late. The big man had Jake, holding him by the shirt with both hands.

From the description Jake had given him the day before, he knew this was the man from Dallas. But even more enlightening was the manner the big man operated—it was painfully clear this man was a professional.

He'd been following Jake and the assassin since Barry's Pub, stayed behind the pursuer through downtown. He wasn't close enough to help when the assassin crept up on Jake in front of Starbucks, but saw Jake escape. Kaplan caught glimpses through the parade floats, but was on the wrong side of Bull Street while Jake eased past the storefronts at Charlotte's Corner.

When Jake was grabbed and pulled into the stairwell next to Saints and Shamrocks, Kaplan tried to cut through the parade but couldn't find an opening. But he'd seen the other man come down the steps and place a gun behind the head of the man holding Jake.

His first instinct had been to mount a rescue attempt to free Jake. But now the odds had changed.

Kaplan watched and waited for an opportunity.

He saw a gap in the parade, just big enough to allow him through. He darted across the street and pushed through the revelers.

He eased close enough to hear the men talking. That's when he heard the assassin's name ... Ian. The other man was called Sullivan, Michael Sullivan. He could see both of them. Their appearances were strikingly different, yet there was still a slight resemblance. It must be an Irish trait.

After he knocked Ian on the head, Sullivan moved fast, pulling the assassin up the stairs.

Kaplan moved backwards for a better vantage point and saw Sullivan putting the limp figure into a chair. Then Sullivan bolted across the patio and out of sight. Kaplan turned and saw Jake stagger down Bull Street.

He dashed up the stairs to see where Sullivan had gone. There was no sign of him. Revelers on the Knights of Columbus patio were staring at Ian slumped in the chair. Then they looked over at Kaplan. He figured Sullivan had just placed the unconscious man in a chair and escaped across the patio to the exit on Liberty Street. Kaplan ran over to the railing and looked down at the crowd of people on Liberty Street. Sullivan was nowhere in sight.

He turned around and leaned back against the railing, palms down flat to support himself. He glanced over at the table where Ian was sitting and watched as the assassin started to regain consciousness.

The man's head wobbled, and then straightened. He placed his hand on the back of his head, and then looked at his palm. Kaplan watched as he shook off the pain. The man got out of his chair and moved slowly toward the stairwell.

Kaplan kept his distance behind him, following him down the stairs and out onto Bull Street. Jake had already wandered out of sight. The assassin walked across the street and stopped at the corner.

After several seconds of standing there looking up and down Liberty and Bull streets, the assassin headed east on Liberty.

Kaplan followed the man, sure that the assassin would eventually lead him back to Jake.

Kaplan was the first to see Jake standing at the corner of Liberty Street and Abercorn Street talking to someone on the phone. He'd hoped the assassin didn't see Jake, but he knew he had when the man's pace increased and he darted across Abercorn Street about three feet behind a fire truck.

Kaplan yelled as loud as he could to Jake but at that same moment the fire truck blasted out its deafening siren, completely drowning out his voice.

In a move so quick it surprised Kaplan, Jake shoved the assassin in the chest while hooking his right foot behind the man's leg. The move caught the man off guard. Jake knocked his grip loose and the assassin fell backwards, landing flat on his back on the sidewalk. The last thing Kaplan saw was Jake jumping over a wrought iron fence into a cemetery.

CHAPTER 43

Adrenaline pumping, Jake ran toward the southwest corner of Colonial Park Cemetery. The sidewalks were crowded, too crowded for him to get away from Ian. His only escape was through the cemetery.

He saw an empty park bench just outside the fence. He ran hard and fast, landing one foot on the bench and leaping high to grab a tree limb. He swung himself over the fence, barely clearing its pointed iron spears. He let go of the limb once clear of the spears and landed face down inside the cemetery. His left shoulder screamed with pain as did his right side. The move pulled the knife wound open and he felt warm blood ooze down his side.

Instinctively, he clutched his side as he got to his feet and started running again. Stumbling past dozens of visitors reading gravestones and markers, marveling at the dates, Jake ran, looking over his left shoulder for signs of the assassin following him over the fence. His pulse quickened—so did the blood flowing from his side. He felt the warmth of the fresh blood on his already soaked shirt.

Jake hurried down an asphalt path to the center of the cemetery where he stopped for the first time. Dazed, he looked around for an exit, he saw two. One on Oglethorpe Street about midway down the fence row and the other in the northwestern corner of the cemetery, where Oglethorpe crossed Abercorn Street. The old man on the church steps had said the police station was next to the cemetery, so Jake stood there scanning for the station.

Winded and in need of a rest or, at least, a chance to catch his breath, he leaned against a stone bench and stared back across the cemetery. No sign of the assassin. He thought about Beth. Vision blurred legs wobbly—he doubled over until the wave of nausea passed.

Why hadn't the woman named Jillian called back? In all the excitement and noise, he could have easily missed the ringing. He checked his phone. No missed calls.

Jake spotted a flagpole atop a large brick building that lent the appearance of a municipally owned facility. *The police station.*

The way to the exit was unsafe. The assassin was walking up the sidewalk toward the same corner, looking at him with a grin on his face.

He knew he couldn't outrun the man to the exit by the police station but he could outrun him to the side exit on Oglethorpe Street. Running to the far side of several ancient burial vaults, Jake looked back toward the police station. He ducked behind the Graham Vault, a vault that had once held the remains of Major General Nathaniel Greene.

A large crowd had gathered between Jake and the side gate. Using them as a screen, he ran out the exit. He ducked low and ran across Oglethorpe, crossing both lanes. The large azalea bushes in the median and the shrubs on the north side of the street hid him from Ian as he hurried west back toward the police station.

The assassin passed him in the opposite direction on the other side of the street, still looking for him inside the cemetery. When the man turned his head toward him, Jake ducked out of sight below the bushes. The man turned back around and Jake ran west toward the corner.

What he saw when he looked at the building flooded him with disappointment and panic. It wasn't a police station at all, it was a fire station. And it was locked up tight.

Looking back down Oglethorpe, realizing the police station must be back the way he came, Jake saw the assassin crossing the street and cutting off his access. Luckily the man wasn't looking in his direction, which gave him a few short seconds to seek cover before the man turned his head and spotted him.

Running north on Abercorn toward Oglethorpe Square he stopped short at an alley. He guessed he could move east down the alley until he was past the cemetery, then double back to find the police station. It was a good plan—in theory.

CHAPTER 44

Kaplan followed the assassin, the man Michael Sullivan called Ian, around the perimeter of the cemetery. He watched Jake run toward a side exit. Ian, in turn, ran toward Jake but appeared to have lost him in the crowd. Kaplan saw Jake cross Oglethorpe Street and duck below the bushes. When Ian crossed the street, Kaplan stayed back and watched him as he walked away from Jake. Jake went back west. Ian turned east.

Kaplan followed Ian. His worst fears were becoming reality. He had explained it all to Beth. There must be some connection between Annie and Pat McGill—they were from the same town in Ireland and were close to the same age. It was too much of a coincidence. But what was their connection, if any, to the crash? And how did the assassin fit in?

Beth was supposed to meet him in front of Barry's Pub but she never showed up. He'd called the hotel but she wasn't in her room. She had given him her cell phone number, but she wasn't answering that either.

That left only two scenarios. One, Jake told her not to meet with them and she just didn't bother calling back, unlikely. Or two, something bad had happened to Beth. His instincts told him something had happened to Beth. Something very, very bad.

Kaplan followed the assassin down the sidewalk. His eyes widened in shock as the man stopped at the house in the middle of the block. The man named Ian looked around then ascended the steps to the front door.

Standing across the street, partially hidden behind a large live oak, he stared at the man, his hands clenched into fists. Mixed with a shattered sense of betrayal and bitter disappointment, he could think of only one thing ... find Jake. Find Jake before it was too late.

His eyes bleak, he saw the assassin twist the doorknob. Nothing happened. The man banged on the door. A few seconds later a man opened the door and the assassin walked in. The other man leaned out of the doorway, looked around, then retreated inside. The face was one Kaplan had seen before.

A face he would not forget.

Kaplan ran back to the corner, out of sight of the residence, then turned north on Abercorn.

He pulled out his phone, pressed the talk button, then scrolled down the previously called numbers until he reached the one for the Westin. He hit the call button, and when the operator answered, he asked for her room.

The phone rang and rang. After the tenth ring, he hung up and redialed the hotel. "Westin Savannah, how may I direct your call?"

After three minutes of explaining, he got what he was after. He punched in the ten-digit number and pressed talk.

He wasn't a religious man but he prayed out loud. "Please, God, let her answer, Jake's life depends on it."

One ring. Two rings. Three. Then he heard a voice answer the phone.

"Carol Martin."

CHAPTER 45

Jake walked down the alleyway, trying to process everything that had happened. His thoughts bounced from the plane crash to the words Donna Greene said about the events in Dallas. The man from Dallas was here, a foregone conclusion.

He thought about the stranger who was in his room that night and how that same man had saved him from a killer just a few moments ago. How could he have been so stupid as to let the assassin catch up to him again?

Beth. His worries returned to Beth. Why hadn't the woman called back with the picture of Beth?

He pulled out his cell phone and checked for missed calls again. None.

He felt light-headed and leaned against an old green Chevrolet Blazer parked in the alleyway. He had been operating on pure adrenaline—and it was wearing thin. He was losing blood and getting weaker. He needed to stop the bleeding. He needed to rest.

After a couple of minutes his head cleared and he walked on down the alleyway, pausing at Lincoln Street. Looking south he could see the cemetery and the gate he'd run out of trying to escape from his pursuer. An old couple walked by the exit, the woman holding the man by the elbow, the old man using his cane as they strolled down the street. An old concrete street sign with its faded lettering leaned against a telephone pole. He stopped and looked for signs of anyone pursuing him. To the north there were hordes of revelers, but no sign of the big man called Ian.

His left shoulder ached and the pain in his side was overwhelming. He still had his right hand pressed against the wound. He let off pressure and felt the blood oozed out again. A wave of nausea hit him but he fought it off. He knew he needed medical attention but first he had to find Beth.

His cell phone rang. Beth.

He pulled the phone out of his coat pocket while he continued east down the alleyway. He glanced at caller ID but didn't recognize the number. He was expecting a call back from Beth's phone.

He flipped open the phone. "Jake Pendleton."

"Jake, it's Gregg Kaplan. We need to talk, it's urgent. Where are you?"

"I don't really know. Somewhere downtown near a cemetery. Gregg, that man I told you about … he's been chasing me. He caught me a couple of times but somehow I got away. They got Beth, Gregg … they got Beth. Call the police."

"Calm down, Jake—I know. I've been following you and the man chasing you. I followed him until he went inside a house," Kaplan said, talking fast. "Tell me where you are. Find a street corner and tell me where you are and I'll find you."

At that same moment, Jake saw a familiar face smiling at him from a balcony overlooking the alleyway. A beautiful woman with auburn hair and deep green eyes waved at him. Annie Bulloch, Kaplan's girlfriend.

"Gregg, I found a place for you to meet me." His voice slurred a little from exhaustion. "I see your girlfriend. I'll be at her house. Meet me here."

"Jake, wait—"

Nausea overwhelmed him. He lowered the phone to his side and flipped it shut, raised his left hand to wave at Annie. The nausea passed, but his shoulder hurt even more. His right hand still clutched his side. He heard her call to him.

"Inspector Pendleton."

"Ms. Bulloch."

"Please call me Annie. You look terrible, are you okay?"

"No, as a matter of fact I'm not. I need your help."

"Certainly, come on inside and let me get you something. Just come through the back gate," she said.

He opened the cypress gate from the alleyway, walked through and closed it behind him. The back of the house was simple, a narrow red-brick structure with a garage on the ground level and two identical balconies, one directly above the other, on the second and third floors.

Annie leaned over the white railing on the second-floor balcony motioning for him to come through the garage.

She pointed to it and said, "Take the stairs in the garage up to the kitchen. Just come on in."

"Thanks, Annie, you're a life saver."

CHAPTER 46

Kaplan yelled into his phone, "NO. NO."

It was too late. He heard the click and knew Jake had hung up. He slammed his phone closed too hard, lost his grip and the phone crashed onto the concrete sidewalk, shutting down from the impact.

"Shit."

He picked it up. It had shut down.

He tried the on switch, but nothing happened. He removed the battery, then the SIMM card, reinserted both and pushed the on button again.

"Come on—work, dammit, work."

The phone rebooted and went through all the steps to acquire a signal. He ran toward Annie's house, taking a circuitous route so he could approach her house from the end of the alley behind her house.

He hit the talk button twice to send it to last number redial. Nothing happened. The phone had shut down again.

He swore.

*   *   *

Jake entered the garage, his back to the wall as he squeezed past her red Mazda MX-5 Miata. The convertible top was down. Overhead fluorescent lights reflected off the shiny black leather seats. Sunglasses perched precariously on the rear view mirror. A silver lipstick tube stuck out of the ashtray. Her FAA identification badge was on the passenger floorboard, along with the NTSB observer's pass from Annie's visit to the crash site.

The garage floor, painted gray with black flecks, was spotless. Storage cabinets lined the walls and two bicycles attached to pulley systems hung from the ceiling. He wondered if Kaplan and Annie ever used them. The garage looked spacious with just the pint-sized Miata inside, but two full sized cars wouldn't fit.

He reached the top step, stretched out his hand searching for the doorknob when the door opened.

Annie motioned him inside. "Come on in, Mr. Pendleton. Can I get you something to drink?"

"Thanks, Annie. Water would be great and, please, call me Jake."

He walked into the kitchen, noticing the bay window. An open book was placed pages down on the cushion. *Smoke Screen*, by Sandra Brown.

Annie handed him a bottle of water.

"Oh my God, you're hurt," she said, pointing to his side. "What happened?"

He looked down and saw that blood had oozed through the cut in his leather jacket.

"Annie, I need your help. Someone took Beth, my fiancée." His voice broke up in panic. "We've got to call the police."

"Jake, come in here and sit down. Let me look at your side." Annie walked casually to an open door. "The first thing we need to do is stop that bleeding."

He followed her into the living room, dark except for a sliver of sunlight coming through a three-inch opening in the curtains. He walked over to the window and squinted into the bright sunshine outside. Dozens of people, apparently holiday celebrators, sauntered along the sidewalks.

Then he noticed an old black relic of a car on the far corner across the street and a sign nearby that read, "Police Barracks." He saw the gate where he exited and it occurred to him that he had gone to the wrong corner of the cemetery.

His eyes were drawn to the familiar Suburban parked in front of Annie's house with lettering on the side … NTSB.

"What the—"

Annie interrupted, "Let me get the lights. There is someone I want you to meet. Let me introduce you to my cousin."

She flipped the switch on the wall.

In the lighted living room stood Pat McGill.

CHAPTER 47

"Pat! What are you doing here? What's she talking about?" McGill looked grim. "I told you about her in the car on the way down here. I have a cousin in Savannah, remember?"

"The other day at the site, why didn't you say something?" His voice trailed off.

"You didn't need to know," McGill replied.

"A man's been chasing me ... he did this." He opened his jacket to show his blood-soaked shirt.

"They got Beth. A woman called me on my cell phone and ... she ... said ..."

He turned and looked at Annie. Another wave of nausea swept over him. He leaned back against the wall to keep from falling.

"Oh my God, you're Jillian," he whispered. "Pat, what's going on here?"

The woman looked at McGill, then at Jake.

"Beth is fine," she said. "She hasn't been hurt in any way."

"I want to see her now," he said.

McGill looked toward a hallway and said, "Bring her in."

Beth walked slowly into view, a silenced Beretta held to her head. A huge hand gripped her elbow.

When the man walked into view behind her, Jake saw it was the man who had been chasing him.

His knees buckled and he slid down the wall and sat on the floor. His head was spinning. The room went blurry. Ears ringing. He could make out only shapes and silhouettes.

He heard Beth yelling but couldn't understand the words. More ringing. Louder. McGill said something but he didn't understand it either. The pain in his side overwhelmed him. The loss of blood finally caught up to him and the room faded to darkness.

When he regained consciousness, he was lying on the floor with a pillow under his head. His jacket and shirt had been removed. Beth had wiped his knife wound clean and was holding pressure to stop the bleeding.

A wet washcloth was folded and placed on his forehead. He was weak from the loss of blood. He blinked his eyes a couple of times, then he saw Beth.

"Welcome back. That big son of a bitch, Ian, they call him, Ian Collins. He told me that he cut you. It looks deep, I think it'll need stitches."

Jake tried to raise his head and look around. He winced.

"Try to be still. Here, drink some of this," she whispered. "Jillian—or Annie—or whoever she is, gave it to me, it's a lot like Gatorade. It will help. They say they're trying to figure out what they're going to do with us. Ian wants to kill us but Pat won't let him. Ian said some man named Michael knocked him on the head and that's how you got away from him."

"He was the man who was in our room the other night," Jake mumbled. "His last name must be Sullivan. That's what Ian called him."

Beth leaned close to Jake's ear and whispered, "What are we going to do? I'm scared."

"I don't know. But I'll think of something, I promise."

CHAPTER 48

Kaplan watched the back of Annie's house for ten minutes. His first thought had been to call the police. They would no doubt come to the door, yell a few times, then break the door down. By then Jake and Beth may already be dead...and Annie too. No, he had to handle this himself. He was familiar enough with the house to know the entire floor plan and furniture layout. He planned to use that to his advantage.

Getting inside without being spotted might be a problem. He knew she would have someone watching the windows, probably the big man. The only access from the alleyway would leave him exposed as he entered the back yard. Regardless of whether he entered through the gate or climbed over the fence, he would be visible and vulnerable. That left the Oglethorpe Street access, the only blind spot.

The west approach to the house on Oglethorpe was too visible. The view from inside the house offered a clean perspective of the sidewalk. He would certainly be spotted on an approach attempt from that direction.

The east approach from Oglethorpe was the only viable option. It offered protection from the windows' view. The stair access and a large magnolia tree blocked the range of vision from inside the house. Unless someone was on the front steps standing watch, he would be shielded from sight. He was confident no one would be outside.

The mid-afternoon sun was bright and warm. Kaplan had ridden his Harley into town this morning and parked it behind the court-house just a few blocks away. He wore jeans, his riding boots, and a black long-sleeved Harley shirt. He pushed the banded sleeves up toward his elbows in a vain attempt to cool down.

Retreating down the alleyway back to Lincoln Street, he circled north and east to Habersham Street, then back south to Oglethorpe. The houses that lined the block on Oglethorpe were close, very close, usually standing no more than three to four feet apart. This offered access to the backyard between the houses. He knew that a narrow gate belonging to Annie's neighbor blocked the path between the two houses.

He crept west on Oglethorpe toward Annie's house, keeping as close as possible to the neighboring houses to cut off the viewing angle from Annie's windows. No sense risking the only chance he had to get in sight unseen.

Reaching the corner of Annie's house, Kaplan looked at the gate. It was padlocked. The gate had never been padlocked before, so the owner of the home next door must have locked it because of the St. Patrick's Day crowd. It was an older lock but a sturdy one.

He checked the gate's hinges. Solid. To climb over the gate would either draw unwanted attention to him or it would make him clearly visible to the window in the living room where the curtains were slightly open. Neither of which he wanted to do.

He checked the padlock again. A little play in the locking mechanism, maybe enough to break it loose with a hard blow. He looked around and the only thing he saw that might work was a brick. Several bricks were stacked underneath the stairwell landing of Annie's front door. The landing was at the top of a concrete block stairwell leading up to the second level entrance.

He picked up a brick and stood next to the gate waiting, watching for a chance to smash the lock with the brick without being seen or heard. His chance came, no cars or pedestrians approaching, so he swung and smashed the brick down hard on the padlock. Nothing happened.

He turned and looked around, holding the brick behind his back. No one showed any interest. He waited. An elderly couple approached and he smiled at them as they walked by in front of him. They were talking about the weather and the parade and paid him no attention. As they moved out of range, a teenage boy walked toward Kaplan. The boy's head was bobbing up and down and he was singing. He had earpieces in each ear with white wires leading down to his iPod. The volume was loud enough for Kaplan to hear the beat.

After the boy passed, Kaplan turned and smashed the brick against the padlock a second time. The brick crumbled into pieces and fell onto the sidewalk. Then he heard Annie's deadbolt click.

He ducked under the landing. Standing only two feet beneath Annie's door, he heard someone step out onto the landing. He pressed his body as close to the concrete block as possible, ducking slightly under the steps. Then he heard a voice call back into the house.

"No one out here but some kid with an iPod."

The assassin.

The door closed and the deadbolt clicked back into place. He didn't move. After two minutes he moved toward the gate looking for something else to use to break the padlock. Then he saw it. A pile of crumbled brick at the foot of the gate and the padlock hanging open in the latch.

He removed the lock, opened the gate, went inside and closed the gate behind him. The soil beneath his feet was wet. Just wet dirt, no weeds, no grass, no vegetation of any kind.

Damp. Musty. Cold. The narrow strip of dirt between the houses never saw any direct sunlight.

As soon as he closed the gate, he realized he was in the wrong back yard. He scaled the eight-foot privacy fence into Annie's yard, and crept along the back of her house to the garage. He ducked into her garage out of sight.

Just like when he was in Special Forces, reaching his target objective proved to be the easy part, gaining access and entry would be the hard part.

CHAPTER 49

The drapes were drawn closed. The only light in the living room emanated from three lamps and the afternoon glow coming down the hallway from the kitchen windows. Jake saw Jillian walking down the hall from the kitchen with something in her hands. Bright light from the window revealed only her silhouette until she walked into the light from the lamps. She carried four beer bottles, set them on a table and then walked back into the kitchen.

Ian Collins stepped into view from behind her with two beer bottles and a gun.

Jake and Beth were sitting next to each other on the leather sofa. The bleeding had stopped. Jake's blood-soaked shirts had been removed.

Jillian walked in with one of Kaplan's shirts draped over her arm and something in her hand. She asked, "Has the bleeding stopped?"

Beth answered, "Yes, for now."

"Good, let's glue it closed."

"What do you mean?" Jake asked.

"I'll show you. This might sting a little." Jillian took a tube of Super Glue and applied a bead down the length of the cut. Then she applied a piece of white medical tape on top of the wound to cover it, gluing it down as she went.

"There you go. That should hold and keep it from pulling open again."

"Where'd you learn that?" Beth asked.

"Actually, believe it or not, it was Ian's idea. He said he's done it to himself many times and I'm sure he probably has."

Jillian stood, walked over to the table and then walked back and stood in front of Jake and Beth and held out two bottles of Guinness Draught.

"Take these and drink up," Jillian commanded.

"Go to hell." Jake crossed his arms.

"No," Beth knocked both bottles from Jillian's hands sending them crashing to the floor.

Jillian slapped Beth. "Bitch."

McGill stepped forward. "What the hell is this all about?"

"Come on, Pat, we've been over this already. We can't let them live, they know too much," Jillian said.

"That's enough. I'll handle this." Collins stepped into the light and placed the silencer next to Beth's right temple.

His hard eyes looked down at Jake. "Drink up, both of you. If you don't, I'll start with her. I'll make you watch. I'll do things to her, things you won't like. Then I'll kill her, right in front of your eyes. Can you live with that, *Mister* Pendleton?"

"Jake, do something." Beth started crying.

McGill protested, "Ian, put the gun down. This has gone too far. Only O'Rourke was supposed to die, not people on my team. Where does it stop? You already killed the mechanic in Dallas, then Dave. Now you want to kill Jake and Beth too?"

"We agreed. You agreed. From the beginning—that we couldn't leave any witnesses," Collins said. "Have you forgotten our objective is not to be discovered? Think about what this would do to our cause. No witnesses."

Jake stood, wavered unsteadily, and interrupted, "Dave? What about Dave? I thought it was an accident."

Beth stood next to him, holding him steady.

McGill turned to Jake. "No, it wasn't. Ian killed him. You know how Dave was always talking to himself out loud. Ian heard him, he heard him call you, and then he shot him. He dropped the wreckage on top of him to conceal the gunshot wound temporarily. The coroner called this morning and told me what he had found, a bullet in the heart."

Jake lowered his chin and shook his head. "You son of a bitch."
He could hear Beth sobbing. "Why the beer?" he finally said.

McGill's eyes looked puzzled as he faced Jillian. "Yes, why the beer?"

Jillian brought two new bottles of beer. "Tell him. Tell them your great plan."

"Sit down, both of you." The hammer clicked in place when Collins cocked it.

After Jake and Beth sat, Collins walked to the middle of the room, still pointing the gun at them. "Well, it's like this. There's going to be an accident. A terrible automobile accident. Alcohol related, I'm afraid. It seems that a young NTSB investigator and his fiancée will have a little too much to drink on this St. Patrick's Day, then they'll go for a joy ride up in South Carolina in his sporty black GTO. The car his girlfriend drove down from Atlanta. He will drive a little too fast and lose control and crash. You Americans and your obsession with cars.

Collins pulled the hammer of the Beretta back. It made a click. "Now drink up."

*   *   *

Kaplan stood underneath the second-floor balcony. He grabbed a five-gallon fishing bucket from the garage and placed it upside down under the ledge to give him the extra height he needed to reach the balcony. He stood on the bucket and jumped up, catching the bottom of the balcony with his fingertips. He hung there for a few seconds while he scanned the alley and the other back yards, then he pulled himself up to the balcony.

When he could see over the bottom of the balcony, he noticed the kitchen was empty. He heard voices coming through the French doors from the living room. He pulled himself onto the balcony, over the railing and then stood with his back against the wall.

He listened. He heard McGill and Annie arguing. A cautious

glance through the glass. The room was dark and he could barely make out the figures down the long hallway near the front door. But what he saw struck him as odd and out of place. Jake and Beth were sitting on the couch drinking beer.

Then he saw the big man step forward with a gun and tell them to drink. He could see McGill yelling at Annie. Then he saw Annie walk behind Jake and Beth and pour beer on their clothes.

Kaplan turned his head away from the glass, standing flush against the wall, still listening and thinking hard, trying to comprehend what he just seen. He saw a couple walking down the alleyway. He tried to act casual, like he belonged there, but still remain hidden from view from inside the house.

Just as he decided to take another look inside, he heard someone below calling his name.

CHAPTER 50

Jake refused to drink. "I won't do it. I won't make this easy for you. You want me dead, then just shoot me, asshole."

Collins grabbed Beth and pulled her to her feet by her hair. He pulled until she was on her toes, then he jammed the silencer against her cheek.

"You don't drink, I shoot her. Are you ready for that? Can you watch her head explode, knowing you could have stopped it?"

"Okay, okay, just let her go." Jake lifted the first bottle of beer.

Collins held Beth's head back while Jillian poured beer in her mouth. She gagged and gurgled.

Jillian said, "Drink it, if you know what's good for you."

Beth spat the beer in Jillian's face.

"You bitch." Jillian slapped her across the face.

Collins yanked her head back while Jillian poured more beer in her mouth. Then he held Beth's mouth shut and Jillian clamped her nostrils closed with her fingers.

Jake jumped to his feet and turned toward Collins, but Collins was fast—very fast, and Jake was looking down the barrel of the Beretta's silencer.

"Sit down," Collins growled as he pushed Jake down by his left shoulder.

Jake winced. "Just drink it, Beth."

Beth swallowed hard.

Collins relaxed his grip.

Beth spun around and shoved her knee into his groin.

Collins backhanded her across the cheek, splitting her lip open. She fell to the floor dazed.

Jake lunged forward, but Ian was ready and punched him hard in the nose. Blood spurted from both nostrils. Jake fell back and dropped to his knees.

Collins said, "Now we can do this the easy way or we can do this the hard way. I suggest you spare yourselves the pain."

Jake acquiesced. "Alright, we'll drink, we'll drink."

* * *

Collins sent McGill to get more beer. While McGill was in the kitchen, Collins sent Jillian to get the other two pistols, both Beretta 92s with M9-SD sound suppressors, his weapon of choice. He watched as McGill came from the kitchen with beer bottles in each hand.

But something else caught his attention.

Something outside the window, a fleeting shadow that moved across the balcony. It was quick and barely noticeable, but Collins saw it. It wasn't the kind of shadow a passing cloud or an airplane or even a bird would make, but rather the kind of shadow a human would make. Then the shadow disappeared upward.

Jillian walked back into the room. Collins turned to her. "Give Pat a pistol. You two keep an eye on them, I'll be right back."

"Where are you going?" she asked.

Without answering, Collins walked into the kitchen. Scout jumped down from the bay window, ran down the hall and up the stairs. He followed the cat to the foot of the stairs.

He looked back at Jillian and McGill and said, "I'm going to get the keys to the GTO. They're probably in her purse upstairs. Then I'll go get the car and we can get this over with once and for all."

He disappeared up the stairs.

* * *

McGill rubbed his hand across his forehead and looked at Jake, then at Beth, then at Jake again. He hung his head and said, "I'm sorry. I'm truly sorry it had to end this way. I tried to get you to back off. You were just doing your job, but I couldn't warn you. This wasn't part of the plan. Things got out of control."

"What's this all about, Pat? What are you involved in?" Jake asked.

Jillian interrupted, "That's easy. Laurence O'Rourke devastated our families. He's responsible for the death of Pat's parents. He raped my mother and killed my father. Don't you see? He had to die. All of his proclamations of peace and for the peace process—all lies. He's a spy and a murderer and he had to pay."

Jillian stared at the floor, memories of long ago dredging up painful emotions. She wiped away a tear.

"I don't really have many memories of my parents. O'Rourke robbed me of that," McGill said. "When I was very young, my parents went to eat lunch at a little café in a tiny town called Claudy, near Londonderry where we lived. O'Rourke was trying to gain acceptance into the IRA so he planted a bomb in the café, thinking no Catholics would be in there.

"My parents died in the explosion along with seven other civilians. Of course, it wasn't until I was an adult that I found out it was O'Rourke who planted the bomb. That didn't come out until long after we had moved here."

Jillian interrupted, raising her voice. "Meanwhile, O'Rourke had been in the Maze prison outside of Belfast," she said, the words pouring out as though she couldn't stop them. "My father was approached by a friend of his who was in the IRA, about a potential prison break from the Maze. He wanted to know if our family would shelter an IRA escapee for a few days until the IRA could slip him out of the country. My father agreed. We were told that someone would be staying in the basement. We were also told to stay away from him, that only my father could go downstairs and talk to him. When the prison break occurred, O'Rourke was the one who came to our house. We were just teenagers then."

Jillian pointed her gun at Jake and Beth again, motioned with the barrel and said, "Keep drinking."

They hesitated and then raised their bottles to their lips. Beth's eyes were starting to glaze a little.

"Beth, drink slow," Jake whispered. "We're going to need our wits about us soon."

She gave him a puzzled look but nodded.

Jake was starting to feel the effects of the alcohol. It helped mute the pain from his knife wound.

"One day when we came home from school," Jillian continued, "O'Rourke was in the kitchen looking for something to eat. He wasn't supposed to leave the basement but he did anyway. He talked to us for quite a while, and then told us not to tell my father and he went back downstairs."

"Ian was fascinated by him. He skipped school the next day and visited with him in the basement all day."

Jake interrupted, "Ian? He was around then?"

McGill said, "Yes, Ian and I were best friends, more like brothers really, for years. That is, until O'Rourke showed up. Then Ian changed. He became distant. He later joined the IRA as a hit man. Now, that's his living. He's a contract killer, an assassin, hitman, whatever."

Jillian gazed across the room, her eyes dark. "Ian was so excited that night. All he could talk about was O'Rourke and what an exciting life he lived. Ian envied O'Rourke for exactly one day, and then Ian despised him. Despised the mere mention of his name, just as we all did."

Jillian stopped talking. Her green eyes filled with tears—one rolled down her cheek. She took her left hand and wiped it away. She tucked her hair behind her ear. "Ian skipped school the next day too. That was the day O'Rourke left. Pat and I came home from school and found them. O'Rourke had beaten and raped my mother. He hurt her. Broke her cheek bone, gave her two black eyes and a broken wrist. She was a small woman, like me, not very strong.

"While O'Rourke was raping her, Ian showed up. He tried to stop him, but O'Rourke was stronger then and beat him up. O'Rourke broke his nose and one of his ribs. Tied him up and gagged him. Then he turned back to my mother and raped her again. This time he made Ian watch."

Jillian started sobbing. "That's not where it ended, though. My father couldn't deal with it, that my mother was raped … so we left Ireland and moved here to Savannah. My mother, Pat, and myself."

Jake stared at her, trying to shake off the blurriness clouding his mind.

McGill stood up and walked over to Jillian, placing his arm around her.

Jake was still trying to put all the pieces together and make sense out of what was happening. Too many things still didn't make sense. Too many things still seemed logistically impossible.

McGill said, "It's a long story, but maybe you'll understand why Jillian and I got involved in all this. O'Rourke supposedly resigned his post with the IRA the next year and joined forces with Sinn Fein. But he didn't really sever his ties with the IRA. No, he still secretly served as the IRA's Quartermaster General. He was also on the IRA Nutting Squad. That was like IRA internal affairs, you know, policing their own.

"O'Rourke ordered the bombing of a shop on Shankill Road. A Loyalist area. He was targeting a meeting of the Ulster Freedom Fighters in a room above the shop. Ten people died and fifty-seven more were injured. The Loyalists responded by entering a pub in Greysteel on Halloween night, yelling 'Trick or Treat' and spraying the pub with a machine gun. Jillian's father was in the pub that night. He died because of the retaliation from an attack O'Rourke had ordered."

When McGill paused, Jillian added the final chapter. "Then the biggest of all the news broke not long ago," she said.

"All this time, O'Rourke was a spy for the British Secret Service. A sleeper who infiltrated the IRA and Sinn Fein, gave away their secrets, and undermined their causes. He'd been proclaiming peace but he didn't know what peace was."

Jillian went silent. She wiped her face with her shirt sleeve and took a couple of deep breaths. She looked Jake in the eyes, "Don't you see, we had no choice? O'Rourke had to die. He didn't deserve to live another moment."

CHAPTER 51

Kaplan stood on the second-floor balcony railing, balanced precariously nearly twenty feet above the ground. He reached above him and gripped the decking on the third-floor balcony. Then he pulled himself up to the next level, threw his legs over the railing and positioned himself flush to the wall and out of sight of the French doors.

Just two minutes prior, he had feared he would be exposed when Annie's neighbor saw him on the balcony and hollered out a greeting. Kaplan had given him the hi-how-are-you wave and a grin, and then acted nonchalant until the neighbor disappeared inside.

After waiting for more revelers below to move out of sight down the alleyway, he had jumped onto the railing and climbed the twelve feet to the third-floor balcony where he now stood, silent and waiting.

He peeked through the glass into Annie's bedroom. The room looked empty. Then he saw something move. Moments ago, he'd seen Scout perched in the bay window downstairs. Now she was walking through the room toward him, her mouth making the familiar *meow* motions. He stifled the curse that wanted to burst through his lips. She must have seen him jump the balcony, and had run upstairs to play. If he didn't silence her, someone inside the house would investigate.

He eased the door open. Scout tried to exit onto the balcony but Kaplan pushed her back inside the room, then he stepped inside, gently closing the door behind him.

Scout rubbed against his legs. He picked her up, rubbed her head, then placed her back on the carpet and motioned the cat to shoo. Scout sauntered out the doorway and then took off down the stairs as if spooked by something.

Kaplan stood behind the doorway, glancing down the stairwell. He heard voices downstairs. He could hear Jake asking questions. He heard McGill and Annie answering.

He heard Annie say, "O'Rourke had to die. He didn't deserve to live another moment."

He felt sick to his stomach. Betrayed by the woman he loved. The woman he thought he knew was part of a scheme that had killed several people and might very well kill several more.

His mind clouded with a thousand thoughts. He quickly moved to the night stand next to Annie's bed. He opened the drawer where she kept a loaded handgun. The handgun was gone. He reached for the phone to dial 911 but the handset was gone. His cell phone was broken, the result of his carelessness when Jake had hung up on him. Then he heard Jake call her Jillian.

Jake. He had to free Jake. And Beth. The truth had to come out. Annie, or was it Jillian—whoever—and McGill and the big man...they had to be stopped.

He quietly slid his feet as he moved across the room in an attempt to keep the hardwood flooring from creaking. He eased from the bedroom doorway onto the landing to evaluate his next move.

He heard it and felt it simultaneously. Cold steel against his temple and Collins's voice saying, "You so much as blink and I'll splatter your brains all over the wall."

CHAPTER 52

Jake needed to buy them some time, he needed a distraction. His mind was filling with questions. Questions about the logistics of the murder of O'Rourke. He needed to keep them talking while he formulated a plan.

He noticed Jillian was in tears, her hands shaking. She had broken down as she explained the events that caused her intense hatred for Laurence O'Rourke. She motioned to McGill to watch Jake and Beth while she went into the bathroom.

"I'll be back in a couple of minutes," she said. "Keep an eye on them and don't do anything stupid or Ian will kill you too."

"They're not going anywhere," McGill replied.

"Pat, I don't understand how you could possibly have coordinated all this. The bomb, the weather in the northeast, the Skyhawk. How could you be sure it would all fall in place?"

McGill turned toward him and Jake sensed his internal conflict. Clearly, the entire situation had snowballed out of his control.

"The bomb was the easy part," McGill said, after a pause. "Ian had information about O'Rourke's movements. We knew he was coming here from Dallas to disclose some sort of information he claimed would expose the New Northern Ireland Assembly as a sham, and he threatened to expose the parties as a bunch of liars.

"Ian has sources, reliable sources in Ireland that know every move O'Rourke makes before he makes them and they were worried about this 'revelation' that O'Rourke had. Ian was hired with a contract on O'Rourke, to take him out in Savannah. His employer codenamed it the Savannah Project.

"Ian first contacted Jillian, who in turn called me," McGill went on. "He wanted to know if we wanted to exact our revenge. He said he would split his take with us three ways if we helped him. Jillian and I didn't really care about the money. Our vendetta was different."

McGill glanced away toward the door, as though checking to make sure Ian wasn't standing there.

"He said he would handle all the details. All we had to do was follow his instructions. A few weeks ago Ian went to Dallas and researched the airport and the operators. He posed as a mechanic and got a job. I don't know how he does most of the stuff he does, but he is good at it," McGill said. "He had all the pieces shipped to him for a radio-controlled bomb. He had the transmitter sent here, to Jillian. She's the one who detonated the bomb, from her car at the airport."

Jake interrupted, "What about the Skyhawk? How could you plan that?"

"We couldn't," McGill said. "That was dumb luck. He was a victim of 'wrong place, wrong time.' It was perfect for us, though. It would have helped to explain away the whole accident if you hadn't kept going behind my back. I could have closed this out in a couple of more days, we could have gone home and none of this would be happening now."

"How could you know the Go Team from D.C. wouldn't come down?" Jake asked.

"I didn't. I actually had planned on the D.C. team coming down. But I also knew I would be assigned to the investigation and would come down from Atlanta. I figured I had enough pull to steer the investigation along in a certain direction and could compromise any evidence that would suggest otherwise. I knew it wouldn't be easy, but I could have handled it. The snowstorm just made it easier."

Jake slowed his drinking but kept mimicking intoxication while he worked on Pat's resolve. He would try to wear Pat down, and then maybe he could appeal to Pat's conscience.

"What about Dave? Why did you let him kill Dave?"

Jake set his bottle down. He reached over and took Beth's hand, worried that she was so silent. She was staring down at the floor, looking almost dazed. He pulled a tendril of hair away from her face and tucked it behind her ear, "Beth, are you okay?"

Beth looked at him with watery eyes and nodded. A tear ran down her cheek.

He wiped the tear away with his finger.

"That wasn't supposed to happen. Dave's death was unfortunate," said McGill. "Ian had followed the wreckage over to Gulfstream and somehow got past the guards. He saw Dave examining the area under the forward part of the cabin, the same area where Ian had placed the bomb. Dave pulled some stuff from the kit and started taking samples. When he heard Dave call you, Ian overreacted and killed him. I didn't know about it until it was too late. That was never part of the plan—none of this was."

McGill lowered his head.

Jake was making progress, Pat was becoming remorseful but Jake needed a little more time—then heard something move behind him.

"What the hell are you telling them?" Collins said. "They don't need to know anything."

Collins shoved Kaplan forward, forcing him to sit beside Jake on the sofa along with Beth. Jake stared at Kaplan.

Kaplan shrugged his shoulders. "Sorry, I didn't figure out about Annie until this morning. That's why I called." He looked at the beer bottles. "What's this?" He motioned with his head. "A little early for drinking, huh, Jake?"

Jake surprised himself when he shot back, "Yeah, well, it beats the hell out of dying."

Jillian came out of the kitchen and immediately saw Kaplan.

"Gregg," she ran across the room toward the sofa.

Collins stepped in front of her and said, "Stay away from him."

"No, let him go. He doesn't know anything."

"I caught him sneaking in from the third-floor balcony. He wouldn't be here if he hadn't figured out what's going on?"

Collins pushed Jillian away from the sofa.

McGill yelled, "Dammit, Ian, you just keep making the situation worse. We can't get away with killing all of them."

"Yes, we can and we will. We have no choice," said Collins.

Jillian placed her hands on her hips. "What are you going to do? Plan *another* accident?"

Collins moved over next to Jillian and McGill, still pointing the gun at the three prisoners sitting on the sofa when a voice called out from behind Ian.

"Drop the weapons, all of you."

Jake's face froze. He knew that voice.

CHAPTER 53

Jake looked up from the leather sofa at the man holding a silenced Heckler and Koch USP 45CT pointed at Collins. It was the first time he had gotten a good look at Michael Sullivan. His previous encounters had been in the cover of darkness or from behind, offering no visual clues, only a voice. This was the second time Sullivan had rescued him from Ian.

Sullivan walked into the room behind Collins and McGill and Jillian. "Place the guns on the floor, each of you. Now with your right foot, slowly kick your guns over toward the sofa."

McGill and Jillian kicked their guns toward the sofa. Collins made no move.

Sullivan placed the silencer close to Collins' head and said, "Do it now."

Collins tried to make a move—a move Sullivan had already anticipated. As Collins spun around, the butt of Sullivan's H & K smashed against his right temple. He fell to the floor unconscious, blood running down the side of his face and around his ear.

Sullivan pointed his gun at McGill and Jillian. "You two, back away from Ian."

They backed up two steps from where Ian lay. Sullivan kept his gun trained on Ian.

He looked at Jake and motioned. "You, pick up the guns and bring them here. Carefully."

Jake stood up. He staggered when he moved, a combined result of the loss of blood and the effects of the alcohol. He picked up McGill's and Jillian's guns first and handed them over to Sullivan.

He leaned over toward Collins' gun, stretching his arm out as far as he could to pick up the gun, trying to keep as much distance from the man as possible, just in case.

Jake pointed the gun at Collins. "I should shoot you right now. Save a lot of people a lot of trouble. But then I'd be no better than you, would I? You're going to jail, pal."

He took two steps away from Collins and then pointed the gun toward McGill. "So are you."

Then Jake pointed the gun at Jillian. "And so are you."

He looked at Sullivan. Jake was looking straight down the barrel of Sullivan's H&K.

"Don't be stupid. Give me the gun, Mr. Pendleton," Sullivan said.

"Why don't you let me keep it til the cops get here?"

"Give me the gun—now."

Jake hesitated and then lowered the gun, turned it around and handed it over to Sullivan, butt first.

Sullivan took the gun.

"Okay, move back over to the sofa," he said.

Jake didn't move. "You said we'd call the police after they were neutralized. I'd say that's now."

"All in due time," Sullivan said. "Now sit down."

Jake sat down between Beth and Kaplan.

Kaplan leaned over to Jake. "Hey, sailor, next time you have a gun—use it."

Jake cut his eyes at Kaplan. "How about next time you mount a rescue attempt, you bring one."

Sullivan placed the Berettas taken from Jillian and McGill on the table behind him. He held Collins' Beretta in his left hand and his own H&K in his right hand, both trained toward the occupants of the room.

Sullivan turned his head slightly, then called out, "Room secure."

Footsteps echoed down the hallway toward the living room. Heavy footsteps,

All eyes from the sofa looked down the long hallway as the silhouette of a tall, thin man in an overcoat came down the hall toward the living room.

The bright light behind him from the kitchen obscured recognition until he entered the living room and the light from the lamps revealed the man's identity.

CHAPTER 54

Jake saw a shocked expression cross their faces. McGill and Jillian looked like they had seen a ghost. Jake didn't recognize the well-dressed man but realized he must be looking at Laurence O'Rourke.

McGill was the first to speak. "O'Rourke! How did you—"

"You bastard." Jillian said. "All those months of work, planning and organizing. You're supposed to be dead,"

"And I would be if it hadn't been for Michael here," O'Rourke said gently. "He is the one you should thank for my being alive."

McGill and Jillian looked at Sullivan.

"How could you know?" Jillian asked.

Collins started moving on the floor. Sullivan pointed toward Collins with his H&K. "That was easy. Ian tipped me off."

"What?" McGill and Jillian said at the same time.

"No. Ian wouldn't do that," said McGill. "He wouldn't betray us like that, not over something as important to us as this."

"There's a lot you don't know about Ian," Sullivan said.

"I've known Ian all of my life," McGill replied. "Even though we haven't been close since we were teenagers, he wouldn't betray us. He's like a brother to me."

O'Rourke said, "Ironic you should phrase it like that. Ian couldn't just stand by and let his brother be killed—to be blown up."

"You're his brother?" Jillian asked O'Rourke.

Sullivan interrupted, "No, Ian's *my* half-brother. We share the same father. We didn't meet until we were in our twenties. We were both in the IRA. Our father introduced us after he made his peace with Ian."

"That's a lie. Ian's father died when he was a child," McGill said.

"No, his father left them. He left them for my mother and a different life. His father's death was just a lie Ian's mother concocted so Ian would never go looking for him," Sullivan said. "Ian knew I worked for O'Rourke and knew what you had planned, so he tipped me off."

"You switched in Longview, didn't you?" Jake stood from the sofa.

Kaplan stood next to him and said, "This the dead guy?"

Sullivan raised his gun and pointed it toward them.

O'Rourke looked at Jake. "Very good, Mister ... uh ..."

"Jake Pendleton."

"Right, Mr. Pendleton. NTSB investigator working for Mr. McGill here, I believe. You're very good. How did you come to that conclusion?"

"Too many witnesses saw you get on the plane in Dallas, yet you're here. Therefore your pilot's story about the cabin door warning light and the precautionary landing in Longview was just a ruse so you could get off the airplane. You must have switched with someone, a double or look-alike or something ... someone who was the same size and shape as you. Someone you were willing to sacrifice. He died in the crash, along with everybody else."

Jake's voice held contempt for the man who willingly let innocent people die.

O'Rourke's face showed no emotion. "A regrettable loss—but one that could not have been avoided. You see, now I am officially dead, so no one will come looking for me. I have made a lucrative deal that will allow me financial security for my very long life. So now I'll just disappear to a place far away. But first, I'm going to expose the truth to the entire world.

"The New Northern Ireland Assembly is a sham, a farce. The IRA lied, Sinn Fein lied, the Ulster Defense Association lied, the British ... they all lied and I have proof. You aren't the only ones who wanted me dead, there are many others."

He laughed. "I'm going to take them all down. I'm going to

expose them for what they really are. And it will be easier now ... because I'm dead, so no one will be looking for me."

Jillian spat at O'Rourke. "You're a British spy. Your betrayal has cost too many lives."

Collins raised his head slowly, pushed himself up with his hands and knees attempting to stand when Sullivan put his foot on Collins' back and pushed him back to the floor.

"Not so fast, Ian, you're safer on the floor. Just stay there and keep your hands out flat on the floor where I can see them."

Jillian kicked at Collins. "You pig. You betrayed us."

Collins mumbled from the floor, "I needed O'Rourke alive, for now anyway. He has information I need, information I will get. Then I will kill him, slow and painful. I will do to him what he did to me."

O'Rourke laughed, "Oh yes, the Ridge of Two Demons. A place you will never see, I'm afraid."

"Don't overestimate your momentary upper hand," Collins scoffed. "This situation will change and when it does, I will take great pleasure in killing you."

"Haven't you been paying attention? I'm already dead. So, I would say the odds are not in your favor right now, Mr. Collins ... or do you prefer Shamrock? You see, Michael's allegiance is still with me and if he has to choose between letting you get to me or killing you—well, I'm afraid you lose."

"He's right, Ian," Sullivan said. "My allegiance is with Laurence. You saved my life by warning me about the bomb and for that, I am grateful. But make no mistake, I will not let you kill Laurence, just like I wouldn't let you kill Mr. Pendleton here. Half-brother or not, you will die if you make one more move in that direction. I knew you must have been up to something when you warned me. We've never been like brothers and we were never going to be, so there was something else. I didn't have to dig deep to figure out what you had planned."

O'Rourke smiled. "You two went to a lot of trouble to plan my death. Your mistake was getting mixed up with Ian. He is a ruthless killer. He has no loyalties. Did you think he was renewing his old friendship? No, he was just using you. And you were going to take the fall. I know why Ian was part of this but what I don't understand is your involvement."

McGill said, "A café bombing in Claudy. Both my parents were killed. You planted that bomb. I was only five years old. I had to move in with my aunt and uncle and my cousin Jillian in Londonderry."

Jake watched Jillian dab away her tears away with her shirt sleeve. She stepped toward Kaplan and reached for his hand.

Kaplan pulled away from her, stepping closer to Jake.

McGill continued, "Then you broke out of the Maze. You stayed in a cellar in Londonderry. That was our house." He pointed at Jillian and back at himself.

"You beat up my best friend." McGill gestured toward Ian lying on the floor.

"Then you raped my aunt, Jillian's mother. Ian saw everything. He watched you raping her and heard her as she pleaded for you to stop."

Jillian dropped to the floor, sobbing.

Beth started to cry.

McGill kneeled down and put his arm around Jillian. He glared at O'Rourke, "Then Jillian's father was gunned down on Halloween night in Greysteel as retaliation for a bombing you ordered. All along you were a spy for the British Secret Service."

O'Rourke lowered the gun to his side, looked over at Sullivan and then glanced down at McGill. "The Troubles claimed the lives of hundreds of Irish men and women. Your parents were only two of them. It was war, survival."

O'Rourke looked at Ian. "You, I should have remembered you—the hair and the eyes. I never put the pieces together. You were so young and foolish. You had some idealistic image of what could be accomplished. It was rather naive."

O'Rourke's eyes moved to Jillian. "Your mother... I remember your mother. I remember her well. She was the most beautiful woman I had ever seen. The most beautiful woman I think I have *ever* seen. I had been in the Maze for a long time, locked up like an animal. I hadn't seen a woman for months, much less touched one."

O'Rourke paused. Jake could tell he was studying Jillian. Jillian's mascara had streaked down her cheeks below her puffy eyes.

"You know, you look like her." O'Rourke said. "The red hair, soft white skin, tiny freckles, brilliant green eyes—your mother's eyes. As I recall, you were just a skinny little lass. Now you've become a most desirable woman."

Jillian flushed with rage. Her body trembled. She sat on the floor and glared at Laurence O'Rourke and screamed, "I hope you rot in hell."

"Shut up." O'Rourke turned to Sullivan, "Michael—kill them. Start with her." He pointed to Jillian with his pistol. "Kill them all." He swept the barrel across the room.

CHAPTER 55

Kaplan watched as Jillian lunged toward O'Rourke, both fists clenched tight.

Before O'Rourke could raise his gun, Michael Sullivan had fired his H&K .45 caliber at Jillian, hitting her chest dead center.

Blood soaked through her blouse. Her body fell backward toward the sofa, crashing onto the coffee table and landing right in front of him.

Her lifeless green eyes still open stared up at him. Blood ran from her chest onto the table, down one of the table legs and onto the polished wood floor.

Kaplan dropped to his knees and grabbed a handful of her hair, "Annie ... no ... Annie." He looked at Sullivan. "You bastard, I'll kill you for this."

Collins made a hard sweep with his legs, knocking Sullivan's legs out from under him. Sullivan fell to his left, and the H&K and the Beretta tumbled into the middle of the room. Both guns landed out of reach of Collins or Sullivan—but right in front of McGill, Jake, and Kaplan.

Sullivan retreated on hands and knees behind a large leather chair and crawled toward the table where he had earlier placed the other two Berettas—next to where O'Rourke stood. Sullivan grabbed O'Rourke's pants leg and motioned for him to get down out of the line of fire. He grabbed one of the Berettas, spun around, then raised himself above the leather chair back.

Kaplan had let go of Annie and dove over the coffee table, grabbing the H&K. He tucked and rolled over to his right. He rolled into a kneeling firing position and fired a shot at Collins.

The bullet from the H&K hit Collins in the left shoulder just above his armpit. Collins clutched his left shoulder as he fell over.

* * *

At the same time Kaplan moved, Jake and McGill both dove for the Beretta. Jake beat him to the gun. He raised it and pointed the barrel toward McGill.

"Don't move, Pat," he yelled. "This has got to end."

McGill stepped back away from him.

Then Jake heard two quick popping sounds.

He watched as McGill fell back against the front door, blood gurgled from his chest. McGill slid down the door, falling to a sitting position as his legs failed him. A smeared trail of blood followed him down the door. Sunlight beamed through two bullet holes in the front door.

Jake turned around and saw O'Rourke holding his H&K gun pointed at McGill. He fired a shot at O'Rourke. Missed. He hit the leather recliner, pieces of foam and leather flew in the air.

O'Rourke dove behind the chair.

Jake moved closer to McGill.

"Pat, Pat," he said. Jake checked his neck for a pulse. "Pat, hang on, Pat."

McGill looked at him, then grimaced. His eyes remained open as his head fell to the left.

Collins dove toward the Beretta, grabbed it and rolled away from Jake.

Kaplan was running toward Jake when O'Rourke fired.

The H&K's bullet missed Kaplan but hit Beth in the side of the neck. The bullet passed through her neck. Blood spurted from her neck as she fell back onto the sofa.

Jake turned toward her and yelled, "Beth!"

He ran to the sofa, where blood was pooling on the leather upholstery and running down the front cushion onto the floor. He grabbed Beth's neck, holding pressure on it. Blood gushed through his fingers. "No. Beth, no." He kept his hands on her neck and pulled her into his chest and sat on the floor.

"Beth ...Beth. Hold on, Beth, hold on. I'm so sorry I got you involved in this."

Sullivan fired three rounds at Collins, as Collins rolled across the floor. Sullivan missed three times. One bullet shattered a lamp, one hit a bookcase and the third bullet shot through a window sending shards of glass over the sidewalk. Pedestrians screamed as they scurried away from the house and the gunfire.

Kaplan rose up from behind the arm of the sofa, steadying the H&K. He aimed the pistol at Sullivan and squeezed the trigger. Sullivan's head exploded. Brain matter splattered against the far wall.

Jake winced at the sight.

"Michael." O'Rourke muttered.

Jake saw O'Rourke lean down and grab Sullivan by the shoulder. O'Rourke pulled Sullivan's body upright and yelled, "Michael, Michael."

Sullivan had only half his head. An eyeball dangled from its socket.

The odds had swung.

Jake saw O'Rourke stand and flee down the hall toward the rear of the house.

Jake saw Collins make a move toward Kaplan. "Gregg, watch out."

Kaplan made a leg sweep, knocking Collins down. He kicked the Beretta from Collins' hands.

Then Collins' hands were on Kaplan's gun. He slammed Kaplan's head against the wall and kneed him in the stomach

Kaplan head-butted the assassin in the left shoulder, right on the bullet wound. Blood from Collins' wound smeared across Kaplan's forehead. Jake couldn't tell whose blood was whose.

Collins groaned and loosened his grip on Kaplan.

Jake cradled Beth's head in his lap, rocking back and forth. He knew he had to keep pressure on Beth's wound or he'd lose her. The battle raged in front of him.

Kaplan pushed Collins back but the assassin held onto the gun.

Kaplan elbowed Collins on the side of the head, but the assassin didn't waver.

The two men fell to the floor. Kaplan and Collins now had both hands on the H&K.

Four hands grappling for control.

The two of them rolled across the floor and Collins pulled the gun down between them. Kaplan head-butted Collins in the chin. It didn't seem to faze him.

Jake saw Collins' fingers grabbing at the trigger. Every move Kaplan made, Collins countered. He was good.

And strong.

Too strong.

They rolled over and over, struggling for control of the weapon.

On the third roll the H&K fired.

CHAPTER 56

Jake jumped at the sound of the muffled pop. All he could see was the two men rolling on the floor. The rolling stopped. He heard Kaplan groan.

He used his foot to grab for the pistol lying next to McGill's body. He struggled to reach it and still manage to hold pressure on Beth's neck. With his heel, he slowly slid the gun across the hardwood floor until he could grab it with his spare hand. Jake wrapped his fingers around the butt of the gun and pointed it at Collins.

Collins raised his head and appeared to look around. He stood up and looked at Kaplan.

Collins pointed the gun at Kaplan's head.

Before Collins' finger could squeeze the trigger, Jake fired a shot.

Collins jumped then turned toward Jake.

Jake aimed his pistol dead center at Collins' chest.

Collins eyes were expressionless and he slowly raised the gun.

Jake pushed the barrel closer, stretching out his arm toward Ian. "Give me an excuse to shoot you, you bastard. Now, just put the gun down."

Collins lowered his gun.

"I said put it down."

Collins dropped the gun to the floor.

Before he could move, sirens wailed in front of the house.

Cars screeched to a stop.

Footsteps clambered toward the front door.

Collins looked at the door and ran down the hall toward the back of the house.

"Stop." Jake yelled. He fired a shot at the assassin but the man had already disappeared.

Jake held Beth's head in his lap, still holding pressure against her neck wound. The bleeding had slowed. Beth was barely conscious. Her voice weak, barely audible.

"Jake?"

"Shhh, Beth, don't talk."

"But—"

"Don't talk. You need to save your strength," he said softly.

Jake looked around the room. During the commotion the curtains were pulled slightly apart. The afternoon's fading rays of sunshine beamed through the windows. Long shadows played across the room.

The world seemed at peace, almost serene.

The last few seconds had lasted an eternity. And now it was over.

Jillian Ann Bulloch laid sprawled across the coffee table just two feet from him. Blood pooled on the hardwood floor beneath her.

Patrick McGill had died sitting against the front door. Two bullets had entered his chest and passed all the way through. Blood trailed down the door and ran underneath his body, finding its way under the quarter-round floor molding.

Michael Sullivan lay dead in the hallway, the back of his head missing.

Gregg Kaplan inched forward, clawing his way across the floor toward Annie's body.

Jake became aware of the sound of the police beating on the front door and yelling something he couldn't understand.

Laurence O'Rourke and Ian Collins were gone.

CHAPTER 57

Office of the Director of Central Intelligence
Central Intelligence Agency

The next day, Admiral Scott Bentley sat behind his oversized executive mahogany desk looking at the stack of files his executive assistant, Jean McCullough, left for his reading. Framed photographs of naval vessels and naval aircraft adorned the walls. His mahogany bookshelves brimmed with intelligence manuals, and military books—mostly of United States Navy.

On his desk was his most recently acquired photograph. A picture of the decommissioned aircraft carrier USS *John F. Kennedy*, a prized possession for Bentley. The photograph was signed by all the officers aboard the *Kennedy* at her decommissioning. He walked across the room, framed photo in hand, and hung it next to his other picture of the *Kennedy*, a photo signed by all the original officers on board at the time of her commissioning. He smiled with satisfaction. Now his collection was complete.

He walked around and sat down behind his desk. Morning light glinted through the tinted bulletproof windows of his corner office. He glanced at his messages. On top was a message from Jake Pendleton.

"Urgent, Please call ASAP."

Bentley stared at the message—wondering why Jake would call after all these years.

Several flat panel monitors were mounted on the wall above his bookcases, each tuned to a different news channel and numbered to make volume adjustments easier from his universal remote. The volume was set on monitor number seven, FOX News.

He pulled off the top file, labeled "EYES ONLY," and opened it. The top page was an old letter from the Department of Justice written by former United States Attorney General, Alberto Gonzales. He read the cover letter, then riffled through all the attached pages. He placed the letter back in the folder and closed it.

He pushed his glasses up with right thumb and forefinger and gently rubbed the bridge of his nose, still pondering the mysterious message from Jake Pendleton. He turned to his computer and did a dossier search for Jacob Pendleton. Within seconds, Jake's life history was displayed on Bentley's computer monitor. He studied the information carefully.

Jake had attended the Naval Academy in Annapolis, a political appointment made possible by his father's political influence. Upon graduation, Jake immediately commenced his obligatory service in the U.S. Navy. His tour of duty as a Naval intelligence officer consisted of a one-year stint with the Office of Naval Intelligence at the National Maritime Intelligence Center in Suitland, Maryland, followed by a ten-month tour on the aircraft carrier U.S.S. Mount Whitney, *the* most sophisticated command, control, communications, computer and intelligence ship ever commissioned.

Then Jake was assigned duty at the Pentagon. For nearly two years, he served directly under the Naval and joint commanders. His Pentagon assignment was an obvious result of his father's political clout. He'd served directly under Bentley, then Chairman of the Joint Chiefs of Staff. Bentley's forte was covert operations. The admiral coordinated covert operations with military operations squads from all branches of the armed services and the civilian agencies of the Central Intelligence Agency, the Federal Bureau of Investigation and the National Security Agency.

Bentley looked up from the computer and noticed a crashed

aircraft on the television monitor number three, CNN Headline News. He quickly pressed the 3 button on his remote control, which turned on the volume to monitor number three, automatically muting the sound for all other monitors.

> St. Patrick's Day in Savannah, Georgia, home of the nation's second largest St. Patrick's Day parade, is generally known for its color green. Green river, green fountains, even green beer. But this year St. Patrick's Day in Savannah turned red, blood red, in what will no doubt be one of the bloodiest shootouts in modern-day Savannah history.
>
> I'm Amber Larsen reporting live from Savannah, Georgia.
>
> What started as an aircraft accident investigation in Savannah has left a trail of blood leading all the way back to Dallas, Texas. NTSB investigators from the Atlanta, Georgia, Field Office came to Savannah to investigate the crash of the corporate jet carrying the controversial Northern Ireland peace activist Laurence O'Rourke. In a strange twist of fate, NTSB lead investigator Patrick McGill and his cousin, Savannah air traffic controller Jillian Ann Bulloch, along with friend and alleged former Irish Republican Army assassin Ian Collins, plotted the death of Laurence O'Rourke.
>
> According to the FBI, Collins planted an explosive device in the jet with the assistance of a Dallas mechanic, who Collins later shot and killed. He brutally raped the mechanic's girlfriend.
>
> Savannah air traffic controller Jillian Bulloch detonated the device as O'Rourke's jet was making an approach into the Savannah airport. The motive is suspected to be a personal vengeance.
>
> O'Rourke was scheduled to make a public announcement here today revealing what he described as "proof of the biggest sham against the people of Northern Ireland," and denouncing the parties to the New Northern Ireland Assembly as "liars."
>
> Thus far the death toll has reached a total of ten with three injured. Investigator Jake Pendleton was treated and released for a stab wound and a bruised shoulder. Savannah air traffic controller Gregg Kaplan suffered a gunshot wound to the abdomen and is in stable condition.
>
> Kaplan is reported to be Jillian Bulloch's long-time boyfriend. His part of this conspiracy is under investigation.
>
> Pendleton's fiancée, Catherine Elizabeth McAllister, is on

*life support in a coma after being shot in the neck. The bullet
pierced her carotid artery and she suffered massive blood loss.*

*Among the dead are Jillian Bulloch, Patrick McGill, and
Laurence O'Rourke's long-time assistant and bodyguard
Michael Sullivan. Other fatalities include Duane Sanders, the
Dallas mechanic, and Dave Morris, an NTSB investigator,
believed shot by Collins yesterday.*

*Also killed were two pilots and a flight attendant, all from
the Dallas area, and three passengers aboard the jet, including
O'Rourke's decoy double. Identifications are still outstanding
for those three, who are also believed to be from Northern
Ireland.*

*At this hour the whereabouts of Laurence O'Rourke and
Ian Collins remain a mystery. The FBI believes both to be
fleeing the United States and has activated a tight web of
surveillance in an attempt to capture them before they can
escape the country.*

Amber Larsen, CNN Headline News, Savannah, Georgia.

Bentley remembered Jake and now understood why he left him
the urgent message. He recalled that three months prior to the end
of Jake's tour of duty with the Navy, Admiral Bentley sat him down
and confided to Jake that he was about to tender his resignation from
the military. That proclamation solidified Jake's decision not to reen-
list.

Jake's dossier went on to outline how he came to be employed
with the NTSB. Within a week of Bentley's resignation, the chairman
of the NTSB offered Jake a position as an accident investigator at the
Atlanta Field Office, a less than subtle intrusion into Jake's affairs by
his father.

Less than a year later, Bentley had been named the new Director
of Central Intelligence for the CIA in Langley, Virginia, the first
African-American to hold that position.

Bentley pressed the buzzer on his phone system paging his secretary and said, "Jean, come in here, please."

"Yes, sir," the pleasant female voice replied through the speaker
phone.

Jean McCullough walked in with her pencil and steno pad. She raised a hand to flip back her smooth strawberry-blond hair, which bobbed on her shoulders as she walked. At fifty-six, she still had a shapely figure. She wore black dress pants that fit snugly against her hips and a gold leopard-print top underneath her black jacket.

"Yes, sir?" she asked.

"Call Flight Ops and have them prep the jet. Tell them I'm going to Savannah, Georgia ASAP and I don't know how long I'll be there. They'll need to be prepared to stay overnight. Also find out what hospital a Catherine McAllister was taken to in Savannah."

"Certainly, sir. Will there be anything else?"

Bentley scribbled two file names on a Post-It note and said, "Yes, have Fontaine bring me these two files. I'm taking them with me."

THE SAVANNAH PROJECT 227

CHAPTER 58

Collins fled Jillian's house in hopes of spotting O'Rourke. O'Rourke should be dead, but he was still alive. He had sent Sullivan the message to ensure O'Rourke's safety, knowing Sullivan would devise a ruse to keep O'Rourke alive.

He also had known he would eventually encounter O'Rourke in Savannah. That's when he intended to kill O'Rourke, but not before extracting from him the location of the "grey fortress near the ridge of two demons," the only information one of his employers had given him. He had no idea what that meant but he knew O'Rourke and Sullivan did.

Collins's plan didn't go as designed, thanks to the meddling of Jake Pendleton. *Revenge will be sweet.*

He had watched as his half-brother's head was blown off in the fire fight at Jillian's house. He'd wanted to kill Kaplan for shooting his brother, but Pendleton had stopped him.

His ambivalent emotions about his brother and the deaths of his childhood friends had flamed into numbness. Now, he truly had no one. No friends. No relatives. Alone.

His rage had narrowed into a searing weapon aimed at only one person—O'Rourke.

He drove around the Savannah area in his Escalade for nearly an hour trying to spot any sign of O'Rourke. A nearly impossible task with the throngs of revelers leaving town after the festivities. Once again, O'Rourke was a ghost.

He had lost the trail in Savannah but knew where he could pick it up again, Belfast. That's where O'Rourke would go. That's where he had to go. He figured he had the luxury of time because O'Rourke was in the same predicament he was in, getting out of the United States and back to Ireland without getting caught. Both of them were now wanted men and no doubt the FBI would turn up the heat at all the airports. His advantage was there were no photos of him. The authorities would be working from sketches. O'Rourke didn't have that edge.

But Collins knew a way out, a covert way out, a way to avoid the FBI and Homeland Security dragnet. An avenue he had used before and would likely use again. Payment from a past job in the form of a bartered exchange with the client. Paid with transportation. Anywhere, anytime, anyplace—a valued asset in his line of work.

He laid low in a truck stop café near I-95 for a couple of hours while he pieced his plan together and then drove out of Savannah, heading south down U.S. Highway 17.

By midnight, the pain in his shoulder became too unbearable to continue any farther. He stopped at a third-rate motel in Yulee, Florida. Before entering the lobby, he put on a clean jacket to conceal his wound and rang the after-hours buzzer over and over. After three minutes of buzzing, an irritated clerk came out of the back room and checked him in.

In room number seven, Collins cleaned and dressed his wound with the rudimentary supplies he purchased at the convenience store next to the motel. The bullet needed to come out but he wasn't going to be able to do that by himself, he needed a doctor but that would have to wait. He took a handful of prescription pain pills. He carried with him on all jobs. Then he pulled out his Blackberry. He calculated the time difference and sent a message to a client.

He arranged himself on the bed, pulling the pillow out from underneath the cheap tropical print bedspread. He was asleep in less than five minutes.

The ring on his Blackberry woke Collins. The answer to his message—his way out of the United States.

His client owned a Libyan shipping company that had been seized by a larger company in a hostile takeover attempt. That is, until the Greek owner of the larger shipping company mysteriously died an untimely death. His heirs had offered Collins' client the opportunity to buy them out at an incredibly low price. Now his client owned the largest shipping company in the Mediterranean, shipping to hundreds of ports worldwide.

The reply to Collins' message was welcome, but he had less than one hour to make it to a Jacksonville port to board a freighter to Portugal. He tossed everything he had haphazardly into a duffel bag and hurried to his vehicle.

Collins drove to the terminal and parked his leased Cadillac Escalade in a nearby convenience store parking lot. He walked to the security gate at the Blount Island Marine Terminal, a vast complex with exactly one mile of berthing space. He reached the ship with little time to spare.

The anxious captain greeted him at the gangway. "You almost didn't make it this time," he said. Then he escorted Collins to his room. The room was familiar enough, he had been on this ship before, several times. Same captain, same crew, same horrible stench. He told the captain he needed to see the ship's doctor, and the captain said that as soon as the ship sailed, the doctor would come to his quarters.

He pulled out his laptop, inserted his cellular wireless modem card and went online to check his accounts. The deposits were there, three of them. Two for the death of Laurence O'Rourke and a considerably smaller one for the death of Michael Sullivan.

The time zone difference worked to Collins' advantage. The news of O'Rourke's escape hadn't reached his clients in Europe yet but it wouldn't be long before his Blackberry started buzzing with angry messages. It was his first failed attempt and he vowed it would be his last. But this was far from over. He made himself a vow. He would see this to its end. He would get the information he needed then he would kill Laurence O'Rourke.

He felt the ship pull away from the terminal. The tugboats weren't gentle but they did their job. As the ship pulled farther away from the dock, another tug moved in between the dock and the ship and pushed the bow around, guiding the big freighter out into the channel.

Soon the ship's doctor would arrive, but not soon enough for Collins. He placed his hand on his wound and could feel the heat. He's had worse wounds, he'll survive this one too.

He turned off his laptop and lay on the cot. It was smelly and uncomfortable but it would have to do for the next few days while he was incommunicado.

CHAPTER 59

The white sterile room in Candler Hospital's critical care unit was filled with sounds. Mechanical sounds. A respirator thumping back and forth forced breath and life into Beth. The pumping and hissing of the blood pressure cuffs contracting and deflating at regular intervals interrupted the slow beeping of the heart monitor.

Beth's mother, Rebecca, was a Southern lady. She had been a debutante in her teenage years, and her mother was a Daughter of the Confederacy. She sat next to the bed holding Beth's hand, dried tears on her face. Her weeping had finally stopped but her eyes were still red and puffy, a tissue balled up in her fist. She had thick chestnut hair, brown eyes and dark tanned skin like her daughter.

Mike McAllister had indulged his only child with the finest of everything. Spoiling her rotten was part of the fun. The son of an Irish immigrant, self-made millionaire and President-CEO of the First Commerce Bank of Newnan, McAllister could certainly afford the excesses he spent on his daughter. He was a large robust man, somewhat intimidating at first, with a stern manner and a seemingly emotionless state. This was the exception, he wore this emotion on his sleeve. Visibly shaken by the ordeal. His only daughter, his pride and joy, lay next to death in a coma in front of his eyes, the victim of an innocent trip to Savannah gone awry.

Jake sat in a chair beside Beth's bed, opposite Mrs. McAllister. His left arm in a sling and his chest bandaged under his shirt. The knife wound had required eight internal stitches and fifteen external stitches, a blood transfusion, an IV of antibiotics followed by ten days of oral antibiotics, and his chest taped to prevent him from pulling out the stitches. He had laughed after the doctor cleaned and stitched his wound, and then applied the hospital's version of Super Glue followed by a strip of medical tape—the same remedy the assassin recommended. *How ironic.*

Jake held Beth's right hand in his. Their wedding was scheduled for early June and now she lay in a coma in critical condition. All the plans they had made, all the traveling they would do. He couldn't bear to see her like this.

Her dark hair was tangled and matted from the blood. The nurses and doctors wanted to cut it but Mrs. McAllister wouldn't allow it. They settled for pulling it into a ponytail and wrapping it in a hospital hair net.

Penrose drains protruded from underneath the gauze bandage wrapped around her neck. Pads at the end of each tube caught the drainage and required regular changing.

Beth was pale and her tanned skin looked jaundiced. A nurse came in every fifteen minutes to check her vitals. Logged them on the charts, then retreated to the nurses' station for another round of hospital gossip. Leg cuffs inflated and deflated in an attempt to keep the circulation in her legs moving.

A light rap on the door broke the monotony of the machinery. The door opened slowly and a tall man in a trench coat walked in. He was about Mike McAllister's age, early sixties, well groomed, wearing a coat and tie and holding a crocodile skin portfolio brief-case. His nearly unlined, light brown face was grave.

Both McAllisters looked at him, obviously thinking the man was in the wrong room, when Jake jumped to his feet, letting Beth's hand drop to the bed.

Jake snapped to attention, automatically throwing a military-style salute.

"Admiral Bentley, sir."

"At ease, Jake, we can dispense with those trifles. How is she doing?" He motioned toward Beth.

Jake relaxed a little. "Not good, Admiral. She's barely hanging on."

Bentley turned to McAllister. "Scott Bentley. I'm terribly sorry about your daughter. My prayers are with you and Mrs. McAllister." Bentley turned and tilted his head toward Beth's mother.

"I know who you are, Mr. Bentley, and I appreciate your concern," replied McAllister, "but what I don't understand is why the Director of Central Intelligence would come all the way from Washington to check on my daughter's health?"

With his usual authoritative voice and calm demeanor, Bentley explained, "Jake and I go back quite a ways. Jake worked for me at the end of my military career. Best damned intelligence officer I ever trained. Your daughter is important to Jake, therefore she is important to me. If there is anything I can do, please don't hesitate to ask."

Mrs. McAllister walked over to Bentley and gave him a hug. "Thank you, Admiral, from both of us. It's been a trying time and we're both exhausted and scared."

"I certainly understand." Bentley looked at Jake. "Jake, maybe we could give them some privacy and you and I can take a walk?"

"Yes, sir. I'll be right there, sir."

Bentley turned and walked out, closing the door behind him.

Jake grabbed Beth's hand, leaned down and kissed her cheek and said, "Baby, I'll be right back."

Jake stood in the hall without moving until Beth's door closed. The nurse glanced up, and then returned to the mounds of paperwork the hospital's administration required of them.

He walked over to Bentley, who had already removed his coat and draped it over his arm. Glancing back at Beth's room he could see Beth's father moving toward her bed. The room was nothing more than a glass-walled cubicle, offering no privacy except on those rare occasions when the curtains were drawn closed.

"Admiral." Jake stuck out his hand. "It's been a long time."

Bentley gave him a firm handshake. "Yes, Jake, it has. I'm truly sorry this happened to your fiancée."

Bentley motioned down the hall and they both walked slowly, yet deliberately, toward an unknown destination, catching up on each others' lives through small talk.

They ended up in the cafeteria, sitting at a table after ordering a round of coffee. The cafeteria was empty with the exception of one couple sitting in the corner. The evening shift was wiping tables in preparation for closing.

Jake shifted his sling around on his arm. He winced at the pain. The doctor had told him it was a mild shoulder sprain and should heal quickly after the cortisone injection.

Jake spoke first. "Admiral, you could have just returned my call. You didn't have to come all the way down here to see me in person."

He looked Bentley in the eyes. "But you didn't come here to check up on Beth, or me either for that matter, did you, Admiral?"

Bentley nodded.

Jake continued, "You know, I'm kind of surprised Nurse Nazi up there even let you in the room. Hell, it took an act of Congress just to get me in there."

"I just flashed my pearly whites and she waved me right through. Of course, the ID badge helped a little too." Bentley chuckled. "Jake, after I saw your message and heard the news report I knew this visit needed to be face to face.

"I believe I know why you called. Maybe it was in desperation, maybe not. I have quite a few questions myself, which will probably lead us to the true purpose of your call."

Bentley placed his briefcase on the table, unzipped the main compartment and slid out two folders with CLASSIFIED stamped on the outside of each in red ink.

"Jake, you held a much higher security clearance when you worked for me, and your NTSB personnel folder shows you currently holding only a 'Secret' clearance. I'm raising that now. Do you still remember what that entails?"

Jake nodded. "Yes, sir, I remember well."

"Good."

He opened the first folder. Inside the folder were several pictures of Laurence O'Rourke taken over a period of many years.

Bentley spun the folder around and laid it on the table in front of Jake. "You recognize him, of course. We'll get to him in just a minute."

He opened the second folder, turned it around and placed it directly on top of the first one. There was no photograph, just an image of a green shamrock with a bullet hole in the center—some CIA analyst's idea of a joke, no doubt. One word was stamped on the top of each page. *SHAMROCK.*

"Notice something, Jake? Or rather the lack of something? This file belongs to an assassin who calls himself Shamrock. We've confirmed only two contract kills in the United States, but we've confirmed dozens in Europe, Africa, the Middle East, one in New Zealand and even a couple in Japan. He never leaves any witnesses alive to give a description. We have no idea what he looks like. We can only recognize him by his calling card—"

Jake interrupted, "Wait, let me guess, a shamrock?"

"That's right. We can also recognize him by his MO. It's like his murder fingerprint. He has a very distinctive style of killing. It's like a 'tell' in poker. We don't really need him to leave a shamrock any more in order for us to know who did it.

"We have his fingerprints and his DNA, he's never been shy about leaving either or both on his victims. I've ordered the fingerprints from the FBI here in Savannah and likewise in Dallas. I'm convinced they will match those we have on file for Shamrock."

"O'Rourke called Collins "Shamrock" right before all hell broke loose yesterday."

"I'm sure the fingerprints will confirm all that," said Bentley.

"And you want a physical description from me?"

Bentley nodded.

Jake slumped his shoulders—not what he was expecting from Bentley. He had hoped the Admiral had come for a different reason. He wasn't certain what he had hoped for when he placed the call to Bentley's office. Maybe some answers, maybe an idea to exact revenge. But certainly more than just to give a witness statement and description. He could have just given that to the FBI.

"Yes, from you and from that air traffic controller who got shot. Did you know he used to be Special Forces?"

"I did. We discussed it during the controller interview portion of the investigation. He was the controller working the airplane when the bomb went off."

"I know it's no consolation, but nice work on that investigation."

"Thank you, Admiral. I'll be happy to help out any way I can."

"Do you mean that, Jake? Will you help out *any* way you can?"

"Yes, sir, of course I will."

Bentley closed the Shamrock folder and slid it underneath the O'Rourke folder.

"What about him, Jake? Will you help me nail O'Rourke?"

"Admiral, O'Rourke is the bastard who shot Beth. If I could I would kill him. I'd really like to be the one to take him down."

Bentley slammed the folder closed, placed both folders back in his portfolio briefcase, and then stood up.

"Jake, that's all I needed to hear. How about you and I take a little trip?"

CHAPTER 60

The next day, the CIA photographer set a backdrop behind Jake. "Mr. Pendleton, would you stand over here please. This will only take a moment."

He snapped several digital photos of Jake, plugged them into a laptop computer and began processing them. The Security chief took a digital scan of his fingerprints and downloaded them into the same computer. Jake was then given a retinal scan, which was also downloaded into the computer.

Jake had anguished over leaving Beth in Savannah while she was still on life support and barely clinging to life. Her parents took the news of his leaving Savannah with mixed emotions. Rebecca McAllister didn't understand it at all and felt Jake should stay at Beth's side. Mike McAllister's response was quite the opposite.

Jake told McAllister that he was going to Virginia with Bentley to assist in locating and apprehending O'Rourke and the assassin. McAllister's reaction was simple. He wanted revenge for his daughter. He only said one thing to Jake before he returned to Beth's side: "Jake, if you get the chance, promise me you'll kill that bastard."

Jake sat in the briefing room adjacent to Bentley's office. He had been rushed into the briefing room, where he was met by a CIA photographer, the head of Security, Bentley's executive assistant Jean McCullough, and a CIA analyst who handled the O'Rourke file and the Shamrock file.

Within forty-five minutes, Jake was outfitted with a new CIA badge, a new passport under a new name along with the supporting credentials, and granted limited access to several areas at the Headquarters via thumbprint and retinal scan by the CIA's central computer—unheard of for an outsider—but ordered by Bentley.

Jake couldn't help but see it as overkill for an operation that would keep him at the CIA facility for less than three days, but Bentley had insisted.

Bentley cleared the room except for Jake and an analyst named George Fontaine, a man in his early fifties with a crooked nose and a muted Jay Leno chin. It was only then that Jake learned Bentley's true intentions for him.

For the rest of the day, he received thorough briefings on Laurence O'Rourke and Shamrock. Coincidentally, there were quite a few similarities between the two men's backgrounds. O'Rourke and Collins had both started as hit men for the IRA, O'Rourke only after a failed first attempt to join the IRA.

Both men had served on the Irish Republican Army's Internal Security Unit referred to as the "Nutting Squad." The similarities ended there. Collins had earned one of the more notorious reputations on the squad for his ruthless but effective tactics. O'Rourke's time on the Nutting Squad was short-lived as he quickly ascended the ranks to Quartermaster General.

Collins' reputation with the IRA as a skilled, masterful killer was unmatched by any other. His flawless executions were still held in high acclaim. One day Collins had approached the IRA Chief of Staff and resigned his commission with the IRA. He disappeared and was believed to have been killed by the IRA.

O'Rourke had served in an official and an unofficial capacity as Quartermaster General for the IRA for a number of years. During the heyday of arms acquisitions, O'Rourke amassed huge caches of weapons of all sorts and stored them in several secret locations throughout Ireland and Northern Ireland.

An artist came in and spent several hours with Jake sketching a drawing of Ian Collins, aka Shamrock. Bentley brought in the FBI sketch from Kaplan's description and held them side by side. They were nearly identical.

The two images were scanned into a computer, then morphed

together and a new image created. The resultant image was then sent to Interpol for distribution throughout the European countries' law enforcement agencies with orders to "capture and detain."

Jake spent the next two days in accelerated training at the CIA's Camp Peary Special Training Center, known as "The Farm." Although never officially acknowledged by the U.S. government, this nine-thousand-plus-acre facility was located in York County near Williamsburg, Virginia. During World War II, Camp Peary was used as a Seabee training base and a stockade for special German prisoners of war. In 1972, the *Virginia Gazette* reported that the CIA trained its assassins at The Farm, but the CIA dismissed this as nonsense because it didn't have "assassins."

The first day's training lasted several hours. The primary focus of the day was The Farm's main impetus, basic tradecraft skills of weapons handling, explosives, infiltration techniques, and exfiltration techniques. Jake was fed and told to get some rest before reporting back at midnight for four hours of "night ops" familiarization training.

Jake found his prior Navy training helpful. The intelligence portion of training was the easy part for Jake, more like a refresher course, whereas the hand-to-hand combat and firearms training sessions were grueling. His anger and determination to get the man who shot Beth carried him through it.

The same helicopter that had brought him to The Farm took off from the five-thousand-foot runway at Camp Peary, and delivered him to the lawn landing pad at CIA Headquarters in Langley. A driver was waiting for him when he arrived and took him back to Bentley's office.

Bentley was waiting for him in the conference room. Also in the room were the head of Security, the head of the Office of Intelligence and Analysis, the head of the Office of Clandestine Service, a female CIA operative named Isabella Hunt, and Gregg Kaplan.

Jake shook his head in amazement and started toward Kaplan. "What the hell are you doing here?"

Kaplan stood, wearing blue jeans and a black t-shirt, and extended his hands palm up..

"I'm going with you to Ireland."

"You can't go, you have a gunshot wound. Shouldn't you still be in the hospital?"

"The bullet didn't hit anything. It just hurt like a son of a bitch. I rubbed some dirt on it." He made circular motions over his wound. "And now I'm fine. I've been hurt a lot worse than this in the Army. Besides, you need me."

"You were a lot younger in your Army days. I don't need you. Maybe you've forgotten who saved your ass at Annie's house?" Jake realized what he'd said. "Gregg, I'm sorry. I'm really sorry about Annie."

"Don't be, okay?"

Jake turned to Bentley. "You called Gregg?"

Bentley shook his head.

Kaplan interrupted, "No, Jake, I volunteered, during the interview after the shooting. With everything that happened I feel I have unfinished business that needs my attention. Same as you do.

"Besides, what's left for me in Savannah? Go back to work like nothing ever happened? Have to listen to all the gossip at work? I don't think so. I've talked to my last airplane."

Jake said nothing.

Bentley spoke up, breaking the awkward silence.

"Jake, you and Gregg are the only ones who have seen Ian Collins and are still alive to tell about it. You two are the only people who can recognize him and give me a positive ID."

Bentley nodded toward the woman at the table as he went on. "You will accompany Ms. Hunt here to Ireland to locate Laurence O'Rourke and Ian Collins. You two will assist her in apprehending both men."

Jake and Kaplan looked at Hunt at the same time, then glanced at each other.

Jake turned back to Bentley and asked, "Why didn't you send

Gregg to Camp Peary with me?"

"I didn't really see a need. I accessed his military records and after reviewing them, I felt Gregg was fully capable of handling himself without any further training. His Special Forces training far exceeded anything he could have been given at the Farm."

Isabella Hunt spoke for the first time, as her hazel eyes glinted at Jake. "I'm going to need you and Kaplan to help me locate O'Rourke and Shamrock. Then *I'll* apprehend them."

Jake kept his mouth shut and his face expressionless as he gave Hunt a closer look. She was attractive, he had to admit, with long, straight, black hair and glowing bronze skin. About five-foot-five, she was trim—maybe a hundred twenty-five pounds, Jake estimated, and she had an attitude. An attitude no doubt fostered from years struggling as a woman in a male-dominated occupation.

Jake rolled his eyes, then looked at Kaplan. "I know you were Special Forces, but what *exactly* did you do in the Army?"

Kaplan furrowed his brow. "Jake, there are some questions people ask and they really don't want to hear the answer. I think this is one of them."

"Oh hell no! I want an answer. I want to know what makes you so special you can just waltz in here and go off with no training or anything else. What *did* you do in the Army?"

Kaplan leaned in close to Jake. "Black ops. Satisfied?"

Jake said nothing.

* * *

The next three hours were spent on detailed mission briefings and planning. During the briefing by the CIA analyst Fontaine, Jake's mind wandered back to Savannah and Beth.

The recesses of his mind registered something familiar as Fontaine addressed the group.

"What did you just say?" Jake asked.

Fontaine sighed, and then repeated his last remark.

"Laurence O'Rourke has a brother named Sean who works with the Provisional IRA, or the Provos, but his whereabouts are unknown at the present time."

"No, no, no. Before that, something about a ridge."

"The ridge, oh yeah," Fontaine said. "The O'Rourkes own property throughout County Leitrim that has been in the O'Rourke family for centuries. Laurence and his brother Sean own a house in a small village called Dromahair. The SIS file says that means 'the Ridge of Two Air Demons.'"

Kaplan raised an eyebrow. "O'Rourke said something about a ridge to Collins right before the shoot-out, didn't he?"

Jake stood up. "Yeah, he did." He looked at the specialist and said, "Can you show me that on the map?"

Bentley interrupted, "Jake, does that mean something to you?"

"It might, it just might."

Fontaine pointed to the area on the map. Jake leaned over and studied the map.

"This is it, Admiral." Jake looked up at Bentley. "This is where we need to go. Like Gregg mentioned, O'Rourke said something to Collins right before the shooting started. Something about the location of the Ridge of Two Demons. Collins wanted to know where it was and once he found out, he was going to kill O'Rourke. This is where we need to go—the answer is here and that is where we will eventually find O'Rourke."

Isabella Hunt interrupted. "How can you be sure? It sounds to me like you're just playing a hunch. If you're wrong, we end up at the wrong place, wasting time while O'Rourke gets away."

She turned to Bentley. "Director, we can't just gamble on a hunch. We need to go to Belfast and wait. We're positive he'll show up there. When O'Rourke shows up, we grab him."

Bentley took off his reading glasses and placed them on top of his head. "Jake, I need you to be sure about this before we make a move."

"Admiral, can Gregg and I speak to you alone?" Jake asked.

Hunt banged her fist on the table. "Director, with all due

respect—"

Bentley raised his hand, then excused everyone from the briefing except for Jake and Kaplan. Hunt, lips tightened into a hard line, stood and walked stiffly out of the room.

"She'll get over it, she always does. She's very dedicated and probably feels a little uncertain about you two, maybe threatened a bit by my prior association with Jake," said Bentley. "She's one of my best, though."

"Way to go, Jake," Kaplan said. "A pissed-off woman with a gun. I don't like our chances."

Bentley walked around the table, put his glasses back on and looked down at the map laid out across the table.

"Can you be sure, Jake? Can you be sure O'Rourke will return here?"

"If you give me a couple of hours on the mainframe, I think I can prove it."

"Okay, Jake. You've got two hours."

CHAPTER 61

Jake returned to Bentley's office exactly ninety minutes later with several printed documents stuffed inside five folders, one each for Bentley, Fontaine, Kaplan, Hunt and himself. If Bentley and Fontaine accepted the information Jake had gathered, Kaplan and Hunt would be briefed.

He laid the folders across the big desk and Bentley and Fontaine opened theirs and studied the documents.

Bentley removed his reading glasses and rubbed the bridge of his nose. "Jake, are you sure about this? Al Qaeda, Nasiri? Can you fathom the implications here?"

"Yes, sir, unfortunately, I'm very aware of all the implications. But I'm also quite certain."

"How certain?" Bentley asked.

"Admiral, I'd bet my life on this one."

"Odd choice of words, Jake—you may very well be doing just that."

"He's right, sir," Fontaine said. "I don't know why I didn't see it before, and Dromahair is the perfect location."

"Well," Bentley said, "I see you haven't lost your touch for thoroughness. I always trusted your instincts before. Alright, let's do it."

Bentley leaned over, pushed the intercom button and summoned Jean McCullough into his office to give Jake an update on Beth. She had been tasked to make periodic calls to the Candler Hospital in Savannah and receive updates on Beth's condition.

"Jean, I'm sure Jake would like to know how Beth is doing. Do you have any news?"

"Actually, sir," she replied, "I have Mr. McAllister on the line right now. Shall I forward the call in here?"

Bentley saw Jake's eyes light up and said, "Yes, Jean, please do and send Mr. Kaplan and Ms. Hunt in here too."

Jake spent the next five minutes on the phone with Mike McAllister getting caught up to speed on Beth and bringing McAllister up to date on those things he was allowed to discuss. The others waited patiently as Jake concluded his call.

Jake looked at Kaplan and saw the hint of a smile on his face. Suddenly Jake was glad Kaplan would be with him in Ireland.

As Jake placed the receiver down, Bentley asked, "Well, how's she doing?"

"She seems to be stabilizing, which is good. Her father said she had some ups and downs and she's still unconscious but her vitals are improving."

"Jake, Gregg, I need to make sure you two fully understand your place in this operation," said Bentley. "You are back-up and support for Isabella. You are also there for positive identification of O'Rourke and Collins, if he should show up. This is Isabella's operation and you will take orders from her. Is that understood?"

Hunt glanced up from the folder and smirked, which didn't go unnoticed by the others in the room.

"Yes sir, Admiral. I understand perfectly," Jake replied. "I have no problem with that. I'm just glad I get to be there when O'Rourke goes down."

Kaplan said firmly, "No problem, sir."

Bentley tapped his finger on the table and leaned toward them. "Just remember, this is 'capture alive' for both O'Rourke *and* Collins. Keep your heads about you at all times. I don't like making phone calls with sad news to relatives. I did enough of that in the Navy. It's no easier now that it was then."

He looked at Jake. "And I don't want to have to call JP. This isn't anything like what you did when you worked for me. This is front-line stuff. It can be a deadly game and you're going after two very dangerous killers."

"Yes sir, Admiral. I'll keep my head low."

"One more thing and this is of the utmost importance. The IRA ceasefire and peace in Northern Ireland are very important to the President. He wants the sanctity of the New Northern Ireland Assembly protected at all costs."

Bentley closed the folders in front of him.

"We can't afford a public display. This is to be covert and quiet. Get in, confirm what you say is correct and then get out. Report in ASAP. I'll have our janitors sanitize the place before O'Rourke even shows up."

Jake nodded. "Yes sir. Discretion is the word."

Bentley stood up and shook hands with Jake and Kaplan. "Isabella is a very competent operative, you can trust her with your life."

"Yes sir," Jake and Kaplan replied in unison.

Bentley held the door open as the three walked out of his office. "Good luck."

Once they were through the door, Fontaine closed it and turned to Bentley, "Do you think they can pull this off?"

"I sure as hell hope so—or this will be the biggest pile of horse-shit I've ever stepped into."

CHAPTER 62

At the late hour, the Stormont Parliament Building was usually empty except for the cleaning crews, but on this night there were occupants in the office of the Secretary of State of Northern Ireland.

"How long before O'Rourke surfaces?" the Secretary asked.

The Commander stood at his usual place by the window looking down at the two rows of street lights leading up to the Stormont Parliament Building. The night air was clear and cold. An occasional automobile headlight shone in the distance to the south passing by the guarded entrance at Upper Newtownards Road, one mile down Prince of Wales Avenue. The ancient walls of Stormont Castle were lit up by several massive floodlights dominating the view to the southeast of the Parliament Building.

In 1858 local architect Thomas Turner was commissioned by the Cleland family to revise and remodel an existing dwelling into a castle. This flamboyant castle later served as the Belfast headquarters of the Secretary of State of Northern Ireland. The Stormont Estate also housed the Stormont Parliament Building, opened in 1932 by Edward, Prince of Wales. The original architectural plans were to resemble the United States Capitol in Washington. Those plans were scrapped after the 1929 stock market crash and a smaller dome-less version was erected.

"It should be a couple more days. He couldn't possibly escape the United States authorities and get all the way here undetected in such a short period of time." The Commander turned from the window.

"I hope you are right—he could ruin everything we have worked for for so many years."

"I have taken extra precautions. I have increased the guards and hired an asset on the outside to take care of O'Rourke when he shows up again."

"I hope he's better than Shamrock. He failed us *and* took our money."

"Shamrock is out of business. His reputation is now damaged beyond repair. No one will hire him again. Our asset was overjoyed when I mentioned the elimination of Shamrock after he finishes with O'Rourke."

*   *   *

The Persian's Blackberry announced the arrival of another message on the Iranian singles web site. He logged in and retrieved his message. It instructed him to fly to Dublin, Ireland, and check into the Clarion Hotel at the Dublin Airport. He was to wait for further instructions. The message was signed by Laurence O'Rourke.

The Persian considered his alternatives and opted to follow the instructions. The payoff would certainly be worth the risk. Besides he was a careful man, and a ruthless businessman—the odds were in his favor.

CHAPTER 63

O'Rourke drove by the Prince of Wales entrance to Stormont Estate in his stolen car. He noticed the increased security measures, extra guards posted at each entrance and extra security guards patrolling the grounds.

He knew a way into the estate that would keep him clear of the guards. His only concern was whether the Commander would also remember and post guards, or worse, cut off the access altogether.

He turned north off Upper Newtownards Road onto Stoney Road, the eastern boundary of Stormont. As he drove, he noticed to his right that a thin layer of fog had settled onto the fairways of the darkened Knock Golf Club. He drove past the Stoney Road entrance to Stormont Estate, where he noticed an increase in security as well.

He continued north, circling east around the golf course until he found a suitable place to hide the car. It had been many years since he had been to Stormont and the landscape had changed, but he was hopeful the location would still be available for his covert entry onto the grounds.

He wore all black clothing to help conceal his movement across Stormont property. Soon he located the drainage ditch from the Knock Golf Club. The drainage ditch caught the runoff of rain and irrigation from the golf course and routed it through a four-foot diameter drain pipe that ran under Stoney Road through the Stormont Estate property, then north off the back of the estate property. The only security measure previously left in place was a removable grate on the golf club side that was used to catch debris.

The runoff ditch made a fifty-foot pass under the security fence. This was O'Rourke's access to the estate.

Wading in nearly eight inches of water and debris, he slowly moved the rusty grate away from the pipe opening, allowing the debris to float through. He wore black assault boots designed for waterborne operations. Their ventilated quick-dry capabilities would allow him to move quietly across the yard.

He ducked down low and into the pipe, pulling the grate closed behind him. He pushed his way through the forty-foot pipe. Rats scurried about, disturbed by his intrusion into their habitat.

Reaching the other end of the pipe, he encountered a new obstacle—a section of chain-link fence over the opening. Rats squeezed through the openings in the fence. He felt along the fence, and then gave it a push. The flexible fence gave at the bottom and with another hard push it started to pull loose from the sides. He pushed harder and the fence gave way, creating a gap large enough for him to squeeze through.

Hunched over in the ditch, he traversed forty yards before climbing out at the tree line. He remained in the forested parts of the grounds, moving swiftly yet quietly around the eastern side of the castle. Then he headed north through the woods, arriving at the large parking lot east of the Parliament Building, exactly where he planned to make his initial approach to the building.

Crouched in the bushes, O'Rourke studied the building. He could detect cleaning crews moving from room to room, turning on the lights when they entered, turning off the lights when they left. He noticed lights that stayed on in one room on the third floor.

The two shadows moving around the room were not those of the cleaning team. One shadow appeared to pace back and forth across the room, while the larger shadow stood at the window that looked out over the lawns. His memory told him this room was his target destination, the office of the Secretary of State.

He circled the perimeter of the parking lot until he reached the Portland stone sarcophagus of Sir James Craig, also known as Lord Craigavon, who had served as the first Prime Minister of Northern Ireland from 1921 until his death in 1940.

O'Rourke used the griselinia hedge surrounding the sarcophagus as cover while he worked his way toward the east side of the Parliament Building.

When he reached the building he encountered his greatest obstacle—floodlights. Thousands of watts of bright light flooded down from the heights of the building, illuminating the proximity as if daylight were upon him. He crawled to the edge of the parking lot immediately adjacent to the building, and then made a dash for the rear service entrance where he knew he could slip into the building undetected.

CHAPTER 64

Jake leaned forward and removed the aircraft emergency booklet from the pouch next to his seat, looked at it, then laughed.

He jabbed Kaplan on the shoulder, held the booklet in front of him and said, "Small world, isn't it? Kind of ironic that this whole thing started with the same type aircraft we're sitting in, a Challenger 600."

Kaplan laughed. "I just hope it's not an omen."

The CIA jet aircraft had picked up Jake, Kaplan and Hunt at Dulles International Airport with a destination of Sligo Airport in Strandhill, Ireland.

Neither Strandhill nor Sligo was to be their ultimate destination, but rather a town east of Sligo called Dromahair, a town, according to CIA and SIS surveillance records, Laurence O'Rourke visited numerous times over the course of the last twenty years.

"According to my research," Jake said. "Land records showed several properties in County Leitrim owned by O'Rourke, including a well maintained homestead on the outskirts of town, a place where O'Rourke visits and disappears from sight for days at a time. The O'Rourke family also holds claim to a heritage entitlement to the historic site of The O'Rourke Banqueting Hall, directly adjacent to the ruins of the old O'Rourke Castle."

Jake pulled out another folder and opened it up for Kaplan to see. "According to the CIA records, Dromahair, or Droim Ath Thair, was a historical stronghold for the O'Rourke clan from the late 8th century until the 17th century. The O'Rourkes built the Dromahair Castle and the Creevelea Abbey, which served as the 16th century O'Rourke family chapel.

The O'Rourke Banqueting Hall was built and enlarged during the 10th and 11th centuries and formed a fortified complex. The family's feasts at the banqueting hall became legendary throughout the region. The hall has supposedly remained undisturbed for over the last three hundred years."

Jake opened another folder. "Records of British Secret Intelligence Service, SIS, or MI6 as it is sometimes called, indicated numerous appearances in Dromahair by O'Rourke during and since his appointment as Quartermaster General of the IRA. The purpose of these visits isn't known."

When the news broke of Laurence O'Rourke's alleged association with the British government and the suspicions of his spying on the IRA, his affiliation with Sinn Fein was terminated, and the IRA hired assassins with orders to kill O'Rourke in a "messy and public" manner. An example needed to be made.

Jake saw Kaplan looked bored. "Are you getting this or did I lose you along the way?"

Kaplan smiled. I don't know, Jake. That's a lot to take in. You sound like my 9th grade history teacher…boring. Is this shit really important?"

"This shit should be important to you. You might have to improvise in the field and having full background information will help you make better decisions. I always made sure I gave the Navy Seals a thorough briefing before each mission."

"I knew you worked for Bentley, is this what you did?"

"Sometimes. When I worked for Bentley I mainly did research and wrote reports for him. He'd brief the Joint Chiefs and the President. Before Bentley though I worked in the field and briefed face to face on occasion."

Kaplan sighed. "Okay, go on."

"According to SIS records, O'Rourke had been recruited as a spy by a man known as the Commander. He's not a commander at all but rather a behavioral psychiatrist, who once worked for British Intelligence as a handler for British operatives. O'Rourke had shown much promise but proved to be the Commander's ultimate failure. The Commander now works in Belfast for the Northern Ireland Secretary of State, who just also happens to be a former director of British Secret Intelligence and had been the director when O'Rourke was recruited by the Commander."

"Now isn't that coincidental?" Kaplan said.

"O'Rourke's objectives as specified by SIS were unclear, but it is believed that he went rogue. Since he became such a high-ranking public figure, SIS had left him alone until he announced he had earth-shattering news that would bring the New Northern Ireland Assembly to its knees. That announcement was made six days ago. Right before the attempt on his life in Savannah—"

Kaplan interrupted. "Something we now know had nothing to do with O'Rourke's plan to undermine the Assembly."

"Exactly."

Jake reclined in his leather seat and closed his eyes. His wounds were healing. It'd only been four days since the shootout but with the marvels of modern medicine, and the help of a CIA physician, his shoulder only ached. His side was tender to the touch but not really painful. Otherwise, only mental and emotional scars remained from the St. Patrick's Day mayhem.

The drain of the last few days caught up with him fast. Within minutes he was asleep, the aircraft emergency booklet still in his hand.

CHAPTER 65

O'Rourke entered the Parliament Building through a rear service entrance after timing the rounds of security guards. He knew where he was going, he had done this before—many times.

The five chandeliers in the Great Hall had been turned off for the night. One large chandelier, made from cast iron and gilded in twenty-four-karat gold was accompanied by four smaller replicas. Without the illumination from the chandeliers, the walnut, cream and golden Italian marble floor lost most of its luster and charm.

He climbed the east stairwell behind the Senate Chamber to the third floor. He opened the door slightly to peer out. He heard voices and saw some of the cleaning crew waxing the floors. When the cleaners were out of sight, O'Rourke darted across the hall into a utility closet, where he found coveralls matching those worn by the maintenance personnel. He also found something extra, the third-floor electrical circuit box.

O'Rourke knew the element of surprise would work in his favor, giving him a clear upper hand.

He had arrived back in Ireland faster than anticipated. He'd driven all night from Savannah to Hartford, Connecticut, where he stopped to rest, paying for a five-hour day-stay at a small motel. He had proceeded on to his source—an ally from earlier days—in Quebec City, Quebec, Canada, where he'd boarded a twin-engine turboprop owned by his ally and equipped with long-range fuel cells for the trans-Atlantic flight.

The Beechcraft King Air 350 had landed at Ronaldsway Airport just outside of Castletown on the Isle of Man, a territory of the United Kingdom located in the Irish Sea halfway between England and

Ireland. After clearing Customs with the fake identification supplied to him by his source, O'Rourke had hopped a train to Douglas where he boarded the afternoon steam packet ferry to Belfast.

There, under the cover of darkness, he had hailed a taxi to take him to the Belfast Airport. When he found a suitable, nondescript vehicle in the long-term parking lot, he broke into it, hotwired it, and drove to Stormont Estate.

He cracked open the door to the utility closet, dressed in coveralls and carrying a toolbox, he scanned the hallway. Nobody. He noticed the stairwell door across the hall slowly opening and pulled the closet door shut leaving only a tiny crack.

He stood in the dark closet staring through the thin slit of light from the crack in the door. He spotted a man, dressed in black, carrying a silenced pistol. O'Rourke couldn't tell what type but it really didn't matter.

He didn't recognize the man but he knew who he was. An assassin paid to kill him.

*   *   *

The man in black entered the room, and both the Commander and the Secretary of State jumped in unison.

The Commander's face furrowed in irritation. "What the hell are you doing here?"

The man said nothing, just looked around the room.

"Who is this man?" the Secretary asked.

"This is the asset we hired to take care of O'Rourke and Collins."

"What's he doing here? He can't be seen here. We have too much to lose."

The Commander looked into the intruder's eyes. "Like I said, what are you doing here?"

The man moved to the window and parted the sheers with his silencer. "He's here. He's in the building."

"What? Who's here? O'Rourke?" the Secretary shouted.

"Where is he now?" The Commander's voice rose.

"He's on this floor. I followed him into the building and up the stairwell," said the man in black. "He's here somewhere. I came in here because he will be here soon."

The Commander walked over to the coat rack and rifled through his coat pockets. He pulled out a small pistol and tucked it inside the back of his waistband.

"Well, I guess we better get ready for him then before he—"

The room went dark.

The exterior floodlights of the Parliament Building left the room with just enough light to see shapes and figures against the stark white walls.

"What happened?" yelled the Secretary.

The man in black said, "It's him. He's cut the power, but only to this floor. See, the outside lights are still on."

The Commander lifted the phone off the hook. "Phones are dead as well."

The Secretary raised his voice. "What are we going to do?"

The Commander and the man in black said in unison, "We wait."

*   *   *

O'Rourke watched the man in black go into the Secretary's office. He had to take action and he knew he had to do it quickly. He couldn't afford to allow the three men time to formulate a plan.

He decided to smoke out the rats. He saw a one-liter can of acetone in the closet. The irritant and flammable properties of the acetone made it his best option. He grabbed the can from the closet, removed the screw-on cap and stuffed a rag into the spout. The rag quickly absorbed the acetone. He could feel the vapors burning his nostrils.

He moved down the darkened hallway to the Secretary's door. He knew his next few moves were critical, life or death moves.

His own life or death.

He lit the rag with a lighter, then kicked open the Secretary's office door and threw the acetone fire bomb inside. The can ricocheted off the wall sending a plume of flame against the wall and across the floor. The sheers on the windows went up in a blaze.

He had only a few seconds left now. The smoke would soon activate the fire alarms and the Parliament Building would be swarming with responders, cutting off any chance he had for escape.

He caught his first break. He could hear the Secretary shouting for someone to extinguish the fire. The first movement he saw through the doorway was that of the man in black. The man moved toward the flaming sheers as O'Rourke came through the doorway.

Before the man could turn around, O'Rourke fired three shots into his chest. The man fell backwards, his arms extended up in the air from the impacts to his chest. His silenced pistol flew out of his hand and slid across the floor, landing only a foot from O'Rourke's feet. The man fell to the floor only three feet from the flames.

O'Rourke quickly moved into the room, pointing his weapon toward the only place the Commander and Secretary could be. His swiftness caught them off guard and they watched in fear as the man in black died.

Flames spread quickly casting an amber glow in the office. When the two men looked up, O'Rourke stood with his gun aimed in their direction. The Secretary threw up his hands to surrender. The Commander didn't.

The Commander and O'Rourke stared each other in the eyes.

O'Rourke leaned down to pick up the hit man's gun without breaking his eye lock with the Commander. The Secretary lowered his arms and reached toward his desk drawer. O'Rourke raised the hit man's gun and fired a bullet dead center into the Secretary's forehead. A faint shadow flew from the back of the Secretary's head as his body fell to the floor.

The room filled with smoke and O'Rourke knew his time was running out. The Commander shouted, "Laurence, that's enough. Put the weapon down. That is an order."

O'Rourke laughed. "I don't take orders from you anymore, old man."

"Look, I can still salvage this. I'll tell them the asset shot the Secretary. You can just leave. Leave now while you have a chance."

"What?" O'Rourke chided, "Are you afraid of dying?"

"It doesn't have to end this way," the Commander said. "We can come to an arrangement."

"Sorry, there will be no arrangements. I will discredit Sinn Fein. I will discredit your dead Secretary. I owe you nothing. You did nothing but use me to do your dirty work, then left me hanging when your ill-conceived plans backfired. Because of you, I have no safe place to go.

"Fortunately though," O'Rourke continued, "I planned ahead. I have enough documentation to bring down the entire New Northern Ireland Assembly. I have proof of all the lies. All your lies."

O'Rourke motioned to the lifeless Secretary of State with his pistol. "All his lies."

O'Rourke smiled for the first time. "I'm going to expose everything, then I'm going to disappear forever. I have the money to live the life I deserve. I'm going someplace out of the reach of the SIS, the CIA, and everyone else."

The fire alarm sounded, interrupting his diatribe. O'Rourke raised the hit man's pistol and fired twice. The first bullet struck the Commander in the chest. The second shot hit him in the right temple. He was dead before he hit the floor.

CHAPTER 66

Jake dreamt of Beth. The last few days rolled over and over in his unconscious mind. She lay in his blood-soaked arms. The yellow shirt stained with her blood. She was dying. Then the faces appeared. O'Rourke. Collins. McGill—eyes open but dead. Then he heard Sullivan talking to them from the darkness of their room at the Savannah Westin. He had no head.

He felt himself shaking. A woman was calling his name, a soft unfamiliar voice.

"Jake, wake up. Jake, Jake, wake up."

He opened his eyes. Isabella Hunt's large hazel eyes met his. They looked like Beth's eyes. She gave him a warm smile.

"You were having a bad dream," she whispered.

"I wish it was a bad dream. Unfortunately it was real," he replied. He looked at Kaplan's empty seat and asked, "Where's Gregg?"

"He's in the back. He couldn't sleep so he went back and laid out the maps and files on the table. He's been going over them for hours."

He turned around and saw Kaplan studying the information he gave him at CIA Headquarters.

"We just received word from SIS in London," said Isabella. "They spotted O'Rourke in Belfast. An operative followed him to Stormont. He lost him but found where O'Rourke hid his car. He'll wait for O'Rourke to return, then follow him.

"They read your dossier. Bentley faxed it to SIS on a scrambled fax line. They believe your assessment is correct and will have an SIS operative meet us in Sligo. Langley said the SIS is, and I quote, 'at our disposal.'"

"How long before we get there?" he asked.

"The pilot said we're less than two hours out. We caught a nice tailwind in the jet stream and are making good time."

Hunt had been with the CIA Clandestine Service for seven years. She started as an analyst and moved up quickly when she got a break on a case she had researched. A female operative on the mission was injured. Due to time constraints, Hunt was allowed to go undercover as her replacement. She won a commendation from her superiors and was recruited as a full-time operative.

The thirty-five-year-old daughter of an interracial marriage, she was fluent in several languages. She had an athletic build, with firm, muscular arms and legs, a result of her years on a swimming scholarship at Amherst College in Amherst, Massachusetts.

Her physical appearance, along with her language skills, made her versatile in mission assignments. Her dark complexion and black hair had allowed her to blend in with the locals on missions in Central and South America, as well as Egypt and the Middle East. Her hazel eyes were easily concealed with brown contacts. She had been credited with seven kills, all flawlessly executed and four "extractions." Extraction being a politically correct way of referring to abduction, kidnapping, whatever term one wanted to use.

He unbuckled his seat belt and said, "I'm going to talk to Gregg."

Hunt smiled at him and said, "Okay, I'll be there in a minute. I need to make a call to Langley first."

"You know, behind that gruff exterior is a likable Isabella—just waiting to get out."

"Yeah? Well, don't get used to it."

He walked toward the back of the jet. He noticed Kaplan staring at something in his hands. As he got closer he noticed it was the gold cross Annie had been wearing around her neck the day she died.

"Gregg, are you okay?"

"Oh yeah, I'm fine." Kaplan quickly put the cross in his shirt pocket.

"I know it must be hard losing Annie. I don't know what I'd do if Beth died."

"Jake, you can't lose something you never had. Obviously, I didn't know her at all."

"Gregg, you once told me you were a good listener. Well, I think I'm a damn good listener too, if you want to talk about it."

*   *   *

Kaplan surprised himself as he began to tell Jake about his past. There was something about the young investigator that he liked. Maybe it was because, despite his privileged upbringing, he remained humble. Maybe it was because Jake didn't want to ride on his father's coattails and worked hard to prove himself. Or maybe it was because Jake was one of the few honest people he'd ever met—honest to a fault.

Hunt sat down across from Jake and Kaplan. She pulled out the folder Jake had made for her and held it up. "Why don't you go over this with us now and how you came up with it?"

"When Kaplan and I were in Savannah, the day Beth was shot," Jake paused, then went on, "Collins asked about some location and O'Rourke mentioned 'the ridge of two demons.' Well, that's the name of the town called Dromahair. It means Ridge of Two Demons and O'Rourke owns property there. In fact, the O'Rourke clan has owned property there for centuries."

"Yeah, I got that much in the briefing at Langley," Hunt said. "They also said that every time O'Rourke was stopped, both coming and going, he was clean. Maybe he was just going home to visit family or something."

"Okay, follow me here with a little history and some folklore or legend about the O'Rourke clan and the Friary at the Abbey of Creevelea."

Hunt nodded and leaned forward to look at the files while Jake talked.

Kaplan listened.

After thirty minutes and several interruptions from Hunt, Jake finished and asked, "Any questions?"

"Yeah, two. Number one, how accurate is this history?" asked Isabella.

"Fair question," Jake said. "As with older history, there will be minor variations in dates and names and beliefs among historians. For the most part, though, it is all historically accurate."

"What about the folklore?" she asked.

"It's really more like mythical folklore or urban legend. Folklore gets started somewhere, and usually, probably most of the time, there is an element of truth to it. Stories or rumors handed down over time. Undocumented, word-of-mouth-only secrets that have been handed down from generation to generation.

"But somewhere along the line in that hand-me-down chain, someone leaks the secret outside the privileged circle. Sometimes it is pure fiction, never happened, never existed. But other times, historical facts lead to the plausibility of the myth or legend. Did that clear it up for you?"

"Oh yeah, clear as mud, Jake." Hunt smiled.

"I have another question."

"Another one?" Jake asked. "Go ahead, ask away."

"Okay, last question, for now." she said. "How the hell did you come up with an Al Qaeda connection?"

CHAPTER 67

Collins watched O'Rourke run through the darkness of the Stormont Estate back to the car he had hidden on Stoney Road. Flames burst from the third-story windows along the front of the Parliament Building. What he couldn't see nor did he care about were the dozens of people responding to the fire. Guards, janitors, firemen—all running through the Stormont grounds. Fire trucks rushed up Prince of Wales Boulevard toward the Parliament Building and would find a gruesome scene.

The scene would eventually be reported as the assassination of the Secretary of State of Northern Ireland. The news would also state that the assassin, mortally wounded by the Secretary's assistant, had fatally shot the man known as the Commander, and then died, lying in a puddle of his own blood.

Standing in the shadows beside the estate, Collins noticed someone.

Someone else was watching O'Rourke.

He had been in this business long enough to realize that this new stranger was either an assassin or, more likely, an MI6 operative tasked to follow O'Rourke to his ultimate destination. Either way, the threat had to be neutralized.

Collins's journey to Belfast was fast, thanks to his client having flown out to the trawler in a Bell 427 helicopter equipped with long-range tanks. After refueling, the client flew him to his villa in La Coruña, in the northwest corner of Spain.

The client refueled the Bell helicopter and flew him to Wexford, Ireland. There, he arranged a car for Collins and a substantial sum of cash. He then sent Collins on his way, calling the score settled and severing their relationship.

Collins was now a tainted commodity.

He watched O'Rourke get into the car, turn around and head back down Stoney Road toward Upper Newtownards Road. He saw the man in the other car turn around with his headlights off and follow O'Rourke down Stoney Road.

Collins, in turn, drove slowly along Stoney Road in the cover of darkness, waiting for the right opportunity to eliminate the intruder.

He pulled out his Blackberry, checked for new messages. The tone of the new messages was the same as those he had received before he left the United States.

Angry and threatening.

He had to make it right. He had to capture O'Rourke and discover his secret, then kill him. Then he would have fulfilled all of his contracts. He knew his future business had been all but destroyed by Jake Pendleton's interference. A debt he promised himself to repay later.

While he drove, tailing the stranger and O'Rourke, he typed in message after message on his Blackberry. Inquiries for information along with reassurances to others were the bulk of his messages.

He received a reply from his message to his Provisional IRA contact.

Contract on O'Rourke withdrawn.

* * *

Dozens of cars sped westward on the M1 expressway leaving the lights of Belfast behind.

O'Rourke was unaware he was being followed but knew he had to be mindful about his trip to Dromahair. He couldn't arouse any suspicions, he couldn't afford to be stopped. Normally a much shorter trip, the one-hundred-seventy-six-kilometer drive would take him over three hours. The media reports had made him too easily recognized—plastering his picture across every television screen and

'ound the globe. He had seen the newscasts, he knew he
l man. He could no longer travel in anonymity.

... .t concerned with the headlights behind him. There were
too many cars on the expressway. A tail would be nearly impossible
to detect.

The M1 expressway ended at Dungannon, turning into the A4
highway. The number of cars on the highway had thinned down
considerably on this rural section at the late hour. The rolling grassy
hills with their ancient stone walls were hidden from view by the
cover of darkness. He noticed several cars behind him, some turned
off the highway, some turned onto the highway.

Two cars turned off the A4 in Augher, but three more joined up
at Clogher. All the cars on the A4 looked the same, headlights behind
him and taillights in front of him.

His first stop was Enniskillen, County Fermanagh, to make sure
he wasn't tailed and to conduct some business. He pulled out his cell
phone, checked for service, then placed a call.

He left the A4 in Enniskillen and navigated his way to High
Street. His destination was the Demon's Lair Bar and Bistro. He
parked across the street which was about a hundred feet away from
the bar. Cars moved up and down the street. Several patrons stood
in the doorway smoking, drinking and laughing. The muffled sound
of a band could be heard from the back of the bar.

He got out of the car, put on his overcoat and cap, flipped up the
collar, and walked in the front door. The dim lighting and his tweed
cap helped him conceal his identity, not that any of the revelers were
on the lookout for Laurence O'Rourke.

It was very late and the crowd had thinned to nothing but the
hard-core drinkers. A heavy haze of cigarette smoke, thick enough to
permeate clothing and skin, hung in the air. The band in the back bar
announced the last call for drinks.

He looked at the bartender and motioned to him with a slight
nod of the head. The bartender gave him a similar nod and O'Rourke
moved nonchalantly up to the balcony. Five minutes later the

bartender walked up with a pint of Irish ale in each hand. He handed one to O'Rourke, then sat down and sipped on the other.

*   *   *

Collins drove down High Street, spotting both O'Rourke's car and the car of the man who had followed O'Rourke. The man sat in the dark gray Saab 9-5 sedan waiting for O'Rourke to return from the bar.

Collins parked a block away and walked back toward the unmarked Saab. Whoever the man was, he was a potential threat. One he had to eliminate. *He* needed to get to O'Rourke first.

The stranger had parked in the dark shadows in an attempt to conceal his presence. The car was parked too close to the bar for Collins to use his gun, the flash would attract unwanted attention. He devised an alternative plan. One he had successfully used before.

Three years earlier, in Germany, Shamrock was contracted to kill a drug dealer on the outskirts of Berlin. The man had three bodyguards, two escorting him inside an office and one outside waiting in the vehicle. The mark had gone into a bookkeeper's office. It was late one winter afternoon, and Shamrock used the drunkard's ruse to get close to the bodyguards without raising suspicion. The ruse worked because he was seen as a drunken annoyance and not as a threat. It worked so well, gaining close access to the bodyguard in the vehicle that he used it to access the office where he pulled two silenced automatic pistols and shot the two remaining bodyguards, the mark and the bookkeeper.

Down the street from the Demon's Lair pub, he pulled out a cigarette, pantomimed looking for a lighter, then staggered along the sidewalk pretending to be drunk, singing an Irish drinking song.

He continued singing as he approached the bar. The few revelers standing in the doorway looked toward his approaching shadow. He threw his hands up at them, enticing them to join in the song. They sang in unison.

The revelers' voices were trailing away when he staggered onto the slate gray Saab. He leaned against the sedan as if he was too drunk to go any further. Then he tapped on the driver's window.

The driver, a tall bald man, lowered his window and pushed Collins away from the car.

"Okay, pal, get away from my car. Move along," he yelled.

Collins leaned in close, held out his cigarette and slurred, "Do you have a light?"

"No, I don't smoke. Now get away—"

Before the man in the Saab could react, Collins reached into the window, placed his hands on each side of the man's head and continued singing.

As the man protested, Collins jerked the man's head hard to the right. The man fell limp in his seat.

Collins felt a twinge shoot through his left shoulder. He put his hands on the man's neck and felt for a pulse on the carotid artery. Nothing. He propped the man back up in his seat.

He reached into the dead man's pocket and retrieved his wallet and identification. He located the man's pistol, slipped it into his pocket and then he staggered back the way he came, still singing.

Collins walked back to his car and moved it so he could spot O'Rourke as he exited the Demon's Lair. He opened the wallet and looked at the bald man's ID. SIS. He had just killed an SIS operative.

A smile spread across his face. It wasn't the first one he'd killed and likely wouldn't be the last. He pulled the man's pistol from his pocket—a Walther PPK—the James Bond weapon of choice.

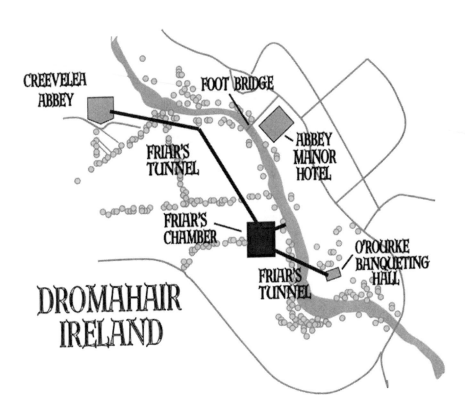

CREEVELEA
ABBEY

FOOT BRIDGE

ABBEY
MANOR
HOTEL

FRIAR'S
TUNNEL

FRIAR'S
CHAMBER

O'ROURKE
BANQUETING
HALL

FRIAR'S
TUNNEL

DROMAHAIR
IRELAND

CHAPTER 68

The CIA jet descended from forty-one thousand feet into the Sligo Airport at Strandhill, Ireland. The Challenger lined up for a straight-in approach to Runway 11.

The jet touched down just before four a.m. local time, and taxied to a section of the ramp where a car was waiting for them. The only sign of life at that time of morning in Sligo.

The night sky was clear and dark and the air was cold and biting. No hint of dawn. The only sounds were those of the turbine engines winding down to a stop, crackling in the cold air as they cooled.

Hunt, Kaplan and Jake stepped from the aircraft stairs to the tarmac and were greeted by a man with a strong British accent, who flashed his credentials. "Matthew Sterling, SIS."

He looked at Hunt. "You must be Isabella Hunt." Throwing a quick glance at Jake and then Kaplan, he said, "And one of you must be Jake Pendleton."

Jake stepped forward and stuck out his hand. "I'm Jake."

Hunt immediately took the lead. "Let's get started, we're running out of time. Did you get the headsets I asked for?"

Sterling nodded. "All business, I see."

"Always. That way she won't forget she's in charge," Jake jabbed.

Kaplan stuck out his hand. "She has no manners either. I'm Gregg Kaplan."

The three men laughed.

She ignored them. "What about O'Rourke—any more word on him yet?"

Sterling looked from Jake to Hunt and said, "We spotted him at Stormont last night, our operative followed him to Enniskillen where our guy last reported in. We haven't heard from him since and that's been over an hour."

"We're cutting this one closer than I thought," Jake said. "I really didn't think he could get here that fast."

"So much for in and out before he arrives, huh, Einstein?" Kaplan laughed.

Sterling paused and gave Hunt a grim look.

She said, "And what?"

"There was a fire at the Stormont Parliament Building a few hours ago, about the same time O'Rourke was there. We found the Secretary of State, his assistant, along with another man, shot to death. It was made to look like an assassin shot the Secretary and his assistant and then was shot by the assistant in the melee. We think O'Rourke probably killed them all and staged the room before setting it on fire."

Jake interrupted, "The body bag count just went up again. In a week and a half, O'Rourke has managed to be involved with what, fourteen deaths that we know of?"

"That we know of," she said.

"I say it's time for *Operation Elimination*." Kaplan said.

Hunt said, "Alive, Kaplan—not dead or alive."

"I'm just saying. People are dying and I don't plan on being a statistic for his body count."

"Remember the rules of engagement. Bentley was clear about that," she said.

Sterling motioned toward the car. "The radios you asked for are in the car. We'll ready them on our way to Dromahair. I suggest we get moving. O'Rourke could feasibly be there by now."

Before they left Washington, Jake, Hunt and Kaplan had been outfitted with operative mission gear. They wore all black clothing, cargo-style pants and shirts made by Blackhawk with the new Integrated Tourniquet System, black assault boots with molded insoles, armored vests, flashlights, penlights, and strap-on headlamps.

The mission was planned to be a covert extraction of Laurence O'Rourke and removal of whatever contents the secret location held.

Upon his capture, O'Rourke's transfer to London would be by CIA jet. The need for a quiet withdrawal was deemed appropriate by SIS and the CIA.

Hunt, Jake and Kaplan had been issued Sig Sauer P226 Tactical 9mm pistols, each with three, fifteen-round clips and equipped with a threaded screw-on silencer. Sterling was armed with the stereotypical MI6 silenced Walther PPK.

When they arrived at Dromahair, they parked across the street from the locked gates to the ruins of the O'Rourke Banqueting Hall and killed the lights to the car. A gray Fiat rental was parked across the street and appeared to be empty in the dark street. Sterling used night vision goggles to detect any movement. There was none. It was approaching five a.m. and still no sign of dawn.

His adrenaline flowed fueling his nervous energy. Jake leaned forward toward Sterling. "Take us over to the abbey and let us start scouting around while you two stay here. Gregg and I know what to do. O'Rourke will show up here first, not the abbey."

"Wait," Kaplan said urgently, keeping his voice low as if he could be heard outside. "We've got company, car lights coming."

The four of them ducked low in their seats trying to hide from the beams of the headlights. As the car approached, it flashed its lights from low beam to high beam twice. The apparently abandoned Fiat across the street flashed its lights on and off.

"Sterling, I thought you said that car was empty?" Hunt said.

"He must have been ducked down. I didn't see anyone in there."

The approaching car slowed and a man jumped out of the parked Fiat and climbed into the arriving car with a backpack in his hand. The car moved slowly by the gates to the banqueting hall, then sped off. Taillights could be seen on the Derryvogilla Bridge going over the River Bonet, then out of sight.

"That was him," Jake yelled, now holding the night vision goggles. "I got a good look at him, no mistake about it. That was that son of a bitch O'Rourke. He's here already and there's someone with him—he looked Middle Eastern."

"I don't freakin' believe it. Was it Nasiri?" she asked.

"I couldn't tell for sure, O'Rourke's head blocked some of my view. He was definitely Middle Eastern though."

"Farid Nasiri? The Al Qaeda arms dealer?" Sterling asked. "What would *he* be doing *here*?"

"I'll tell you in a minute." Hunt turned around and peered over the seat of the car at Jake. "Bentley was right about you. You are good."

"One other thing though," Jake said. "He's knows we're here. He looked right at us. Whoever it was in that car must have told O'Rourke about our arrival. We have to assume they know we're onto them. We should reassess our planned operation."

"You're probably right, Jake. Now we have to improvise. Quick change of plans," she said.

"Jake, you and Kaplan check out the banqueting hall and Sterling and I will follow O'Rourke and Nasiri. You know what to look for, you're the one who told me. Just keep listening to the radio and stay out of sight. Sterling and I will handle O'Rourke and company."

Before she could finish, Jake and Kaplan jumped out of the car and raced for the gate to the ruins. By the time Sterling turned the car around to follow O'Rourke, they had disappeared over the high stone wall and into the ruins of the O'Rourke Banqueting Hall.

"We're in," Kaplan said. "I'm in anyway. Navy boy's still stuck on the wall. But I'm sure he'll be along shortly."

"I'm coming, I'm coming." Jake said. "I had to give Kaplan a boost or he'd never have made it over the wall."

Jake's earpiece crackled, then Hunt's voice said, "That was fast. Now you two quit horsing around and find that entrance."

"Yes, ma'am." Jake said. "Be careful—people have a bad habit of dying around O'Rourke and Nasiri,"

Sterling and Hunt drove over the Derryvogilla Bridge using the very faint light of the moon as their only illumination.

* * *

Another car was parked nearby. Its driver watched the game of cat and mouse unfold in front of him. He smiled and chambered a round into his Beretta.

CHAPTER 69

At O'Rourke's insistence, the Persian had shed his traditional Muslim garb for the attire of the Western world. He wore jeans, black t-shirt, a brown leather jacket and black athletic shoes.

The Persian had jumped into O'Rourke's car and quickly informed him of the vehicle with the three people in it. "Ah, the ghost of Laurence O'Rourke, even the Americans are chasing you now."

"You must be the Persian, the one who will make me a very rich man," O'Rourke replied.

"I don't want any trouble with the Americans. Can you lose them?"

"This is my town. I will lose them and we'll be out of sight before they can react. There is no way they could possibly find us after that. What you want is hidden in a very secure place. After you have checked it out and paid me, then you can figure out how to remove it."

The Persian looked over at him and sneered. "Let's hope for your sake nothing goes wrong. You're a very confident man, Laurence O'Rourke, but too much confidence can make a man careless."

O'Rourke caught a quick reflection in his rearview mirror as the other car turned around. The nearly full moon caught the windshield at just the right angle to catch his attention. He watched as a shadow crossed the Derryvogilla Bridge behind him, and he knew he was indeed being followed.

He needed to get to the abbey, but the other vehicle following too closely. He needed more time to get the Persian and himself into the friars' tunnel without revealing the secret entrance from the abbey.

He stopped and turned the car around in a driveway. He knew he could catch his pursuers off guard and get a jump on them into town. He pressed the accelerator and sped back toward town, darting past the Saab, which had already pulled over to the side of the road. O'Rourke raced over the Derryvogilla Bridge and turned onto Main Street.

He sped through town past the Banqueting Hall, and turned into the Abbey Manor Hotel. He pulled into the rear parking lot and parked between two larger cars, concealing the Peugeot from the view of Main Street. He grabbed two items from the back seat—the only items he would need, a flashlight and a gun.

He scanned the parking lot for any signs of movement, motioned to the Persian to follow him, and quickly made his way to the northwest corner of the parking lot where a footbridge would take them over the River Bonet.

They reached the footbridge and he turned on his flashlight and followed the gravel pathway up the hill toward Creevelea Abbey. The eastern sky was waking up as dawn approached. Not a cloud could be seen on the horizon. The ruins of the abbey were barely visible in the pre-dawn light.

Creevelea Abbey, the last Franciscan friary founded in Ireland before the suppression of the monasteries by Henry VIII, was founded by Eoghan O'Rourke and his wife Margaret in 1508. Brian Ballach O'Rourke partially restored the abbey, which was unsuccessfully suppressed again in 1539. The friars retained possession of the abbey for another half-century, despite ongoing threats of suppression.

During the tumultuous decade between 1545 and 1555, the friars had secretly tunneled from the abbey to the O'Rourke Banqueting Hall. They also built a chamber room large enough to house dozens of friars for extended periods of time more than forty feet underground.

Access to the secret room was either through the nearly fifteen-hundred-foot tunnel from the abbey or through a four-hundred-foot tunnel from the banqueting hall. In 1575, the friars built a one-hundred-fifty-foot third tunnel—a small escape tunnel that led to a wooded area on the banks of the river. Its exterior exit was kept covered with stones.

The bond between the O'Rourkes and the friars remained sacred. The existence of the tunnels and the room had been handed down by word of mouth from generation to generation. No one outside the O'Rourke family knew for certain of its existence.

Laurence O'Rourke and Farid Nasiri slipped quietly into the ruins of the abbey. O'Rourke hadn't used the abbey entrance to the tunnel for over thirty years due to its open exposure and relentless pounding of tourists. His usual access had been through the banqueting hall but that was too risky now with the intrusion of the Americans.

The lichen-covered stone walls and archways of the Abbey of Creevelea stood mostly in ruins. The tower still hovered high above the ground. The grassy grounds of the interior courtyard had become a cemetery over the years, now dotted with tombstones and grave markers. Mounds of broken boulders, now overgrown with grass, littered the Abbey landscape.

O'Rourke moved along the main perimeter wall shining his flashlight at each name on the tombstones, searching for the secret access. He stopped at a gravestone bearing a single last name and a family crest. No one was buried under that marker. It was a full-length gravestone engraved with the name "O'Brien" but bearing the O'Rourke escutcheon inlaid in the stone. O'Rourke brushed away the pebbles next to the stone, revealing two narrow three-foot-long stone strips that extended perpendicular to the gravestone.

The stone was designed and built by the friars to conceal the entrance to the tunnel. O'Rourke leaned over the stone, placing his hands firmly on the golden O'Rourke crest. The locking mechanism required a ninety-degree counterclockwise turn followed by a clockwise turn of one-hundred-eighty degrees, the same sequence as the banqueting hall entrance. The crest barely moved.

"What's the matter?" the Persian asked.

"It's just stiff, probably hasn't been used in thirty or forty years. It most likely has some sand and pebbles jamming the mechanism."

He heard a click and the blade of a knife flashed in O'Rourke's face. He jumped back and stared at the Persian.

"My patience is wearing thin," the Persian said. "Here, use this to dig out around the edges of the crest."

O'Rourke took the knife. "Dammit, you scared the devil out of me."

"It will take more than a knife to exorcise you."

O'Rourke smiled and then used the blade to clean around the crest. He leaned onto the headstone again, placing as much of his body weight as he could onto the crest. He turned the crest slowly to the left until he felt it catch, then as quickly as he could back to the right. When the crest reached the right spot they heard a muffled thump. The gravestone moved slowly across the thin stone strips, grinding as it inched across.

Then it stopped. It had opened a space only eight inches wide when it ground to a halt.

O'Rourke moved to the side and pushed on the gravestone. The heavy stone slid ever so slowly onto the narrow perpendicular stone strips. Below him were stone steps leading down into a dark, dank abyss.

"Hurry, we don't have much time. It will be light soon," O'Rourke said, motioning the Persian toward the opening.

Nasiri grabbed his backpack and descended the steep stone steps.

He followed the Persian into the stairwell. A four-inch-diameter stone protruded from the wall of the stairwell. He pushed hard against the protrusion and it slid into the wall. The gravestone slowly slid itself back into place, plunging O'Rourke and the Persian in total darkness.

A beam of light shot forth at the click from O'Rourke's flashlight. "It's a long way from here. Maybe half a kilometer, but it's narrow and cramped and wet—it'll seem more like two."

"Laurence, if this isn't everything you've claimed, you'll never see the light of day again."

CHAPTER 70

Jake and Kaplan scaled the twelve-foot stone wall with relative ease.

They landed hard and fell to the ground next to each other.

A stabbing pain shot through Jake's side. "Ouch, son of a bitch, that hurt."

Kaplan groaned, holding his side. "I know. That hurt me too."

"Not a word to Hunt. Deal? She already thinks we're a liability." Jake grinned.

"Deal. Now lead the way, Navy boy."

Jake heard the sound of Sterling accelerating the car to catch up with O'Rourke. He thought he heard another car drive by slowly.

His research had indicated that the O'Rourke Banqueting Hall, built beside the River Bonet, was believed to be part of a 10th-through 13th-century castle complex. The fortified walls were built from limestone that came from quarries outside of Dromahair, creating a central stronghold surrounded by defensive walls. Walls that were now rubble.

Jake and Kaplan moved slowly through the ruins, looking for any sign of an entrance. Vines of ivy covered most of the remaining structures. Collapsed stones outlined the exterior walls of the main hall.

"Anything yet, Gregg?" Jake asked.

"Not yet. Just a bunch of broken rocks."

"There must be a hidden access panel to a chamber beneath the hall, or all of my research was incorrect and we're on a wild-goose chase." Jake said.

"It wouldn't be the first time I've been on a wild goose chase courtesy of Uncle Sam." Kaplan laughed.

Castles and other structures of that time period were well known to have had secret chambers built below them for storage or as a means of escape in the event of an attack. The remains of the arched doorways still stood on the north and south walls. The other walls, destroyed by time, were piles of rubble.

Jake's headset filled with the voices of Hunt and Sterling.

"Blast, he's turning around," Sterling whispered.

"Pull over. When he passes, let me out. I'll run over to the abbey, you follow O'Rourke and Nasiri. Whatever you do, don't let them get away," Hunt ordered.

She continued, "Jake, are you getting this? The son of a bitch doubled back on us. He may be coming toward you two now."

"Yeah, we got it. The hall is a mess. Almost leveled by time. Just a few stone ruins, mostly piles of rubble. This may take longer than I anticipated. Daylight would help but we might not have that long—"

"There has to be an access of some kind," Sterling said. "We have had visual contact of O'Rourke going into the hall and not coming out. Sometimes for hours, sometimes for a day or two at a time. It's there. Keep looking."

Jake looked at Kaplan. "You go clockwise, I'll go counterclockwise. Holler if you find something."

"Right. I'm looking for a secret passage in a pile of rubble. Should be a piece of cake." Kaplan said.

Jake paced around the ruins scanning every detail, every fallen stone, every opening.

Jake's headset came alive again with Sterling's voice. "I found O'Rourke's car. He's parked at the Abbey Manor Hotel. It looks like they took the footpath up to the abbey. Isabella, are you in position?"

"Yes, I'm in position but I don't see anything yet," she replied.

Jake noticed the largest structures still standing in the banqueting hall were the stone fireplaces. They were also the only structures large enough to conceal an access to a tunnel or chamber below. That was where he and Kaplan concentrated their attention.

"Jake, over here—I think I found what you're looking for."

Jake moved quickly, stepping over boulders and remnants of stone walls until he reached the fireplace where Kaplan stood. "Where?"

Kaplan pointed to the north wall fireplace. Ivy had completely covered the stones. A hidden protrusion had pushed the ivy out at one spot. As he separated the curtain of ivy with his hand he found an inlaid crest six inches below a stone mantle. Kaplan shone his light onto the crest. The gold inlays glistened in the light. "That it?"

"Gotta be. It's a coat of arms inlaid into the chimney."

Jake pushed on the crest.

It moved inward.

Nothing else happened.

Jake grabbed the crest and tried turning it to the right. It turned but without results. Jake then turned the crest to the left. Nothing. He turned the crest further to the left until it stopped, then back to the right until it stopped again.

Still Nothing.

Kaplan moved closer to Jake. "Hurry up, Jake. We're losing precious time here. What's the problem?"

Jake shot Kaplan a look. "If I knew, we'd be in already."

Jake studied the golden crest. "It pushed in but nothing happened and it turned but nothing happened. The range of motion for the crest is ninety degrees to the left and ninety degrees to the right."

"Combine your efforts. Maybe if you pushed it in and turned it at the same time," Kaplan said.

"It's worth a try. Did you learn that from your Special Forces days?"

"Nope, saw it on *National Treasure*."

They both laughed as Jake leaned into the crest, turning it to the left as he pushed. He reached the ninety-degree mark and heard a click. He felt the excitement build inside him but nothing else happened. He looked at Kaplan.

"Turn it back to the right now."

He pushed as he turned it back to the right. All the way to the right. The crest stopped.

They heard a thud followed by the sound of stone grinding on stone. The noise was right in front of them, behind the ivy curtain. They felt the vibration as the stone wall in the fireplace slowly moved open.

"I'll be damned. It worked. I've got to watch more movies." Kaplan said.

"Something worked, let's see."

Jake reached his hand out toward the wall and parted the curtain of ivy with his flashlight.

Kaplan shone his light into the fireplace and they saw an opening in the five-foot-thick stone wall just large enough to crawl inside. The beam lit up the opening, revealing steep stone steps circling straight down into the darkness.

Jake spoke into his headset. "We found it, we found it. The steps lead straight down below the north wall." He gave Hunt the sequence of steps to unlock the entrance. "We're going in."

She whispered, "Roger that. I've got something too. O'Rourke and Nasiri are here. He's hunched over some sort of gravestone or something and pushing. Wait, they're gone. They just disappeared. Just like that. Jake, you and Kaplan wait there for Sterling. I'm going in here. Jake, did you hear me?"

Jake and Kaplan didn't hear Hunt. They were already twenty feet below the banqueting hall, descending the stone steps into the tunnel.

* * *

Collins watched as O'Rourke and the Persian disappeared. Disappeared into some sort of hole in the abbey. Now there was someone else. A small dark figure dressed in black moved toward the exact spot where O'Rourke disappeared.

Earlier, Collins had spotted the tail on O'Rourke and watched as O'Rourke doubled back. When the tail doubled back, he followed the second car to the Abbey Manor Hotel.

Now, he reasoned that someone must have gotten out of the tail car when O'Rourke doubled back, and whoever it was had run the half mile to Creevelea Abbey from the road.

Collins had followed the tail car into the parking lot and watched as a man dressed in black followed O'Rourke and the Persian across the footbridge and up the path toward the abbey. Something was wrong though. The figure he was looking at now was not the same person that followed O'Rourke and the Persian.

The small dark figure shined a flashlight on the gravestone. The backdrop of light from the approaching dawn had brightened the sky just enough for Collins to recognize the figure as that of a woman.

He waited patiently as the woman worked on the stone. She knelt down, then hunched over the stone. Thirty seconds later she disappeared in the same spot as O'Rourke and the Persian had.

Collins knew he had the location. This had to be it. He didn't know what the location held, and he really didn't care. All that was left was to execute the remainder of his contracts. He walked over to where O'Rourke and the woman disappeared and found an opening revealing stone steps leading down into the depths below the abbey.

Collins took out his Blackberry to send his last message, the location of O'Rourke's secret.

No service.

*   *   *

Jake and Kaplan descended into the dingy depths below the O'Rourke Banqueting Hall, their headlamps illuminating the way. The steep steps wound down in a circular fashion, damp and slick with mold. The air—stale and musty.

Jake knocked down several spider webs as he descended.

Hunched over because of the low headroom and sharp turns, the taller Kaplan slipped before reaching the bottom, banging his shin on the stone steps.

They reached a chamber around forty feet below the surface. Stone walls lined the fifteen-foot-square room. It was empty, left vacant for centuries and now the home of rodents and spiders. The only way out, other than the way they came in, was through an arched doorway on the western wall that appeared to lead to another tunnel.

Movement on the floor caught Jake's eye, rats scurried in the damp darkness. Beady little eyes glowed from the beam of the flashlight. A cold chill ran through him. Jake shivered.

"God, I hate rats," Jake said. "We need Hunt. She probably eats them for snacks."

"You don't like her very much, do you Jake?"

"I like her as much as she likes us. It's kind of a toss-up—rats or Hunt. Not much difference as far as I can tell."

Kaplan laughed.

Jake moved through the doorway into the tunnel. It was barely three feet wide and only about six feet high. He unconsciously hunched over as he walked down the narrow tunnel, with Kaplan a few feet behind.

"Hey, squid, are you claustrophobic too?"

"No, I'm not. But thanks for asking."

Their bantering seemed to ease the tension.

They felt the slope in the floor.

"Looks like we're headed downhill?" Jake asked.

"Yeah? What was your first clue? The fact that it's getting sloppier with every step. Be careful."

The stone walls became moist, then wet. They stopped and listened. Standing in roughly an inch of water, they could hear the sound of the River Bonet rushing overhead.

"Do you hear that?" Jake asked.

"I'm not deaf. The river's directly above us."

"How do you think the tunnel survived all these years without caving in?" Jake asked.

"How about you stop giving off negative vibes while we're below it. I didn't bring my water wings."

They pushed on for about another hundred yards, noticing they were walking slightly upgrade. The tunnel opened into a larger space. Using their flashlights, they surveyed the chamber.

Kaplan studied the room. "I guess I expected something a little bigger, Jake."

"Gregg, look." Jake pointed toward the ceiling.

Bare light bulbs were strung from the stone ceiling. As Jake and Kaplan moved farther into the room, they found a table and chair, a radio with wires he guessed ran up to the surface, a small refrigerator and a gas camping stove.

Jake moved his hand to the left. "Look over there—boxes of supplies stacked next to the refrigerator."

Kaplan moved to the side and shone his light behind the refrigerator and supplies. "Hey Jake, back here I got a generator. It looks like it's vented to the outside. And next to it is a large bank of batteries. That explains O'Rourke's extended disappearances. All the comforts of home."

"Yeah, a big rat living with his little buddies."

Next to the table was a file cabinet. Jake walked over and opened the top drawer. He heard Kaplan walk off behind him. The next few minutes he spent rifling through the folders, reading the files as quickly as he could. Absorbing the details. He realized O'Rourke hadn't made a veil threat. He did indeed have documentation that could destroy the New Northern Ireland Assembly.

"Gregg, you're not going to believe this shit. There are several folders, each containing notes and records from secret, unmonitored meetings between Sinn Fein and the Democratic Unionist Party. And look, here's a hit list, an IRA/Ulster hit list, names of individuals from both sides whose existence was considered a deterrence to the peace process and a hindrance to true power-sharing in Northern Ireland."

Jake pulled out the list. His headlamp shone on the files while he read down the list of names. The Ulster list had about forty names. All but four had been lined out. The IRA list had almost twice as many names. Again, all but four were marked out. An asterisk indicated that the lined out names had been eliminated. Several of these names he recognized by the media reports of their deaths.

He noticed that one name on the IRA list without an asterisk was circled in ink—Laurence O'Rourke.

Jake put the folder back and opened the second drawer. In the front of the drawer was an IRA weapons list. He studied it closely, then called for Kaplan, "Gregg, come here and look at this."

Kaplan stepped behind him. "What have you got there?"

"It's a list of the 'official' and 'unofficial' weapons depots for the IRA. The list contains the weapons storage facilities' locations and a detailed listing of the weapons contained in each. Here's a copy of a memorandum issued to the DUP and the Independent Monitoring Commission, the watchdog agency monitoring the Northern Ireland paramilitary groups.

"Look, it lists the locations of only the 'official' weapons storage facilities. It includes a statement declaring that the weapons listed here are all the IRA had in its cache, and that the IRA now considers itself in full compliance with the cease-fire agreement."

Kaplan scanned the list of storage facilities. "Jake, this place isn't on either of those lists, and look at the signature on the bottom of the memorandum—'compiled, authorized and signed by Laurence O'Rourke, Former Quartermaster General, Irish Republican Army.'"

"Okay, I give. Why would this place need to be on here?"

Kaplan started back across the room. "Come here, Jake. I'll show you why."

Jake placed the folder on top of the drawer before turning around. He scanned the large room with his flashlight. Kaplan was standing in a doorway opposite the tunnel entrance shining his flashlight into a black void.

"What is it?"

Jake walked over to Kaplan and aimed his light into the void.

Kaplan said, "I figure it's roughly a hundred fifty feet by two hundred feet."

Jake was dumbfounded. "Holy shit."

To his left was a huge assortment of boxes and crates. Boxes of different sizes and shapes stacked to the ceiling filled the large room. The boxes and crates created a maze of walkways throughout the chamber room.

"Stone columns, evenly spaced. And look at the notches in the walls—just large enough to be bunks for the monks." Jake laughed. "Bunks for monks. That rhymes."

"Idiot. Look up, the ceiling has vents in it too. These monks sure knew what they were doing. You were right, Jake, the Friars' Chamber indeed does exist."

Jake walked over to where Kaplan stood, beside the shortest stack of boxes, about chest high, and read the markings on the side.

50 lbs. SEMTEX

SEMTEX. Plastic explosives. Jake totaled the boxes, three thousand pounds of explosives.

Kaplan said, "I don't really know that much about SEMTEX, but I'd bet this is enough to destroy this entire town."

They stepped to the next stack, seventy wooden crates. Stamped on the side of each crate were the words:

Grenade Launchers
10 Count

Jake and Kaplan separated and hurried around the room, checking the crates and boxes and making a quick mental inventory of what they'd found. In addition to the Semtex and the grenade launchers, they found one hundred forty-two shoulder-launched SAM-7 surface-to-air missiles, four hundred fifty American-made

Barrett .50-caliber rifles, six hundred Armalite M-16A2 rifles, thirteen hundred AK-47 rifles, thirty Browning rifles, nine hundred Belgian FAL rifles, thirteen hundred forty Makarov pistols, twelve hundred fifty Webley .455-caliber service revolvers and nearly two hundred .50 caliber and .30 caliber machine guns.

They gave up counting about halfway through the chamber, noting the crates and boxes of weapons and ammunition were marked as originating from places all over the globe ... the Soviet Union, Libya, Syria, Britain and the United States.

Kaplan looked at Jake. "After just reading the lists of weapons stored at the other facilities, do you realize that this Friar's Chamber contains more weapons and explosives than the entire 'official' and 'unofficial' weapons storage facilities *combined?*"

Jake now understood what O'Rourke's secret was and why so many must be after it. The SIS records of the Persian's arrival in Dublin, Ireland, had thrown up a red flag when Jake did his research. His insight, which was really nothing more than a hunch, about the connection between Laurence O'Rourke, a former Quartermaster General for the IRA, and the Persian, an Al Qaeda arms dealer working directly for Bin Laden, was right on the mark. A hunch he drew only after recalling something O'Rourke said right before Beth was shot ... *I have made a lucrative deal that will allow me financial security for my very long life.*

"Well," Jake said, "this explains the presence of Farid Nasiri with O'Rourke. The ramifications of letting these weapons fall into the hands of Al Qaeda are too great to sit by and wait for the cavalry. We need to find Hunt and Sterling and find them fast. We're going to need more help."

"I think you're right. Let's go find them."

The generator roared to life behind them.

Before they could move, all the lights illuminated in the enormous chamber room.

The first thing Jake and Kaplan saw was Laurence O'Rourke standing only ten feet away with a gun pointed at Jake's head.

CHAPTER 71

"Well, well. What have we here? Mr. Pendleton, we meet again. Seems like I'm always pointing a gun at you."

O'Rourke held the gun steady. The obese Iranian was sweating and winded from the long walk through the tunnel.

"Yeah, yeah. You point your gun, you lose your gun." Jake motioned to Kaplan.

Kaplan started to move.

O'Rourke fired a shot. "Stay where you are. Both of you. I'm rather surprised to see you, of all people, intruding into my private chamber. Who are you really working for? Certainly not the NTSB. No doubt the U.S. Government. But who? CIA? FBI, maybe? Maybe your newly founded Department of Homeland Security? And all this time I thought you were merely a stupid aircraft accident investigator." O'Rourke looked at Kaplan. "And you—you're the redhead's boyfriend, aren't you? What are you doing here?"

"I'm catching up on my Irish history. You know, the kind not found in travel guides," Kaplan said.

"Oh, you Americans, always making lame attempts at humor. Well, your history lesson is over. This time you won't live to haunt me again. First things first, Mr. Pendleton. Take your gun out nice and slow and place it on that crate over there." O'Rourke motioned with his empty hand. "Don't be stupid and try something you'll regret."

Jake removed his weapon and placed it on the wooden crate next to him.

"Very good. Now step away a few steps."

Jake took five steps away from the crate.

"Now you," he motioned to Kaplan. "You do the same."

Kaplan obliged and followed the same routine that Jake just had.

"Now let's go." O'Rourke motioned with his gun.

Jake needed to stall for time—time to allow Hunt and Sterling to find the chamber.

"What is this about?" Jake asked, raising his arm and sweeping it around the room. "What is all this about?"

"You are so naive. This is about power, control, and freedom, among other things. I don't expect you to understand, you're American. This is Ireland. This is about something you could never understand."

"You're wrong. I may be an American but I do understand. I understand that you're a traitor to your own country, to your own people." Jake pointed to Nasiri. "And now you're helping terrorists. You are nothing more than an assassin who would kill his own mother for money. You can't expect to get away with this. You can't expect that no one will come after you."

"No one come after me, are you joking? Pay attention. Everyone is already trying to kill me because I know too much or," O'Rourke waved his gun over the cache, "they want this. Some want to use it, others want to destroy it and pretend it never existed. Either way I can never live in peace again without always looking over my shoulder wondering is today the day somebody gets lucky? Is today the day I die?"

Farid Nasiri walked up and stood next to O'Rourke. O'Rourke waved his gun and said, "But you're right about one thing. This is only about money now. And he has a lot of it—which is going to be mine soon."

Jake felt the rage building inside him. "You better be looking over your shoulder. You shot Beth. I left her in Savannah, struggling for her life."

"An unfortunate accident, I assure you." O'Rourke alternated pointing his gun at Jake and then Kaplan. "I was aiming for your smart-ass friend here."

"You asshole, that unfortunate accident will cost you your life—"

"Except that I'm holding the gun on you," O'Rourke panned the gun back and forth. He looked at Kaplan. "What is your name anyway?"

"Kaplan."

"And why are you here, Mr. Kaplan?"

"To keep Jake company. Why else? He gets lonely when he travels by himself."

"Shut up. I'm growing tired of your humor."

"Who are these Americans?" Nasiri asked. "Kill them and let's get on with our business." Nasiri spat at Kaplan's feet.

Kaplan stared at the overweight man. The Persian stepped back.

"Not yet. They're no threat to us now. They're not armed and we are. Mr. Pendleton doesn't understand how brilliant I am. This has taken many years of careful planning. I'm sure you were briefed that I served as Quartermaster General for the IRA for quite a few years."

Jake's reply was an icy stare.

O'Rourke smiled. "I acquired weapons for the IRA all over the countryside. I even had three stockpiles in Britain. It was safer than trying to transport them. It made strikes against the British on British soil so much easier—"

Kaplan said, "Why weren't all the weapons caches surrendered or even reported?"

"As you Americans like to put it, backup. I…we needed a backup plan in case the cease-fires and the peace agreements fell through. If the IRA surrendered all their weapons and the agreements were broken, we would be defenseless and subject to a slaughter."

"You're talking out of both sides of your mouth," Jake argued. "You said the IRA needed a backup plan but you are a British spy, spying on the same people you are now talking about protecting. You truly have no allegiance, do you?"

"I never wanted to be in the IRA. In my late teens, I wanted peace. I thought the Troubles were nothing more than the senseless slaughtering of our people by our own people, a wasteful civil war, as it were. Peer pressure forced me to try to join the IRA. My first mission backfired and I was arrested.

"That's when I was approached by an SIS handler. While I was in prison, he convinced me that the way to peace was for the IRA to be crippled internally. That the piecemeal army would fold up and just die out. So I went along and infiltrated the IRA. Later, I actually started getting sympathetic to the IRA cause and even sabotaged some of my handler's plans."

Kaplan was silent and his stance looked casual, but Jake could tell by his eyes he was looking for an opportunity. Jake nodded to encourage him to keep talking. *Come on, come on, Isabella,* his mind screamed. *You show up before he blows my brains out, I'll be your friend for life.*

"Finally, my last assignment was to infiltrate Sinn Fein. The British government hates Mairéad Brady and views Sinn Fein as just a puppet of the IRA. They want her out of the picture. She is viewed as nothing more than a terrorist herself, running a terrorist organization," said O'Rourke,

"Once inside, I was supposed to leak information back to my handler that would permanently discredit Sinn Fein and remove Brady from authority or, better yet, find something that would send her to prison. But, sadly, there was nothing."

Jake interrupted, "That's a nice history lesson but that doesn't explain all this. Why keep all this?"

"I already told you, you're American, you won't understand. I am a man with no place to go. The IRA, what's left of them, wanted me dead because I was a spy for the British and they hold me responsible for the deaths of my fellow IRA members. Sinn Fein wants me dead for the same reason. The only difference is the IRA wants this stockpile location so they have access to arms again."

"What do you mean, access to arms again? There are several other weapons storage facilities, your 'unofficial' ones."

O'Rourke glanced at the file cabinets. The top drawer still open. "I see you've done some reading since you got here, so you probably also realize that the other sites are miniscule compared to this one. Sinn Fein wants this stockpile destroyed so they can disavow its existence and the IRA will have lived up to their full disarmament. And, of course, I won't be around to say otherwise. The British government wants me dead because I can publicly implicate them in the sanctioning of the murders of several Brits."

O'Rourke stopped, and then took a few deep breaths.

"First and foremost, Mr. Pendleton, I'm an Irish Catholic. I have arranged a deal with the Provisional IRA for protection in exchange for the evidence I have accumulated against Sinn Fein and the British government. That is to include the factual documentation, which I have in my possession, that, despite both parties' denials, Sinn Fein and the Ulster Defense Association were negotiating behind the scenes on deals that included the deaths of certain, shall we say, notorious figures from each side of the table.

"Besides, the UDA didn't give up any weapons, only made the false claim to disarm *after* the IRA disarmed. So now the IRA has disarmed but not UDA … Something doesn't seem quite right now, does it, Mr. Pendleton?"

"And you're just going to sell all these weapons to Al Qaeda so they can kill innocent men, women and children all over the world?"

"Quite frankly, I don't care what Nasiri does with all this. I say good riddance. I'll be a rich man living a life in seclusion."

From behind O'Rourke came the sweetest words Jake had ever heard. "Not if I have anything to say about it, O'Rourke. Now, drop the gun."

CHAPTER 72

He heard the voices in front of him but stayed concealed in the darkness of the tunnel while he assessed his next move. He watched from behind as the woman held the gun on O'Rourke. He heard the man's voice but didn't have a clear view of him.

Collins had followed the woman through the tunnel, crouching because of the low overhead clearance. The tunnel had continued for about a quarter of a mile before emptying into the large chamber room filled with crates. The room was very large, lit only by five or six dozen low-wattage bare bulbs hanging from the stone ceiling.

His vantage point wasn't clear. Somewhere in the maze of crates, he knew O'Rourke stood, with the woman's gun aimed at him. But who had O'Rourke been talking to before she arrived, and where was that person standing? Who else was in the chamber with them?

Just as he was about to make his move, he heard a voice shout from across the room, "Drop the gun, lass."

He saw the woman flinch at the sound of the voice. She turned her gun slightly.

Pop.

She grabbed her left leg as the bullet pierced slightly above the kneecap. She fell to a squatting position, still keeping her gun trained on O'Rourke.

A dark figure of a man dove over a short stack of crates, followed by three more shots from a different gun. He heard footsteps running away from the fracas.

The voice in the back of the room said, "Next one's in the head, my dear."

The woman's gun clattered onto the stone floor.

He heard the man's voice say, "That's nice, very good."

"Are ye alright, Laurence?" the same voice asked.

Before O'Rourke could answer, the woman asked, "Who are you?"

"The name's Sean O'Rourke. I'm Laurence's brother and the new Chief of Staff for the Provisional IRA."

* * *

Jake moved toward Hunt.

"Stop right there!" yelled Sean O'Rourke. "Not another move."

"She's been shot. I'm unarmed, let me help her." Jake said.

"Okay but no tricks or you're both dead."

Jake knelt down beside Hunt. "How bad is it? Do you need to use the tourniquet?"

"It hurts like a son of a bitch but I don't think it's too bad."

"I'm just getting my field first aid kit, okay?" Jake reached down and opened the pocket on his cargo pants.

"Do it slow. I want to see your every move."

Jake opened the kit and pulled out a wad of padding and a Velcro strap. He placed the padding on the wound and wrapped the strap around her leg and tightened it enough to hold the wadding in place.

"I'm sorry, Jake. I didn't see the other man."

Jake's hands were covered in her blood so he wiped them on his pants legs and then he helped Hunt to her feet. "Actually, the distraction helped Kaplan get away."

The bullet had just grazed the outside of her left lower thigh. The injury looked worse than it was, even though the wound bled profusely. He held her up with his left arm while she stood on her right foot, clutching her left leg with her hand.

O'Rourke trained his gun on Hunt and Jake. He motioned to the Persian. "Mr. Kaplan got away. You need to find him. Find him and kill him. I'll take care of these two."

Nasiri smiled, his eyes glinting wickedly, and then he darted out of sight with his gun cocked and ready.

O'Rourke turned to his brother. "Well, Sean, I really didn't expect to see you here this soon," he said. "I expected you to wait a few days, but I'm happy you decided to come when you did."

Sean replied, "You said you wanted me to see if anyone was following you when you left the Demon's Lair. No one did that I could tell. But I saw a car sitting nearby with someone in it. It had been there too long so I went to check it out, and found a dead man with his neck snapped.

"And, brother, I've only owned the Demon's Lair for a few months and I really don't enjoy finding dead people outside my bar. It's not good for business, you know. So, I figured it was probably related to you and decided I better drive over and check up on you."

Jake caught movement to the left, and saw another man come around a stack of Kalashnikov AK-47s and into view.

Ian Collins.

Collins looked Jake in the eyes and said, "I ought to kill you here and now."

The O'Rourke brothers had both jumped and turned their guns toward Collins when he suddenly rounded the corner of the boxes.

"Stop right there. Who are you?" Sean yelled.

"Shamrock." The voice was cold, expressionless.

"You shouldn't be here," Sean said. "I withdrew the contract. You received my message, correct?"

"I received your message but you have it all wrong. The Provos weren't paying me to kill Laurence, they hired another assassin for that. I was only to find this location and relay it to my Provo contact, which I presume is you. Consider that contract fulfilled," said Collins. "I expect the remainder of your payment as soon as we get out of this hell hole."

"I know very well what the contract was for. When I took office, I didn't need the contract. I already knew about this place. The contract was useless, so I cancelled it. It remains cancelled. There will be no more money. I cancelled the other contract also."

"With everything I've gone through, you'll pay the money or you'll die in this chamber." Collins smiled.

"I'm sure we can come to some kind of accord," Sean said.

"We'll talk after I get what I came for," Collins said.

"And what is that?" Sean asked.

"First, I want him." Jake saw Collins pointing a gun at him, then he heard Hunt scream.

It felt like a sledgehammer struck him twice in the chest, in rapid succession. He felt himself tumbling between two sets of wooden crates.

Jake landed on top of Hunt.

CHAPTER 73

"Second, I want your brother." Collins fired several shots into the crates before ducking behind a stack of Browning rifle crates.

The O'Rourke brothers retreated behind some crates marked Barrett .50 CAL.

"Son of a bitch." Jake grabbed his chest. He was wearing his armored vest. He would be sore but he would be okay.

Jake saw Hunt crawling out to her gun, dragging her left leg behind. As she reached the Sig P226 and lifted it, he yelled.

Collins fired two rounds into her already injured left leg. She screamed in pain. Her gun bounced and landed at Jake's feet.

Jake picked up the gun and leapt out from between the walls of crates, rolling across the floor. As he rolled into the clearing, he fired twice.

The first bullet struck Collins in the right side, almost the same spot where he had stabbed Jake. *How fitting*, Jake thought in a split second.

His second shot missed and ricocheted off the stone wall. Collins darted out of sight as if the bullet hadn't fazed him.

Behind him on the other side of a wall of crates, he heard voices arguing. The O'Rourke brothers were fighting over who would get the cache of weapons stored in the Friar's Chamber.

He heard someone yell, "Freeze." It was Sterling's voice.

Jake jumped at the sound of more gunfire.

Then Laurence O'Rourke yelled, "Sean ... no! You son of a bitch."

Sterling answered, "It's a superficial wound, he'll live. Now drop your weapon and lie down on the floor beside your brother with your hands where I can see them. The next shot will be to kill."

Jake yelled, "Sterling watch out. There's another one over here."

It was too late. Collins stepped into Jake's view and fired a shot toward O'Rourke and Sterling. Sterling fell to the stone floor with a bullet hole in his side.

When he saw Collins, Jake fired off two more shots. The first bullet hit the top of a crate, wood splinters flew in the air. Collins turned his eyes toward Jake as Jake squeezed off another round.

The bullet struck Collins on the right side of the head. Blood spattered onto the crate of AK-47 rifles. He went down and didn't move.

Jake pointed the Sig P226 in the general direction of the O'Rourke brothers and fired as he ran toward Hunt. Grasping her right arm, he pulled her out of the line of fire while emptying his clip in the direction of the O'Rourkes.

Jake ejected the empty clip, inserted a fresh one, put a round in the chamber, and leaned down to check on Hunt. She was bleeding and in pain. "Hunt, are you alright?"

"My leg's hurt bad, Jake."

"Use your tourniquet. I'll be back in a minute."

"Jake, remember. Collins and O'Rourke alive. Bentley's orders."

"We're way past a capture mission now. This is survival. Kill or be killed." Jake ran out of sight and ducked behind a crate.

Jake heard running and shuffling sounds and knew the O'Rourke brothers weren't going to let him walk out of there alive. He had to neutralize them both. It was him or them.

The hunt was on.

He crouched behind the crates and moved quickly to the left near the tunnel where Hunt and Collins had entered. Collins' bloody body lay still on the stone floor. He couldn't tell if Collins was alive or dead. He looked dead. His face was pale, his white forelock covered in blood.

Jake heard a wooden crate being pried open. He knew he had to move quickly or the O'Rourkes' two-to-one advantage would escalate rapidly in their favor. He crawled on hands and knees toward the sound, his pistol tucked in his holster.

He came upon Sterling, a puddle of blood growing underneath him. Sterling's eyes were closed. He felt for a pulse and found one—weak, but he was alive. He had to move him to a safe location.

*   *   *

Kaplan had dived over the boxes and run about a hundred feet through the maze of crates. He was unarmed, his gun still on the crate where O'Rourke made him place it. He heard gunfire as he ran and hoped—no, prayed that Jake hadn't been shot.

He had been in tighter spots in the Army but that was many years ago. He was surprised by the rush of adrenaline and anger. He remembered it well.

It drove him.

He found a smaller stack of crates and climbed on top. Climbing higher as he jumped from stack to stack. Jump, then lie low and listen. On the third stack, he heard someone shuffling along the stone floor. His vantage point put him around fifteen feet above the floor. High enough to see well, but low enough to be easily seen if someone looked up.

He waited until the steps passed by him, held his breath, and peeked over the edge of the crate to get a glimpse of who it was.

The Persian.

He moved silently along the tops of the crates, stalking his prey. When he was in the right position, he dove toward the Persian from six feet behind and ten feet above.

The Persian heard him too late and Kaplan knew it. By the time the Iranian spun around, Kaplan was on top of him, knocking the gun free from his hands. The gun slid twenty feet down the floor and out of reach for both of them.

Now it was hand-to-hand combat, Kaplan's forte. The two men rolled on the floor and Kaplan punched the Persian mercilessly in the kidneys, bruising them. He groaned. Kaplan landed his right elbow into Nasiri's jaw, knocking out three teeth.

The Persian grunted and rolled over on his stomach, spitting blood and teeth onto the stone floor. He pushed himself up with his hands and knees.

Kaplan moved forward and kicked him with tremendous force in his enormous gut. The Persian fell on his back.

He stepped back, rubbing his fist. He heard another gunshot, and glanced in that direction as he heard Laurence O'Rourke yell. A good sign, he hoped.

Kaplan heard the Persian move and then heard a familiar click. He wheeled around to see the Persian make a roundhouse swing at Kaplan's mid-section with a switchblade.

He instinctively arched his body and jumped back at the same time, barely avoiding the sharp blade of the knife. He hated knife fights. He'd been in his fair share in Panama. Statistically, his chances were better against the gun. When shooting at a moving target, people miss more often than they hit. A knife is different. If it touches, it cuts. It cuts veins and vessels and arteries and tendons and ligaments. A knife can do debilitating damage even with little or no skill.

The Persian slashed at him feverishly while Kaplan ducked and dodged, evading the switchblade. Kaplan's boot slipped slightly causing him to double-step to catch his balance. The Persian jabbed the blade straight into Kaplan's chest. The tip of the blade stuck in his vest.

Kaplan had his opportunity and took it. He turned, grabbed the Persian's wrist with one hand and placed his arm over the man's arm. Now they stood side by side. He jammed Nasiri's wrist into his own upward moving knee, knocking the switchblade from the man's grip—shattering the bones in the Persian's wrist.

Kaplan shoved Nasiri backward with his extended leg, laying him flat on his back. With his free hand, he picked up the knife and plunged it into the Persian's abdomen just below the navel. With a downward thrust, Kaplan arced the six-inch blade severing the man's intestines.

The Persian lay on the stone floor of the Friar's Chamber bleeding profusely as entrails pushed through the large gash in his abdomen.

Kaplan pushed himself away, pulled the blade out of the Persian's gut and wiped it on the Persian's clothes. The man yelled something at Kaplan in Farsi. Even though Kaplan couldn't translate it, he knew its meaning well by the tone in the large man's voice.

Kaplan leaned over him, placed the tip of the knife blade between two ribs on Nasiri's chest and said, "Time to go see Allah, you towel-headed son of a bitch."

He plunged the knife blade into the Persian's heart.

*   *   *

Jake looked around the crate of SAM-7 launchers and saw Sean O'Rourke prying open a wooden crate with a crowbar in one hand while the other hand clutched his left side, blood oozing through his fingers.

Jake's heart raced as he saw the words stamped on the side of the crate: 50 CAL Machine Guns.

In the distance, Jake heard the Persian make a blood curdling scream. *Kaplan has done his job.*

O'Rourke looked in the direction of the Persian's scream, his back to Jake. Jake had to move fast before O'Rourke turned around— he only had a second.

He stood up from behind the crate, aimed at Sean and fired. The bullet struck the man in the right side of his chest. Sean O'Rourke dropped to the stone floor.

O'Rourke spun around as his brother fell to the floor. Then he looked at Jake.

Jake fired. The bullet struck O'Rourke in the left shoulder. The Irishman fell forward striking his head on a wooden crate, then fell to the floor.

He heard O'Rourke's gun bounce across the floor.

Jake stood up. His adrenaline was pumping. He couldn't believe his good fortune. Two shots, two O'Rourkes.

He walked over toward where Sean fell. The man looked up, agony all over his face. *Uncanny,* Jake thought. *A change of hair style, glasses and a few pounds and Sean and Laurence could pass as twins.*

He stared at Sean O'Rourke, the resemblance of the brothers fueled his rage once again and the events played through his mind. He saw Beth fall to the floor, blood spurting from her neck. He could hear himself screaming again. The same light-headed feeling overtook him and he wobbled slightly on his feet.

As Jake faltered, Sean stretched out his hand toward his gun.

Jake never flinched. "Oh no you don't." He raised his gun and fired one round into Sean's forehead.

Jake walked around the corner of the crates, gun pointed toward the place where the other O'Rourke had fallen.

The spot was empty except for a puddle of blood on the stone floor.

CHAPTER 74

Hunt heard the popping of silenced gunfire. Excruciating pain in her left leg consumed her. Jake had moved her out of the line of fire then he disappeared. He *was* better than she'd given him credit.

The first bullet in her leg had grazed the outside of her lower thigh, in and out, a clean wound. It would leave a scar but it didn't hit any muscle.

She had taken two more shots into the same thigh. One had grazed the outside of her leg just below the hip bone. It was a flesh wound.

The other was much more serious. That bullet buried itself deep inside her upper thigh. It did damage going in. It hit bone, she was sure. Her leg was on fire. She felt the back of her leg, no exit wound.

Jake told her to use the integrated tourniquet system imbedded in her Blackhawk clothes. She had never used it before now. Hunt lifted the flap on her cargo pants and flipped over the carbon fiber bar. She pulled the tactical nylon tight, then slowly started turning the twist bar until she noticed cessation of blood flow in her wounds.

She heard more popping sounds of silenced gunfire and secured the twist bar.

She worried about Jake and Kaplan. They were in way over their heads. What happened to Sterling? Where was he? She was sure she had heard his voice.

Jake and Kaplan were along as backup and support for Hunt as well as for identification purposes, but she realized they made a good team. She could tell Jake was a smart man and a quick study, but he wasn't an operative and had received only cursory training at best. She feared his training might give him a false sense of security and his overconfidence in his abilities might be his undoing.

And now he and Kaplan were in a shootout with an assassin, a known IRA hit man, the Chief of Staff of the Provisional IRA, and the ruthless Persian, Farid Nasiri. Even a seasoned operative in the clandestine service wouldn't stand much of a chance stacked against those odds. Hunt knew Jake couldn't last long unless Kaplan's Special Forces training saved him.

She was still wearing her headset and started calling for Jake. He didn't answer. She called for Kaplan—no response.

Hunt heard footsteps. The footsteps kept getting closer. She pushed herself backwards across the cold stone floor, dragging her limp left leg. Her energy was draining fast. She pushed until her path was blocked by a wall of crates, each crate marked Makarov Pistols. She had backed herself into a corner with no avenue of escape.

Gregg Kaplan came around the crates, carrying Matthew Sterling over his shoulder. He placed Sterling on the stone floor next to her.

"Where's Jake?" Kaplan asked.

"I don't know. He moved me in here then took off. Where's Nasiri?"

"I'm afraid Al Qaeda will have to look for another arms dealer."

He stood up, saying, "If you're okay, I'm going to find Jake—and a gun."

"I'm okay. Kaplan, find him before they do. Bentley will kill me if something happens to him."

As Kaplan turned around to run, they heard a muffled *pop.* Kaplan grabbed his leg and fell to the floor. "Shit," he yelled.

Blood oozed through his fingers.

Another *pop.*

Blood flew from his shoulder. He fell back against the crates with a heavy grunt.

"Kaplan, no!" Hunt screamed.

Pop, pop.

Kaplan's body bounced as two more shots slammed into his

chest. His head dropped as he fell unconscious.

She saw a tall figure walking toward her, pointing his gun directly at her.

Laurence O'Rourke.

Panic filled her body.

She was going to die.

They were going to die.

O'Rourke raised the gun and pointed the silencer at her head.

She closed her eyes.

She heard the *pop, pop,* and flinched.

CHAPTER 75

Jake watched O'Rourke fall to the stone floor of the Friar's Chamber. Blood spurted from both sides of his neck. The same wound he'd inflicted on Beth.

How fitting. An eye for an eye.

A flood of guilt washed over Jake as he realized he was so far from Beth.

Jake walked to O'Rourke and stood over him. The Irishman's throat gurgled as the blood drained from his body. The puddle under his body now flowed all the way to the man's shoes. He opened his mouth to speak but nothing came out but blood.

With each remaining breath, O'Rourke sucked in blood, then coughed, spewing blood over his face.

Jake knelt down next to him. "It's time for you to die, asshole. And I want your killer's face—my face—to be your last memory on earth. The depths of Hell are waiting for you."

He watched O'Rourke turn pale, then ashen as all the blood left his body. He'd be damned if he would lift a finger to save O'Rourke. Jake had played this scenario over and over in his mind. Revenge.

He'd wanted it desperately, but now … he felt nothing.

A crimson river ran along the stone floor disappearing beneath a crate of Armalite M-16A2 rifles.

Laurence O'Rourke died with his pistol in his hand. Jake picked it up and tucked it inside his belt.

Jake turned away from him and stood up. He walked over to where Hunt was lying. He found Kaplan and Sterling next to her—the men unconscious.

"Are they alive?" Jake asked.

"I think so. Sterling looks pretty bad though."

"How's your leg?"

"Hurts like hell, but I think I'll live."

He checked for blood flow and saw very little. "I need to get you to a hospital soon or you might lose that leg."

"Check on them first. They need your help more than I do right now. Then we'll get out of here."

He checked Sterling's wound. A nasty gunshot to his side. The entry point, not so bad, but the exit wound was a mess.

Kaplan groaned as he regained consciousness. The shoulder wound was superficial, the leg wound more serious.

He grabbed Kaplan's ITS flap and said, "You want me to do this for you or can you handle this one yourself?"

"I'll handle it, sailor boy," he grinned.

Kaplan motioned with his head, "The bad guys, all dead?"

"The O'Rourke brothers are dead. I watched them both die. What about the Persian?"

"Let's just say Nasiri didn't have guts enough to fight. What about Collins? Did you see him anywhere?"

"I shot him in the head. I thought he was dead, didn't you see him over there when you came up?" Jake pointed to where he shot Collins.

"No. Are you sure that's where you shot him?"

"Shit." Jake looked around. "He may still be alive."

"Jake, be careful." Hunt said.

"Right." Jake stood up, unholstered his pistol and walked around the stack of crates to where Collins had fallen.

Ian Collins was gone.

Jake followed the smeared trail of blood. It led to a third smaller tunnel. He retrieved his flashlight from the pouch on his pants leg, then proceeded to follow Collins' blood trail.

Thirty feet into the tunnel he could hear the sounds of the River Bonet reverberating through the tunnel. That's all he could hear. Jake kept the beam of the light shining forward until the ambient light near the end of the tunnel lit the rest of the way.

When he reached the end of the tunnel, he noticed several large rocks and stones had been pushed to one side. Blood smeared on the rocks assured Jake that Collins had indeed escaped the secret chamber through this friars' tunnel.

Dawn had come and gone and the early morning sun was bright. The sky was clear. A cool gentle breeze blew through the river valley. The only sounds were those of the waters of the River Bonet cascading over the rocks in the river bed and the birds chirping in the trees.

The blood stains led down a steep rocky bank to the river, where they stopped. Jake walked upstream and downstream but couldn't find any trace of Collins.

The one man CIA Director Scott Bentley desperately wanted to capture alive had now disappeared into thin air. Again.

Ian Collins, aka Shamrock, was a man on the run and, for now, a free man.

CHAPTER 76

Two days later, Jake entered Sligo General hospital. He knocked on Kaplan's door as he walked in. "How's the leg?"

Kaplan was fully dressed, sitting in a chair holding Annie's cross. He closed it tight in the palm of his hand. "It's fine. In no time, I'll be back on the dance floor."

Jake looked at Kaplan's closed fist. "You miss her?"

"I have mixed emotions. We were together a long time. Of course, I'll miss her. Annie and I had a lot of good memories. But she kept her past a close secret. She never let go. Everybody has baggage in life, it's always there. But most of us put the baggage in the trunk where it belongs, not in the front seat where it gets in the way."

"Damn, Gregg. That's some pretty deep shit. Where'd you come up with that? Is it some of that Army psychobabble?"

"Nah, I think I heard it on Dr. Phil. It didn't make sense then either."

"Well, are you going to be able to put her behind you? Can you put this in the trunk?"

"How about I start with my back pocket and go from there?" Kaplan leaned forward and slipped the cross into his back pants pocket.

Jake smiled. "Let's go see Isabella."

"Okay."

He rapped on Hunt's hospital room door as he opened it. "Isabella, it's Jake, can I come in? I brought Gregg with me."

"If I say no, will you go away?" Hunt laughed.

He walked in, with Kaplan two paces behind him on crutches.

She smiled. "The doctors said I can leave tonight as long as the

Company puts me in the hospital as soon as we arrive in D.C."

"I figured as much when Bentley said he would see all three of us tomorrow morning," Jake replied. "What did they say about your leg?"

"Two were flesh wounds. Physical therapy for the other. When the doctors retrieved the bullet they said it was a clean wound with minimal damage to muscle tissue. It lodged against the bone, but didn't do any damage. He said I was lucky, another centimeter and the bullet would have hit an artery and I would have bled to death." She paused. "Thank you, Jake. Thanks for saving my life. Thanks to both of you. I couldn't have done this without you."

She looked at Kaplan. "What about you? How are your injuries?"

"The shoulder's nothing but a scratch. My leg hurts like hell, but the doctor says it's not that bad. Certainly nothing like yours. I'll be as good as new in no time."

Hunt's brow furrowed. "Have they cleaned up the mess in the chamber?"

Jake looked at her. "The housekeepers came and the place is spotless. Everything's gone. Weapons, files, wires. It's like the friars left it—dusty. All the entrances have been closed and permanently sealed. Orders are 'nothing was found.' You were shot trying to stop an assassination attempt. The assassin fled the scene."

Hunt smirked. "My, my, isn't SIS efficient."

"It was our housekeepers, not theirs," Jake replied. "There will be a news release about it later today."

"What about Sterling? How's he doing?" she asked.

"He was in bad shape," Jake replied. "They already flew him back to London."

"And Collins? Did they pick up a trail?"

"No," Jake lowered his head. "Shamrock seems to have vanished in thin air."

"I hate to hear that. What about Beth? How's she doing?"

Jake smiled. "She's doing great. She came out of the coma. She's weak and anemic from blood loss but she'll recover now. They moved her out of Intensive Care and put her in a private room. I talked to her last night.

"She sounded good. I can't wait to get home and see her. I was so worried she wouldn't make it and I was going to be way over here." His voice wavered. He paused. "I don't think I would have ever forgiven myself."

"Don't be so hard on yourself, Jake. You and Gregg saved a lot of lives—maybe even hundreds or thousands by keeping those weapons out of Al Qaeda's hands. Look at the bright side, you killed the man who shot her."

"Yeah, Jake. You turned into a regular Dirty Harry." Kaplan smiled.

Hunt grinned and held up her thumb in a victory gesture.

Kaplan laughed and patted Jake on the back.

Jake's eyes felt scratchy from the lack of sleep and he was sore, as well as tired, but he smiled at both of them.

It felt good.

CHAPTER 77

Beth hung up the phone beside her bed. Jake had just called from the flight phone on the jet to say he was coming home. He would be in Langley, Virginia, early the next morning where he'd undergo a debriefing with DCI Admiral Scott Bentley. Admiral Bentley promised to fly Jake down to Savannah the moment they were finished so he could be with her.

She was happy now. Jake was coming home. When she had come out of her coma, she was scared and angry that he was gone. After her father had explained Jake's decision and told her that he supported Jake's move, she understood but still wished he was with her.

Jake had promised to fill her in on all the gory details when he arrived. He told her to watch CNN tonight to get a glimpse into what had transpired. She grabbed the remote control and flipped through the stations until she found the channel. Just as she did, she caught the announcement for the upcoming news segment.

And coming up on CNN News, Amber Larsen brings us up to date on the death of Laurence O'Rourke.

At eight-thirty, the floor nurse came into her room. She picked up the clipboard from the foot of the bed. She checked Beth's pulse and blood pressure, then took her temperature with their new digital thermometer. After noting all the vital signs on the clipboard, the nurse handed Beth a tiny paper cup holding three pills. The same three pills she'd taken the night before, two painkillers and a sleeping aid. The nurse left her room just as quickly as she entered.

Beth saw the introduction for the news segment beginning and turned the volume a little louder. She readjusted her pillow and rolled onto her side.

> *Laurence O'Rourke is dead. I'm Amber Larsen. Just over a week ago I reported the bizarre and bloody story of Irish peace activist Laurence O'Rourke. At that point the death toll had reached eleven. Well, now the death toll is up to fourteen and some sources believe as high as seventeen.*
>
> *The bodies of Laurence O'Rourke and his brother, Sean O'Rourke, were found in an abandoned home jointly owned by the two O'Rourke brothers in Dromahair, Ireland, last night in an apparent assassination. One SIS agent was found dead in his car parked outside of Demon's Lair Bar and Bistro in Enniskillen, Northern Ireland, a pub owned and operated by Sean O'Rourke, and another agent was shot and seriously injured here in Dromahair near Creevelea Abbey. Authorities believe the death and the shooting to be attributed to the assassin Shamrock, whose true identity is now known as Ian Collins of Londonderry, Northern Ireland. Interpol has initiated an extensive manhunt for Collins.*
>
> *A week ago I reported that Laurence O'Rourke declared he had earth-shattering news that would destroy the New Northern Ireland Assembly. Well, now we may never know what that news really was.*
>
> *When asked her opinion on this whole O'Rourke episode, Sinn Fein President Mairéad Brady said, "Although we had our differences, Laurence O'Rourke was a true fighter for the peace process. He will be missed."*
>
> *An unnamed source had a different theory altogether, claiming that Laurence O'Rourke killed the Northern Ireland Secretary of State, his assistant, and his bodyguard. The same source claimed that Laurence and Sean O'Rourke were killed by an agent of the U.S. Government. The informant also claimed that Collins was wounded in a shootout and is now seeking refuge elsewhere in Ireland.*
>
> *SIS authorities had no comment on these allegations. The United States Government authorities denied any involvement whatsoever.*
>
> *I'm Amber Larsen reporting live from Dromahair, Ireland.*

Beth's eyes closed as the effects of the sleeping pill took hold. She knew she would dream of Jake and spies, but her thoughts were peaceful. Jake would be home tomorrow.

*   *   *

At midnight, a doctor stepped into Beth's room. He was wearing his full-length doctor's jacket, skullcap and surgical gloves. Beth was sound asleep, courtesy of the sleeping pill. He pulled out her charts, put his reading glasses on and studied her charts.

He gently placed the clipboard back in the bracket and removed a syringe from his coat pocket. He injected its contents into her IV line. He threw the syringe into the red hazardous biological waste box and left the room.

The doctor walked past the nurses' station. They paid him no attention. He walked toward the exit. He rounded the corner and ripped off his white coat and stuffed it into a garbage can. He removed the skullcap and gloves, pushed them into the garbage can as well, and then walked through the exit door.

*   *   *

Beth woke up. She felt like her chest would explode.

Her chest pounded with each beat.

Her body temperature rose higher.

She grabbed her call button then glanced at the heart monitor. It read 72.

It must have been a nightmare. She told herself.

Her body temperature returned to normal.

She placed the call button down beside her.

She relaxed and closed her eyes again. She quickly fell back to sleep.

60.

50.

40.

30 …

Alarms sounded in her hospital room. She couldn't hear them. A shamrock lay next to her head on the pillow.

AUTHOR NOTES

This book is a work of fiction. Names, characters, places and incidents are products of the author's imagination or are used fictitiously. Any resemblance to actual events, locales, or persons, living or dead, is coincidental.

The aviation accident investigators of the National Transportation Safety Board have a complex and sometimes gruesome job filled with detailed procedures, guidelines and techniques that are utilized to accurately determine the probable cause in aircraft accidents. This arduous journey takes many weeks and months to accomplish and not days as in this book. The procedures in this book have been drastically abbreviated and simplified and are only a superficial representation—at best. Their job is too complex to do it justice in any novel.

As is the case with most authors of fiction, certain liberties are taken with the truth. Here is where I'll try to separate the fact from the fiction. I have listed several areas my readers inquired about accuracy and truthfulness. I suggest you wait until after you have finished reading The Savannah Project before you read what follows.

THE H.M.P. Maze prison existed and was used to house paramilitary prisoners from 1976 to 2000, when it was closed. The conditions were reported by most as deplorable.

The "Graveyard Tour" at the Savannah International Airport is real as is the plaque that is embedded in the asphalt on the east/west runway.

References made in Chapter 43 to General Noriega's second-in-command Raul Diego and the prostitute Angelina Vasquez are a fabrication of the author's imagination.

Stormont Castle and Stormont Parliament Building are real—the floor plan of the Parliament Building and the drainage canal are a fabrication.

Enniskillen is an actual town in Northern Ireland on the A4 highway and High Street is an actual street in Enniskillen. The truth ends there. Demon's Lair Bar and Bistro and all the descriptions that accompany it are a product of the author's imagination.

Dromahair, Ireland exists and has been called the "ridge of two demons." Creevelea Abbey and the O'Rourke Banqueting Hall also exist.

The Friars' Chamber and the Friars' tunnels do not exist and are fictitious—as is any cache of weapons and documentation eluding to collusion between the parties involved in the New northern Ireland Assembly. Pure fiction.

The O'Rourke clan is real and did occupy the Dromahair region. The O'Rourke clan did build the O'Rourke Banqueting Hall. However, Laurence and Sean O'Rourke are fictitious—their creation and surname was entirely coincidental and was used for convenience.

Chuck Barrett, a graduate of Auburn University, is a veteran pilot and air traffic controller. *The Savannah Project*, Barrett's first novel, interweaves his aviation expertise, a long-held passion for writing and a keen sense of suspense. He currently resides in Northeast Florida.

www.chuckbarrett.org

CPSIA information can be obtained
at www.ICGtesting.com
Printed in the USA
FFOW02n1127260614
6044FF